Thomas Leland

The History of the Life and Reign of Philip

King of Macedon, the Father of Alexander

Thomas Leland

The History of the Life and Reign of Philip
King of Macedon, the Father of Alexander

ISBN/EAN: 9783337236076

Printed in Europe, USA, Canada, Australia, Japan

Cover: Foto ©Raphael Reischuk / pixelio.de

More available books at **www.hansebooks.com**

THE HISTORY

OF THE

LIFE AND REIGN

OF

PHILIP

KING OF MACEDON;

THE FATHER OF ALEXANDER.

BY

THOMAS LELAND, D. D.

FELLOW OF TRINITY COLLEGE, DUBLIN.

THE SECOND EDITION.

IN TWO VOLUMES.

VOL. I.

LONDON:

Printed for E. JOHNSTON, in Ludgate-ſtreet.

MDCCLXXV.

THE
PREFACE.

THE histories of ancient times, which seem most likely to engage the general attention, are such as abound with extraordinary and surprising events, great and glaring actions, astonishing viciffitudes of fortune, and striking instances of succefs, apparently difproportioned to the powers and abilities, or even to the expectations, of thofe, whofe bold attempts were thus wonderfully crowned. The history now prefented to the reader, it must be confeffed, is of another nature. It leads him on gradually through a feries of actions and events, many of them feemingly inconfiderable, but all operating regularly to produce one of the greateft revolutions of

A 3

power,

power, which the annals of the heathen world afford. The flow and painful fteps, by which PHILIP king of Macedon warily and fagacioufly proceeded, with a patient refolution, to ftrengthen and to aggrandize his kingdom, to incorporate it with the illuftrious nation of Greece, to fubdue that nation, and to place himfelf at the head of its united powers ; as they difcover no lefs merit and abilities than that rapidity of conqueft, which cafts fuch glory round his fon, and other heroic characters ; fo they may poffibly appear no lefs worthy of attention, although the detail be frequently addreffed rather to the judgment than to the imagination.

In this cafe indeed, the tafk of the hiftorian is by far more difficult : his errors and imperfections more obvious and ftriking. Great and furprifing actions fupport themfelves, and animate the writer with that fpirit and energy with which they fhould

be

be defcribed. But to conduct the reader through the labyrinths of policy; to trace the progrefs of an artful, penetrating, and fagacious prince, furrounded with dangers and difficulties, exactly and inceffantly attentive to his defigns, and wifely chufing and proportioning his inftruments and means to the great ends which he propofed; to difclofe the latent caufes of the declenfion and ruin of nations, of the grandeur of kings, and the eftablifhment of empires;---thefe call for all the accuracy, all the judgment, of a writer.

In difplaying the difficulties of his tafk, the author means not to infinuate, that he is poffeffed of any extraordinary abilities; but to befpeak the indulgence and pardon of the reader, for thofe imperfections, which his tafte and judgment may, or rather muft, neceffarily difcover in the following work; however the writer hath endeavoured, by a painful and laborious application, to avoid the guilt of any essential omissions. And he may possibly appear to have a better claim to this indulgence, when it is considered from what a variety of authors the following history is collected; and that his materials lie detached, and dispersed through so many of the great writers of antiquity: which were to be collected with care, united with propriety, and reconciled, where they disagreed, with truth, or at least with the appearance of probability: a task which required attention and accuracy, and other still higher accomplishments.

THEOPOMPUS, an historian cotemporary with PHILIP, collected a large and copious account of this prince's actions, of which time hath unhappily deprived us. The fragments of this historian, which Athenaeus hath preserved (if genuine) confirm the representations, which we find in ancient writers, of the severity and acrimony

of

of Theopompus. Poffibly, the corruption of thofe with whom Philip contended, as well as many parts of this prince's conduct, (whatever greatnefs of foul, or elevation of genius, he poffeffed) might have juftly merited this feverity. Had we not been deprived of his work, or even if Photius had tranfmitted to us the plan and general heads of his hiftory, poffibly we might have had many particulars both to admire and cenfure in this hero, which are now buried in eternal oblivion.

DIODORUS SICULUS, in his fixteenth book, hath given an abftract of the hiftory of PHILIP, collected, not only from Theopompus, but fome other ancient writers, whofe names only have defcended to us. His detail is frequently interrupted by the hiftory of the affairs of Sicily; fo as, in fome fort, to diftract the attention of the reader, by the variety of objects. But this cannot fo properly be cenfured as a fault,

since

since the scheme of his history was general;
and, whatever errors or omissions may be
discovered in his account of PHILIP's actions, by comparing him with other writers, yet we must justly acknowledge our
obligations to him, both as an historian,
and as an accurate chronologer.

TROGUS POMPAEUS intitled his uni-
versal history, HISTORIA PHILIPPICA,
either in imitation of Theopompus, or from
a particular veneration for the king of Macedon. " Although he hath employed"
(saith Olivier, an author of whom we shall
immediately give some account) " but three
" books in reciting the actions of this
" prince; yet he was persuaded that these
" gave a new appearance to the affairs and
" interests of the world. And, in effect,
" the empires formed on the ruins of that
" of Alexander, owe their foundation to
" men trained up and taught by PHILIP.
" It is to be presumed, that Trogus pre-
" served

" ferved many particulars which his abbre-
" viator hath neglected. There is even a
" literal proof that this latter did not value
" himfelf on his accuracy. Among fome
" ancient manufcripts is found a fummary
" of the Philippic hiftory, called Periochae
" Trogi: from which it appears, that Ju-
" ftin hath not contented himfelf with re-
" verfing the order of facts, with omitting
" feveral effential ones, and adding others:
" but that he hath related fome, in a man-
" ner totally different from his author."—
If this be fo, it affords an additional reafon
to juftify the author of this work, in fometimes neglecting, and fometimes contro-
verting, his authority.

AND, if Juftin endeavoured to diffufe
fome portion of the fpirit and acrimony of
Demofthenes into the hiftory of Trogus,
Paulus Orofius hath proceeded fomewhat
further. His point was to prove, that the
miferies and enormities of the pagan world
exceeded

exceeded thofe which mankind felt, from the time that Chriftianity was firft propagated: and his zeal to fupport his argument hath rendered his account of PHILIP's actions rather bordering on an invective, than a difpaffionate hiftory: although he hath collected the facts from Juftin into a fmaller compafs, with fufficient art; and hath been rather more careful to preferve the order of time.

THOUGH we have no life of PHILIP written by Plutarch; yet in thofe of Pelopidas, Phocion, Demofthenes, and Alexander, we have many particulars relative to this prince. And, had fuch a valuable piece of antiquity defcended to us, we might have found it rather made up of private anecdotes, calculated for marking out the temper and character of PHILIP, than a regular detail of facts, which might fully explain the whole fcheme and fyftem of his conduct. In the lives of Phocion and Demofthenes,

mofthenes, he feems, as ufual, to fuppofe the reader already acquainted with the hiftory of their time, which he relates in fuch a manner, as that no common reader, who hath not recourfe to other works, can form a clear idea of it: and fometimes in a manner by no means confiftent with other accounts of high authority. A regular and ample comment on his truly valuable Lives, to fupply his defects, and to correct his inaccuracies as an hiftorian, might make him to be read with greater fatisfaction and utility. But, at prefent, the reader is to guard not only againft thefe, but fometimes againft his prejudices: at leaft, critics have attributed his unfavourable re-prefentations of PHILIP, in his Lives, to this latter caufe. In his moral works, however, he frequently does him fufficient honour. He dwells on his maxims and fallies of wit, on the inftances of his con-defcenfion and humanity, with feeming pleafure: and hath preferved many agree-

able

able anecdotes, which it would have been unpardonable in a modern compiler to pass over, whatever pains the collecting and introducing them might cost.

BESIDES the historians now mentioned, we are considerably indebted to others of the ancient writers, from whom many particulars are collected relative to the present subject. Such are Athenaeus, Strabo, Pausanias, Lucian, Ælian, Polybius, Seneca, Pliny, and others. But the greatest lights, the amplest supplement to the omissions and defects of history, are furnished by the noble and valuable remains of the great Athenian orators. And here the author must bespeak all the candour of the learned reader, in judging of the use he hath made of their materials. They were undoubtedly the most capable of giving the clearest and most authentic account of affairs, in which they themselves had so considerable a share. Yet, in ascertaining the

force

force and extent of their teftimony, in
diftinguifhing between truth and artifice,
between the real or probable ftate of facts,
and the reprefentations of a vehement,
impaffioned, and perhaps interefted fpeaker,
judgment, fagacity, and attention, are
required : and here the defects of a writer
muft be particularly obfervable : not to mention the difference of fentiment which neceffarily arifes in fuch a cafe. If Ifocrates
reprefents all the actions and defigns of
PHILIP in the faireft and moft advantageous light, the learned and judicious may
not be entirely agreed, how far this is to
be afcribed to the inexperience and unfuf-
pecting honefty, the benevolence and fim-
plicity, of a reclufe rhetorician, unacquainted with the wiles of policy, and the
corruptions of the great world. If, on the
contrary, Demofthenes burfts forth into the
moft animated indignation and abhorrence
of this prince;   he loads him with the
blackeft imputations; it may not be agreed,

how

how far we are to guard againſt the extravagance of an honeſt zeal, or the artifice of
a popular leader. When two great rivals
are contending for reputation, power, and
all that is valuable in human life, if not for
life itſelf, although the diſpute happily fur-
niſhes us with many particulars of their
public conduct, as well as that of their co-
temporaries; although it hath preſerved
many important inſtances of the policy,
abilities, ſentiments, and paſſions, of the
great actors in that ſcene in which the contending parties were engaged; yet what
credit is to be given to their different repreſentations, may ſometimes be thought by
no means eaſy to determine, but a matter
which may admit of ſome variety in opinion. When two competitors are violent
againſt each other; when their moſt momentous intereſts are concerned in the conteſts; when they know that ſucceſs depends
in a great meaſure on the preſent impreſſion
made on the paſſions and imaginations of
their

their judges; they muſt have more than ordinary integrity, if they are not tempted to paſs the bounds of truth and juſtice. And the contentions between Demoſthenes and Æſchines have diſcloſed ſome particulars, which render the integrity of both at leaſt ſuſpicious. Even in their repreſentations of facts, which might be ſuppoſed not ſo liable to fallacy and deception, we are often embarraſſed by the weight of contradictory evidence, and tempted to believe, that they ſometimes aſſerted, with a deliberate purpoſe of deceiving. Of this I ſhall take the liberty of laying before the reader one among many inſtances.

IN that oration of Demoſthenes, in which he accuſes Æſchines of corruption and miſconduct in his management of a treaty which the Athenians concluded; in order to load his rival with public odium, he relates a particular incident highly to his diſhonour; and dwells upon it with all poſfible aggravations, and all the appearance of truth and fincerity. He fays, that, during his refidence in Macedon, he (Æfchines) was invited to an entertainment by one of his friends: that, in the courfe of the feftivity, a woman was introduced, a native of Olynthus, a city which had been in alliance with Athens, which PHILIP had lately fubdued, and whofe inhabitants were now generally in a ftate of flavery. 'This woman, faith Demofthenes, was treated with the liberty which her prefent diftreffed condition feemed to allow, not with the decorum due to her former fortune. As fhe was not yet enured to feverities, fhe expreffed her uneafinefs and refentment; which fo provoked Æfchines, and fome other guefts, that, with unparalleled barbarity, they called in an attendant flave, who was ordered to lafh her without mercy; and would have put her to death, had it not been for the interpofition of one man, to whom fhe flew, imploring his protec-

6

tion ;

tion; and who, with great difficulty, faved her from their drunken rage.—This the orator infifteth on as notorious; declares that it had raifed the utmoft indignation in Arcadia and Theffaly, where it had been commonly fpoken of; and offers to produce Diophantus, an Athenian of fome eminence, as a witnefs to the truth of a fact, with which this citizen was well acquainted, and which he had before mentioned in the affembly.—One would imagine that nothing could be afferted more plaufibly, and with a greater appearance of truth and candour. Yet, when Æfchines comes to make his defence, we find him afferting, that the bare mention of this had raifed the utmoft fury and indignation againft the falfe accufer; that Demofthenes had actually attempted to fuborn one Ariftophanes, a native of Olynthus, to bear teftimony to his malicious falfehood; that Ariftophanes had rejected the infamous propofition with horrour; and, to atteft

the

the truth of all this, he produces the evidence not only of this Olynthian, but of two citizens of Athens.—Other paffages may be obferved in both the rival orators, which afford good reafons for receiving their teftimony with all due caution. If the author fometimes appears to be determined to one particular fide, and to affume the reprefentations of one of the parties as authentic ; it would be prefumption to expect that the fentiments of the learned reader, who examines his authority, muft be ever exactly confonant to his: and, if he fometimes contents himfelf with relating the different reprefentations of the orators, without attempting to decide between them, this is a method which the hiftorians of times and actions lefs remote and obfcure are fometimes obliged to purfue.

The orator Ariftides, who lived about five hundred years after the death of Philip, made two orations againft this prince,
which

which are yet preferved. They are written in the character of an ambaffador fuppofed to be fent to Thebes, to engage this
ftate to unite with the Athenians againft
Macedon. Had the oration which Demofthenes really delivered on this occafion
been preferved, it might have afforded many
illuftrations of the hiftory of his time, as
well as many noble proofs of his art and
power of fpeaking. But the topics on
which Ariftides enlarges, are common and
well known; and fcarcely any new materials can be extracted from him.—His abilities, as an orator, it is not to the prefent
purpofe to examine.

GEORGE Gemifthius Pletho, a modern
Greek, wrote a continuation of the hiftory
of Xenophon down to the death of PHI-
LIP; a work fufficiently accurate and well
connected. Had he read thofe authors
which are now loft, it might have been
of confiderable ufe; but his materials are

taken

taken entirely from writers well known, Diodorus Siculus and Plutarch: and therefore we are not to expect any new lights from him, or any information which may not be as well obtained by drawing from the same sources.

THE modern compilers, who have treated this part of ancient history, are perhaps already well known to the reader. Monsieur Tourreil, in his learned preface to his translation of the Philippic Orations of Demosthenes, proposes to supply the loss of Theopompus, by collecting and uniting together the scattered remains of PHILIP's history. But his collection is by no means suited to so magnificent a promise. It is confined within the compass of a very few pages, and is by no means so perfect and accurate as that of the learned Puffendorf, who hath given us short but excellent and exact heads of this prince's actions, in the second of his *Dis-*

sertationes

sertationes Academicae selectiores, intitled, *de Rebus gestis Philippi.*

THE labours of Rollin, on this subject, deserve great commendations, whatever inadvertencies or omiffions may be found in them. The nature of his work did not permit him to give it the full extent, which he himself thought that it merited; as appears by his wishing that some modern would undertake it particularly, and collect all the scattered remains of antiquity relative to the history of PHILIP. The fame may be said of the authors of the UNI-VERSAL HISTORY, who, in their account of this prince, have discovered taste, judgment, and learning, amidst some lefs material errors, and some omiffions, which might have been avoided, even consistently with their plan.

WHAT Monsieur Rollin wished to be executed, was undertaken by one of his

a 4

country-

countrymen, Claude-Matthieu Olivier, a native of Marfeilles, and Member of the Academy of Belles Lettres of that city: and fome time after this writer's death, which happened in the year 1736, his work was publifhed in two fmall volumes, under the title of *Hiftoire de Philippe*, &c.: a work to which the author muft acknowledge himfelf greatly indebted, and whofe publication makes it neceffary for him to offer fomething in juftification of his prefent attempt.

OLIVIER appears plainly to have employed great affiduity in making his collection of materials, nor hath he difcovered lefs genius and judgment in ufing them. It is faid that his attention to this work haftened his diffolution: and, unhappily, his papers fell into the hands of perfons by no means fo well acquainted with the fubject of them as the author himfelf. This feems to have been the reafon that his authorities

thorities are frequently not quoted at all; scarcely ever with any degree of accuracy; and, in general, the quotations even ridiculously defective and erroneous; which in a great measure defeats the advantages which a subsequent writer might derive from his labours. Had this author lived to finish and polish his history, a careful revisal of the writers from whence he drew it, might have suggested to him many alterations, improvements, and corrections. As it stands at present, several inaccuracies appear to have escaped him; many, and some material omissions; authorities sometimes wrested from their real and natural purport, or stretched beyond their due bounds, together with many faults in his arrangement, where we find the order of facts and actions disturbed and reversed. Some of these imperfections the reader will find occasionally pointed out in the following history: by which he will judge, whether the author hath been severe in his

censure,

cenſure, or raſh in diſſenting from Olivier; of whom he ſpeaks with greater freedom, as he apprehends that a writer is not entirely accountable for the faults of a piece, to which he hath not put the laſt finiſhing hand. But there is one objection to be made to the whole tenour of this writer's hiſtory, and that is an objection which lies againſt moſt biographers : I mean, a ſtrong prejudice and partiality in favour of his hero. " Unhappily" (ſaith he) " for " the reputation of PHILIP, the city which " oppoſed his deſigns with moſt obſtinacy, " was that which gave birth to the great- " eſt orators of Greece : ſo that many " know PHILIP only as a prince, againſt " whom Demoſthenes delivered the maſter- " pieces of eloquence."—The deſign of Olivier, therefore, was to form an *apology*, (as he himſelf ſpeaks) for this prince. And how far he was tranſported by his zeal, appears remarkably in his ingenious compariſon between PHILIP and ALEXANDER;

in

in which his love to his hero hath betrayed him into some violations of historical truth, and even into some contradictions to his own history. The author's first intention was to have added this comparison, as well as that of Tourreil, between PHILIP and Caesar, to the present work; but, upon reflection, he resolved rather to deprive his history of these ornaments, than seem to take too great freedoms with the labours of other writers.

AND, if the observations he hath now made on the French writer do not exceed the bounds of truth and candour, it cannot be deemed presumption, that he was not discouraged, by his work, from the pursuit of a design, undertaken some time before he had been made acquainted with it. At the same time that he hath endeavoured to give this history a greater extent and copi-ousness than Mr. Olivier hath bestowed on the subject, to avoid his errours, and to

supply

fupply his omiffions; he freely acknowledges the affiftances he hath received from
his learning and judgment; and, if at any
time, in the courfe of this work, he hath
neglected fuch acknowledgment, he hopes
that this declaration will free him from all
fufpicions of fo defpicable a crime as plagi-
arifm. He is not confcious of attempting
to impofe on the public by a tranflation, or
even a paraphrafe, of the French hiftory.
He hath followed the author of it, where
this author himfelf followed the beft leaders; he hath quitted his guidance, where
he had any fears of being mifled.

As to the importance and ufefulnefs of
the fubject itfelf, the learned reader is not
to be informed of thefe: and, as to the
manner in which he hath treated it, nothing that might be here faid could excufe
or atone for its defects. From the nature
of the work, it is impoffible that every part
of it can be equally interefting and engag-

ing.

ing. The judicious reader will be determined by the whole, and then pronounce
equitably and candidly.—To prepare him
for the perufal of the following hiftory, in
which the council of Amphictyons acts fo
confiderable a part, it feemed neceffary to
lay before him the nature and conftitution
of this famous body. Of thefe he will find
a general account prefented to his view, in
the form of a Preliminary Differtation;
which is prefixed, not fo much for the fake
of refining on thofe learned men who have
already treated of this fubject, as to fave
the trouble of turning to other books.

I CANNOT clofe this preface, without
acknowledging my obligations to thofe who
have been kind enough to think my application to this fubject merited their favour
and encouragement. I am bound particularly to declare, that I owe the warmeft
and fincereft gratitude to the friendfhip of
the Reverend Doctor SAMUEL MAD-
DEN,

DEN, a name which muſt be ever honoured and revered in *Ireland*, while it feels the happy effects of his extraordinary zeal and generous public ſpirit. And, whatever may be the fate of the author and his performance, he muſt ever reflect, with pride and pleaſure, that he had an opportunity of declaring thus publickly, that there is *another perſon*, by whom he hath been highly and particularly obliged; and that this work was undertaken at the deſire, and introduced to the world by the favour and patronage, of the generous friend to every uſeful and ornamental art, every attempt to improve or pleaſe mankind, the Right Honourable JAMES Lord Viſcount CHARLEMONT.

PRELIMINARY DISSERTATION

ON THE

Council of AMPHICTYONS.

ANCIENT Greece was inhabited by people, whofe origin and language were the fame; but their manners, cuftoms, inftitutions, and forms of government, in many refpects, totally different [A].   Yet,

[A] Licebat Athenis eodem patre natam uxorem ducere, uterinam vero in matrimonio habere non folum nefarium erat, verum etiam inceftuofum: contra, Lycurgus, qui Lacedaemoniis, populo finitimo, leges tulit, germanarum incefta effe conjugia voluit, uterinarum confuetudinem indulfit. Rurfus huic populo quem ultimo memoravi, in ufu et moribus fuit, ea quae pro legibus obfervarent, non literis, fed memoriae mandare: in illo autem viciffim, ex legibus non fcriptis jus dicere, cum capitis periculo conjunctum effe videbatur. Nemo erat Thebis Boeotiis tam nobilis imp. qui non et gratia et laude dignum duxit fcienter tibiis canere, et pari effe in muficis ac in bellicis fama: contra, ab Athenienfium moribus haec omnia aberant, et partim infamia, partim humilia atque fervili homine digna habebantur. TAYLOR. Com. ad Marmor. Sand. p. 53.

amidft

amidſt this diverſity, their general principles were alſo the ſame, an ardour for
liberty, and a ſtrict regard to the public
good. " The Grecians," ſaith the learned Biſhop of Meaux, " were naturally poſ-
" ſeſſed of genius and valour, which were
" timely cultivated by thoſe kings and colo-
" nies which came from Egypt, who, by
" ſettling early in ſeveral parts of Greece,
" ſpread through the whole country the
" excellent polity of the Egyptians. Hence
" were learned the exerciſes of the body,
" wreſtling, racing on foot, on horſeback,
" and in chariots, and all the other exer-
" ciſes which were brought to perfection
" by the glorious prizes of the Olympic
" games. But Greece derived ſtill more
" important advantages from the Egyp-
" tians, that of wiſe laws and inſtitutions;
" that of being taught a rational ſubmiſſion
" and amenable deference to rightful power;
" that of being formed to a juſt conception
" and ſtrict attention to the public inte-
" reſt. Its particular inhabitants did not
" confine their regards to their own private
" affairs. They did not conſider public
" dif-

" difficulties merely as they affected their
" own tranquillity, or that of their families;
" which they were inftructed to confider
" as parts of a more extenfive body, that
" of their ftate or community. Such fen-
" timents were conftantly tranfinitted from
" the fathers to their children, who, from
" their infancy, were taught to confider
" their country as a common mother, to
" whom they belonged no lefs than to their
" natural parents. The word CIVILITY,
" among the Grecians, did not barely fig-
" nify that fweetnefs and mutual deference
" which render men fociable : their ΑΝΗΡ
" ΠΟΛΙΤΙΚΟΣ was the man who confider-
" ed himfelf as a member of the ftate ; who
" fubmitted his conduct to the laws ; who
" acted entirely under their direction ; who
" confpired with them in promoting the
" general good; without any attempt to
" encroach on the rights of individuals, or
" to violate the juft equality of citizens in
" the fame community. The ancient
" kings, who reigned in the different parts
" of Greece, Minos, Cecrops, Thefeus,
" Codrus, Temenes, Crefphontes, Eury-
    VoL. I.   b   " fthenes,

" sthenes, Patrocles, and others, diffused
" this laudable spirit through the whole
" nation. They gained popularity, not by
" flattering the people, but by procuring
" their good, and establishing the just au-
" thority of law."

A number of neighbouring societies, thus formed and modelled, became gradually to be considered as one body or nation, composed of so many distinct members, all united and connected together by interest and affection. As the good of each individual was subservient to that of his community; so the good of each community was considered as subordinate to that of the whole nation. Hence arose a similar species of CIVILITY, if it may be so called, which each society owed to the general assemblage. Even amidst those contests and disorders which unruly passions, or the accidental clashing of interests, might produce, war had its laws and limitations; the universal interest of Greece was professedly at least the first and greatest object of attention; the attempt of any state to extend its power beyond the juſt and equitable bounds was conſidered as an injury to Greece in general : juſtice, moderation, equality, were ever ſtrenuouſly enforced, and all military conteſts carried on among the Greeks in a manner ſomewhat ſimilar to judicial controverſies in private ſocieties : and, while it was allowed thus to ſeek redreſs of particular injuries, the general rights of the contending parties were ſecured by the national laws, and demanded a juſt and ſcrupulous attention, even amidſt all the confuſion and violence of arms. Thus the great Athenian orator deſcribes the principles and ſentiments of the Greeks, ſpeaking of the ancient wars of Athens and Sparta :

Οὑτω δ'αρχαιως εἶχον, μαλλον δε ΠΟΛΙΤΙΚΩΣ, ὡσ]ε ὐδε χρημα]ων ὠνεισθαι παρ ὐδενος ὐδεν· αλλ' ειναι ΝΟΜΙΜΟΝ τινα καὶ προφανη τον πολεμον. *Such was their ſimplicity, or rather their* CIVILITY, *(that is, their deference to the general laws of Greece, and their attention to the common good of that nation)* that corruption was never made the inſtrument of their ſucceſs; but they carried on a *LEGAL* and an open war.

Dem. Phil. 3. ſect. 13. Ed. Dub. Æd. Acad. 1754.

b 2　　　WHILE

WHILE thefe principles preferved their due vigour and influence, Greece continued a really united body, happy in itfelf, and formidable to its enemies. Many circumftances contributed to form this union; and many inftitutions were fuggefted, by the fagacity of ftatefmen and legiflators, to fecure and confirm it. Of thefe, the famous COUNCIL OF AMPHICTYONS deferves particular regard; whofe origin and conftitution are here to be explained, that the reader may come duly prepared to underftand the hiftory now prefented to him, in which this auguft body makes fo confiderable a figure.

THE council of Amphictyons, like other inftitutions of the fame kind, was at firft but inconfiderable; nor did it arrive to its full ftrength and luftre but by gradual advances, and in a long feries of years. Its firft origin we are to afcribe to Amphictyon, the fon of Deucalion, an ancient king of Theffaly, as the authority of the Arundelian Marbles warrants us to determine. Their teftimony is full and explicit, and on

account

account of the high antiquity of this monument, deferves particular attention.——
Αμφικτυων Δευκαλιωνος ἐβασιλευσεν ἐν Θερμοπυλαις, και συνηγε λαους περι του ὁρον οἰκυντας,
και ὠνομασεν ΑμΦικτυονας, και Πυλαιαν, οὑπερ
και νυν ἐτι Θυουσιν ΛμΦικτυονες.——" Amphic
" tyon, the fon of Deucalion, reigned at
" Thermopylae, and collected the people
" bordering on his territory, and called
" them Amphictyons, and *the affembly,*
" Pylaea, in the place where the Amphic
" tyons facrifice to this day." Dionyfius *
of Halicarnaffus, in the fourth book of
his Roman Antiquities; Theopompus, as
quoted by Harpocration on the word Αμ
Φικτυονες; and Androtion, an ancient writer
quoted by Paufanias * in his defcription of
Phocis; all concur with the Marbles of
Paros, in afcribing the inftitution of this
council to Amphictyon. Dionyfius indeed
makes him the, fon of Hellen the fon of
Deucalion. But to this we may juftly oppofe the authority above mentioned, as well
as that of Philoponus, in his treatife on
the Greek Dialects. Androtion afferts, that
the convention was at firft held at Delphi,

b 3

and

Prideaux.
Mar. Ox.
p. 160.
Ed. Ox.
1676.

* p. m. 230.

* p. m. 323.
Ed. Franc.
fol. 1683.

and compofed only of thofe who lived in the neighbourhood of this city, and who were called not from Amphictyon, but Αμφικτιονες, *the neighbouring inhabitants.* But to this again we muft oppofe the high authority of the Marbles, which feems to be confirmed by the names Πυλαια and Πυλαγοραι, by which the council and its members were ever called, in whatever place they were convened in fucceeding times.

THE intention of Amphictyon, in inftituting this affembly, was, that the children of Deucalion, who, at his deceafe, divided the kingdom between them, fhould have a common tribunal, to which they might appeal in all private contefts, and a council, in which they might concert all meafures neceffary for their defence againft their foreign enemies. And for thefe purpofes, befides thofe laws by which each particular city was governed, he enacted others of general force and obligation to all, which were called Amphictyonic laws. By means of thefe, faith Dionyfius *, the people, thus united, continued in ftrict and mutual amity; regarded

each

each other as real brethren and country-men; and were enabled to annoy and ftrike terrour into their barbarous enemies. Ther-mopylae was the limit which divided the territories of Amphictyon and Hellen, the two brothers; here, therefore, they built a temple to Ceres at the common charge, near the mouth of the river Æfo-pus, in which the members of the Am-phictyonic council affembled to offer their facrifices, and to confult about their com-mon intereft, twice in every year, in fpring and autumn; and hence the names Πυλαια εαρινη και μετοπωρινη, the vernal and au-tumnal convention.

Prideaux
Not. ad
Chron. Mar.
p. 122.

THE affembly, thus formed, was at firft but fmall, being wholly compofed of thofe people whom Deucalion had commanded, and who, from his fon Hellen, were called ΕΛΛΗΝΕΣ. The Dorians and Ionians, who were defcended from the pofterity of this Hellen, as yet had no being; nor were any of the Peloponnefians now accounted Hellenes, but were called Pelafgi; neither were they difpofed to unite with the fons of

Ibid.

b 4

Deuca-

Deucalion, by whom they had been deprived of Theffaly, and all that part of Greece which lay beyond the ifthmus. As Greece improved, and the Hellenes increafed in number, new regulations became neceffary: and accordingly we find, that, in fome time after the original inftitution, Acrifius, king of Argos, when, through fear of Perfeus, (who, as the oracle declared, was to kill him) he retired into Theffaly, obferved the defects of the Amphictyonic council, and undertook to new-model and regulate it; extended its privileges; augmented the number of its members; enacted new laws, by which the collective body was to be governed; and affigned to each ftate one fingle deputy, and one fingle voice, to be enjoyed by fome, in their own fole right; by others, in conjunction with one or more inferior ftates: and thus came to be confidered as the founder of this famous reprefentative of the Hellenic body.

FROM the time of Acrifius, the Amphictyons ftill continued to hold one of their

annual

annual councils at Thermopylae, that of autumn. But it was now made a part of their function (and, in time of peace, became the moft confiderable part of it) to guard and protect the national religion. The vernal affembly therefore was held at Delphi, the great feat of the Grecian religion; the object of univerfal veneration ; whither all people, Greeks and Barbarians, reforted, to feek the advice and direction of the famous Pythian oracle. The immenfe quantity of wealth, the number of rich votive offerings, which the fuperftition of fo many ages and nations had lavifhed on the temple, demanded the exacteft care and moft vigorous protection. The prodigious concourfe which attended there, at particular feafons, naturally produced many contefts, and required a well regulated polity, and the frequent interpofition of a refpectable and powerful jurifdiction. The Delphians themfelves were entrufted with the poffeffion and general guardianfhip of the temple : they attended entirely on the fervice of the god, and were folely employed in the ceremonials of his religion :

they

Dem. de Coron. fect. 51.
Ed Fouike
& Fieind.

Van Dale
Differtat. de
Conc.
Amph.

they were accounted in some sort sacred; the priests, the attendants, and as it were the family, of Apollo. So they are called by Lucian (in Phalarid. 1.) ἱεροι τε και παρεδροι τε Πυθια, και μονονε συνοικοι και ὁμοροφιοι. But although they enjoyed certain powers and privileges with respect to the temple, and could even grant some honours and favours to particular persons, such as that of the Προμαντεια, or right of precedence in consulting the oracle, as appears from an imperfect inscription preserved by Spon and Wheeler, and quoted by Van Dale [B]: yet still were they subject to the inspection

[B] The inscription according to Spon:

     . . . . ΑΔΕΛΦΟ
     . . . . . ΑΝ. ΠΑΤΡΟΝΑ
     . . . . . ΕΥΔΟΡΩΙ
     . . . . ΤΑΡΧΟΣ. ΒΟΙΩΤΟΙΣ.
     . . . ΤΑΝΑΓΡΑΣ ΑΥΤΟΙΣ.
     ΕΓΓΟΝΟΙΣ. ΠΡΟΞΕ
     . . . . ΠΡΟΜΑΝΤΕΙΑΝ.
     ΕΛΕΙΑΔΑΣΥΛΙΑΝ.
     ΠΡΟΕΔΡΙΑΝ. ΠΡΟΔΙΚΙ . . . .
     ΑΝ. ΕΠΙΤΙΜΑΝ. ΚΑΘΑΠΕΡ.
     . . . ΔΕΛΦΟΙΣ. ΑΡΧΟΝΤΟΣ.
     ΘΟΙΝΙΩΝΟΣ. ΒΟΥΛΕΥ
     . . . Ν ΓΩΝ. . . . . . ΣΩΠΟΔΟΡΟΥ.
     . . . ΡΑΚΛΕΙ . . . . ΑΔΑΜΟΤ . . . . .

I

and

and jurifdiction of the Amphictyons, who were the great confervators and protectors of the fhrine; and who, befides their general care, appointed certain of their members, either by lot or rotation, to prefide over the temple; an honour which, according to Van Dale, was alfo called by the name Προμαντεια.

THE times of affembling we have faid were two in each year. The following hiftory however affords an inftance of the Amphictyons affuming a power of affembling oftener, on fome extraordinary emergencies. But this feems to have been a corruption introduced by time, or the power of particular parties; and as fuch we fhall find it condemned and difcountenanced. Here, however, we are to diftinguifh between the Συνεδριον Αμφικτυονων, the regular affembly formed of thofe deputies only who had a right to vote, and who had thefe ftated times of meeting; and the Εκκλησια, which muft be here explained. Whenever or wherever the council of Amphictyons

was

Æsch. in Ctef. fect. 39. Val-lois. Dif-fert. fur les Amph. Vol. 3. Mem. des B. l. p. 207.

was affembled, a great concourfe attended from all parts of Greece, to fhare in the public games and fpectacles which this council inftituted and fuperintended; and to expofe their wares and merchandizes to public fale. Thefe Greeks were always allowed to be prefent in the affembly, to obferve the conduct of their reprefentatives, to affift, direct, and inftruct them. When the council met at Delphi, the concourfe was ftill further increafed, by the numbers who came to confult the oracle, among whom were many perfons refpectable by their ftations and characters; and parti-

Ibid. p. 226.

cularly the Θεοροι, or men commiffioned to repair to Delphi by each ftate, together with its Amphictyons, in order to confult the oracle, to offer facrifices, and to affift in religious rites. All thefe perfons were not only permitted to be prefent in the council, but on extraordinary occafions were fummoned to attend. Thus an af-fembly extraordinary was fometimes form-ed of the ufual and ordinary Amphictyonic deputies, and thefe additional numbers,

called

called Εκκλησια. The learned Vallois is perfuaded that thofe Greeks, who attended on the fervice of the gods, are marked out by the words το κοινον των Αμφικτυονων, which occurs in one of the decrees quoted by Æfchines. And, if fo, they feem not to have been excluded from voting in fuch extraordinary affemblies; all refolutions were at leaft paffed in their name, as well as in that of the ordinary Amphictyons. Εδοξε τοις Πυλαγοραις και τοις συνεδροις των Αμφικτυονων και το ΚΟΙΝΩ ΤΩΝ ΑΜΦΙΚΤΥΟΝΩΝ. *Dem. de Coron. fect. 51.* " It is decreed by " the Pylagorae and affeffors of the Am- " phictyons, and the community of Am- " phictyons."

THE alterations, made in the council of Amphictyons at different times, feem to have occafioned the difference in hiftorians as to the number and names of the people who had a right to fend reprefentatives to that affembly. Agreeably to the difpofitions made by Acrifius, twelve cities only were invefted with this right, according to Strabo. Æfchines and Theopompus

alfo

also confine it to twelve people, whom the orator * calls, not πολεις, cities, but ἐθνη, a word denoting a collection of several particular communities. Pausanias † also calls them γενη, a term of like signification.

* Æschin. de falsa Leg. sect. 36. Ed. Brooke.

† in loc. cit.

THE AMPHICTYONIC PEOPLE.

According to Æschines.	To Theopompus.	To Pausanias.
THESSALIANS	IONIANS	IONIANS
BOEOTIANS	DORIANS	DOLOPES
DORIANS	PERRHAEBEANS	THESSALIANS
IONIANS	BOEOTIANS	ÆNIANS
PERRHAEBEANS	MAGNETES	MAGNETES
MAGNETES	ACHAEANS	MALEANS
LOCRIANS	PHTHIOTES	PHTHIOTES
OETEANS	MALEANS	DORIANS
PHTHIOTES	DOLOPES	PHOCIANS
MALEANS	ÆNIANS	LOCRI EPICNE-
PHOCIANS	DELPHIANS	' MIDES.
	PHOCIANS	

ÆSCHINES, we see, enumerates but eleven; yet he asserts the number to be twelve. By which it seems probable, that some copyist was guilty of an omission, in leaving out one name, possibly that of the Dolopes. The OEteans, in his list, are the same fame with the Ænians in the others, who were fo called, from their vicinity to mount Oeta. And, amidſt all this diverſity of repreſentation, we may perceive there are ſome people whom all acknowledge as members of this council. Theſe are the Ionians, Dorians, Magnetes, Phthiotes, Phocians, and Maleans. Difference of times and circumſtances might have produced many alterations; but the general intention of this aſſembly, and the invariable objeɕt of all its modellers and direɕtors, was to form a complete repreſentative of all Greece; and accordingly it is called by Demoſthenes το κοινον των Ελληνων Συνεδριον, and by Cicero, who exaɕtly tranſlates him, commune Graeciae concilium.

We are not therefore to imagine, that the twelve principal cities in the ſeveral diſtriɕts, only, continued to ſend their deputies to the Amphiɕtyonic council, (whatever might have been the caſe in earlier times) or that the twelve ΕΘΝΗ were ſo many diſtinɕt and ſeparate ſocieties, which had a right to ſend juſt twenty-four deputies

ties (for the number of deputies from each ftate was doubled in fome time after Acrifius). Each of thefe diftricts, on the contrary, contained a number of Amphictyonic ftates, each of which, either by themfelves, or in conjunction with others, had an equal right of fending their reprefentatives. This cannot be better illuftrated, and, at the fame time, more fully proved, than by quoting the paffage from Æfchines *, to which we are indebted for this information : Κατηριθμησαμην δ᾽ εθνη δωδεκα τὰ μετέχοντα τυ ιερυ· Θετ]αλυ᾽ς, Βο.ωτυς, υ᾽ Θηβαιυς μονους, Δοριευς, Ιωνας, Περῥαιβυς, Μαγνητας, Λοκρυς, Οιταιυς, Φθιωτας, Μαλεεῖς, Φωκεῖς· και τυτων ἐδειξα ἑκαςον ἐθν℗ ισοψηφον γενομενον, το μεγιςον τω ἐλατ]ονι, τον ῾ηκοντα ἐκ Δωριυ και Κυτινίυ ισον δυναμενον Λακεδαιμονιοις, δυο γαρ ψεφυς ἑκαςον φερε. ἐθν℗, παλιν ἐκ των Ιωνων τον Ερετριεα και Πριηνεα τοις Αθηναιοις, και τυς ἀλλυς κατα ταυτα. " I " enumerated the twelve people who had a " right to fhare in the guardianfhip of the " temple; the Theffalians, the Boeotians, " (not the Thebans alone) the Dorians, Io- " nians, Perrhebaeans, Magnetes, Locrians, " Oeteans,

" Oeteans, Phthiotes, Maleans, Phocians.
" Of thefe I fhewed that each particular
" ftate had an equal right of fuffrage, the
" leaft with the greateft; the deputies of Do-
" rium and of Cytinium the fame with the
" deputies of Lacedaemon: two voices to
" each ftate: and again, of the Ionians, the
" Eretrian and Prienean deputy an equal
" power with the Athenian: and fo of the
" reft."

WE find a remarkable paffage in the life
of Themiftocles by Plutarch, which exactly
agrees to this.   The hiftorian relates, that
the Lacedaemonians endeavoured to have
all thofe cities excluded from the Amphictyonic council, that had refufed to unite in
the war againft the Perfians; and that Themiftocles, who conceived this to be a fcheme
for throwing the whole power of the council into the hands of the Lacedaemonians,
oppofed it ftrenuoufly, and prevailed on
the pylagorae to reject the propofition :
διδαξας ὡς τριακοντα και μια μοναι πολεις εἰσιν
αἱ μετασχουσαι του πολεμου, και τουτων αἱ
πλειες πανταπασιν μικραι· δεινον οὐν εἰ της ἀλλης
Ἑλλαδος ἐκσπονδου γενομενης, ἐπι ταις μεγιςαις

δυσιν η τρισι πολεσιν ἐςαι το Συνεδριον: "Shewing that but one and thirty such "cities had shared in the war; and of these "moft were very fmall; fo that it would "have alarming confequences, if the reft "of Greece fhould be excluded from the "council, and fo the whole influence of it "devolve to two or three principal cities." Here, then, we find, that one and thirty cities made but a part of this council in the time of Themiftocles. Non credo, faith Van Dale *, quod omnes iftas xxxi civitates tunc fingulas jus illud fuffragii reverà poffediffe, fed id voluiffe Themiftoclem, ut, fi hae omnes iftud jus obtinerent, reliquas non poffe excludi, quod aeque civitates Graeciae effent. "I do not believe, "that every fingle city of thefe thirty-one "really enjoyed the right of fuffrage: but "that the meaning of Themiftocles is this, "that if they were all to be admitted to "fuch a right, the others could not be ex-"cluded, as thefe were equally ftates of "Greece." But where is the difficulty of believing what the hiftorian afferts, and what is fufficiently confirmed by collateral evidence? The queftion was not whether

any

* Differt. de
Conc.
Amph.

any new right fhould be conferred on the cities which had joined in the war, but whether the others fhould be deprived of the right which they had before enjoyed. A few lines above the paffage quoted, we have this fentence : Φοβηθεις μη Θετ]αλυς και Αργειυς ἐτι δε Θηβαιους ἐκβαλλοντας του Συνεδριου, κ. τ. λ. " apprehenfive left if the " Theffalians and Argians and Thebans " fhould be excluded from the affembly," &c. But it is plain the Argians and Thebans fat in the council, as members, the one of the Dorian, the other of the Boeotian body. Again, we find the Athenian orators fpeaking of an Amphiffaean, an Arcadian, a Pharfalian, as haranguing and acting in the Amphictyonic council : which cannot be naturally accounted for, but by fuppofing them to have been the reprefentatives of certain Amphictyonic ftates which the twelve general diftricts contained, all of which had an equal right of being reprefented. This might be thought a point too well eftablifhed to require to be enlarged upon, if the writers upon this fubject had

not

not either abfolutely denied it, or admitted it only with certain limitations and reftric-tions. Prideaux *, for inftance, afferts that no more than twenty-four members fat in this council: but how can this be recon-ciled with the declaration of Æfchines, that Dorium, Cytinium, Prienea, Eretria, had each two voices as well as Lacedaemon and Athens? Again, Van Dale fuppofes that the principal ftates only fent their deputies conftantly, while the inferior cities were admitted to this privilege, at fome particu-lar times, which were determined by ro-tation. But it may be doubted whether this fuppofition can be thoroughly reconciled to that equality of power and fuffrage, that ισοψηφον, which Æfchines fpeaks of. In the time of Paufanias * indeed, fuch a re-gulation obtained as Van Dale mentions; and certain inferior cities were allowed only to fend reprefentatives by turns, (as we fhall hereafter have occafion of obferv-ing:) but this feems to have been a new re-gulation, which had not obtained in any former times, but was eftablifhed on mo-delling this council in a new manner.

WE

* Not. in
Chron Mar.
p. 124.

* in Phoc.
ut fupra.

WE fee, then, how this famous council was formed. The whole nation of Greece was divided into twelve diftricts or provinces : each of thefe contained a certain number of Amphictyonic ftates, or cities, each of which enjoyed an equal right of voting and determining in all affairs relative to the general intereft. Other inferior cities were dependent on fome of thefe, and, as members of their community, were alfo reprefented by the fame deputies : and thus the affembly of the Amphictyons became really and properly the reprefentative of the whole Hellenic body : το κοινον των Ελληνων Συνεδριον.

THIS idea of the Amphictyonic council may poffibly ferve to explain a remarkable paffage in Diodorus Siculus *, which the interpreters and commentators feem to give up as totally inexplicable. It is in that decree which the Amphictyons made againft the people of Phocis, at the conclufion of the famous facred war. One article of which runs thus : Των δ' εν Φοκευσι τριων πολεων περελειν τα τειχη, και μεδεμιαν κοινωνιαν ειναι

* Lib. 16. fect. 60. Ed. Amft. 1746.

τοις

τοις Φοκευσι τυ ιερυ, μηδε τυ Αμφικτυονικου Συνεδριου. Utque trium in Phocide urbium moenia deftruantur ; nec templi deinceps, et Amphictyonum curiae Phocenfes fint participes. The word τριων feems fo very difficult to be explained, that it is fufpected to be an interpolation : but, even upon this fuppofition, it is obferved by the commentators, that the article cannot be reconciled to another in the fame decree, which imports, not that the citics of Phocis, or three cities of Phocis, fhould be difmantled, but that all the Phocian cities fhould be razed to the ground. The article, now quoted, I would tranflate in this manner : " That " the walls of THE three cities of the Pho- " cians fhall be pulled down ; and that the " Phocians fhall have no further commu- " nication with the temple, or the affem- " bly of the Amphictyons." By THE THREE cities, fo called by way of eminence, I would underftand the three Amphictyonic cities of Phocis, or at leaft the three Amphictyonic cities which had fhared in the guilt of facrilege. The oath which each deputy in this council was obliged to

take

take (as we fhall immediately find) forbad
the deftruction of any one of thefe cities.
Out of refpect therefore to this oath, and
to the right which thefe Amphictyonic
cities of Phocis formerly enjoyed, I fuppofe that a diftinction was made between
thefe three, and the Phocian cities in general: and that, while the reft were totally
demolifhed, their walls only were pulled
down. And that fuch a diftinction was
really made, and that, while a great number of cities in this ftate were razed to their
foundations, fome were fuffered to continue, appears from this, that, fome years
after this decree, Elataea, one of the cities
of Phocis, was accounted a poft of fuch
confequence, that all Greece was thrown
into the greateft confternation when Philip
king of Macedon poffeffed himfelf of it.
And this interpretation not only reconciles
the two articles of the decree, which were
deemed repugnant to each other, but alfo
explains the addition of the fecond claufe
in that now quoted, *and that the Phocians
fhall,* &c. which muft otherwife appear

c 4

not

not fo natural at leaft, if not difficult to be accounted for.

EACH of thofe cities, which had a right to affift in the Amphictyonic council, was obliged to fend its deputies to every meeting; and the number of thefe deputies was ufually and regularly two: the one entitled HIEROMNEMON, to whom was particularly entrufted the care of religion and its rites. His office was annual, as appears from feveral decrees, in which his name is joined with that of the Athenian archon $\epsilon\pi\omega\nu\nu\mu\sigma\varsigma$; and he was appointed by lot. The other deputy was called by the general name PYLAGORAS, and was chofen by election for each particular meeting. Each of thefe deputies, however differing in their functions, enjoyed an equal power of determining all affairs relative to the general intereft. And thus the cities which they reprefented, without any diftinction or fubordination, each gave two voices in the council of the Amphictyons, a privilege known by the name of the DOUBLE SUF-
FRAGE;

Suidas, Harpocration, et al.

Dem. de Coron. fect. 51. Arifteph. in Nub. Dem. in Finoc. Æfchin. in Ctef. fect. 30.

FRAGE; which term, so frequent in the ancient writings, is thus fully explained, without any refinement or difficulty. But, although the number of deputies seems to have been settled originally so as to answer to the number of votes which each city was allowed, yet, in process of time, we find, that, on some extraordinary occasions, the principal cities assumed a power of sending more than one pylagoras to assist in a critical emergency, or to serve some purpose of a faction. Thus we shall find, in the following history, that the Athenians, at one particular time, nominated three pylagorae, Midias, Æschines, and Thrasicles. Prideaux asserts, that Demosthenes also was joined with these; and speaks with severity of those who deny it. And yet possibly some arguments might be brought to disprove this assertion, if, notwithstanding the positive manner in which it is advanced, it was not sufficiently discredited by coming entirely unsupported by any authority. But, in all cases where the leading cities took the liberty of enlarging the number of their deputies, though such

procedure

procedure might ferve to increafe their
fecret influence, yet their power of voting
continued the fame.   This was exactly
afcertained, without any regard to differences of grandeur or power in the different
ftates.   Each enjoyed two voices, the leaft
as well as the greateft; they who fent but
two deputies, and they whofe affairs required a greater number.

WHEN·the deputies, thus appointed, appeared to execute their commiffion, they in
the firft place offered up their folemn facrifices to the gods; to Ceres, when they
affembled at Thermopylae; when at Delphi, to Apollo, Diana, Latona, and Minerva : and, before they entered on their
function, each deputy was obliged to take
an oath, which Æfchines hath preferved,
or at leaft fome part of it ; and which was
conceived in thefe terms :

AEfch. de
fal. Leg.
fect. 35.

    " I SWEAR that I will never fubvert
" any Amphictyonic city : I will never ftop
" the courfes of their waters either in war
" or peace. If any fuch outrages fhall be
                              " attempted,

" attempted, I will oppofe them by force
" of arms, and deftroy thofe cities who
" may be guilty of fuch attempts.   If any
" devaftations fhall be committed in the
" territory of the god; if any fhall be privy
" to fuch offence, or entertain any defign
" againft the temple; I will make ufe of
" my feet, my hands, my whole force, to
" bring the offending party to condign pu-
" nifhment."

To render this oath ftill more folemn,
the following awful imprecations were fub-
joined :

" IF any one fhall violate any part of
" this folemn engagement, whether city,
" private perfon, or country, may fuch
" violators be obnoxious to the vengeance
" of Apollo, Diana, Latona, and Minerva
" the provident.   May their lands never
" produce their fruits: may their women
" never bring forth children of the fame
" nature with their parents, but offsprings
" of an unnatural and monftrous kind:
" may they be for ever defeated in war,

Æfch.
in Ctef.
fect. 36.

5

" in

" in judicial controverſies, and in all civil
" tranſactions ; and may they, their fami-
" lies, and their whole race, be utterly de-
" ſtroyed: may they never offer up an
" acceptable ſacrifice to Apollo, Diana,
" Latona, and Minerva the provident ; but
" may all their ſacred rites be for ever re-
" jected."

As the hieromnemon was particularly
entruſted with the affairs of religion, the
dignity of his function gave him a ſuperiority over the pylagoras, who appears to
have been obliged to pay him ſome kind of
deference and ſubmiſſion.   There is a paſſage in Æſchines * which ſeems to warrant
this : Πεμψαμενۛ δε ὁ Ιερομνημων ἠξιου με εἰσελ-
θειν εἰς το Συνεδριον, και εἰπειν τι πρὸς τους Αμφικτυονας ὑπερ της πολεως, κ. τ. λ.   " The
" hieromnemon ſent for me, and ſignified
" his directions that I ſhould go into the
" aſſembly, and ſpeak to the Amphictyons
" in behalf of the ſtate, &c."   But this
doth not fully prove that it was the peculiar province of the pylagoras to ſpeak in
the council, as M. de Vallois ſuppoſes :

I
for,

* in Cteſ.
ſect. 38.

'for, at this particular time, the hieromne-
-mon was fick; and we may as well fuppofe
that his directions to Æfchines were occafioned by his prefent inability of appearing
and fpeaking, as that it was not a part of
his office and power to fpeak in the council.
Indeed the principal weight of bufinefs
feems to have fallen on the pylagorae, who,
as they were chofen by election, were ge-.
nerally men of abilities; and from this
caufe feem to have become the fpeakers
(οἱ πεμπομενοι ἀπο των πολεων εἰς Αμφικτυονιαν
ρηλορες. " Men fent from the feveral ftates
" to the Amphictyonic council as fpeak-
" ers," as Suidas calls them) rather than
from any particular power annexed to their
office. As the hieromnemons, on the contrary, were appointed by lot, this office
muft have fometimes devolved on men unacquainted with public bufinefs, and un-
fkilled in politics. And, when intrigue
and corruption began to prevail in the Amphictyonic council, many inconveniencies
muft have arifen from this. Artful ftatefmen, and factious leaders, by affecting an
high veneration for their authority, by
alarming

alarming them with the real or pretended dangers to which religion was expofed, abufed their honeft, though mifguided, zeal ; and made them the dupes of their craft and policy. Thus we find Demofthenes * complaining, το μελλον ου προορωμενους τυς Ιερομνημονας πειθει ψηφισασθαι, κ. τ. λ. " He perfuaded the hieromnemons, who " did not forefee the confequences, to vote, " &c."

* de Coron. fect. 49.

It was the peculiar privilege of one of the hieromnemons to prefide in the council. He collected the votes ; he reported the refolutions : he had the power of convening the Εκκλησια, or general convention : (as we learn from Æfchines *: Κοτ]υφος ο τας γνωμας επιψεφιζων, εκκλησιαν εποιει των Αμφικτυονων. " Cottyphus, who collected the " voices, convened a general affembly of " the Amphictyons.") His name was prefixed to every decree, together with his title, which was that of fovereign pontiff or prieft of Apollo. Of this Demofthenes * furnifhes us with fome inftances : Επι Ιερεως Κλειναγορου, εαρινης Πυλαιας εδοξε τοις Πυλαγοραις,

* in Ctef. fect. 39.

* de Coron. fect. 51.

γοραις, κ. τ. λ.   " In the pontificate of Cli-
" nagoras, the vernal affembly, it is de-
" creed by the pylagorae, &c."   This honour of prefiding doth not feem to have
been a privilege granted to power or grandeur, or to have been confined to the deputy of any one ftate.   We find in the
Athenian orators, that Cottyphus, the pre-
fident of the council, was the deputy either
from Arcadia or Pharfalia, places of inferior note.   It is probable, therefore, that
the hieromnemon of each Amphictyonic
ftate enjoyed this power in rotation.   Such
feems to be the language of the following
ancient infcription taken from Gruther,
p. 129 and 1021, (if the infcription be copied accurately :)

ΘΕΟΙΣ.

ΕΠΙ. ΑΡΙΣΤΑΓΟΡΑ. ΑΡΧΟΝΤΟΣ. ΕΝ.
ΔΕΛΦΟΙΣ. ΠΥΛΑΙΑΣ. ΗΡΙΝΗΣ. ΙΕΡΟ
ΜΝΗΜΟΝΥΟΝΤΩΝ. ΑΙΤΟΛΩΝ. ΠΟ
ΛΕΜΑΡΧΟΥ. ΑΛΕΞΑΜΕΝΟΥ
ΔΑΜΩΝΟΣ.

                              BUT,

BUT, whatever honours might have been annexed to the office of hieromnemon, the real equality of power was still fcrupuloufly obferved; and even all appearances of fuperiority, all forms of fpeaking or writing, that might point out any difference between the members of the council, avoided with particular delicacy and politenefs. Of this we have an inftance in the form of an Amphictyonic decree, as it is explained by M. de Vallois: Εδιξε τοις Πυλαγοραις, και τοις Συνεδροις των Αμφικτυονων, και τω κοινω των Αμφικτυονων. " It is decreed " by the pylagorae, and *the other* affeffors " in the Amphictyonic council, and by the " community of the Amphictyons." By the Συνεδροις, according to this author, muft be underftood the hieromnemons, as the council was compofed only of the two orders. Here, then, we find the hieromnemons named after the pylagorae. And the reafon feems to him to be this: The office of the former was to collect the votes, to pronounce the decrees, and to reduce them to writing. To name themfelves in the

firft

Dem. ut fupra.

firſt place would have been a violation of that decorum to which the Greeks ever carefully adhered; and, at the ſame time, their prerogative was to be preſerved. They therefore choſe to ſubſtitute the term Συνεδροι, in the place of their title Ἱερομνημονες, in order to preſerve the reſpect due to their collegues, and, at the ſame time, not to derogate from the honour annexed to their own rank. As to the laſt clauſe, το κοινον των Αμφικτυονων, it hath been already explained.

Such was the conſtitution of this famous Grecian council. As to the diſputes of particular perſons, it was accounted beneath the dignity of the Amphictyons to take cognizance of them. Nor do we read of any private man ſummoned to appear, or condemned in this aſſembly, except Ephialtes, who, when the Spartans poſſeſſed themſelves of Thermopylae, under the command of Leonidas, conducted the Perſians over the Oetean mountains into Greece. But all offences againſt religion,

Prideaux
Nor. in
Chron.
Marm.
P. 125.

Vol. I.   d   all

all inftances of impiety and profanation, all contefts between the Grecian ftates and cities, came under the particular cognizance of the Amphictyons, who had a right to determine, to impofe fines, and even to levy forces, and to make war on thofe who prefumed to rebel againft their fovereign authority. The ancient writings afford us feveral inftances of the interpofition of this their authority, fome of which it may not be improper to lay before the reader.

AFTER the famous naval victory at Salamis, where Themiftocles deftroyed the fleet of Xerxes; and the battle of Plataea, in which the Perfians received a total overthrow by the arms of Greece, conducted by Paufanias the Spartan, and Ariftides the Athenian; the Greeks confecrated a golden tripod to Apollo, in acknowledgment of two fuch fignal fucceffes. Paufanias, who was chofen to depofit this offering, from an arrogant ambition of immortalizing his own glory, and that of his country, affumed to himfelf the whole honour of this offering,

Demoft.
in Neaer.

offering, and infcribed the following verfes on the tripod :

Ελληνων αρχηγος, επει στραℸον ωλεσε Μηδων,
Παυσανιας Φοιϐω μνημ' ανεθηκε τοℸε.

" Paufanias, general of the Greeks, when
" he had deftroyed the army of the Medes,
" dedicated this memorial of his victory to
" Apollo."   The people of Plataea, who had contributed confiderably to the fuccefs, conceiving a juft indignation at this procedure of Paufanias, fummoned the Lacedaemonians to appear before the Amphictyons, who condemned them to pay a finc of a thoufand talents to the confederates, who had been injured and infulted by this infcription.   It doth not appear whether or no this fine was rigidly exacted : but it is certain that the Lacedaemonians were obliged to efface this infcription, and, in the place of it, to fubftitute the names, not of the Plataeans only, but of all the confederate cities, which contributed to the expence of the votive tripod, and the fuccefs

d 2

which

which had occafioned this offering to be made. Thucydides indeed, towards the end of his firft book, and from him Plutarch, at the end of his treatife on the Malignity of Herodotus, afferts that the Lacedaemonians voluntarily effaced this infcription, when they had been informed of the general indignation with which the Greeks received it. But fuch a confeffion of their fault doth not feem to agree with the fierce and haughty temper of this people; and the implacable refentment, with which they purfued the Plataeans, feems an argument of the reluctance with which, on this occafion, they fubmitted to a fuperior authority.

Vid. Taylor. Comment. in Marm. Sand. p. 19.

ANOTHER inftance of the power and authority of the Amphictyons appears in the conteft between the Athenians and Delians, concerning the patronage of the temple of Apollo in Delos. This ifland had long acknowledged the jurifdiction of the Athenians, who affumed the whole care of the temple, which Eryficthon, the fon of Cecrops,

crops, was faid to have erected; and, in many inftances, exercifed a tyrannic power over the inhabitants. About the end of the Peloponnefian war, the Delians made fome ineffectual remonftrances againft the injuftice of the Athenian claim to the property of their ifland, and the guardianfhip of their temple; but, in the hundred and feventh, or hundred and eighth Olympiad, they brought their caufe before the Amphictyonic council, encouraged poffibly by the enemies of Athens. On this occafion Hyperides was, by the interpofition of the Areopagites, appointed to defend the right of his country, and deliver his famous Deliac oration; and probably with fuccefs, though the ancients do not particularly inform us of the event of this difpute.

Dem. de Coron, fect. 42.

PLUTARCH, in the life of Cimon, takes notice of the inhabitants of the ifland Scyros being fined by the Amphictyons, for a violation of the law of nations, in plundering thofe who brought merchandifes into their own port.

THE

The same author, in the conclusion of his treatise intitled Κεφαλαιων καταγραφη Ελληνικα, hath recorded, that, at a time when certain of the Peloponnesians were deputed to repair to Delphi, in order to confult the oracle, in their way they stopped at Megara, and difposed themselves, with their wives and children, in their carriages, in order to pafs the night. The Megareans, with a brutal infolence and cruelty, which were partly the effects of drunkennefs, overturned thefe carriages into an adjacent lake, by which fome of the Peloponnefians were drowned. This was an outrage which particularly demanded the interpofition of the Amphictyons, as religion was affronted by the violation of the reverence due to the perfons and commiffion of thefe Peloponnefians. This council therefore exerted its authority, and inflicted fevere punifhment on the Megareans; condemning fome capitally, and banifhing others who had not fhared fo largely in the offence.

QUINC-

QUINCTILIAN informs us, (in his fifth book and tenth chapter de Inst. Orat.) that, when Alexander demolished Thebes, he there found an authentic record, by which it appeared that the Thebans had lent two hundred talents to the Thessalians: and that, in consideration of the services he had received from the Thessalian cavalry, he cancelled the deed. When Thebes had been restored by Cassander, this state demanded the repayment of the loan; and brought its suit before the council of the Amphictyons.

CICERO (de Inventione, l. 2.) relates, that the Thebans, having gained a victory over the Lacedaemonians, instead of setting up a slight trophy, which might continue but for a time, according to the ancient moderation of the Greeks, erected one of brass, and were accused of this insolent attempt to perpetuate the memory of Grecian discord, before the council of the Amphictyons.

THESE

THESE two laſt inſtances indeed may poſſibly have been no more than fictions, invented by the teachers of oratory, as ſubjects for declamation, in order to exerciſe their ſcholars. The power of this council is however fully proved by the other examples, and much more by thoſe religious wars which were undertaken by their authority, and which the reader will find related at large in the following hiſtory.

WHILE the generous principles, on which this illuſtrious body was firſt formed, continued to preſerve their due vigour, the Amphictyons of conſequence were reſpectable, auguſt, and powerful. When the nation itſelf began to degenerate, its repreſentative of courſe ſhared in the general corruption. Selfiſh, luxurious, and venal conſtituents committed the care of their intereſts to men who gratified their paſſions, with an intent to abuſe the truſt repoſed in them. We find that, in the time of Philip, the popular leaders, in one particular ſtate, were ſo totally loſt to all ſenſe of decency,

Dem. Phil. 3. ſect. 8.

that

that they openly avowed their proſtitution and corruption, which were made a matter of mirth to their fellow-citizens. And, as the degeneracy was in a great degree univerſal through Greece, it ſeems highly probable, that moſt of thoſe, who were deputed to ſit in the council of the Amphictyons, came prepared to earn the wages of iniquity, and to devote themſelves entirely to the ſervice of a crafty and enterpriſing prince, who could pay them liberally, without regard to their own honour, the intereſt of their community, or the general good of Greece. And the natural and neceſſary conſequences of ſuch depravity were weakneſs and contempt.

THE decline of this council we may therefore date from the time when Philip king of Macedon began to practiſe with its members, and prevailed to have his kingdom annexed to the Hellenic body. It continued, however, for ages after the deſtruction of Grecian liberty, to aſſemble and to exerciſe ſome remains of its autho-

VOL. I.   e   rity.

rity. Not only the Phocians, but the Lacedaemonians, and all the Dorians, are said by Paufanias * to have been excluded from the council at the conclufion of the fecond facred war. The Phocians, however, afterwards recovered their feat by the fervices which they performed in defence of Delphi, when that city was befieged by the Gauls. When Auguftus, the Roman emperor, had built Nicopolis, in honour of his victory at Actium, he ordered that this new city fhould be admitted into the council, and enjoy the power of fuffrage, which was before poffeffed by the Magnetes, Maleans, Ænians, and Phthiotes (who were now ordered to unite, and to make one Amphictyonic ftate with Theffaly) and by the Dolopes (a people at that time loft). In the time of Paufanias, who lived in the reign of Antoninus Pius, the Amphictyonic cities were thirty; but of thefe the cities of Athens, Delphi, and Nicopolis, only fent their deputies conftantly, the reft at particular times in rotation. But as their care was now entirely confined to the rites of
their

* in loc.
cit.

Ibid.

Prid. Not.
in Chron.
Marm.
p. 127.

their idolatrous worſhip ; and as theſe came
to be forbidden in the time of Conſtantine ;
this famous council of Amphictyons ſeems
to have fallen, together with their temple
and their religion.

THE

THE HISTORY

OF THE

LIFE AND REIGN

OF

PHILIP

KING OF MACEDON.

BOOK THE FIRST.

Vol. I.   B

BOOK I. SECTION I.

CONTENTS.

MACEDON described.—The original settlement of Caranus at Edessa.—He founds the kingdom of Macedon.—The regal power; religion; manners; and original boundaries of his kingdom.—His successors.—Perdiccas the first.—Argaeus.—Amyntas the first.—The deputies of Megabyzus entertained at his court.—Alexander the first.—His merit and abilities.—Perdiccas the second.—His policy.—Original establishment of the united states of Olynthus.—History of Amphipolis.—Archelaus.—His character.—Is killed by Craterus.—Orestes. Æropus.—Pausanias.—Amyntas the second, father of Philip.—Is supported by Derdas.—Marries Eurydicè.—Defeated by the Illyrians, who establish Argaeus on the throne.—His kingdom exposed to the incursions of Thessaly and Olynthus.—Amyntas resigns the remaining part of his territories to the Olynthians: but is restored by the Thessalians, and reclaims them.—Favoured by a particular event.—The birth of PHILIP.—*Sparta and Macedon unite against Olynthus.—The conduct of Sparta explained.*

B 2

—Euda-

THE

4

THE
LIFE AND REIGN
OF
PHILIP
KING OF MACEDON.

BOOK THE FIRST.

SECTION I.

THE founder of the Macedonian great-ness, whose actions are to be the sub-ject of this history, was by no means of the number of those princes who were affisted by the advantages of an illuftrious country, who inherited the opulence and force of fplendid and extenfive dominions, or were ftrengthened by the acquifitions, and animated by the atchieve-ments, of a long train of renowned anceftry.

B 3
To

To his own abilities alone did PHILIP owe his elevation; and appears equally great, and equally the object of admiration, in furmounting the difficulties attending on his infant power, as in his maturer and more extenfive fortune. But before we proceed to relate thofe actions in which his vigour, courage, and policy, were fo eminently difplayed; before we attempt to trace his gradual progrefs through all the various obftacles which furrounded him, to that confummate greatnefs which his ambition prefented as the proper object of his views, and his abilities happily acquired; it will be previoufly neceffary, to detain the reader for a while, by a brief account of that kingdom which he governed, and of thofe actions of his predeceffors, which tend more immediately to illuftrate THE HISTORY OF PHILIP.

THE kingdom of Macedon, in its moft flourifhing condition, (as a comparifon of the different defcriptions which antiquity affords directs us to determine) contained all that extent of territory, which lies to the north of Theffaly and Epirus, feparated from the one, by the mountains Pelion, Olympus, and Offa; and from the other, by Pindus and the Chaonian mountains. The river Neffus, and the Egean fea, divided by three peninfulas, into

the

3

the Thermaic, Toronaic, Singitic, and Stry-
monic bays, were its eaftern boundaries. On
the north, the mountains Pangaeus, Hoemus,
Orbelus, and Scardus, divided and protected it
from the Dardani, Triballi, and Illyrians. On
the weft it was wafhed by the Adriatic and Io-
nian fea, extending on that fide from the river
Liffus, to the Chelidnus, and the entrance into
Epirus. Within this tract, the ancient geogra- Plin. Hift.
Nat. l. 4.
phers recount no lefs than one hundred and fifty c. 10.
different people, who, in the earlier times, lived Pomp. Mela
de fitu Orbis
independent of each other; enacted their dif- l. 2. c. 3.
tinct laws, and adminiftered their feveral go-
vernments, while their habit, language, and
unpolifhed manners, were the fame. Nor did
Macedon acquire that extent which hath been
defcribed, but by a flow and gradual progrefs,
and in a long feries of years: when the abilities
of that prince, who is the fubject of this hiftory,
enabled him to reduce all the neighbouring powers; to extend his territories far beyond their
ancient limits, and to add his country, hitherto
obfcure and barbarous, to the renowned body
of Greece.

Caranus, an Argian by birth, and a defcen- Caranus.
Juftin l. 7.
dant from Hercules in the fixteenth degree, ac- c. 1.
cording to * Velleius, is faid to have been the * l. 1. c. 6.
original founder of this kingdom. The difficul-
B 4 ties

Book I.
Juftin ut fu-
pra.

ties of his family, or his own ambition, deter-mined him to forfake his native country, accord-ing to the cuftom of thofe early ages, to feek fome new fettlement, and to create that power and fortune for himfelf, which his native land denied him. At the head of a chofen band of Greeks, whom fortune had obliged, or glory animated, to the undertaking, he marched out, and pierced into the midland part of that di-ftrict which hath been defcribed, then called Emathia; and encamped in the neighbourhood of Edeffa its capital. On a fudden, the fky was overcaft, a great ftorm arofe, and a herd of goats was obferved to fly for fhelter to the city. The oracle was faid to have promifed, that " goats fhould conduct him to his fettlement:" the prefent accident recalled this prediction to his mind; and, thus encouraged, his men flew after thefe their deftined leaders; and furprized Edeffa. In commemoration of this event, Caranus, now lord of the city, changed its name to Ægae: and goats, which are called by that name among the Greeks, were appointed the enfigns of his army, and of his new country. The neighbouring people foon rofe up in arms to oppofe this new fettlement, but proved une-qual to Caranus and his valiant Greeks. * Pau-fanias, in his defcription of Chaeronea, records a tradition, which hath been thought worthy

* In Book.
p. 315.
Univ Hift.
Fol. Vol. 3.
p. 271.

Sect. I.

to be obſerved, as it is an inſtance of the manner by which maxims and cuſtoms come to be eſtabliſhed in kingdoms, and of which poſterity frequently find it difficult to aſſign a reaſonable cauſe. Among other princes, againſt whom Caranus was obliged to turn his arms, he attacked Ciſſaeus, the ſovereign of a ſmall territory, ſouth of his new kingdom, and having defeated him, erected a trophy according to the Grecian cuſtom. An enormous lion, which hunger had driven from a foreſt in the neighbourhood of mount Olympus, fell on this trophy, overturned and demoliſhed it. This the conqueror underſtood as a warning from heaven to treat the vanquiſhed with a juſter moderation, inſtead of inſulting and irritating them by thoſe monuments of their defeat. From that time, therefore, it became an eſtabliſhed rule never to erect a trophy, and was obſerved as a maxim of ſtate by his ſucceſſors. But whether Philip and Alexander paid a ſtrict attention to this maxim, as the author abovementioned aſſerts, may come to be conſidered hereafter.

From henceforward Caranus ſought to gain the affection of the neighbouring nations, and to reconcile them to his government, rather than to oppreſs or extirpate them. In their de- Juſt. l. 7. fence, or to repel a danger which threatened his

ſettlement,

settlement, he is said, by the abbreviator of Trogus, to have driven out Midas king of Phrygia, who had possessed himself of some part of the adjacent territory: and thus having gradually reduced or persuaded the several neighbouring states to a submission, he laid the first foundations of the Macedonian empire *.

* An. M. 4387, according to Euseb.

THE adventurers, who attended Caranus, must have had that valour which the enterprize demanded: his new subjects were possessed of the same virtue, the most obvious and striking proof of merit among a barbarous and unpolished people, and necessary in a disordered age of violence and bloodshed. The king boasted a descent from an illustrious hero, the deity of the warlike, and patron of hardy and brave atchievements. Valour therefore naturally became the great distinguishing character of this new kingdom, and was necessarily cultivated and encouraged, as the qualification essential to its very being.

THE principles of civil government which Greece had taught, her sons adopted; and, in all the institutions which the present settlement demanded, a just attention was paid to the subject's liberty and welfare. Though the form was monarchical, yet the regal power was circumscribed.

cumfcribed. The king governed according to the exacteft rules of natural equity; fo that the Macedonians, faith * Arrian, preferved as great, or greater liberty, than was enjoyed under moft of the Grecian commonwealths: and Lucian, in his dialogue between Philip and Alexander, calls them freemen. This was the original conftitution; nor was it fubverted but with the kingdom. In war the king, though abfolute in his command, was yet obliged to treat his foldiers with tendernefs and affection; in peace he adminiftered juftice, and heard and redreffed the grievances of his fubjects in perfon. The prefent hiftory will afford inftances of this cuftom; and the hiftorian * Livy affures us, it was obferved by Perfeus, the very laft of the royal race of Macedon. The lives of the people were by no means at the difpofal of their king: nor even to their lateft times could a Macedonian be regularly and legally put to death, until his fentence was confirmed by the people in time of peace, or by the army in the field [A].

THEIR religion was alfo borrowed from Greece, with all its rites and ceremonies. Ju-

[A] De capitalibus rebus vetufto Macedonum modo, inquirebat exercitus: in pace erat vulgi: nihil poteftas regum valebat nifi prius valuiffet auctoritas.

CURTIUS in loco citat.

piter

piter their protector, Hercules the founder of the royal race, and Diana the goddefs of hunting, the fport of the manly and robuft, were held in particular honour by the Macedonians, as appears from many of their coins. Manners, cuftoms, and inftitutions, were alfo eftablifhed, to infpire refolution in the mind, and to give vigour and ftrength to the body [B].

Thus was the kingdom of Macedon fo modelled by the principles of equity, juftice, and moderation, in the prince, and valour, and national loyalty, in the people, as to promife happinefs and ftability; but in its infancy was furrounded by many fecret or avowed enemies, many jealous and wavering allies and dependents, equally fufpecting and fufpected. On the weft lay the Lynceftae and Elimiotae; on the north the Pelagonians, Eordians, and Edonians; the Bottieans and Pierians on the eaft; and on the fouth the Magnetes and Dolopians. Moft of thefe people had their particular fove-

[B] Thus we learn from Athenaeus (l. 1. p. 18.) that among the Macedonians no one was admitted to lie down at fupper, until he had killed, with his fpear, a wild boar, in hunting. And thus Ariftotle (de Rep. l. 7. c. 2.) hath recorded, that every Macedonian, who had not yet killed his enemy, was obliged to wear a kind of collar, as a mark of his noviciate in military affairs.

reigns,

reigns, who acknowledged their dependence on Sect. I.
Caranus and his fucceffors, or rofe up in arms
againft them, according to the different viciffitudes of their fortune and power.

Among the earlier kings of Macedon, Per- Perdic-
cas I.
diccas, the firft of the name, feems to have been
a prince endued with abilities, and favoured by
fortune. His hiftory is obfcured by the fhade Herod. l. 8.
c. 137.
of fiction, a circumftance which fhould per-
fuade us that he had real merit, and that his
actions, which we find magnified and diftorted
by fable, were really worthy of being faithfully
recorded, as they were thought worthy of exer-
cifing the imaginations of the early writers.
The fame of his predeceffors was fo far loft in the
fplendour of his reputation, that he is accounted
by * Herodotus the firft of the Macedonian * in loco
cit.
kings. When full of days he is faid to have
fhewed to his fon Argaeus the place where he Juft. l. 9.
c. 2.
wifhed to be interred, and where, he likewife
directed, that, in all fucceeding ages, the bodies of all the royal race fhould be depofited ;
declaring, that till this cuftom was abolifhed,
there fhould not be wanting one of his line to fit
upon the throne.   And hiftorians have been
fuperftitious enough to fuppofe, that this prediction was accomplifhed by the interment of
Alexander in Babylon.

Argaeus,

Book I.

Argaeus.

Juſt. l. 9.
c. 2.

ARGÆUS, the ſon of this prince, together with his immediate ſucceſſors, are only diſtinguiſhed by the wars in which they were engaged with the Illyrians, the old and inveterate enemy of the Macedonian power, and other neighbouring nations. Theſe continual wars confirmed the valour of his people, improved their diſcipline, and extended their reputation: yet checked and awed on one hand by the ſeveral ſtates of Greece, who exerted their increaſing power, and endeavoured to extend their dominions, both by ſea and land; terrified and controuled on the other, by the new erected empire of Aſia, formed by the junction of the Median and Perſian power in the perſon of Cyrus; and, at the ſame time, ſurrounded by ſecret enemies, or avowed rivals; the abilities of the Macedonian princes, and the valour of their ſubjects, ſeem to have been for a long time exerted rather for the defence, than the enlargement of their boundaries.

Amyntas
I.

Herod. l. 5.
c. 17.

AT the time when Darius was obliged to make an ignominious retreat into Aſia, after his Scythian expedition, he left Megabyzus in Europe with a large army, in order to make ſuch conqueſts as might retrieve the honour of his arms, and conceal their late diſgrace. In purſuance of his inſtructions, this general ſent his ambaſſadors to all the neighbouring nations to demand earth

and

and water, the marks of fubmiffion and vaffal-
age.   Amyntas, who then reigned in Macedon,
received the fummons; and readily confented to
acknowledge his fubjection to a power fo vaftly
fuperior to his own.   The Perfian emiffaries were
entertained with all the magnificence which his
court could difplay; and, at their defire, the
Macedonians fo far complied with the Afiatic
manners, that women were introduced to add to
the feftivity.   The indecent freedoms with which
thefe were treated by the Perfians, infolent in
their acknowledged fuperiority, and inflamed
by wine, were beheld with filent grief by king
Amyntas, but by his fon Alexander with a live-
lier and more dangerous indignation.   He defired
leave for the women to withdraw, under pretence
of preparing for the entertainment of thefe guefts,
and in their places introduced as many youths,
difguifed in female habits, who inftantly returned
the lewd careffes of the Perfians, by plunging
their daggers in their hearts.   And when Megabyzus fent Bubaris, one of his principal officers, to enquire after the ambaffadors, the young
prince contrived to elude the enquiry, by capti-
vating Bubaris with the charms of his fifter.
With her the Perfian wedded; the maffacre was
paffed over in oblivion; and the Perfian court
acknowledged the Macedonians as faithful and
honourable allies.

ALEXANDER

SECT. I.

Herod. l. 5.
c. 21.

Alexander had ſucceeded to his father's throne, when Xerxes invaded Greece. The alliance made with an illuſtrious and powerful Perſian, ſecured him from all the dangers of this invaſion, and gained him a peaceful poſſeſſion, and even [c] an enlargement of his territories. Nor doth hiſtory

[c] The earlier ſtate of this kingdom, and the gradual enlargement of it, which was partly the work of this Alexander, will be diſtinctly conceived by attending to the following paſſage of Thucydides.—Τῶν Μακεδονων εισι και Λυγκηται και Ελειμιῶται, και αλλα εθνη επανωθει, ἁ ξυμμαχα μεν ιτι τετοις και ὑπηκοα, βασιλειας δ᾽ ἐχει καθ᾽ αυτα. Τὴν δὲ περι θαλασσαν των Μακεδονιαν, Ἀλεξανδρος ὁ Περδικκε πατηρ, και οἱ προγονοι αυτε Τημενιδαι το αρχαιον ὀντες ἐξ Ἀργυς πρωτοι ἐκτησαιτο, και ἐβασιλευσαν, αναστησανλες μαχη ἐκ μεν Πιεριης Πιερας.——Ἐκ δε τῆς Εστιας καλεμενης Βοτλιαιες, οἱ νυν ὁμορι χαλκιδεων οἰκεσι. Τῆς δε Παιονιας παρα τον Ἀξιον ποταμον, γενην τινα καθηκεσαν ἀνωθεν μεχρι Πελλης και θαλασσης ἐκτησανο· και περαν Ἀξιε, μεχρι Στρυμονος, την Μυγδονιαν καλεμενην, Ἠδωνας ἐξελασανλες, νεμονλαι. Ανεστησαν δε και ἐκ τῆς νυν Ἐορδιας καλεμενης Ἐορδες. (ἁν οἱ μεν πολλοι διεφθαρησαν, βραχυ δε τι αυλων περι φυσκαν καλωκηλαι) και ἐξ Αλμωπιας, Ἀλμωπας. Ἐκραλησαι δε και των ἀλλων ἐθνων οἱ Μακεδονες ετοι, ἁ και νυν ἐτι ἐχεσι, τον τε Ἀιθεμεντα και Γρηγωνιαν και Βισαλλιαν, και Μακεδονων αυτων πολλην. ὁ δε ξυμπαν Μακεδονια καλειλαι, και Περδικκας Ἀλεξανδρε, βασιλευς αυτων ἠν, ὁτε Σιταλκης επηει. In the general name of Macedonians, are comprized the Lynceſtians and Helimiotians, and other nations lying upwards, allied to, and dependent upon, the reſt, yet governed as diſtinct kingdoms. The dominion over the maritime Macedonia was firſt obtained by Alexander, father of Perdiccas, and his anceſtors the Temenidae, who derived their original from Argos. Theſe, by a ſucceſsful war, had

hiſtory attribute the proſperity of his kingdom, more to the protection of Perſia, than to the virtues and abilities of Alexander himſelf, which were known and celebrated through Greece. When a youth, he had paſſed over into that country to learn and practiſe thoſe arts which were eſteemed ornamental and honourable. He appeared at the Olympic games, amidſt the robuſt and accompliſhed champions and competitors for glory : whence the national pride of the aſſembly would have removed him as a foreigner and barbarian. But the prince boldly aſſerted his right of aſſiſting at thoſe famous

Herod. l. 5. c. 2.

had driven the Pierians out of Pieria.—From the region called Bottia, they alſo expelled the Bottiaeans, who now live upon the confines of the Chalcideans. And further, they ſeized in Paeonia, near the river Axius, a narrow tract of land running along from the mountains down to Pella and the ſea ; and got poſſeſſion of that which is called Mygdonia, lying between the Axius and the Strymon, by driving away the Edonians. They expelled the Eordians out of what is now called Eordia, (of whom the greateſt part were deſtroyed, but a ſmall number dwell now about Phyſca ;) and out of Almopia, the Almopians. Theſe Macedonians alſo conquered other nations, of which they are ſtill in poſſeſſion, as Anthemus, Greſtonia, and Biſaltia, and a large part of the territories belonging to the other Macedonians. But this whole tract of country hath the general name of Macedonia : and Perdiccas, ſon of Alexander, reigned over them, when Sitalces formed his invaſion.

SMITH.

games, as being by defcent an Argian, and was
admitted even to contend in the exercifes, and
bore away the prize from thofe who had defpifed
him as unworthy of fharing in the Grecian entertainments. A prince of genius and renown,
admired in Greece, beloved and revered in his
own kingdom, and refpected by the Perfians,
both on account of his own virtues and his fifter's
marriage, was efteemed by Mardonius a fit ambaffador to negociate a feparate peace with Athens,
that he might thus weaken the force of Greece.
In this negociation, though the propofitions were
Herod. l. 8. rejected with a difdain which hiftory hath re-
c. 140. corded with wonder and applaufe, yet the ambaffador himfelf was acknowledged as a friend.
And however his prefent intereft might oblige
him to adhere to Perfia, yet a prince of his en-
dowments' could not but admire and love the
l. 9. c. 43, Grecian virtue. He foon after difcovered his
44. real attachments, by informing the Greeks, even
at the hazard of his life, of the intentions and
motions of Mardonius [D].

[D] This prince's actions are here related with a brevity
which would be unpardonable, were it my prefent purpofe
to give an accurate hiftory of the earlier ftate of Macedon.
The delightful account which Herodotus gives of thefe tranfactions, will abundantly reward the learned reader, who
may turn to the paffage quoted in the margin.

He

He had three fons, Perdiccas, Alcetas, and Philip Tharaleus. The firſt ſucceeded to the throne; but his brothers diſputed his pretenſions, and roſe up in arms to diſpoſſeſs him. The neighbouring nations beheld, with envy and diſcontent, the acceſſions of territory which Macedon had received in the reign of Alexander. The Athenians were powerful by their colonies and allies, their dependent towns and diſtricts on the ſea-coaſts; and either to ſecure, or to enlarge their territories, found it convenient, to aſſiſt his rivals. Greece was at this time in commotion: the Lacedemonians began to think of eſtabliſhing a power in Thrace; while the Perſians, hitherto the great ſupport of Macedon, were weak and contemptible. A kingdom thus circumſtanced, required a prince of vigour and abilities: and Perdiccas ſeems to have inherited all the virtues of his father. He ſupported himſelf againſt his rivals and neighbouring enemies: and, by his art and policy, made both Athens and Lacedemon ſerve to ſtrengthen his power, at the time when he appeared, and profeſſed, to aſſiſt them in the eſtabliſhment of their own.

The mutual jealouſies ſubſiſting between theſe two ſtates and king Perdiccas, was one great cauſe of the Peloponneſian war. The actions

SECT. I.
PERDIC-
CAS II.

Thucyd.
l. 1.

of

of this prince, and the share which he bore in the Grecian contest, are distinctly recorded by Thucydides: here it is only necessary to point out some particulars, tending more immediately to illustrate the present history.

At the first rise of the famous Peloponnesian war, the Athenians, as hath been observed, had a considerable power on the coasts of Thrace; and controuled the King of Macedon by their tributary and dependent towns and districts, bordering on his territories. All that tract, which lay towards the coast between the Thermaic and Singitic bays, was inhabited by Greeks originally from Chalcis, a city in the island Euboea, who all acknowledged the jurisdiction of Athens, afforded that state the convenience of their ports and harbours, and aided and secured its commerce with the upper Thrace. But when the Corinthians and Corcyraeans began to quarrel about Epidamnus, and that the Athenians took a part in this contest, the Corinthians persuaded Potidaea, one of the chief towns in the Chalcidian region, to revolt from Athens; while Perdiccas, to revenge himself on a people who had supported the pretensions of his competitors, urged the other Chalcidians to abandon their settlements on the coast, to fortify Olyn-thus,

thus, a city about sixty stadia from Potydaea, built near the river Strymon, and which preserved a communication with the sea, by means of the port of Myceberna; to make this their residence, and to shake off their dependence on the Athenians. His instances were so far successful, that Olynthus was made the chief seat of their power; and all the other cities united in interest, and were governed by this their capital. Such a revolution was considered by the Athenians as an outrage on their lawful authority. They declared war against the Olynthian confederacy, and laid siege to Potidaea. This city was, after some difficulties, reduced; but the Chalcidians found means to support their independency, and protracted the war to a considerable length. These practices of Perdiccas, however necessary and politic at this time, yet in the end proved the means of raising up a powerful and dangerous rival to the Macedonians; and had lasting and important effects, both on that kingdom, and on Greece. In the course of the disputes, which thus arose, the attack of the famous city of Amphipolis, of which so frequent mention must be made in the progress of this work, is also worthy of particular notice.

This city was seated on the Strymon, in that narrow gut, where the river divides into two branches,

Book I.

Thucyd. l. 4.

branches, wafhing the town on each fide, and falling into the fea at the diftance of two ftadia. At the mouth of the principal of thefe branches ftood Eion, a fmall town, which ferved as a port to Amphipolis, and rendered the commerce with the upper Thrace eafy and convenient. The place where Amphipolis ftood, was originally called Enneodoi; that is, the nine ways;

Olivier Hift. l. 1. p. 67.

poffibly becaufe the roads which led through Macedon and Thrace, iffued from that point. Ariftagoras of Miletus attempted to fettle there, after his revolt from the Perfians; but was prevented by the Edonians, a people of Thrace,

Thucyd. l. 4.

who then inhabited that diftrict. The Athenians, fully fenfible of the value of its fituation, took care to affert a claim to it, and deduced

Efchin. de falf. leg. fect. 14.

their title from Acamas, the fon of Thefeus, who they faid received it as a dowry with his wife. Thirty-two years after the attempt of Ariftagoras, they fent thither a colony of ten thoufand men, who drove out the Edonians: but attempting to pufh their victory to the upper Thrace, they were furrounded, and cut to pieces, by a general confederacy of the people of that country, who fufpected the new colony.

Thucyd. l. 4.

At length, Agnon, the fon of Nicias, eftablifhed himfelf in this place, with a colony which the Athenians fent thither twenty-nine years after their firft attempt. He expelled the Edonians,

and

and raifed a fortification round from one arm of the river to the other; fo that the new fettlement had now the form of a triangle, whofe bafe was towards the fea, and whofe two fides were defended by the branches of the Strymon, which was confiderably deep, and formed a morafs at the upper angle. Here the Athenians continued peaceable poffeffors till the Peloponnefian war broke out; and Perdiccas fpirited up the Lacedemonians to carry their arms into thefe parts, and to endeavour to difpoffefs them from a fettlement of fuch importance to their commerce; from whence, befides a large pecuniary revenue, they drew all their materials for building their fhips; and which he muft neceffarily have regarded with uneafinefs and jealoufy, as it abfolutely commanded his kingdom on that fide. Hither, therefore, Brafidas, the Lacedemonian general, was now fent: and partly by force of arms, partly by addrefs, and an equitable attention to the liberty and welfare of the inhabitants, wrefted Amphipolis from the Athenians; who, fully fenfible of their lofs, and naturally impatient of every difappointment, banifhed Thucydides the famous hiftorian, who had been unfuccefsful in his attempts to fecure the city. And when Perdiccas fhewed fome inclination to defert the Lacedemonians, another army was fent from Athens to recover Amphi-

Thucyd.l.4.

C 4

polis,

Book I.

Thucyd.l.5.

polis, under the command of Cleon; which produced the engagement where the general on each side fell. The people of Amphipolis interred Brafidas in the moft honourable manner, acknowledged him as their real founder, and demolifhed all the monuments of Agnon the fon of Nicias; yet the city was yielded the next year to the Athenians, by a treaty concluded with Lacedemon, and continued under their jurifdiction, until the deftruction of their liberties, by the victory of Lyfander.

In all thefe difputes, Perdiccas had a confiderable fhare; and appears to have acted a part, which the intereft of his own kingdom recommended; but which, by no means, difcovered a ftrict and honourable adherence to his engagements.

Arche-
laus
in Gorg.
P. 471.

He was fucceeded by Archelaus, his illegitimate fon, according to Plato, who fpeaks with great feverity of this prince; the blood which he fhed, to fecure the poffeffion of his throne, having fullied thofe great qualities which he afterwards difcovered. As his meafures for fortifying and ftrengthening his kingdom, alarmed

Diod. Sic. l.
13. fect. 49.

the neighbouring powers; Pydna, a city of fome confequence on his confines, endeavoured, by the affiftance of Athens, to fhake off its dependence

ence on Macedon. But, in defiance of all the
support which that state detached to her new ally,
Archelaus befieged and reduced Pydna to his
obedience; and, in order to cut off all future
intercourfe between this city and the Athenians,
he obliged the inhabitants to remove * twenty
stadia further from the fea.

Sict. I.

* About
two miles.

But this prince was for nothing fo remarkable, as his attachment to learning, and its pro-
feffors. Socrates was invited to, and Euripides
entertained at his court. Painters were employed to adorn his palace; and men of genius,
of every kind, careffed, rewarded, and encouraged to honour his kingdom by their refidence.
But the advantages which Macedon might have
derived from his temper and abilities, were all
cut off by his untimely death. Diodorus relates, that he was killed accidentally in a chace
by his favourite Craterus. But the reprefenta-
tion of Ariftotle * has been thought more probable, who afcribes the death of Archelaus to
the ambition of Craterus, and his refentment at
being denied his daughter in marriage. The
murderer afcended the throne; but, in a few
days, met with the fame fate; and was removed
by an affaffination.

Stoboeus
Serm. 237.
Arift. Rhe.
l. 2. c. 29.
Plut. Apoph.
Ælian, hif.
var. l. 14.
c. 17.

Diod. Sic. l.
14. fect. 37.

* Polit. l. 5.
fect. 19.

Ælian,
l. 8. c. 9.

THE

Book I.

Orestes.
Diod. l. 14.
sect. 37.

Æropus.
Solinus, l. 9.
Diod. l. 14
& 15.

Pausani-
as.

Amyntas
II.

Thucyd. l.
4.

Diod. l. 14.
sect. 89.

The peace of Macedon became now totally subverted. Orestes, the infant son of Archelaus, was scarcely seated on the throne, when he fell a victim to the ambition of his tutor Æropus. The disorders and frequent revolutions, which now rose in Macedon, have occasioned a difference in the representations of historians, as to the order of succession. But it is agreed, that Pausanias usurped the throne, either directly, or soon after Æropus; and, after a reign of one year, was succeeded by Amyntas, father of that prince, to whose actions we are now hastening. Amyntas was (according to Thucydides) the son of Philip, the brother of that king Perdiccas, who had so considerable a share in the affairs of Greece, during the course of the Peloponnesian war. He had found means, by the assistance of Sytalces, king of Thrace, and the Athenians, to disturb the reign of Perdiccas, by his attempts to dispossess him. These attempts, however, proved ineffectual; but now having taken the opportunity of the weakness of the throne, and the confusions of the kingdom, to assert his old pretensions more effectually, he attacked, dethroned, and killed Pausanias.

The succession of Amyntas to the throne of Macedon, seemed to promise a more settled state

of peace and tranquillity to a kingdom so long
harassed by intestine wars and commotions. Sect. I.
His brother Derdas governed the province of Xenop. His.
Grae. l. 5.
the Elimiotae; and their mutual harmony contributed to their mutual support. The prince
of the Lynceftae, a neighbouring people, then
independent on Macedon, Amyntas contrived
to attach firmly to his intereft, by his efpoufal
of Eurydicè, the grand-daughter of that prince, Strab. l. 7.
p. 326.
and one of the family of the Bacchidae of the
royal race of Corinth.

For five years, the vigilance and abilities of
Amyntas preferved the peace of Macedon, and
defeated all the attempts of Argaeus, the brother of Paufanias, who afferted his title to the
fucceffion; and practifed with the Macedonian
nobles, and the neighbouring powers, to engage
them in a revolt. But now Bardyllis, king of
the Illyrians, a warlike nation, trained, exercifed, and improved, by the activity and long
experience of their fovereign, invaded Macedon
with all his powers; and, while he affected only
to fupport the title of Argaeus, determined to
gratify his own ambition, by reducing the king- Diod. l. 14.
fect. 92.
dom to a ftate of fubjection and dependence on
Illyria. The courage of Amyntas, and the efforts of his foldiers, proved ineffectual againft
this formidable enemy. He was defeated in two

feveral

several engagements: the enemy seized his capital, and placed Argaeus on the throne, who readily consented to govern under the direction of Bardyllis, and to render the kingdom of Macedon tributary to Illyria.

IN this time of general distraction, the cities of the Chalcidian district, being now united into one formidable body, of which Olynthus was the head, seized the occasion of enlarging their territories. They began with the city of Potidaea, which had been reduced under the power and jurisdiction of Athens; fell on the eastern parts of Macedon, and pushed their conquests even to Pella, a city of importance by its situation, and afterwards rendered illustrious by the birth of Alexander. The Thessalians, on their part, though in alliance with Amyntas, seemed resolved to forget their engagements, and to share the spoil of his dominions. The southern provinces were exposed to their invasion, and soon became their prey. Thus despoiled of almost all his dominions, and without hope of being restored, he endeavoured to provide for the peace and security of those places which still continued firm to him, by making a formal cession of them to the Olynthians. They were the only neighbouring power that could dispute them with the Illyrians; and Amyntas deemed

it

Xenop. Hist. Grae. l. 5. p. 554.

Dem. in Aristocrat.

Diod. l. 14. sect. 89.

it lefs dishonourable to fee them dependent on a
confederacy, compofed of Grecian cities, than
to expofe them to the fury of a barbarous enemy, or the refentment of a rival, who muft confider an adherence to their prince, as in the
higheft degree criminal. The Olynthians took
poffeffion of them, and maintained their title
againft all the attempts of Illyria and Argaeus;
ftill continuing to receive the revenues of thefe
provinces, which they had thus annexed to their
own dominions, during the fhort interval of Diod. l. 15.
fect. 19.
Argaeus his power.

Thus was Amyntas, for fome time, compelled to yield to the prefent ftorm, and to retire in
expectation of better fortune. When his rival,
according to fome hiftorians, had enjoyed the l. 14. fect.
royal title and authority for two years, the 92.
Theffalians were prevailed upon to give fuch
affiftance to Amyntas, as enabled him once more
to afcend the throne. What were the induce-
ments which now moved this people, hiftory
hath not mentioned; but poffibly they might
have been difappointed in the advantages they
propofed from the diforders of Macedon; and
envied thofe, whofe attempts to difmember that
kingdom, had been more fuccefsful; or even
found it neceffary, for their own fecurity, to
check their increafing power. But though the
king

Diod. l. 15.
fect. 19.

king had, by this affiftance, refcued a part of his dominions from the Illyrians, yet ftill a confiderable part remained in the hands of the Olynthian league, a people who feemed determined to fupport that right, with which the neceffity of his affairs had obliged Amyntas to inveft them. His honour, and even his fafety, called on him to endeavour to recover thefe territories: he firft began by negociation, and formally reclaimed them, as if his ceffion had been but temporary and occafional: the Olynthians, on their part, peremptorily rejected his demand, and declared themfelves fully refolved to maintain their poffeffion by force; when commotions arofe in the Chalcidian diftrict, highly favourable to the interefts of Amyntas, and which greatly facilitated his defign of reducing the Olynthian power.

As Olynthus had erected itfelf into a kind of fovereignty over the other neighbouring cities, fome of them feem to have beheld with impatience their fplendour diminifhed; and thofe advantages, which all had joined to acquire, and all had equally a right to fhare, confined, for the moft part, to that which now called itfelf the ruling city. Apollonia and Acanthus, the two moft confiderable, next to Olynthus, had expreffed their jealoufies and diffatisfactions; and,

Xenoph.
Hif. Grac.
5. p. 554,
555.

and, having shewn some inclination to detach
themselves from the confederacy, were threatened by the Olynthians with force and severity.
These two cities, therefore, consulted for their
security and revenge, by sending deputies to
Sparta, in order to alarm that state with apprehensions of the increasing greatness of Olynthus.
This city, they observed, had already possessed
itself of a considerable part of the Macedonian
territories, and even of Pella, the place of
greatest consequence in that kingdom. ' Inso-
' lent in these important acquisitions, the Olyn-
' thians began to treat the rest of the confederacy
' as subjects and vassals; were endeavouring to
' strengthen themselves by an alliance with
' Athens and Boeotia; a junction which could
' not but have the most important consequences;
' that it became the Spartans to consider how to
' guard against the danger with which they
' themselves were threatened by so formidable a
' coalition; to redress the injuries, and maintain
' the independency of the Chalcidian cities;
' and to crush the ambitious efforts of Olyn-
' thus, before any further accessions of power
' might frustrate all such attempts.'

SPARTA made no difficulty of undertaking
this quarrel; and, encouraged by the prospect
of

of so powerful an assistant, king Amyntas collected his forces, and declared war against Olynthus. His fortune began to wear a fairer aspect. His wife Eurydicè had already born two sons, Alexander and Perdiccas: and now his third son Philip, destined by providence to raise his paternal kingdom to a degree of greatness far beyond all present expectations, first saw the light.

* Petav. v. 2.
* Euseb. Chron.

† l. 16, p. 572.

Chronologers * and historians generally agree in fixing the birth of this prince to the second year of the ninety-ninth Olympiad. Strabo † hath assigned Pella as the place of his birth. If so, the apprehensions of the Spartan invasion must have determined the Olynthians to evacuate this city. As Pella is said to be in their hands in the speech of the Acanthian deputy at Sparta, recorded in the fifth book of the history of Grecian affairs by Xenophon, the French author of the history of Philip concludes, that he was born near Mount Pindus, at the time of his father's exile; and warns his readers against what he apprehends to be a mistake of Strabo, and such modern compilers as have been guided by his authority. But, whatever difficulties or objections may be suggested about the place, the time of his birth is clearly ascertained, and will by no means agree to the time assigned by this writer; as it appears by the account of * Diodorus,

Oliv. l. 1. p. 13.

* l. 14 p. 92.

dorus,

dorus, and is agreed by chronologers, that the restauration of Amyntas must be fixed to the second year of the ninety-seventh Olympiad.

Every addition to the family of Amyntas, must have been regarded by him, and his adherents, as an omen of happy fortune; as the oracles pronounced, that Macedon was to be eminently flourishing under the reign of one of his sons. They are even said to have pointed out the new-born prince by name, as the destined instrument of the happiness of this kingdom [B]. An ancient Sibylline verse is recorded by * Pausanias, importing, that the first grandeur, and the final ruin of Macedon, were both to be the

Sect. I.
Euseb.
Chron.
Petav.

Justin. l. 7.
c. 6.

* in Achai.
p. 214.

[B] Αυχοῦνίες βασιλεῦσι Μακεδονες Αργεαδησιν,
  Ὑμιν κοιρανεων ἀγαθον και πημα Φιλιππος.
  Ἠτοι ὁ μεν πρὁτερος πολεσιν λαιοῖσι τ' ἀνακίας
  Θησι· ὁ δ' ὁπλότερος ἰιμην ἀπο πασαν ὀλεσσι;
  Δμηθεις ἑσπεριοισιν ὑπ' ἀνδρασιν ἠωοις τε.   Pausan.

What boots the pride which high descent inspires?
And what, thy race, from royal Argian sires?
Hear Macedonia!—From a Philip's reign,
Expect thine happiness: expect thy bane.
The first, great prince! shall distant lands obey;
And realms confess his delegated sway.
The last, O fatal name! what woes attend!
With him thy conquests, honours, all shall end:
From east, from west, behold thy foes arise!
And in one hapless hour thine empire dies.

Vol. I.   D   work

work of a Philip. It is too clear and explicit not to have been made after the event: however, it still might have been the interest of Amyntas, in a season so critical, at the eve of a dangerous and hazardous war, to amuse and encourage his barbarous and ignorant subjects, with predictions and oracles; and to improve this incident, of the birth of his son, into a pledge of future happiness, vouchsafed by heaven itself.

While he was thus encouraging his subjects, collecting his army, and making every provision in his power for war, he had the pleasure of finding, that the Spartans concurred so warmly in his views, that, in conjunction with their allies, they declared war against Olynthus; resolved to raise ten thousand men for this service; and, in the mean time, dispatched Eudamidas, with two thousand Lacedemonians, in order to keep those cities firm in their revolt, or disaffection, which were declared, or secret enemies to Olynthus. To have the clearer conception of the nature and reasons of the conduct of Sparta on this occasion; a conduct which had the most important consequences, and proved the source of many great events, which the following history must display; it will be conve-

Xen. Hist. Grac. l. 5. p. 556.

nient

nient to recall to the reader's mind the character, difpofitions, and prefent circumftances, of this famous people.

Whoever is in the leaft acquainted with Grecian hiftory, muft know, that their legiflator, by the feverity of his inftitutions, formed the Spartans into a robuft, hardy, valiant nation,, made for war; that their early atchievements, in the field, foon raifed their military reputation; infpired them with exalted fentiments of glory, and vaft defigns of power; and that under the appearance of a rigid difcipline, manners ftrictly corrected, and a life of frugality and labour, they concealed an inordinate ambition. The victory of their general Lyfander, over their great rival ftate, feemed to have confirmed them in that fupreme authority, to which they had inceffantly afpired, from the moment that their foreign enemies had been driven out of Greece. An intemperate and tyrannical abufe of power, was the immediate confequence of this fuperiority, which, joined with an unreafonable partiality in favour of their own form of government, (now arbitrarily and cruelly impofed on all the ftates which they had reduced to fubjection) made them foon regarded as the odious and haughty mafters, not as the protectors, of

D 2

Greece.

Greece.   A natural love of liberty, animated by the patriot zeal of one illuftrious Athenian, foon overturned the power of thofe tyrants, whom they had impofed on that ftate.   The other Greeks faw this event with fecret fatisfaction, and fome even dared to deny their affiftance to fupport the tottering dominion of the thirty, and to rivet the chains with which their country-men (for fo the Greeks regarded each other) were cruelly loaded.   But, although the original conftitution was thus re-eftablifhed at Athens, ftill the Spartan fovereignty was acknowledged and felt in Greece.   The genius of this ftate, and the fupport of this its fovereignty, required a continued courfe of action and war.   Difputes and contefts were perpetually excited; and the Grecian ftates attacked, haraffed, and oppreff-ed, by a people, whofe domeftic courfe of feve-rity rendered them infenfible to the diftreffes of their neighbours.   Their reftlefs ambition, at length, prompted them to fend their king Age-filaus into Afia; there to extend his conquefts, and the glory of his country, under pretence of fupporting the independency of the Grecian co-lonies.   The king of Perfia, alarmed at his progrefs, and well informed and experienced in the method of fecuring his own peace, by arm-ing the Grecians againft each other, wifely

fends

fends his emiffaries to foment the difcontents already conceived againft Sparta; and, by the power of money, to induce the ftates to rife up againft an odious, oppreffive dominion. The Thebans were the firft to embrace the defign; the Athenians eagerly concurred; Argos and Corinth joined in the confederacy; a pretence of quarrel was foon found out; and the defeat and death of Lyfander, the foul of all the ambitious defigns of Sparta, obliged this ftate to recall Agefilaus to the defence of his native land. This prince, while yet upon his march, receives an account of the naval victory gained at Cnidus by Conon the Athenian; the fatal ftroke to the ambition and power of his country: whofe allies now began to revolt. Sparta itfelf was forced to that mortifying meafure of making overtures of accommodation to Perfia; and, by the peace of Antalcidas, to renounce all the advantages gained in Afia, to abandon the Afiatic colonies to the Perfian, and to acknowledge the right of all the feveral Grecian ftates to freedom and independency.

Thus controuled, difmembered, and reduced, Sparta ftill retained a paffion for pre-eminence and fovereignty; exerted an affected fuperiority over the leffer ftates; and, under pretence

of

of supporting the late accommodation, dictated such terms, and, by force of arms, made such dispositions in the several communities, as might raise her own reputation, and convince others of their weakness; at the same time fully sensible how essentially the late events affected her real strength and grandeur, and retaining the most inveterate resentment against Thebes, whose practices had obliged the Spartan arms to retreat from Asia, and had produced the late revolutions of power, by which their old rivals had been once again enabled to dispute the sovereignty of Greece.

From this affectation of appearing the supreme umpire and general protector of the injured, and with these dispositions of resentment and revenge against their late opposers, the Spartans now engaged in the war with Olynthus. Eudamidas, their general, fortified some towns in Thrace, secured their attachment by his garrisons, and became master of Potidaea; which, by its voluntary submission, seems to have been displeased with its new masters. In the mean time Phoebidas marches to reinforce his brother Eudamidas with a powerful body. He encamps near Thebes, and there renders his expedition famous, by boldly and unexpectedly, in time

Xenop. Hist.
Grae. l. 5.
p. 556.

P. 557.

time of peace and fecurity, feizing the [F] citadel of Thebes; an action which hiftory hath
juftly branded as the great difgrace of Spartan
integrity, and which proved the fource of thofe
calamities, which afterwards fell on this ftate,
as a punifhment of fo outrageous a violation of
public faith. With an unaccountable and ridiculous inconfiftency the Spartans kept poffeffion
of the citadel, yet cenfured and recalled Phoebidas; and Teleutias, the brother of one of
their kings, was fent to command in the expedition againft Olynthus.

THIS general urged king Amyntas to unite
his force with that of Lacedemon againft their
common enemy. His brother Derdas was alfo
warned of the danger to be apprehended from
the ambition of Olynthus, and invited to affift
in crufhing a power which might prove as dangerous to his peace, as to that of the Macedonians. Thefe two princes embraced the favourable occafion of fighting in their own caufe
with the arms of Sparta, and took the field with
a well-appointed body of horfe, which proved

[F] It was an ancient fortrefs built by Cadmus, 1519
years before the Chriftian era, and called after his name
Cadmaea. The city of Thebes was afterwards built round
this place, and thus the Cadmaea became its citadel. Oliv.
l. 1. p. 16.

D 4

of

of confiderable fervice. Derdas, who commanded in perfon, difplayed both abilities and valour; the Olynthians were defeated, and obliged to fhelter themfelves, within the walls of their city, from the purfuit of the victorious army. This action clofed the firft campaign. Derdas and his Macedonians were difmiffed with the refpect due to their conduct, but did not fpend the winter inactively. This warlike prince found a favourable opportunity of fallying forth from Apollonia, on a large body of Olynthian cavalry who were ravaging the adjacent country; whom he defeated, and drove to their very walls with confiderable flaughter.

Xen. Hift.
Grae. l. 5.
p. 560, 561.

The next feafon proved more favourable to the Olynthians. Teleutias appeared at the head of his troops, and began to lay wafte their territories; when the enemy iffued out, and feemed difpofed to give him battle. The Spartan general, with contempt and indignation, ordered fome light-armed forces to charge them: thefe the Olynthians, by an affected retreat, drew on, till they had paffed a river which cut them off from all affiftance; then furioufly attacked and deftroyed them, together with their commander. Teleutias, naturally warm and impatient, now loft all remains of temper, and hurried on with his main body to attack the enemy; who ftill

retired,

retired, and were purſued with paſſion and reſentment, rather than with caution and diſcipline.
The Spartans ſoon found themſelves before the
walls of Olynthus, in confuſion and diſorder,
attacked by miſſive weapons from the fortifications, and furiouſly charged by a general ſally;
unable either to oppoſe the enemy, or to retreat
with any order or ſafety. Here Teleutias, by
his fall, paid the price of his temerity; and his
army fled with precipitation to the adjacent cities
in the intereſts of Sparta and Macedon.

BUT this defeat neither diſcouraged the Spartans nor Macedonians. Ageſipolis, one of the
kings of Sparta, was ſent to purſue the war;
and Amyntas, and Derdas, both united with
him, and exerted extraordinary and ſucceſsful
efforts. The ſickneſs and death of Ageſipolis,
for a while, ſuſpended their operations. Poliſti-
ades, his ſucceſſor, for whom the deciſion of this
quarrel was reſerved, ſhut up the Olynthians
within their walls, and ſoon obliged them to demand a capitulation. Their deputies were ſent to
Sparta, where a peace was ſoon concluded, upon
terms rather more favourable than their preſent
difficulties could claim. They were obliged to
acknowledge thoſe as their allies, with whom Lacedemon was thus connected; to aſſiſt this ſtate,
and to march under its ſtandard. Theſe conditions

Xen. Hiſt.
Grae. l. 5.
p. 564.

p. 565.

Excerpt.
Strab. p.
330.

ditions secured Amyntas in the peaceful possession of his kingdom; restored a considerable
part of his territories, and enabled him to appear with splendour. He fixed his residence at
Pella, the city of greatest figure and consequence in Macedon: and here his young son
Philip received his earliest education. His alliances in Greece were the means of deterring
his barbarous neighbours from disturbing the
tranquillity of his government; and the jealousies of these barbarous neighbours, rendered it necessary for him to be ever careful
to embrace all occasions of strengthening those
alliances; to have a constant attention to the
affairs of Greece; and, according to the different fluctuations of power, to attach himself to
that state which appeared most likely to afford
him an effectual protection. The Spartans, by
the reduction of Olynthus, seemed to have attained the full summit of authority and grandeur.

Plut. in
Pelop.
Corn. Nep.
in Epami-
non.

They counted among their allies, that is, their
dependents and subjects, almost all the communities in Greece. Athens, though enabled to
maintain its liberty, was still incapable of contending for superiority: and Thebes was secured
by the Spartan garrison, which commanded its
citadel, and the Spartan governors who ruled
the city; and who had banished all those that
had been suspected of the least design to disturb
the

the prefent fettlement. But the fortitude and
patriotifm of Pelopidas, one of thofe illuftrious
exiles, raifed an unexpected ftorm, which firft
fhook, and, in the end, overturned all this great
fabric of power. This man, feconded by Epa- Plut. in
minondas, that truly great and virtuous Theban, Pelop.
and affifted by fome other of his gallant countrymen, determined to relieve his native land
from the prefent oppreffion ; killed the Spartan
tyrants, and (fupported by fome forces which Diod. Sic.
the Athenians had fent to affift this daring en- l. 15.
terprife, againft the enemies of their power,)
recovered the citadel, reftored liberty to Thebes,
and laid the foundation of its future greatnefs.
The better to fupport the war which this event
produced, the Thebans determined to engage
the Athenians in a conteft with their common
enemy, and by fecret practices prevailed on the
Spartan general to make an attempt to feize the Xen. Hift.
Athenian port. Juftly incenfed at this injurious Grae. l. 5.
attempt, fired with revenge, jealoufy, and am- Diod. l. 15.
bition, Athens determined to feize this favourable opportunity of joining in a confederacy
againft her rival, which had a fair profpect of
fuccefs; engaged vigoroufly in the war, and,
by her repeated fuccefses, recovered the empire
of the fea, and this in a manner which had a
fair and popular appearance, and enabled her Dem. in
orators to declaim on her generous concern for Phil. 2.
& alibi.

relieving

relieving the oppreſſed, and her invariable attachment to the liberty of Greece. Thus did the Athenians divide the ſovereignty with Sparta; but ſaw, with ſome concern, the riſing greatneſs of the Thebans, and therefore were obliged to uſe their advantages with moderation: and when the king of Perſia, who had occaſion for ſome Grecian troops to aſſiſt him in a war againſt Egypt, ſent his ambaſſadors to recommend a renewal of the late peace, an accommodation was readily embraced, and a convention held to adjuſt ſuch terms as might ſecure the tranquillity of Greece.

Xen. Diod. et ſupra.

THE king of Macedon, duly attentive to theſe events, thought it neceſſary to gain the friendſhip and alliance of the Athenians, who now appeared the great riſing power of Greece; and, for this purpoſe, preſented an advantage to their view, the moſt flattering and agreeable, the recovery of Amphipolis. From the time of Lyſander's victory, this city had continued to enjoy its independence under the protection of Lacedemon. A conſiderable number of Lacedemonians had taken their reſidence there, and lived in amity with the original inhabitants. But now their late ſucceſſes had encouraged the Athenians to renew their old pretenſions to a place of ſuch conſequence to their ſtate; and, in the

Philippi Litt. ad Athen.

convention

convention held to settle the affairs of Greece, their right to Amphipolis was by them asserted, and acknowledged by the whole assembly. It was even resolved, that they should be reinstated, in full possession, by the general force of Greece, in case of any opposition. Amyntas was the first to confess the justice of their claim, and, by his apparent zeal, so far wrought on the Athenians, that they thought themselves bound to acknowledge him as their friend and ally.

But while the prince was thus wisely engaged in providing for the security of his government, and his policy seemed to promise a perfect and undisturbed tranquillity; in his own family he found that uneasiness and distraction which his foreign enemies could not occasion. His wife Eurydicè, a princess of exalted genius, but of passions evil and ungoverned, having conceived a violent affection for a young nobleman of Macedon, to whom she had given her daughter Euryonè in marriage, formed the detestable project of dispatching her own husband, and giving her son-in-law possession both of his bed and throne. But whether the Macedonian looked with horror on a design so shocking, and, in his surprise and tenderness, communicated it to his wife; or, whether this princess discovered the unwarrantable correspondence and conspiracies of her mother and

husband

Sect. I.

Eschin. de falf. leg. sect. 14.

Justin, l. 7. c. 4 & 5.

husband by accident, she defeated the infernal scheme, by disclosing it to Amyntas. The king, too tender in his nature to inflict the full severity of punishment on the mother of his three young princes, was prevailed on to forgive the offence: and history hath suggested, that this proved a fatal weakness; and that his death, which happened soon after, was occasioned by the wicked arts of Eurydicè, who suspected the sincerity of his pardon, (conscious how little her offence deserved it) and calmed her apprehensions by dispatching Amyntas.

ALEXANDER, the eldest of his three legitimate sons, succeeded to the throne; unable, however, to support his dignity with splendour or security.

The Illyrians once more rose up in arms, and obliged the king to purchase peace by a tribute, which he agreed to pay, and gave his brother Philip as an hostage and security for the performance of his stipulation. The Illyrians, on their part, seem to have been soon convinced of the integrity of the king of Macedon; as it will appear, that the young prince was, in some time after, sent back to his court, where the wickedness of his mother, and the ambition of Ptolomy, raised such disorders, as utterly subverted the peace and security of the kingdom, which

Amyntas had long endeavoured to establish.

This

This Ptolomy is called by * Diodorus the son
of Amyntas. But, as † Justin doth not mention
him, in recounting the offspring of this prince;
as he is also called ἀλλότριος τοῦ γένους, ' an alien
from his race,' in another author; and as we
find him, in Plutarch's life of Pelopidas, promise to keep the kingdom for the brothers of
Alexander, without mentioning any affinity of
his own, we must suspect some mistake, or at
least some inaccuracy of expression, in the abovementioned historian. It is suggested by a learned
commentator on Diodorus, that he was the hufband of Euryonè, for whom Eurydicè conceived
her unlawful passion. By the secret practices of
Eurydicè, or of Ptolomy, (for historians are not
agreed in their relations) Alexander died, after
a reign of one year. The conjecture of Pal-
merius may enable us to reconcile their differences, by making the death of this prince the
effect of a conspiracy formed by the queen and
her adulterer. And, that there really was some
combination formed to destroy him, appears from
Demosthenes, who, in his oration on the embassy, mentions Apollophanes, a citizen of Pydna, as one of the accomplices.

WE find it asserted, in the fourteenth book of
Athenaeus, from an historian called Marsyas, that
Alexander

SECT. I.

* l. 15. sect.
7'.
† l. 7. c. 4.

Dexippus
in Syncell.
Chrono.
p. 24.

Jacob. Pal-
merius in
Diod. l. 15.
p. 49.

Justin, ut
supra.
Athen. l. 14.

De falsa
leg. sect. 58.

l. 14. p.
629.

Eſchin. de
falſ. leg.
ſect. 13.

Alexander fell, by the hand of Ptolomy, in a
martial dance, in which the performers were
armed: if ſo, the murderer did not reap the
fruits of his cruelty and treachery. For Pauſanias, a prince of the royal blood, but from
another branch, took advantage of the preſent
confuſion, and returned to Macedon, from
whence ſome former attempts to diſturb the government had occaſioned him to be baniſhed.
Here he found many friends and adherents. He
poſſeſſed himſelf of Anthemus, Therma, and
Strepſa, with ſome other towns, and aſſumed
the royal title. The friends of Perdiccas, the
ſecond ſon of Amyntas, who now became the
lawful poſſeſſor, were gained over or intimidated; and the intereſts of the family of king Amyntas began to appear totally deſperate, when, happily for the young princes, Iphicrates, the Athenian general, appeared in Macedon, upon an
important commiſſion from his ſtate. Amphipolis, as hath been already obſerved, was, by
the general voice of Greece, conſigned to the
Athenian juriſdiction. But the preſent inhabitants had ſo long taſted the pleaſures of independence, (and poſſibly were influenced by the
Spartans) that they refuſed to ſubmit to the ſentence of the Grecian convention, or to return to
a ſtate of ſubjection. The Athenians, on their

part,

part, determined to affert their right by force of arms. But firft, they fent their general, whofe character gave weight and dignity to his reprefentations, with a few fhips, to try the gentler methods of perfuafion and remonftrance, as well as to inform himfelf of the prefent condition of the city, and the meafures fit to be purfued, if an open rupture fhould prove neceffary. Iphicrates had been fome years before in Macedon, when charged with an expedition againft fome barbarous natives of Thrace : on which occafion Amyntas had expreffed his refpect to this illuftrious Athenian and his ftate; and had entertained him at his court with due magnificence and politenefs. A friendfhip and affection grew from this incident, which the people of that age would have deemed it the utmoft bafenefs to forget. Eurydicè therefore now fought an interview with this general; he was entertained at her palace, and there furprifed by an action, which could not fail to have the utmoft influence on a humane and polifhed mind.

Plut. in Apoph. Cor. Nep. in Iphic.

THE queen, with her two fons, whofe age, ftation, and misfortunes, rendered them objects of attention and refpect, appeared fuddenly before him in all the marks of grief and calamity. The elder fhe gave to his hand; Philip, the

 younger, was placed on his knee. " Here,"
said Eurydicè, " behold the tender pledges of
" that friendſhip which Amyntas always felt,
" always expreſſed, for Iphicrates.   To you he
" was a father; you he conſidered as his child.
" Your city he loved and revered; and you the
" moſt reſpectable of that city.   Theſe helpleſs
" orphans are your brethren and your friends.
" To you they fly for protection and aſſiſtance.
" Pity their tender years, oppreſſed by cruel
" uſurpation; pity their weeping mother, who
" thus begs redreſs of her own, and her chil-
" dren's injuries; relieve the dear remains of
" of your ancient friend, and reſtore the peace
" that kingdom, which hath ever merited the
" kindeſt offices from Athens."

   Iphicrates, affected by this addreſs, readily
engaged to reinſtate the ſon of Amyntas in the
throne of Macedon.   Pauſanias was ſoon obliged
to yield to his power and authority : Perdiccas
was acknowledged ſovereign : and, during his
minority, the adminiſtration was entruſted to
Ptolomy.   This diſpoſition could not at all contribute to abate the ambition of Ptolomy, who
was by no means contented with the power and
dignity of a regent.   Fired with the hopes of
aſcending the throne, he began with forming
                                        his

his alliances and connexions in Greece, fo as to facilitate his fecret defigns. The Thebans were by this time become eminent and powerful. The implacable refentment of Agefilaus, who never could forgive the people that ftopped the glorious progrefs of his arms in Afia, kindled up the flames of a war with Thebes, which proved fatal to his country. At Leuctra the Spartans loft one of their kings, the choice of their troops, and the reputation of their arms. The Thebans, conducted and encouraged by Epaminondas, purfued their advantage, and almoft all Greece crowded to their ftandard; the Athenians excepted; who envied and dreaded their rifing power; and, in order to preferve the balance, united with Lacedemon. The Thebans, therefore, Ptolomy determined to gain; and, to recommend himfelf to their alliance and protection, oppofed the Athenians in their attempts to recover Amphipolis. Thus ftrengthened, as he imagined, by the alliance of a ftate now in the full fplendour of its glory, this turbulent and ambitious prince began to avow his defigns, and openly claimed a right to the fovereignty of Macedon. A confiderable party was brought over to his intereft, and the whole kingdom fell once more into confufion and diforder, by the contentions of the two competitors to fupport their different claims: when a particular event put

Sect. I.
X n. Hift.
Grae. l. 6,
7.

Æfch. de
fal. leg.
fect. 14.

Plut. in
Pelop.

an

 an end to this confusion, and greatly contributed to lay the foundation of that greatness, to which Philip, the younger prince, afterwards attained.

THE Thessalians had for some time groaned under the oppression of a family of usurpers. Jason, the Pheraean, who had at first seized the government, was a prince of merit, genius, and sagacity. His assistance had been of the utmost consequence to the Thebans in the war with Sparta; and both the contending parties he had endeavoured to manage in such a manner as to prevent either of them from growing too great, so as to obstruct those vast designs of power and grandeur which he had meditated for himself and Thessaly. His abilities reconciled the Thessalians to his usurpation, and might have had important consequences, had he not been suddenly cut off by a conspiracy. The respect due to his memory induced the Thessalians to acknowledge his two brothers, Polydorus and Polyphron, as their rightful sovereigns. The latter, impatient of a divided power, stabbed Polydorus; but soon after met with the like fate by the hand of Alexander, son, or, according to Diodorus *, the brother of the murdered prince. This action might have been considered as the effect of a just resentment; but the conduct of Alexander left

Xen. Hist. Grae. l. 6. p. 601.

* l. 15. sect. 61.

no

no room to extenuate his crimes. His ambi-
tion and cruelty were equally outrageous, and
equally oppreffive to the Theffalians, who foon
found themfelves obliged to implore the good
offices of Thebes, to relieve them from fo intolerable a tyrant. His outrages had even reached
to the Thebans and Athenians; and all mankind
feemed concerned to reprefs tne cruelties of this
deteftable monfter.   The Thebans, therefore,
fent Pelopidas, their illuftrious citizen, into Theffaly to reftore the tranquillity of that country.
His reputation rendered him revered and dreaded; the principal cities opened their gates to
him; and the tyrant fled before him.   At firft,
he endeavoured, by the gentle methods of perfuafion and addrefs, to infufe fuch principles
into the breaft of Alexander, as might prove
more friendly to mankind; but finding him incapable of reformation, and receiving repeated
complaints of his cruelty and abandoned fen-
fuality, he thought it neceffary to threaten him
with the feverity of his power, which fo intimidated the tyrant, that he retired privately with
his guards, and left his countrymen freed from
his oppreffion.

To Pelopidas, who was ftill in Theffaly, and
who feemed formed for reftoring the peace of
E 3 kingdoms,

Xen. ut
fupra.
Plut. in Pe-
lop.

kingdoms, and redreſſing the injuries of the oppreſſed, the Macedonians now applied. Nor could the two contending brothers refuſe to ſubmit their cauſe to the determination of an umpire, no leſs diſtinguiſhed for his equity, than for his other glorious accompliſhments. On this occaſion, his ſentence ſeemed entirely conſonant to the ſtricteſt rules of juſtice and moderation. Thoſe, whom the violence of party had driven from their country, he cauſed to be reſtored, both on one and the other ſide. Perdiccas he declared ſole king of Macedon, and obliged Ptolomy to relinquiſh his pretenſions, and to profeſs a cordial reconciliation with his lawful prince. The king, whom he had now eſtabliſhed on the throne, engaged to act, in all particulars, as a friend and ally to the Thebans; and, as a ſecurity for his performance of every thing required on his part, Philip [G] his brother, together with thirty youths of the firſt diſtinction in Macedon, were committed as hoſtages to the hands of Pe-

[G] THE hiſtory of this prince's earlier years is embarraſſed with many differences and inconſiſtencies in different hiſtorians. By weighing and comparing their ſeveral accounts, I have endeavoured to form a conſiſtent narration, without entering into any particular diſcuſſion of the relations of thoſe writers, who ſpeak of his confinement in Illyria and Thebes; which might add to that tedifouneſs which the reader may have already found in the introductory part of this hiſtory.

lopidas,

lopidas, and by him conveyed to Thebes. A transaction which, as Plutarch obferves, reflected the higheft honour on his country; difplayed the authority which the reputation of the Theban arms had gained abroad, and the opinion which had been univerfally conceived of the juftice and integrity of this ftate.

To the inftances he had already given of his humane and generous difpofition, Pelopidas added that of a ftrict attention to the care and education of the young prince, whom the neceffity of affairs had thus torn from his family and his country. He had now attained the age of fifteen years, the time of life which demanded the exacteft culture and regulation, and when a mind, to which nature hath been bountiful, begins to be fufceptible of folid inftruction. And Pelopidas confulted moft effectually for his improvement and direction, by placing Philip in the family of Polymnus, the father of Epaminondas, who had the happinefs to be ftill living, a witnefs of the glory and greatnefs of his illuftrious fon. The fame tutors, and the fame courfe of ftudy, by which Epaminondas had been formed, were provided for the Macedonian prince. He had now an opportunity of forming his mind by the Grecian manners, the ftandard of politenefs, and

Sect. I.

Plut. in. Pelop. Olymp.102. Y. 4.

Plut. in Pelop. Diod. l. 16. fect. 2. Nep. in Epam.

E 4

the

the fchool of virtue. He had ever before his eyes a character, one of the moft truly great and amiable which the Grecian ftory hath preferved, which he was inftantly taught to revere, and to believe it his intereft and glory to imitate. But it may be neceffary to enter a little more particularly into the character of this renowned Theban, that we may have the clearer conception of thofe advantages which Philip happily derived from his prefent fituation.

Nep. ut fupra.

EPAMINONDAS was born and educated in that honeft poverty, which thofe lefs corrupted ages accounted the glorious mark of integrity and virtue. The inftructions of a Pythagorean philofopher, to whom he was intrufted in his earlieft years, formed him to all the temperance and feverity peculiar to that fect, and were received with a docility and pleafure which befpoke an ingenuous mind. Mufic, dancing, and all thofe arts which were accounted honourable diftinctions at Thebes, he received from the greateft mafters. In the athletic exercifes he became confpicuous, but foon learned to apply particularly to thofe which might prepare him for the labours and occafions of a military life. His modefty and gravity rendered him ready to hear and receive inftruction; and his genius enabled him to learn and improve. A love of truth, a

love

love of virtue, tenderneſs, and humanity, and
an exalted patriotiſm, he had learned, and ſoon
diſplayed.   To theſe glorious qualities he added
penetration and ſagacity, a happineſs in improving every incident, a conſummate ſkill in war,
an unconquerable patience of toil and diſtreſs,
a boldneſs in enterprize, vigour, and magnanimity.   Thus did he become great and terrible
in war; nor was he leſs diſtinguiſhed by the
gentler virtues of peace and retirement.   He
had a ſoul capable of the moſt exalted and diſ-
intereſted friendſhip.   The warmth of his benevolence ſupplied the deficiencies of his fortune:
his credit and good offices frequently were employed to gain that relief for the neceſſities of
others, which his own circumſtances could not
grant them: within the narrow ſphere of theſe
were his deſires regularly confined; no temptations could corrupt him; no proſpect of advantage could ſhake his integrity; to the public he
appeared unalterably and ſolely devoted, nor
could neglect or injuries abate his zeal for
Thebes. All theſe illuſtrious qualities he adorned
with that eloquence which was then in ſuch re-
pute, and appeared in council equally eminent,
equally uſeful to his country, as in action.   By
him Thebes firſt roſe to ſovereign power, and
with him ſhe loſt her greatneſs.

Such

Book I.

Clemens
Alex. in
Paedag.

Diod. Sic.
l. 16. fect. 2.

Such was the accomplished perfonage, in whofe fteps Philip was now taught to tread [h]. A Pythagorean philofopher was alfo given to to him as an inftructor, to form his mind by thofe precepts, whofe effects were already fo eminently difplayed in Epaminondas. But thefe precepts do not feem to have been received by Philip with that due regard to their intrinfic worth, which the virtuous Theban had difcovered. Yet, as reputable and honourable accomplifhments, they fufficiently engaged his attention; and, under the direction of this tutor, he attained to a remarkable proficiency in the Pythagorean doctrine. The fame polite and ornamental parts of education he had alfo the

[h] A severe perfecution, to which the difciples of Pythagoras had been expofed in Italy (of which we have a particular account in Juftin, l. 20. Polybius, l. 2. Plutarch de Gen. Socrat. and other authors) obliged thofe few who could efcape from the barbarity of their enemies, to take fhelter in Greece, where they found protection and refpect; and were employed in inftructing youth in the fevere rules and precepts of their philofophy. Hence Epaminondas found an ufeful and agreeable preceptor in Lyfis; and hence Naufithous, another of that fect, was now at Thebes ready to undertake the important charge of the young Macedonian prince. The poverty of Polymnus may induce us to concur with the Abbè de la Tour, author of the Life of Epaminondas, in fuppofing, that a public penfion was affigned, to defray the expence of Philip's education.

faireft

faireft opportunities of acquiring, and was early taught to admire all thofe arts in which Greece excelled. Eloquence was pointed out, as an accomplifhment highly meriting his regard; and he continued, even in his moft exalted fortune, to glory in the proficiency he was now labouring to gain. The converfation of Epaminondas enriched his mind with knowledge, and taught him the lovelinefs of virtue. High and exalted fentiments of glory were beft fitted to his difpofition; and all the arts and accomplifhments which led to this, he ftudioufly cultivated, and eagerly acquired. From the great Theban he learned activity and vigour in all military operations; addrefs and fagacity in improving all opportunities, and turning every incident to his advantage; but as to the more material parts of this great man's excellencies, faith Plutarch, his juftice, his magnanimity, and his clemency, of thefe Philip poffeffed no fhare by nature, nor did he acquire them by imitation. But, although the conduct of this prince may fometimes give a fanction to this fevere fentence, yet may we reafonably confider the hiftorian as fpeaking from the refentment of a man, whofe country had fuffered by this prince's power. To conceal his faults, and, by a ftrained defence, to convert his moft exceptionable actions into fo many inftances of virtue or abilities, is to deftroy that profit-

able

Sect. I.

Plut. in Alex.

in Pelop.

able inftruction which his hiftory may afford to mankind. But it may be at leaft afferted, without any violation of hiftorical truth, that Philip doth not always appear deftitute of thofe virtues. He was fenfible of the worth and amiablenefs, and never failed to affume the exterior appearance of them; and it may be more confonant to his character to fay, that an inordinate ambition, the firft great paffion of his mind, checked and controuled all the humane and benevolent fentiments which he received from nature and education. Glory was his ultimate purfuit; and, to this, all his virtues were made fubfervient. Hence it is, that we fhall find this prince, who, from many inftances of his conduct, appears by no means infenfible to the dictates of juftice and clemency, yet fometimes acting injurioufly and cruelly; forgetting, or neglecting, thofe noble inftructions he had received, and that example of true greatnefs, which had been pointed out to his imitation.

THAT this young prince, whofe genius now began to fhine out, might want no advantages to complete his education, he was not confined to Thebes, but feems to have been attended by his preceptors into different parts of Greece, where the peace which this country enjoyed in the beginning of the reign of Perdiccas, admitted

ted

ted him to visit the several states, to study the tempers, manners, and dispositions of those people, who then engaged the general attention. The arts, the learning, and elegance of Athens, he seems to have particularly studied, relished, and admired. With the learned men of that city he formed connexions which continued during the whole course of his reign. He revered and admired Plato, as appears from that regard which he ever discovered to his followers: nor doth he seem to have been less regarded by the philosopher. He paid the due respect to the rising genius of Theophrastus; and that intimacy, to which he admitted Isocrates, we shall have frequent occasion of observing. But his intercourse with Athens doth not seem to have been entirely devoted to the adorning his mind, or improving his taste. The political state of that city, the passions, inclinations, and present corruptions of its inhabitants, were objects no less fitted to gain his attention. These he undoubtedly studied with the greatest diligence; for no man appears to have been more intimately acquainted with them. He well knew how to esteem their good qualities, to despise their faults, and to derive the due advantages from their prejudices and weakness.

Ælian. l. 4. c. 19.
Athen. l. 11.
Ælian. ibid.

In

Book I.
Plut. in
Alexan.

In thefe his excurfions from Thebes, he vifited Samothrace, and was there initiated into thofe grand myfteries of Ceres, which were celebrated at Athens, at Eleufis, and in other parts of Greece. Here he firft faw Olympias, the fecond daughter of the king of Epirus; who was alfo initiated into the myfteries, and was now called Myrtalis, a name which the remembrance of their firft affection feems to have preferved, and occafioned it to be frequently repeated. The affinity of their houfes naturally engaged Philip's attention to this princefs.

Paufan in
Corinth.
JulianiCaef.

For Lanuffa, the grand-daughter of Hercules, had been efpoufed by Peleus, the grandfon of Achilles, from whom the kings of Epirus were defcended. And her extraordinary beauty, joined to the natural graces of her tender years, made an impreffion on the young prince, which never was effaced, but by their conjugal difagreements.

Olivier, l. 1,
P. 39.
Rollin.

It is alfo probable, that Philip was permitted to attend Epaminondas in fome of thefe expeditions which have fo highly exalted the military character of that great Theban. Men of diftinguifhed note in Greece thought themfelves honoured by following the ftandard of a general, whofe arms pierced into the very bofom of

Sparta,

Sparta, and who, more than once, made his
enemies tremble for the fafety of their very
city.

WHILE Philip was thus labouring to acquire
all thofe accomplifhments which might render
him great and eminent, the kingdom of Macedon became again diftracted by the ambition of Plut: in
Ptolomy, who was again encouraged to renew _{Pelop.}
his pretenfions to the fovereign power; again
began to opprefs the family of Amyntas; and
obliged them once more to apply to Pelopidas,
their protector.   His honour and his difpofition
both engaged him to fupport his own fettlement,
and to affert the interefts of his friends : but,
as the Theban forces were otherwife engaged,
he was obliged to collect fome mercenary troops;
and, at their head, marched againft the ufurper.
As they approached, Ptolomy contrived to corrupt thofe mercenaries, to engage them to revolt from their general, and to join his own
army: yet the very name of this illuftrious Theban ftruck him with more terror than the appearance of an armed force.   Single, and deferted, as he was, the Macedonian humbled
himfelf before him, acknowledged his fault, and
implored pardon, as from a fuperior : folemnly
promifing, for the future, to confine himfelf to
the duties of a regent; to pay due allegiance to

the

the lawful heir of the throne, and to behave, in every particular, as a faithful friend and ally to the Theban ftate; and, as a fecurity for his conduct, he gave his own fon Philoxenus, with fifty other young Macedonians, as hoftages; who were all fent to Thebes.

Plut. in
Pelop.

THIS expedition, fo honourable to Pelopidas, in the end proved fatal to him. His defire of revenging the treachery of his mercenaries, was the occafion of his falling into the hands of Alexander, the tyrant of Theffaly; (from whence he was delivered by his friend Epaminondas;) and his refentment of the tyrant's cruelty afterwards induced him to lead an army into Theffaly, where his fury and impatience to attack Alexander in perfon, hurried him into the midft of his enemies; and this renowned Theban fell beneath their numbers.

Diod. l. 16.
fect. 2.

PROBABLY the death of Pelopidas encouraged Ptolomy once more to affert his pretenfions; and to raife new diforders in Macedon. At leaft, we find that Perdiccas ftill fufpected his enterprizing temper; and, to fecure the quiet poffeffion of a throne, which he had hitherto enjoyed but in name, recurred to the expedient ufually practifed in this unfettled kingdom, and quieted his apprehenfions by murdering his tur

bulent

bulent guardian. Thus was this prince eftablifhed in an undifturbed poffeffion of the fovereign power : and, from this event, we find
hiftorians date the beginning of his reign.

Sect. I.

Olymp. 103.
Y. 4.

PERDICCAS was a prince who did not want
talents, but wanted the art of regulating and
applying them ; he had more boldnefs than
firmnefs, more cunning than prudence, and
more genius than judgment. He valued himfelf upon his learning, and was paffionately
fond of learned men, without informing himfelf whether their characters anfwered to the
knowledge they had acquired. Not contented
with fupporting them with his bounty, and encouraging them by his favour, he admitted
them indifcriminately into his ftricteft confidence; and even fuffered himfelf to be abfolutely governed by one Eupratus, a philofopher unworthy of the fchool of Plato, where he
had been inftructed ; who poffeffed the prince
with an high opinion of his own proficiency in
fcience, with an affectation of refinement and
fpeculation; collected all thofe about him, who
might flatter this difpofition, and made him pre-
fer pedants to his generals.

Oliv. c. 1.
p. 42.

Athen l. 11.
p. 508.

His connexions with Thebes naturally led
him to oppofe the Athenian intereft. Amphi-

Æchin. de
fal. Leg.
sect. 14.

polis, the perpetual subject of dispute, was still claimed by that people: but Perdiccas peremptorily refused to acknowledge the justice of their pretensions, and prepared to defend the possession of this important city, which he now assumed, by the force of arms. The Athenians, on their part, determined to assert their right, and, for this purpose, sent out a considerable armament, under the command of a general named Callisthenes. Perdiccas found himself unable to oppose this force, which had defeated him; and was on the point of regaining the city, when he was obliged to call in artifice to his assistance, and (possibly by tampering with Callisthenes) obtained an advantageous truce. The Athenians were justly dissatisfied with the conduct of their general, who now returned with disgrace, and some time after fell under the resentment of his countrymen. He was put to death, but without any public declaration, that the truce which he had concluded with Perdiccas, was the real cause of his sentence. The people rather affected a regard to public faith, to adhere inviolably to the act of the man whom they had regularly commissioned, and even to approve of this truce, as a means of bringing the king of Macedon to a just sense of the equity of their cause. Nor had they sufficient

Xen. Hist.
Grae. l. 7.

cient

cient opportunity to aſſert their claim effeƈtually, being now engaged in aſſiſting the Lacedemonians. The united force of theſe ſtates were conquered by Epaminondas at Mantinea, but unhappily the Thebans loſt their glorious general; and, with him, all the fruits of their victory, and all their ſhort-lived power and grandeur.

THE effeƈt which this important loſs muſt neceſſarily have on Thebes, was ſoon perceived by the powers bordering on Macedon, which had hitherto been awed by that ſtate, and prevented from attacking its ally. But now the declenſion of the Theban grandeur, evidently foreſeen, appears to have encouraged the old enemies of the Macedonians to diſturb their peace: The Illyrians had ſtill at their head the ſame brave and experienced prince, Bardyllis, whoſe age doth not ſeem to have abated his vigour, and whoſe arms had already proved ſo formidable. He now ſent to Perdiccas to demand the payment of that tribute which he had exaƈted from ſome former kings; and, on his refuſal, advanced at the head of a powerful army to ſupport his claim; which quickly rouſed the Macedonians, who marched out to oppoſe the invaders. The valour of each army was equal: but the Illyrians were better diſciplined,

SECT. I.

Olymp. 104?
Y. 2.

Diod. l. 16.
ſeƈt. 2.

F 2

and

 and better conducted; and found but little difficulty in gaining a complete victory. The
poor remains of the Macedonian army, of which
more than four thousand, by far the greatest
part of its force, had been cut to pieces, was
obliged to lay down their arms, and submit to
the conqueror. Their king, who had not been
deficient in acts of valour, fell a prisoner into
the hands of his enemies, and there died of the
wounds he had received in battle. His son
Amyntas, who now became his successor, was
yet in his infancy, unable to assume the government, much more to retrieve the disordered and
dangerous state of his kingdom. Thus was
Macedon left exposed to all the consequences of
civil dissension, at the same time that it was
driven to the brink of ruin by the most fatal
calamities of a foreign war.

BOOK

BOOK I. SECTION II.

CONTENTS.

DIFFERENT opinions about the place of Philip's residence at the time of Perdiccas' death.—Complicated distress of Macedon at this conjuncture.—Philip assumes the regency.—The immediate effects of his appearance.—Is raised to the throne in the place of his infant nephew.—Animates his subjects, by his successes, against the Paeonians.—Enforces military discipline.—Institution of the Δορυφοροι.—Philip forms the Phalanx.—Description of that body.—Observations on its form, arms, advantages, and defects.—Philip prevails on the king of Thrace to abandon his rival Pausanias.—Declares Amphipolis a free city.—His conduct explained.—Philip defeats Argaeus.—Concludes a treaty with Athens.—Subdues Paeonia.—His battle with the Illyrians.—The death of Bardyllis.—Philip erects a trophy.—A probable reason of his making this alteration in the Macedonian customs.—Philip projects the siege of Amphipolis.—His address in defeating an intended union between Athens and Olynthus.—He gains over the

F 3

Olynthians

BOOK the FIRST.

SECTION II.

DIODORUS* afferts, that Philip was ftill detained at Thebes, and there refided; when the news of the total defeat of the Macedonians, and the death of their king, fpread through the neighbouring nations, and reached this young prince. Education, example, his youth, and natural ardour, all confpired to render him impatient for fome great occafion of exerting his abilities; and this event feemed, as it were, the fignal for his ftarting forward in the race of honour and glory. According to that hiftorian, he now eluded the vigilance of the guards, to whom the care of his perfon was entrufted; and fled privately away to Macedon; refolved to affift his family and country in their diftrefs; elevated with expectations of renown; and perhaps not without hopes of the throne, to which he afterwards was raifed.

F 4

But,

Book I.

* l. 7. c. 5.

† L. 11. p. 506.

But, according to this account, Philip muſt have reſided for a much longer term at Thebes than three years, which Juſtin * makes the time of his confinement in that city. And this ſeems to favour a relation, which Athenaeus † ha h preſerved, but which he ſpeaks of as obſcure and uncertain. It is ſaid, that Plato conceived ſuch expectations of this prince, that he recommended him to the late king Perdiccas as a perſon entirely qualified for a public truſt; and that, in conſequence of the philoſopher's advice, Perdiccas placed him at the head of one of the Macedonian provinces, that he might there raiſe, train, and diſcipline, a body of forces, by way of a reſerve, on any ſudden emergency. If we may credit this relation, Philip muſt have been in his government at the time of his brother's defeat; and now appeared opportunely in defence of his country, not ſingle or unprepared, but at the head of a conſiderable reinforcement.

Olv l. 2. p. 47.

Diod. Sic. l. 16. ſect. 2.

Circumstanced as Macedon was at this time, a prince whoſe only virtue was courage, muſt neceſſarily have completed its ruin, and one who poſſeſſed leſs of this than Philip could not have attempted to re-eſtabliſh it. The choice of all its forces had been cut to pieces,

or

or made prisoners, in the late engagement; the
remains were totally intimidated; their wounds
still bleeding, and the terrour of the enemy still
strongly impressed upon their minds. The victorious army, which Bardyllis had augmented
by new levies, was every moment expected to
pour down upon them; and nothing was spoken
of, but the necessity of an absolute submission.
The Paeonians, a powerful and warlike people,
accounted, in earlier times, less barbarous and
more considerable than the Macedonians, had
received some cause of offence from Perdiccas;
and were now indulging their revenge, ravaging
and insulting the kingdom without the least interruption or controul. Ancient pretensions to
the sovereignty were at the same time renewed;
and foreign enemies invited to share the spoils of
this unhappy kingdom, under the pretence of
supporting the claims of different competitors.
Pausanias, whom Iphicrates had dispossessed,
openly asserted his right to the crown. The
Thracians he had engaged to support his title;
and was now ready to invade the kingdom, at
the head of a formidable army, which the king
of that country had been prevailed upon to raise
for his assistance. Argaeus, the old competitor
of king Amyntas, looked on the victory of his
friends, the Illyrians, as an event highly favourable to his pretensions; which he also now

avowed

avowed and afferted. His known connexions with the victorious enemy, muft have confiderably increafed his party in Macedon: but his dependence was not entirely on this party, nor on the Illyrians. The people of Athens had conceived an high refentment againft Perdiccas, who had prefumed to difpute their right to Amphipolis; and oppofed their attempts to regain this city. They were by no means favourably difpofed to Philip, the friend of Thebes, and pupil of their enemy Epaminondas. They juftly fufpected that this prince, if once eftablifhed in the peaceable adminiftration of affairs, would not be inclined to make them any conceffion which Perdiccas had denied. Argaeus, on his part, who was grown old in intrigue, knew how to make the moft flattering promifes, when he ftood in need of affiftance: and fo effectually convinced the Athenians, that their intereft was clofely connected with his reftauration to that throne, on which he had for some time fat, that they refolved to exert themfelves in defence of his title; and, for this purpofe, fent out Mantias, one of their commanders, with a powerful fleet, and three thoufand men.

Diod. Sic. ut fupra.

Ibid.

Two pretenders to the crown, and four formidable enemies, now actually in arms, and

2

ready

ready to furround him, were not capable of deterring Philip from affuming the reins of government, under the title of regent and protector to his infant nephew. His eloquence was now firft exerted to roufe the Macedonians from their defpair; to recall to their minds the courage, and the ancient honours of their fathers; to infpire them with hopes of better fortune; and to engage them in a faithful allegiance to the reigning family. All the motives that could poffibly diffipate their terrour, and conciliate their affections, were pathetically and effectually urged by this prince: his own undaunted deportment gave weight to his arguments; and the appearance of his extraordinary merit made them confider fidelity and ftrict adherence to him, not only as their duty, but their true intereft. He poffeffed all thofe qualifications, in an eminent degree, which render a prince amiable in the general eye. His perfon was remarkably graceful, and commanded affection and refpect: his addrefs and deportment were obliging and infinuating: his confummate penetration had not the leaft appearance of referve: he had affability the moft pleafing and flattering; natural and unftudied; without that timidity and hefitating condefcenfion, that awkward and ridiculous mixture of caution and affected opennefs, which the great may sometimes

times

Sect. II.
Juft. l. 7.
c. 5.

Diod. l. 16.
fect. 3.

Æfchin. de
falfa Leg.
Plut. in Apophth. Athenæ & al.

times betray, who know the ufe of affability, and vainly hope to appear what nature forbids them to attempt. He had a temper gay and unclouded; a wit indulged with apparent eafe, but ever well corrected. Such accomplifhments are oftentimes found to be the veil of deep defigns and turbulent paffions; but are frequently known to raife fuch prejudices in favour of the poffeffor, as caution and reflection cannot conquer. The bare appearance, therefore, of fuch a prince, in a time of public danger, muft have had a confiderable effect: and the firft experience of his abilities, in the beginning of his regency, ftrengthened the expectations of the people, and confirmed their attachment to him. But the dignity of regent was by no means fuited to the greatnefs of his ambition, now inflamed by the popular favour, and general good opinion, which his merit had acquired. The oracle was induftrioufly publifhed, which promifed that Macedon fhould arrive to the higheft grandeur, under the reign of a fon of Amyntas: and it was received with all poffible deference. " This " is the man," they cried, " whom we are to " regard as the deftined deliverer of his country. " Let us reflect upon the dangers now impend- " ing over us, and can we hope for any fecurity " but from a king like him, or that an infant " reign can be at all confiftent with the prefent

" ftate

Juftin. l. 7. c. 6.

" ſtate of Macedon? Can it be expected, that
" a young prince, fired with a generous love of
" glory and power, will exert all his abilities in
" defence of the glory and power of another?
" No: let us make our cauſe his own: let us
" offer him a prize worthy to be contended for;
" and let us place that prince upon the throne
" of Macedon, whom the God himſelf points
" out to us, and commands to be received as
" our deliverer." Such ſentiments were, no
doubt, propagated with all diligence by the
friends and partiſans of Philip, and were heard
with all attention. And, as the circumſtances
and inclinations of the Macedonians favoured
the ſchemes of his ambition, the infant Amyntas was ſet aſide, without difficulty, in a kingdom which had frequently been uſed to ſee the
lineal ſucceſſion interrupted; and Philip himſelf
was now inveſted with the royal title and authority.

Thus was he happily and eaſily put in poſſeſſion of the firſt darling object of his aſpiring
hopes. And, having aſcended the throne of
Macedon, he inſtantly began to exert himſelf
with due policy and vigour, for the defence of
his own power, and the welfare of his new ſubjects. His attention was, in the firſt place, Diod. Sic.
turned to the army which had ſuffered ſo ſeverely ut ſupra.

in

in the late engagement: and his firſt care was to reſtore its ſtrength and vigour; and to eſtabliſh and improve its diſcipline.

THE art of war had not, as yet, been duly underſtood in Macedon, though, from the earlieſt ages, the ſoldiers of this kingdom had been remarkable for natural valour: and, in a diſordered ſtate, where many competitors frequently contended for the ſupreme power, and the government was weak and precarious, it is eaſy to conceive that princes might have been tempted to connive at many relaxations in military diſcipline, in order to preſerve the affections of their ſoldiers by this falſe indulgence. But Philip's views were much juſter, and more extenſive. The obſervations he had made, and the inſtructions he had received in Greece, formed him completely in the military art; and taught him to regard an exact regulation of his army, as the ſure foundation of all his future hopes.

Diod. Sic. l. 16. ſect. 3.

He therefore applied to this work with an attention ſuited to its importance. He began with providing a ſufficient quantity of arms for his ſoldiers; and, in the form and management of theſe, made ſuch alterations as his experience and obſervation had ſuggeſted. His forces were conſtantly exerciſed, reviewed, engaged in mock battles; trained and inured to form, to move,

to

to march, with eafe and regularity. Every thing that tended to luxury and indulgence was ftrictly prohibited. Their wives were never fuffered to attend his officers; though [A] he himfelf was yet not careful to inforce this ftrict regard to the difcipline of his camp by his own example. His exact care, in banifhing luxury and effeminacy, continued during the whole courfe of his reign. We learn from Polyaenus *, that one officer was difmiffed from his fervice, for ufing warm baths; and two others for entertaining a finging girl. The men of moft diftinction in his army were not permitted to make ufe of any carriages in their march, either for themfelves, or for their baggage; which was allowed to be no more than their fervants could carry; nor were the number of thefe permitted to be any greater than ftrict neceffity required.

Among the inftances of his attention to the modelling and regulating his army, and training up his foldiers to the military art, we may reckon one which Arrian * and Ælian † both afcribe to Philip: and that is the inftitution of the ΔΟΡΥΦΟΡΟΙ, or fpear-men, as they were called. Thefe were carefully chofen from all the noble families in Macedon; educated and inftructed,

---

[A] Ὁ δὲ Φιλιππος ἀει κατα πολεμον ἐγαμει. Athen. in loco cit.

in all liberal accomplifhments, at the royal court, from their earlieft years, and employed in all offices about the king's perfon. They guarded his chamber-door by turns; they attended him in hunting and in battle; they had peculiar honours and privileges, and particularly were admitted to dine at the king's table. Thus he contrived to keep, as it were, a number of hoftages, to fecure the allegiance of all the nobles in Macedon: and thefe youths, early taught to love and refpect the perfon of their prince, conftantly under his infpection, and, of confequence, fired with emulation to render themfelves worthy of his regard, ferved as a glorious feminary (fo Curtius * calls them) of future generals and officers; on whofe abilities and zeal the king might have the firmeft reliance. And, for this purpofe, it was particularly neceffary that they fhould be enured to an exemplary obfervance of his regulations. Not all the favour which he fhewed them; not all the affability and condefcenfion with which he entertained them, as his equals and companions, was fuffered to encourage them to the leaft relaxation of his rigorous difcipline. One of them, who had left his company on a march, to allay his thirft in a tavern, was feverely chaftifed. Another, who, when he fhould have remained under arms, was tempted to lay them down, for the greater convenience

of

* l. 8. c. 6.

Ælian, ut fupra.

of plundering, was put to death without mercy; Sect. II.
and without the leaft regard to his intimacy
with the king, which had encouraged him to
commit this offence.

And now it was, that Philip formed the fa- Diod. Sic.
ut fupra.
mous Macedonian Phalanx, which afterwards
performed fuch effectual fervices on many occafions; which fo greatly contributed to his
fon's conquefts in Afia, and which appeared fo
formidable to the Romans, at a time when its
figure and its arms alone remained, without the
fpirit by which it was originally animated. Homer was the fource from whence the Grecians
drew all their knowledge: and, from the following paffage of his immortal poem, Philip
is faid to have conceived the firft idea of this
renowned body:

Ασπις αρ' ασπιδ' ερειδε, κορυς κορυν, ανερα δ' ανηρ.
Ψαυον δ' ιπποκομοι κορυθες λαμπροισι Φαλοισι
Νευοντων' ως πυκνοι εφεςασαν αλληλοισι.   Iliad. N. 131.

An iron fcene gleams dreadful o'er the fields;
Armour in armour lock'd, and fhields in fhields.
Spears lean on fpears, on targets targets throng:
Helms ftuck to helms, and man drove man along.
                                        Pope.

Book I.

See note on
the life of
Philip in
the Univ.
Hift.

Polyb. l. 17.

ÆlianTa9.
c. 28.

THUS Diodorus relates: but it hath been fuggefted, and not without reafon, that Philip was by no means the original inventor of the Phalanx, but only new modelled and difciplined a body, with which the Macedonians, as well as all the Grecians, were already well acquainted. In the time of Philip, this Phalanx was compofed of a body of infantry of about fix thoufand men, which ufually formed his main battle. Their arms were a fhort cutting fword, a large fquare buckler, four feet in length, and two and an half broad; and a pike fourteen cubits long, called by the Grecians ΣΑΡΙΣΣΑ. This body was ufually drawn up fixteen in depth: the files were fometimes doubled, fometimes divided, as the different exigencies required: and, in the manner of their evolutions and counter-marchings, on fuch occafions, Philip introduced an alteration which he deemed of confequence, as it tended to encourage his own foldiers, and to intimidate the enemy. The original manner of this counter-march, which the Macedonians invented, was fo contrived, as to have the appearance of a retreat; the new method, which was adopted from the Lacedemonians, had an oppofite effect, and fhewed like a bold and undaunted onfet.

THE

THE space between each Phalangite, on their march, (as Polybius * hath defcribed this body in the time of the Romans) was four cubits; and the diftance between the ranks the fame: as they advanced towards the enemy, the men clofed to half thefe diftances; and, when they were to receive the enemy, they locked ftill clofer, fo that the diftances were but one cubit. Their pikes, as hath been obferved, were fourteen cubits long. The fpace between the hands, and that part of the pike which projected beyond the right, took up four, and, confequently, each pike was advanced ten cubits beyond the body of the foldier. So far did they advance towards the enemy, from the foldiers of the firft rank; while thofe alfo, of all the four fucceeding ranks, projected beyond the front to their feveral proportional diftances. The foldiers of all the other ranks behind the fifth held their pikes, (which could not reach the enemy) raifed and reclining a little over thofe before them, fo as to form a kind of roof to fecure them from all miffive weapons. But this was not the only ufe of thofe foldiers, whofe pikes could not reach the enemy. They were moft effectually employed in bearing up againft thofe who preceded them, and fupporting them with all their ftrength. So that the charge was ever made with the whole united force and impetuofity of

SECT. II.
* l. 17. p. 764—767.
l. 12. 664.

G 2

all

all this mighty body; immoveable and impregnable by its union; and without the least possibility of a retreat for those soldiers who were on every side closely locked in, and pushed forward by their comrades.

THE difficulty of sustaining the weight of this body, appears evidently from its description; the difficulty of opening or breaking it Polybius * thus demonstrates, by comparing it with the disposition of the Roman army. Each Roman soldier, saith this historian, takes up in fight two cubits: the same distance must be allowed for shifting their shields, and wielding their arms. The whole, then, is twice the distance of the Phalangites, when they move to attack the enemy. Every Roman, therefore, opposes two of these, and is obliged to make head against ten different pikes. And, when the Phalanx waits to receive the enemy, the numbers and difficulties are doubled. The efforts of the assailants might indeed sometimes break one or more in this vast forest of pikes. But then, (as Livy * hath observed in one particular instance) the pike, so broken, still continued to fill up the tremendous range, without any vacancy or interval: nor was its broken point incapable of doing execution.

* ut supra.

* l. 32 sect. 17.

A LATE

A LATE author * of a difcourfe on the Roman
art of war is of opinion, that the principal defect of the Phalanx lay in its difadvantageous
armour, and order of battle. " In reality, faith
" he, the pikes of the two firft ranks only were
" ferviceable in an engagement; thofe of the
" reft fcarcely availed any thing. The men of
" the third rank could not fee what paffed in
" the front, nor had any command of their long
" pikes, which were entangled and locked up
" between the files, without a poffibility of mov-
" ing them to the right or left: hence the Ro-
" mans found no great difficulty in furmounting
" an obftacle, formidable indeed in appearance,
" but at bottom very trifling. They had only to
" gain upon the pikes of the two firft ranks,
" that they might join the enemy, and fight
" hand to hand. This they were enabled to
" do by their large bucklers, with which they
" bore up the pikes of the Macedonians, and,
" forcing their way under, reached them with
" their fwords. All refiftance was then at an
" end: the Phalanx, unprovided for defence,
" and rather embarraffed than aided by their
" pikes, could no longer ftand the furious charge
" of the Romans, who made dreadful havock
" with their pointed fwords. We find at the
" battle of Pydna, where Paulus Æmilius gained
" fo complete a victory over Perfeus, that no

G 3

" lefs

" lefs than twenty thoufand Macedonians were
" flain, with the lofs of only one hundred men
" on the fide of the Romans." This, our author adds, it is impoffible to afcribe to any other
caufe, than to the infufficiency of the pike,
when oppofed to an infantry armed with fwords
and bucklers.

It becomes the writer of this hiftory to fpeak
with the utmoft caution on fuch a fubject: particularly as Folard *, from whom thefe obferva-
tions are almoft exactly copied, has pronounced
pofitively on the inconvenience of the Macedonian pikes. But it is obvious to remark, that
the battle, here brought as an example to eftablifh this theory, doth not afford a fingle circumftance in favour of it; but, on the contrary,
doth remarkably confirm that of Polybius. In
the firft place, we find the conful Æmilius ufing
all poffible artifice to bring Perfeus from his
ground, which he had chofen particularly for the
fake of his Phalanx: and to which he obftinately adhered, till accident, or rather the policy of the Roman, obliged him to advance.
The fight of the Phalanx, though defcending
into a lefs advantageous place, ftruck Æmilius
with horror and amazement. It was attacked
with all imaginable gallantry in front, but bore
down all before it with fuch irrefiftible impetuofity,

* Traité de
Colonne.
Polybe.
tom. I.

Livy, l. 44.
cap. 40. cum
Sup. Freinft.

ofity, that Æmilius rent his garments in an agony of grief and indignation. When the inequality of the ground, the immenfe front of this body, and the confufion of the battle, began to deftroy the firm and folid form of the Phalanx; then it was, that this able Roman conceived hopes of fuccefs: then it was, that he ordered his legions to attack it in the intervals and vacancies now laid open. [B] And to this difpofition Livy *, in exprefs terms, afcribes the victory. Had the whole Roman army, faith he, continued to make its impreffion on the front, it muft have run directly on the Macedonian pikes; nor could it have fuftained the weight of this clofe and firmly compacted body.

* cap. 41.

[B] NEQUE ulla evidentior caufa victoriae fuit, quam quod multa paffim praelia erant: quae fluctuantem turbarunt primo, deinde disjecerunt Phalangem: cujus confertae, & intentis horrentis haftis intolerabiles vires funt. Si carptim aggrediendo circumagere immobilem longitudine et gravitate haftam cogas, confufa ftrue implicantur: fi vero ab latere aut ab tergo aliquid tumultûs increpuit, ruinae modo turbantur. Sicut tum adverfus catervatim incurrentes Romanos, et interruptâ multifariam acie obviam ire cogebantur; & Romani, quacunque data intervalla effent infinuabant ordines fuos. Qui fi univerfâ acie in frontem adverfus inftructam Phalangem concurriffent, quod Pelignis principio pugnae incaute congreffis adverfus cetratos evenit, induiffent fe haftis nec confertam aciem fuftinuiffent. Liv. in loco cit.

G 4 THE

Oliv. l. 2. p. 64.

Polyb. ut supra.

THE Phalanx, therefore, appears to have been irrefiftible in almoft every cafe, but where the inequality, or accidental obftructions in the ground, or the unwieldinefs, occafioned by its numbers, made it break or fluctuate. This was the chief inconvenience attending on the Phalanx, which is faid to have been greatly increafed by the later kings of Macedon, who were enabled to augment this body to fixteen thoufand men. Though their divifion of the Phalanx, thus augmented into ten diftinct battalions, feems to have been purpofely intended to obviate this inconvenience. And, if once broken, either by the nature of the ground, or the artifice of the enemy in retiring, and tempting the Phalangites to a diforderly purfuit, or by any other caufe, the mifchief became totally irreparable, as it was abfolutely impoffible for them ever to rally and refume their form.

Livv. l 33. c. 10.

ANOTHER defect of this body feems to have been, that its rear was left entirely expofed and defencelefs. Men armed with long pikes, and exceeding clofely drawn up, could, by no means, if attacked behind, face about readily, and prefent their arms that way. Accordingly, we find, that in the battle of Cynocephalae, where the Roman conful Flaminius conquered Philip,

the

the latter king of Macedon, a legionary tribune,
with a few manipuli, undertook to break through
a formidable body of the Macedonian Phalanx,
which continued, after the difperfion of their
comrades, to fight firmly on the right wing;
and, by attacking them in the rear, eafily effected his defign, cut the hindmoft to pieces, and
obliged the reft to fly.

The Phalanx, thus formed, Philip juftly confidered as his beft and moft effectual refource:
and the foldiers, of which it was compofed, he
treated with every mark of diftinction and regard.
That affability and affection, which he fhewed
to all his foldiers, and which he well knew how
to exprefs, without defcending from his true
dignity, were doubled to them. He gave them
the honourable title of ΠΕΖΕΤΑΙΡΟΙ, his fellow
foldiers, a name invented to animate and encourage them, and to foften the utmoft feverity of
their toils. Such familiarities, faith the French
tranflator of Demofthenes, are eafily practifed,
and coft a prince but little, yet frequently prove
of the utmoft confequence.

Demoft.
Olyn. 1.
fect. 8.
Tourreil
Not. in
Olyn. 1.

But his different enemies were now pouring
down upon him, and made it neceffary to exert
all his efforts and abilities to avert the danger.
In his prefent difficulties he deemed it by no
means

Book I.

Diod. Sic.
l. 16. sect. 3.

means inconfiftent with his honour, to treat, to promife, and to oblige. He began with fending a deputation to the Paeonians; and, partly by bribing fome of their chiefs, partly by fair and artful promifes, (the methods with which he firft began, and always continued to conduct his defigns) he prevailed on that people to grant him a peace, and to leave his territories unmolefted. From this experience of the effectual power of gold, he was induced to try the fame artifice againft the people of Thrace, who had efpoufed the interefts of his rival Paufanias. The wealth of the kingdom had been entirely exhaufted by the public diforders, and gold was now fo exceedingly fcarce in Macedon, that Philip is faid to have regarded an only cup of that metal, as a poffeffion of fuch confequence, that, for the greater fecurity, it was always placed on his pillow. Yet, on this preffing occafion, he ufed all his powers to raife a fum confiderable enough for his defign; and by a magnificent prefent to the king of Thrace [c], engaged him to

Athenae l.
4. p. 155.

[c] We learn from Thucydides, that, among the ordinary revenues of the kings of Thrace, thofe prefents were accounted, which their richer fubjects, neighbouring princes, &c. ufually made to him, as well as to his nobles: and, that Philip, on this occafion, gratified his pride, as well as his love of gold; for that, in Thrace, it was efteemed more honourable to receive than to give; contrary to the cuftom of Perfia. Thucyd. l. 2. fect. 97.

abandon

abandon Paufanias and his caufe. Thus was he Sect. II. extricated from fome of his immediate difficulties, and, particularly, from the moleftation of one formidable competitor.

But Argaeus and the Athenians gave him ftill greater uneafinefs: his interefts demanded the ruin of the one; the others were to be managed with the utmoft addrefs and policy. Although Diod. Sic. ut fupra. their difpofitions were by no means favourable to him, he was fenfible that their great motive for efpoufing the caufe of Argaeus, was the hopes of becoming mafters of Amphipolis, a ceffion which that prince could make no difficulty of promifing, if, by their interpofition, he might be advanced to the throne. By the fame conceffion, Philip might have at once gained their friendfhip: but he clearly faw the danger of invefting thofe, whom he confidered as his enemies, with a place of fuch importance to the peace and fecurity of his kingdom. He therefore could not think of fuffering the Athenians to poffefs it: on the other hand, he was to act with due caution and delicacy, fo as, if poffible, to give no umbrage to this people; and this could by no means be effected, if he ftill continued to keep poffeffion of it himfelf. He therefore determined upon a meafure, dictated by the extent of his genius and policy. He with-

drew

drew the Macedonian forces from Amphipolis; and affected to renounce all claim to that city, by a formal declaration, acknowledging the right of its inhabitants to absolute liberty and independence, as a Grecian settlement, intitled, by the express words and tenour of treaties lately concluded, to the enjoyment of their own laws and privileges, free from the controul of any foreign jurisdiction. By this means, whatever opposition should be made to the pretensions of Athens, was to appear as the act of the inhabitants themselves. And this declaration of Philip had the appearance of such disinterested generosity, that the people of Amphipolis, in the first emotions of gratitude, decreed divine honours to him, as their guardian genius; expressed the

warmest zeal for his support against all attempts to disturb his government at home; while, at the same time, they defended his frontier against all foreign attacks, that might be made on that side.

MANTIAS, the Athenian admiral, was now at anchor before Methonè, the city so called on the Thermaïc bay, forty stadia distant from Pydna; and from thence detached a body of troops to reinforce the Macedonians, who had taken up arms for Argaeus. This prince now

appeared

appeared at the head of his united army, and prefented himfelf before the city of Ægae. He addreffed himfelf to the inhabitants in the manner ufual in fuch difputes; inveighed againft the injuftice of the prefent government; fupported his own title by every argument which his caufe could fupply; and urged every motive of honour and intereft, which might induce them to acknowledge him as their fovereign, and to fight under his ftandard. But thefe people had too juft notions of the merit and abilities of Philip, and of the weaknefs and infufficiency of his rival, to fuffer their allegiance to be fhaken. They, with one confent, determined to adhere firmly to the interefts of the prefent reign, and fhut their gates againft Argaeus. Difpirited by this difgrace, he directed his march back towards Methonè; when Philip, who was now prepared to attack him, fell furioufly on his rear, and cut it to pieces. The reft of his army gained a neighbouring eminence, where they were quickly furrounded, and obliged to furrender themfelves prifoners of war.

In this battle Argaeus fell, and thus freed Philip from all the dangers and commotions which might arife from his pretenfions. His Macedonians, Philip difpofed among his own troops, and freely admitted them to renew their

oaths

oaths to him, with a confidence well calculated to attach them to his intereſt. All the Athenian priſoners he treated with the utmoſt diſtinction and reſpect. He commanded that their baggage ſhould be inſtantly reſtored to them; he expreſſed the greateſt veneration for their ſtate; and the moſt cordial affection, and tender concern, for its citizens; and thus ſent them home, deeply affected with the politeneſs, and humane diſpoſitions, of the young king of Macedon.

Demoſt. in
Ariſtec.

THE Athenian priſoners had ſcarcely arrived at their city, when ambaſſadors from Philip appeared in the aſſembly; where the late conduct of their maſter gained them the utmoſt favour and attention. In his name they propoſed a peace; and a renewal of that alliance, which had formerly ſubfiſted between Athens and king Amyntas. On his part, the faireſt profeſſions were made of regard and amity: and, as to

Polyaen.
l. 4. c. 17.

Amphipolis, his deputies were inſtructed to ſpeak of it as a city to which Philip had no claim, and which was no longer dependent on the crown of Macedon, either to hold, or grant to others. His overtures were received with all attention by a people, who, although they derived conſiderable advantages from their conqueſts and colonies in Thrace and Macedon, yet were greatly difcouraged by the vaft expence of fend-ing out and maintaining their fleets, in order to fupport thefe acquifitions; and were therefore, at prefent, well inclined to make a peace with Philip, on fuch honourable terms as he now offered. Thefe, as they confifted entirely in words and promifes, he made no difficulty of propofing. And they, on their part, did not, as yet, think fo highly of Philip's power, and were not fo well acquainted with his policy, as to imagine that he could not prefume to violate any treaty which they might conclude with him. They therefore contented themfelves with feeing Amphipolis independent on Macedon; per-fuaded that they might, at fome time, recover it by force of arms. Not the leaft mention was now made of it; but the treaty, without any objection, or difficulty, accepted, concluded, and ratified, entirely to the fatisfaction of Philip; who, in the depths of his artifice and policy, confidered it only as a temporary expedient: fully determined, that no engagements, of this nature, fhould raife any obftructions to his fu-ture defigns.

THESE actions engaged the firft year of Phi-lip's reign; and, having thus far provided for the fecurity of his power and kingdom, he

received

received an account of the death of Agis, king of the Paeonians. A fimilar event had encouraged the Paeonians to diftrefs and harafs the kingdom of Macedon; and now Philip, inftructed by their invafion, determined to embrace the fame occafion of oppreffing them. He entered their territories with the choice of all his forces, encouraged and invigorated by their late fucceffes. The enemy who marched out to meet him, were utterly defeated, and the whole nation obliged to fubmit implicitly to the conqueror, and to acknowledge an abfolute dependence on Macedon.

Philip had now one enemy alone remaining, but this by far the moft formidable; Bardyllis, king of the Illyrians. The victories which this prince had gained over the brothers and the father of Philip; the fhameful tribute which they had paid him, and which he ftill demanded; the acquifitions which he had already gained in Macedon, and the danger with which his increafing power ftill threatened the kingdom; all engaged this prince to revenge the injuries done to his family, to affert the honour of his fubjects, and to provide for his own defence and fecurity. He therefore affembled his foldiers; and, by a fpirited difcourfe, inflamed their minds with fentiments of glory; rendered them impatient

tient to engage their old enemy, and to retrieve
the honour of their arms; and, having thus
prepared them for actions of valour, marched
towards the confines of Illyria, at the head of
ten thousand foot and six hundred horse. Bardyllis perceived the approaching storm, but not
without emotion: he would have been well
pleased not to expose his reputation, purchased
by a long life of military toils, to any hazard,
against a prince in the active part of life, of
extraordinary vigour and abilities, and who already appeared formidable by his late successes.
Ambassadors were therefore sent from the Illyrian, with proposals of peace, on condition that
each party should be acknowledged sovereign
of those places which they then possessed. To
these overtures Philip boldly replied, that an
equitable and an honourable peace would be
entirely consonant to his inclinations; that he
could not regard any peace, as either equitable
or honourable, but such a one as should effectually confine the Illyrian within his ancient
limits. That he should immediately relinquish
all his conquests in Macedon, were the terms
which became the king of Macedon to propose;
and these the only terms he was determined to
accept. This spirited answer put an end to all
further negociations. The Illyrian king ordered

VOL. I. H his

Book I.

his troops to march; and, with a due intrepidity, fought out the bold invaders.

Diod. Sic.
l. 16.
sect. 4.

The armies of the two nations were nearly equal, that of the Illyrians being composed of ten thousand foot, and five hundred horse. They were also equally animated, though by different motives. The Macedonians fought to revenge their late disgraces, and to regain the honour of their arms: the Illyrians came on in the pride of former victories, and were eager to support their advantages, and maintain the glory they had already gained. As they approached, each army endeavoured to strike terror into their assailants, by horrid shouts and outcries, according to the ancient custom of these nations. The Illyrians advanced in one large column, of that kind which the Greeks called Plinthion, to fall with all their weight upon the enemy. The right wing and center of the Macedonians were composed of their choicest infantry, and, among these, the Phalanx lately formed.

Fron. Strat.
l. 2. c. 3.

On the left, Philip stationed his cavalry, who were ordered to wheel about and attack the Illyrians in flank; while the prince, at the head of his favourite body, stood firmly in the front, and bravely sustained their charge. Both sides fought with equal valour, and victory remained long in suspence. At length,

length, the Macedonian cavalry began to make
fome impreffion, both on the flank and the rear
of the Illyrians ; while all the boldeft efforts of
the Phalanx, and all the military fkill of their
royal general, were exerted to break their front.
Victory began, at length, to favour, and, after
a long and obftinate conteft, to declare for Philip : repeated charges, directed with due fkill,
and executed with becoming valour, obliged the
Illyrian column to bend and fluctuate : the Macedonians preffed their difordered enemy on all
fides ; on the front, the flank, and the rear ;
and, with great havock, broke and difperfed
the whole army. More than feven thoufand fell
on the field of battle ; and, among thefe, the
gallant old king Bardyllis ; whofe mind and body
ftill retained fuch vigour, that, at the age of
ninety, he fought bravely on horfeback. This
man had raifed himfelf, by his valour, from a
ftate of the greateft meannefs and obfcurity.
Having firft gained a few followers, he fupported himfelf by rapine and plunder ; and, by
remarkable equity and exactnefs in the diftribu-
tion of the prey, attached his followers to his
intereft, and greatly increafed their numbers.
Hence he feems (in this favage nation, where
power was chiefly founded on violence and perfonal bravery, the great mark of merit) to have been
enabled to raife himfelf to the fovereignty. In

Lucian in
Macrobiis.
Photius
Biblio. p.
1579.

Cic. de Off.
l. 2. fect. 2.

H 2

this

 this ftation he acted with becoming vigour; and now fell in a manner worthy of a warlike prince.

THE purfuit was, for fome time, continued with confiderable flaughter; but, as the rout difperfed and feparated the enemy, Philip, who well knew how far to purfue his victory, recalled his foldiers to the field of battle; where he caufed the dead to be interred, and, as Diodorus * hath recorded, erected a trophy in honour of this important victory. It is certain, that this account is not agreeable to the eftablifhed maxim of his predeceffors; and that Paufanias, as hath been already obferved, afferts, that neither Philip nor Alexander ever erected a trophy in honour of any of their many victories. Yet, in the medals which have been preferved, both of the father and the fon, we find a reverfe charged with one of thefe memorials of victory; which feems to favour the account of Diodorus, and to imply, that Philip did really make this innovation in the Macedonian cuftoms; and rather chofe to imitate the manners and ufages of Greece. And if fo, it is a circumftance the more worthy of attention, as it feems to be an indication of the afpiring temper of this prince. His firft great ambition was to

make

* l. 16.
fect. 4.

make his kingdom be confidered as a true and genuine member of the illuftrious community of Greece. This was an honour the Greeks were now by no means difpofed to grant him; and every circumftance of diftinction many of them were fufficiently ready to point out. Hence might poffibly have arifen this affectation of conforming to the Grecian manners : which was by no means accidental, or lightly conceived by Philip; but the refult of deep defign, to place himfelf and his fubjects in a more honourable view than that of barbarians, in which their enemies were willing to confider them; and to abolifh every, even the minuteft, cuftom, which might tend to preferve the memory of a diftinction fo odious and mortifying.

See Demoft. Phil. 3. fect. 6. et alibi.

HOWEVER this may be, the ambitious and daring fpirit of Philip, enlivened and elevated by fuccefs, now meditated ftill greater and more extenfive defigns. The late victory had completely freed his country from the incurfions of a dangerous enemy; and reduced Illyria to the condition of a province dependent on Macedon. His abilities, his fuccefles, his whole deportment, obliging and engaging, both by nature and by art, all confpired to captivate the affections of his fubjects, and to attach them with particular firmnefs to his fervice. They now

Diod. Sic. ut fupra.

H 3   fpoke

fpoke of nothing but the greatnefs of their king; and, under his direction and command, were prepared to undertake the moft hazardous enterprizes. Thus animated, and thus fupported, Philip now determined to go on in that courfe of bold and hazardous enterprizes, which he had hitherto purfued with fo much good fortune; and, not contented with fecuring the peaceable poffeffion of the throne, (which many princes, fituated as he had been, would have thought fufficient for their glory) refolved to render his kingdom much more opulent and flourifhing, much more powerful and refpectable.

Amphipolis he confidered as a city, the poffeffion of which was, in the firft place, neceffary to his future defigns; and which both glory and intereft equally prompted him to reunite to Macedon. But many difficulties there were to obftruct an attempt of this nature, which required the moft confummate policy to furmount. The Athenians had by no means refigned their pretenfions, but prepared to reduce the city by force of arms. The Amphipolitans, on their part, had now tafted the comforts of freedom; and determined, if poffible, to maintain their independence: for this purpofe, they attached themfelves to the Olynthian league, which had

once

once more grown powerful by the ruin of the
Spartans. The people, who formed this confederacy, appeared well-difpofed to defend them,
both againft the Athenians, with whom they
were, at this time, engaged in a conteft; and
againft Philip, whom they juftly dreaded and
fufpected. Iphicrates, the Athenian, was once
more fent againft this city, whofe abilities foon
made him mafter of all the adjacent pofts. The
town was blocked up; when a party of the citizens, in the Athenian intereft, promifed to   Demoft.
deliver up one of the gates to him, and gave   in Ariftoc.
hoftages for the fecurity of their performance.
Thefe hoftages Iphicrates committed to the care
of Charidemus, the commander of a body of
hired troops, who then fought under him, and
was himfelf obliged to return to Athens, whither
the diffatisfaction of his countrymen had recalled him. Charidemus, pretending to refent the
wrongs of Iphicrates, refufed to ferve under
Timotheus, who had fucceeded him; and returned the hoftages to the Amphipolitans. The
Athenians were thus defeated in their hopes of
gaining the city; and Timotheus himfelf was
foon after obliged to raife the fiege, as he had
not forces fufficient to oppofe the Olynthians
and Thracians, with whom he was at once
engaged.

H 4

THE Amphipolitans, thus fecured from their prefent danger, feem to have grown to fome degree of infolence, and to have given Philip real, or pretended, caufes of complaint. The Olynthians plainly perceived, that thefe muft neceffarily produce an open declaration againft them on the part of Philip; and that a place, where many of their fubjects had fettled, was in imminent danger of falling under the dominion of a prince, whofe power was already become formidable to his neighbours. What ufe he might be tempted to make of fuch an acceffion of ftrength; how far their intereft might be affected, and their welfare rendered precarious by it, was uncertain. They, therefore, determined to quiet

all their fufpicions and jealoufies at once, and to provide effectually againft all confequences, by a timely union with Athens; and now fent their deputies to that city, to propofe an accommodation and alliance.

Such a conjunction could not but appear in the higheft degree alarming to Philip; his future hopes entirely depended on defeating the defign; and, for this purpofe, that artifice and policy, which had always fo great a fhare in the fuccefs of all his fchemes, were now effectually exerted. His agents were inftantly difpatched to Athens: the popular leaders, and public minifters,

minifters, were gained; and the people flattered
with the faireft and moft plaufible declarations.
To give thefe an air of greater fincerity, a negociation was commenced, and a formal ftipulation made, that the Athenians, in the firft
place, fhould be put in poffeffion of Amphipolis; and that they, on their part, fhould give
up Pydna to Philip; which, though famous
for its fidelity and attachment to Amyntas; an
attachment carried even to adoration, as we
learn from Ariftides *, yet had revolted from
Philip, and committed itfelf to the protection
of Athens. Under the pretence of preventing
the inhabitants of this city from taking the
alarm, and feeking the defence of fome other
ftate, the whole tranfaction was privately carried
on in the fenate of five hundred, without being
referred, as ufual, to the affembly of the people: and, by this means, there was the greater
room for evafion and fubterfuge, and better opportunity for delays and difficulties. The Athenians, fired with expectations of regaining
Amphipolis, the great object of their wifhes,
fuffered themfelves to be amufed, and, with the
moft infolent contempt, refufed to receive any
overtures from the Olynthian deputies; a treatment which juftly irritated their ftate, and determined it to give all poffible oppofition to the
Athenian intereft.

Demoft.
Olynth. 1.
f.ct. 3.

* Orat. de
Societ. tom.
3. p. 480.

Theopom-
pus in Ulp.
& Suida.

Demoft. ut
fupra.

          THIS

Dem. Phil.
2. sect. 4.

THIS was the disposition with which Philip wished to inspire the Olynthians. He instantly applied himself to them, while yet their resentment was violent; he flattered, he courted, he promised them, and they readily hearkened to his proposals. With an air of the utmost friendship and cordiality, he gave them up Anthemus, a city which separated Olynthus from the sea, and which had, for a long series of years, acknowledged the jurisdiction of the kings of Macedon: and, thus gratified and obliged, the Olynthians made no difficulty of entering into strict engagements with their benefactor. By these means did this consummate master of intrigue dispel that storm, which, had it once burst forth, must have destroyed his rising greatness, and engaged a powerful and important people firmly to his interests, who had ever regarded him with envy and discontent, and were, but a moment before, prepared to unite with his most dangerous antagonists.

STRENGTHENED by this new alliance, he made no scruple of avowing those hostile intentions, which he had, for some time, entertained against Amphipolis. He had art sufficient to persuade the Olynthians, that their interest, as well as that of Macedon, required that he should reduce this city to his obedience. This people

people had alfo fome wrongs to urge againft the inhabitants. It was therefore determined to unite their refentments; and Amphipolis was preffed by a vigorous fiege. The Amphipolitans, more affected by danger, when it had once fallen upon them, than attentive to the means of preventing it, had recourfe to Athens in this emergency, and fent two of their citizens to defire the protection of that ftate. The Athenians had juft now given an uncommon proof of attention to their public interefts. The ifland of Euboea had been, for fome time, under their protection; and its refpective cities were governed by perfons devoted to their fervice. Diforders, however, had arifen; and a fedition, fomented and fupported by the Thebans, whofe forces had been admitted into fome of the cities, threatened the whole ifland with a revolution. Menefarchus, the governor of Chalcis, had been guilty of fome outrages againft the Athenians: Themifon, who governed in Eretria, had alfo given them a particular caufe of complaint. He had taken from them the city of Oropus, fituated on the confines of Attica and Boeotia, and given it into the hands of the Thebans; who ftill obftinately refufed to reftore it to a people, who either could not, or were not difpofed to make ufe of any other

means

Sect. II.

Diod. Sic. l. 16. fect. 8.

Demoft. Olyn. 3. fect. 4.

Æfchin. in Ctef. fect. 31.

means for recovering this city, but thofe of re-monftrating, and pleading the juftice of their pretenfions. Yet thefe chiefs now found them-felves obliged to implore the affiftance of the Athenians, who, notwithftanding all former complaints and quarrels, could not but fee the neceffity of fupporting their intereft in Euboea, which, by its fituation, ferved either to com-mand, or to defend, the country of Attica; and, by its fertility, fupplied it amply with pro-vifions. But, although the attempt of Thebes was fufficiently alarming, yet doubts and delays were arifing; when Timotheus, the great A-thenian general, appeared in the affembly. " What, my countrymen," cried he, " the " Thebans are in the ifland; and are you de-" liberating? why are you not already at the " port? why are you not embarked? why is " not the fea covered with your navy?" So fpirited an addrefs, determined them at once: in five days, they entered Euboea; in thirty, they obliged the Thebans to come to terms, and to evacuate the ifland; and, on their return, Hierax and Stratocles, the deputies of Amphi-polis, appeared before them to implore their aid upon a like occafion. They reprefented the danger of a junction between Philip and Olyn-thus in the ftrongeft light; and earneftly preffed them to fend out their fleet, to take a city under

their

Demoft. de
Cherfon. in
fine.

Æfch. ut
fupra.

Dem. O-
lynth. 3.
fect. 4.

their protection, which they had long defired to
poffefs; and, by that means, to prevent it from
falling under the power of their common
enemy.

THE late inftance of their vigour made Philip fee plainly the neceffity of having once more recourfe to artifice. He therefore addreffed a letter to the Athenians, which he well knew how to draw up in the moft fpecious and infinuating terms. In this he acknowledged their pretenfions to the city, which he now befieged; he renewed the affurances of his friendfhip; he declared, that it was his real intention to furrender Amphipolis to them; and that, for this purpofe, and with this defign alone, he had now laid fiege to it. The Athenians, who were entirely engaged by a general revolt of their allies, and dependent towns, (which produced the war, called the *focial war*) eafily fuffered themfelves to be amufed by thefe reprefentations; and, pleafed with the leaft appearance of a pretence to juftify them in not engaging in an enterprize, for which they were not fufficiently at leifure, abfolutely rejected the propofitions of the Amphipolitan deputies; and refufed to fend fuccours to a city, which they fondly imagined they fhould receive without any trouble. Philip was thus left at liberty to prefs the city with

Demoft. in Ariftocr.

Dem. Olynth. 3. fect. 4.

double

Diod. Sic.
1. 16. fect.
8. Dem.
Olyn. 3.
fect. 6.

double vigour; a breach was made in the walls; the Macedonians entered; and the citizens, finding all refiftance ineffectual, were obliged to furrender themfelves to the mercy of a conqueror, whom they had provoked by an obftinate defence; though, by an unaccountable inconfiftency of conduct, they ftill continued to pay him divine honours.

Diod. Sic.
ut fupra.

PHILIP, now mafter of Amphipolis, contented himfelf with banifhing thofe who had oppofed him with greateft violence, and treated the reft of the inhabitants with fufficient lenity. His defign was by no means to exterminate, but to command them. The fituation and importance of their city, and the extent and conveniencies of its commerce, recommended them to his protection; and determined him to fhew a juft regard to the welfare and tranquillity of fo valuable an acquifition. Far from gratifying the expectations, which the flighteft grounds had been fufficient to make the Athenians entertain, he reunited Amphipolis to Macedon, and refolved to brave all the refentment of that people; yet, ftill with due caution and policy, he judged it neceffary to arm himfelf againft any effects of that refentment; and, for this purpofe, determined to cement the union which now fubfifted between him and the Olynthians.

THEY

THEY were poſſeſſed of a conſiderable power, both by ſea and land. They had conceived high notions of their own importance, and had already diſcovered their jealouſy of Philip's increaſing power, which, though it had for the preſent ſubſided, yet might ſtill break out, on any future alarm. Favours and benefits, therefore, were the only ſure means of confirming them in his intereſt; and he ſoon found opportunities of gratifying them. The revolt of Pydna afforded him a fair occaſion of marching againſt that city, in order to reduce it to his obedience. The ſiege was formed; and the Pydneans, unſupported by their new ſovereigns, were ſoon obliged to ſurrender. Libanus * and Ariſtides † have both aſſerted, that, at the very time when theſe people were performing thoſe ſolemn rites, by which the terms of their capitulation were ratified, Philip ordered his ſoldiers to fall on them without mercy, and thus cruelly maſſacred a conſiderable number of the citizens. But ſuch an inſtance of barbarity would not, it may reaſonably be preſumed, have been omitted by Demoſthenes, who repreſented all the actions of this prince in the blackeſt light; nor is it at all conſiſtent with the tenour of his actions: for, although his humanity was, on many occaſions, made to yield to his policy and ambition, yet unneceſſary barbarity was neither

con-

 confiftent with his temper, nor his intereft. It feems more reafonable to fuppofe, that he accepted of the fubmiffion of the inhabitants, without inflicting any extraordinary feverities, and without difgracing his prefent to the Olynthians, to whom he now gave up Pydna, by putting them in poffeffion of a city, depopulated and polluted by the blood of helplefs wretches, who had laid down their arms, and yielded themfelves up to mercy.

Ibid. Phil.
2. fect. 4.
Diod. Sic. l.
16. fect. 8.

To gratify the Olynthians ftill farther, he, in the next place, turned his arms againft Potidaea. This city had been taken fome years fince by Timotheus, and was now in poffeffion of the Athenians; but, as it had been originally dependent on Olynthus, with profeffions of the trueft affection, he made a tender of his affiftance, in order to reduce it to their obedience. His propofal was readily accepted; and he now marched, at the head of a formidable force, againft a city by no means capable of contending with the united powers of two fuch confederates. The gates of Potidaea were foon obliged to be thrown open to receive the befiegers. The Athenian garrifon, from a vain expectation of relief, retired into the citadel, and there continued the oppofition, till, convinced of their abandoned and defperate condition, they

con-

consented to yield to superiour force, and surrendered themselves prisoners of war. In this siege, Philip affected only to be considered as ally to Olynthus, to be engaged entirely on their account, without any hopes of private advantage. The city, therefore, was instantly given up to the Olynthians: but the Athenian prisoners he took under his protection, as the citizens of a state, for which he professed the greatest veneration and regard. With declarations the most flattering, and with every mark of honour and esteem, he freely dismissed those Athenians, loaded with favours, and conducted, in security, to their city. Thus tempering his very hostilities by a deportment the most obliging and caressing; so as still to have room for palliating his conduct, and disguising his most flagrant opposition, by the specious plea of necessity.

FAME now began to speak loudly of his actions; and all the adjacent states beheld him with admiration and terrour. A spirited and seasonable association might still have crushed his growing power; but his manners and qualifications were admirably calculated to frustrate such designs: his engaging affability, and insinuating address, stole the affections of all who approached him: they who beheld him, could not conceive him dangerous or aspiring: and,

SECT. II.

Demost.
Olynth. 1.
sect. 6.

Diod. Sic.
ut supra.

Dem &
Aesch de
fals. L g.
passim.

when they had once converfed with him, even
the cleareft evidence could fcarcely efface their
prejudices in his favour. His penetration pierced
into their moft fecret fentiments; his caution
and policy concealed his own; while he feemed
implicitly to refign himfelf up to all thofe who
were admitted to his prefence, with an appearance of undefigning confidence, capable of im-
pofing on the moft guarded, and beft experienced in the ways of men. Hence it was, that
the powers, concerned to oppofe him, were perfuaded that they enjoyed, or might eafily acquire, his friendfhip: and, inftead of concerting
meafures for the general defence, each thought
themfelves fufficiently fecure, when his arms were
turned away from them; and, by this fatal infenfibility, fuffered that power to increafe, without any effectual interruption or controul, which
was at length to involve them all in one general
ruin.

Demoft.
paffim.

Philip, on his part, knew how to improve
every opportunity, and every inftance of im-
prudence in his rivals. He had now firmly fecured the friendfhip of the Olynthians, by putting them in poffeffion of fome places, which,
had he kept himfelf, their garrifons muft have
confiderably weakened his army. And, having
thus

Sect. II.

thus provided for the fecurity of his kingdom;
reconciled a powerful neighbouring ftate to his
government, and engaged it in his fervice by
the ties of intereft and gratitude, his active foul
prompted him to take the advantage of thofe
favourable circumftances, and to march out of
his dominions in purfuit of further conquefts.
The people of Thrace had long confidered Macedon as a diftrict rent from their dominions:
they had frequently infefted it, and fometimes
with fuccefs; their late attempt to fet Paufanias
on the throne Philip's art could improve into a
faircaufe, and juftification, of hoftilities. Againft
them, therefore, he now determined to march;
and the character of their king gave him juft
grounds to hope for fuccefs.

Thucyd.l.2;

COTYS, who at this time governed the eaftern Thrace, poffeffed the Cherfonefus, and the
coafts of the Egean fea, as far as the Euxine.
He had at firft difcovered fome wifdom in the
adminiftration of affairs. He ftrengthened himfelf by an alliance with Athens; and gave his
daughter in marriage to Iphicrates; on which
occafion he difcovered fuch fatisfaction, and
thought himfelf fo much honoured, that he even
defcended to wait at table on thofe who were
affembled at the nuptials. He had no fixed re-

Corn. Nep.
in Iphic.
Athenae. l.
4. p. 131.

I 2

fidence

fidence in his dominions; but, as they contained the moſt beautiful foreſts, and were watered by many rivers, whoſe banks were embroidered with variety of fragrant flowers, he ranged about with his attendants, and pitched his tents wherever the beauty of the place invited him. Theſe delightful retreats gave a wild and romantic turn to his mind, ſo that he at length conceived the fancy of being enamoured with Minerva. He quitted his court, and pierced into the receſſes of his groves, to enjoy, as he pretended, the converſation of this goddeſs. All preparations were made for the reception of his divine miſtreſs; and his guards ſent out to ſee whether ſhe was not attending to receive him: their anſwers were fatal to them, whether they ſoothed his folly or declared the truth; in either caſe he revenged the diſappointment, by putting them inſtantly to death. He ordered one of his concubines to aſſume the attributes and ornaments of the Athenian Minerva. In a word, his mind was totally diſordered, which appeared no leſs in his public conduct. He engaged his ſon-in-law to wage war on his country; and, having gained a naval victory over the Athenians, by means of this general, he deprived them of all their territories in the Cherſoneſus, and attacked their colonies on the coaſt of Thrace. To ſup-

port

port this war, he demanded a loan from the people of Perinthus, which they refused. He then defired, that they fhould, at leaft, grant him fome troops to replace his garrifons, that he might be enabled to appear with all his forces in the field. The Perinthians flattered themfelves, that it would be in their power to keep thofe places where they were to be ftationed, as a fecurity for his performing the terms of their ftipulation; and therefore agreed to his demand. But this capricious prince treated their fuccours as prifoners, and refufed to difmifs them without a ranfom.

Sect. II. Arifto'. Oeconom. l. 2. p. 5·8. Ed. Lutet.

Such was the man againft whom Philip marched. The particulars of his expedition are not recorded exactly by any hiftorian now extant: but the Thracian king feems to have fled, with precipitation, at the bare rumour of fo formidable an enemy; for, from a fragment of Theopompus, which Athenaeus † hath preferved, we learn, that, on the third day of their march, the Macedonians poffeffed themfelves of Onocarfis, a delightful refidence, fituated in the midft of a foreft, to which Cotys had opened feveral avenues; and which was moft frequently the feat of his enjoyments. The Thracian prince, thus driven from his favourite fettlement, and

† l. 12. p. 531.

I 3 unable

unable to oppofe an enemy who were now freely traverfing and wafting his dominions, vainly hoped to ftop the progrefs of Philip by a letter. Its contents are not known, but, we muft fuppofe, were in the higheft degree extravagant. The bare mention of a letter from Cotys raifed a loud exclamation of contempt and ridicule among the Macedonian courtiers. "Yes," replied Philip, "from Cotys! doth that excite "your mirth? you little think what demands "he makes."

Plut. in
Apophth.

The arms of this prince were as ineffectual as his negociations. Some few parties of the Thracians were fent out againft Philip, whom he with eafe difperfed, and purfued his march to the fhore. He encamped near Crenidae, a colony of the Thaffians, equally diftant from the mountains of Thrace and from the fea. The beauty of the fituation was fufficiently ftriking: a lake, into which there entered divers ftreams and rivulets, tempered the drynefs of the foil; which produced fruits of the fineft and moft delicious kind, and rofes of a peculiar hue and fragrancy. But Philip, however delighted with the charms of nature, was determined to this refidence, by a much more material confideration. The grand object of his attention were thofe mines of gold

Diod. Sic.
ut fupra.

in

in the neighbouring mountains, of which he had
been well informed, and from whence he promifed himfelf confiderable advantages.   He
drove out the Thracians from Crenidae, which
they had juft built (without any regard to their
alliance with Athens); fettled a colony of Macedonians there, and called the place, after his
own name, Philippi, fo famous afterwards, in
the Roman hiftory, for the defeat of Brutus and
Caffius.   He then proceeded to examine the
ftate of thofe celebrated mines : his foldiers defcended, with their torches, into a vein, which
had not been wrought upon for a confiderable
time.   Here they traced the art and labour of
the ancient poffeffors.   Canals had been contrived, with infinite pains, to drain off the water,
which burft forth into fubterraneous lakes; and
many circumftances appeared to encourage and
to facilitate his defign, though the barbarous
inhabitants had, for a long time, neglected this
important fund of wealth.   Numbers were inftantly employed; and all the contrivances,
which ingenuity could fuggeft, were made ufe
of, in order to work thofe mines to greater advantage than had hitherto been derived from
them.   The fuccefs rewarded his labours; for
he, by this means, eftablifhed an annual revenue of ten thoufand talents, without any burden or impofition on his fubjects.   And, how-

I 4   ever

Sect. II.

Dem. in
Lept.
Diod. l. 16.
fect. 9.

Afclepiodo-
tus in Se-
neca.
Nat. Quaef.
l. 5. p. 763.
Ed. Lipf.

ever severely the philosopher Seneca [D] may have spoken of this transaction, such a resource will not be thought unworthy of the attention of a wife prince. He now struck that celebrated coin, which was called after his own name: it was dispersed liberally to promote his aspiring schemes, and soon became of general high estimation, as formed of the purest metal which these mines afforded. By this he was enabled to reinforce his army with a numerous body of mercenary soldiers, of whom many were found in all the neighbouring nations, ready to

Diod. Sic.
l. 16. sect. 8.

[D] Asclepiodotus auctor est, demissos quamplurimos a Philippo in metallum antiquum, olim destitutum, ut explorarent, quae ubertas ejus esset, quis status; an aliquid futuris reliquisset vetus avaritia: descendisse illos cum multo lumine, & multos durasse dies: deinde longâ viâ fatigatos vidisse flumina ingentia, & conceptus aquarum inertium vastos pares nostris, nec compressos quidem terrâ supereminente, sed liberae laxitatis non sine horrore visos. Cum magnâ haec legi voluptate, intellexi enim faeculum nostrum non novis vitiis, sed jam antiquitus traditis laborare: nec nostrâ aetate primum avaritiam venas terrarum lapidumque rimatam in tenebris male abstrusa quaesisse. Illi quoque majores nostri, quos celebramus laudibus, quibus dissimiles querimur nos esse, spe ducti montes ceciderunt, ut supra lucrum sub ruina steterunt. Ante Philippum Macedonem reges fuere, qui pecuniam in altissimis usque latebris sequerentur; & relicto spiritu libero, in illos se demitterent specus in quos nullum noctium, dierumque perveniret discrimen; & a tergo lucem relinquerent, &c.   SENECA.

receive

receive the pay of an opulent and renowned prince: and this coin he liberally diftributed in all the ftates whofe councils or actions might effect his defigns: where numbers of creatures were thus fecured in an age of luxury and depravity, who confidered themfelves as retained by a generous mafter, and obliged to be ever in readinefs to act, to fpeak, to advife, to influence, juft as his fervice required, and his commands dictated. Having thus projected and prepared the means of facilitating his future defigns; and having made all the neceffary difpofitions for the eftablifhment of his new colony at Philippi, he proceeded to purfue his advantages over the king of Thrace, who, on the other hand, was as violently preffed by the Athenians.

WHEN Timotheus found himfelf obliged to raife the fiege of Amphipolis, fome time before this city was reduced by Philip, that general fell on Thrace, and there made fome conquefts, which might have been improved ftill further, had he been properly fupported by Charidemus. But this commander withdrew his mercenaries, and paffed over into Afia, where he engaged in the fervice of Artabazus, a revolted fatrap. Here he foon found himfelf obliged to fupport his forces, by plundering fome towns dependent on that fatrap, whom he came to ferve. When

the

Demoft. in
Ariftocr.

Book I.

the spoil was well nigh consumed, and no further resource appeared, he pretended to return to the service of the Athenians; and demanded, from their general Cephisodotus, a fleet to convey him back to Europe, with assurances that he would reduce the Chersonesus to the subjection of the Athenians. This people, encouraged by these hopes, granted his request; and Artabazus, by the interposition of Memnon and Mentor, his kinsmen, suffered him to embark.

Demost. in
Aristocr.

CHARIDEMUS, instead of performing his promise, returned to the service of Cotys, and reduced two cities that were under the Athenian jurisdiction; but, the extravagance of this prince increasing with his success, he was assassinated, in the midst of his court, by two brothers, Python and Heraclides, of the city of Ænus in Thrace; to whom the Athenians gave all the honours which they usually decreed to the murderers of tyrants, although they had been entirely prompted by private revenge, as Cotys had, some time before, caused their father to be put to death.

CERSOBLEPTES, Berisides, and Amadocus, were his joint successors; which produced much confusion, by the attempts of Cersobleptes to dispossess the other two. Charidemus espoused

him;

him; Anthenodorus and Miltocythes, who had some petty sovereignties in Thrace, supported the interest of the others. The Athenians, depending on the services of Charidemus sent Cephisodotus into Thrace, with instructions to assist the coheirs, and to attempt the recovery of the Chersonesus. But Charidemus disappointed their expectations, attacked Cephisodotus, and obliged him to sign a treaty, whereby the Athenians acknowledged Cersobleptes sole king of Thrace.

AT Athens this treaty was disavowed, and their general condemned to pay a large fine. Miltocythes, supported by the Athenians, asserted the right of Berisides and Amadochus. But Charidemus caused him, and his son, to be seized; and, as he apprehended the clemency of Cersobleptes, delivered them into the hands of the Cardians, the most avowed enemies which the Athenians had in those parts: and this people put them to death, with circumstances of the utmost cruelty. There now remained only Anthenodorus, who, depending on the assistance of Athens, continued his attachment to the two princes. Athens, however, sent no other assistance than their general Chabrias, with a single vessel; who, as he had no forces, was obliged to accede to all the demands of Chari-

Demost. in Aristoc.

6   demus.

demus. Diffatisfied at this tranfaction, and convinced of their errour, the people determined to correct it. Chares was fent to Thrace with a fleet of fixty fail; who obliged Cerfobleptes to fign a more equitable treaty; and Thrace was divided equally beween the three coheirs.

The king of Macedon was ftrictly attentive to all thefe tranfactions; and, though he as yet deemed it inconfiftent with good policy to ufe open force, in order to difturb any fyftem which the people of Athens efpoufed; yet it was fufficiently apparent, that he ftudied to derive advantages to himfelf from the diforders of Thrace. The Cherfonefus, the great mart of all the Thracian commerce, from whofe ports was derived an annual revenue of no lefs than two hundred talents, was defervedly the principal object of his regards. Here he determined to eftablifh an intereft, by the fecret methods of intrigue, until the terrour of his arms might be more opportunely employed. To the people of Cardia, the principal city of this peninfula, he feems to have applied early; and to have founded his defigns on their averfion to the jurifdiction of the Athenians, who formerly poffeffed, and now claimed the Cherfonefus; though the war, in which they were engaged with the allies, prevented them from effectually fupporting their title.

title. Philip well knew how to take the due
advantage of their embarraſſments. He was
now powerful and formidable; his kingdom
completely ſettled; his frontier ſecured and extended on one ſide to the ſea of Thrace, and, on
the other, to the lake Lycnitis: his finances
were large and well regulated; and all the advantages of commerce abundantly ſecured by the
poſſeſſion of Amphipolis. Situated as it were,
at an advantageous point of view, he ſurveyed
the ſeveral ſtates of Greece; obſerved their different intereſts, tempers, and diſpoſitions, their
errours and corruptions: and, with the utmoſt
reaſon, exulted in the proſpect, that the deſigns
of extenſive power, which his vaſt ambition
dictated, were now ripening to execution.

BOOK

BOOK I. SECTION III.

CONTENTS.

BOOK

BOOK the FIRST.

SECTION III.

WE are now advancing to the period of this hiſtory, when Greece began to be the ſcene of many of Philip's enterpriſes. The affairs of that nation have already appeared to be in part connected with his earlier actions: and from henceforward we ſhall find, that the events, which diſturbed the peace of its different ſtates, or called forth their armies, were many of them the effect of his machinations, and almoſt all determined by his valour or policy. We ſhall find his life one uniform ſcheme of watching their commotions, fomenting their diſorders, and eſtabliſhing his own power on their weakneſs and corruption. The whole body, collectively, hath been already preſented to the reader. And it muſt be deemed a neceſſary part of this work, here to conſider its ſeveral leading members, in order to trace the internal cauſes, the latent ſources, of thoſe events, which we ſhall find gradually operating to the full eſtabliſhment of the Macedonian em-

See prelimi-
nary diſſer-
tation.

pire, and the final ruin of a people, who have ever appeared highly worthy the attention of all ages; and, from whose fall, we may derive some of the most important instructions, which history holds forth to mankind.

THE different fluctuations of power, and the variety of fortune, which the principal states, in their turns, experienced, had now inspired them with the dangerous passions of revenge, jealousy, mutual diffidence, and mutual aversion; and raised that spirit of discord and contention for pre-eminence, which were the great basis on which Philip founded his designs. The states † l. 8. c. 1. of Greece, saith Justin †, while each was ambitious of commanding, all lost that darling object of their wishes: and, while they rushed on with blind fury to the destruction of each other, never perceived, till they were irrecoverably lost, that the distresses of every particular member intimately affected the whole body.

THESE continual struggles for power took their rise from the time that the Persian had been defeated, and were the chief causes of the depravation of manners which then began, and gradually increased, in Greece, down to its final ruin. The contending parties frequently found

it

it convenient to apply to the Perſians for aſſiſtance; a nation whom they had hitherto thought
it their glory to regard with abhorrence and contempt. But their ambition now made them ſer-
vile and complying. In ancient times, their
wars were carried on with the ſimplicity and
openneſs of a generous and honeſt people; but
now intrigue, and cabal, and corruption, began
to prevail among them, though by ſlow degrees.
Bribery crept in, even where the conſtitution demanded and enjoined an utter contempt and dif-
regard for riches: and Perſian agents were ſeen
in every ſtate, practiſing with miniſters, and in-
fluencing the public councils.

But, as all corruption is gradual, the Athenians (particularly) could not at once forget
their original principles, but ſtill expreſſed, on
ſome occaſions, thoſe ſublime ideas of virtue
and integrity, which had been derived from
their anceſtors. When the king of Perſia had
ſent his agent to bribe the Peloponneſians to
take up arms againſt them, inſtead of revenge
and reſentment, they expreſſed the moſt generous indignation at this baſe attempt upon the
integrity of Greece: and thundered out a ſevere ſentence of proſcription againſt the man
who had preſumed to bring gold into Peloponneſus. But ſuch appearances were never laſting,

Dem. Phil.
3. ſect. 9,

K 2

being

being generally affumed to conceal lefs honourable motives, or were, at beft, but the temporary effects of fenfibility and delicacy, which
were foon forgotten with the occafion, among
a people, where refolution and conftancy were
wanting, and where that uniformity and con-
fiftency of conduct were utterly unknown,
which only can render men really good and
great, whatever principles they may have im-
bibed, or whatever character they may affume.

ATHENS was now confeffedly the greateft and
moft eminent of the Grecian ftates. The honours which fhe had acquired in the famous
Perfian war, infpired her citizens with the moft
exalted ideas of virtue and glory. The fuccefs
of their repeated contefts for liberty and pre-
eminence, gave them the higheft notions of
their ftrength and abilities: and all the tranfactions of their country, frequently celebrated by
their writers, and difplayed in all the pomp of
eloquence by their orators, infpired them with a
peculiar national vanity, which continued in its
full ftrength, even in their loweft ftate of degeneracy. Various and inconftant in their tempers and paffions, they were eafily provoked,
faith Plutarch *, and as eafily returned to fentiments of benevolence and compaffion. Ad-
mirers of wit, and encouragers of gaiety and

* in Prae-
cep. Reip.
ger.

6
                                                plea-

pleafantry: but unfortunately to fuch excefs, that a jeft too often determined them in their moft important deliberations, and ridicule became their teft of truth. They poffeffed, in a great degree, and even affected, a quicknefs of conception and penetration; but this was unhappily accompanied with an impatience of attention, and an averfion to deliberate and well-weighed counfels.

When the Thebans triumphed over the power of Sparta, had their general furvived his victories, fo dangerous a rival might have kept the Athenians duly attentive to their public interefts: but hiftory afcribes their ruin to that fatal fecurity with which the death of Epaminondas infpired them. Confirmed in their power, as they thought, and freed from all danger and competition by this event, they now indulged their love of eafe and felf-enjoyment, without meafure or control.

Their affluence had been fucceeded by luxury; and luxury they adorned and recommended by all the arts and refinements of tafte and elegance. Mufic and poetry, public entertainments, and fpectacles, had ever been the objects of their warmeft affection; but were now made the bufinefs and occupation of their

lives.

lives. The lowest of the people were, in a good degree, judges of the polite and fine arts. Men who excelled in those, were invited and encouraged by their taste, and rewarded magnificently by their opulence. A public festival was, in these days, celebrated with more expence, engaged more numbers, and was the object of greater attention, than was granted to the raising an army, or to the equipment of a fleet. To the theatre particularly they had ever been most passionately devoted: and some of their meanest citizens, when in distress and captivity, had been enabled to purchase relief and liberty, by charming their masters with the verses of their admired tragic writers. But now the support of the theatre was become so much the concern of the state, that their more serious and momentous affairs were sacrificed to it, by an astonishing establishment, which will here require to be explained.

In the early ages, the theatre knew not that magnificence, which riches and luxury afterwards introduced. Slight and unadorned edifices were occasionally raised, the people admitted freely to the entertainments, and the right of places and precedence entirely undetermined. The people assembled in a tumultuary manner, and the first occupier thought himself

entitled

Dem.
Phil. I.
sect. 13.

Plut in
Nicia.

intitled to oppofe all attempts to difpoffefs him
of his feat. Hence diforder and contentions
fometimes arofe: to prevent which, the magiftrates ordained, that a fmall price fhould
be paid for places, to reimburfe the expence of
erecting the theatre. Though the tax was low,
the poorer citizens complained; and Pericles, an
able and artful politician, fatally conceived a
fcheme of ingratiating himfelf with them, by
removing this pretended grievance. It had been
agreed, in a time of tranquillity, that one thoufand talents fhould be annually depofited in the
treafury, there to remain inviolable, as a public
refource, in cafe of any invafion of Attica.
This was, for a while, obferved with the attention ufually paid to all new regulations. But
Pericles propofed, that this fum fhould be diftributed among the poorer citizens, to defray
the expences of their theatrical entertainments;
with a refervation, that, in time of war, it
fhould be applied to the military fervice, agreeably to the original intention. Both the propofition and the reftriction were accepted. But,
as relaxations of all kinds degenerate fooner or
later into licence, the people became fo intoxicated at length with the gay fcenes with which
riches and politenefs entertained them, that no
public emergencies could induce them to refign
thefe diftributions; and we fhall foon fee them

Plut. in
Peric. Thu-
cyd. l. 2.

K 4

for-

 forbidding any man, on pain of death, to move for reſtoring what was now called the theatrical money, to the military, or any other public ſervice.

The theatre, for whoſe ſupport they provided thus amply, was infected by the general depravation; and, in its turn, contributed to diffuſe and increaſe the infection. In the early ages, their drama was eminently remarkable for chaſtity of ſentiment. Immorality, even in the mouth of a vicious character, was known to have excited a loud and general indignation in an Athenian audience. But now their ears were accuſtomed to obſcenity and impiety (though theſe, it muſt be allowed, were never made the great buſineſs of the repreſentation; nor were theſe the qualities, which rendered a character the favourite of the audience.) Formerly, they found alluſions in their admired poets, which were, with pleaſure, applied to expreſs their ſenſe of the valour and virtue of their countrymen; now no character, however exalted or honourable, could eſcape the wantonneſs and intemperance of their ſatire. And this unhappy ſpirit of ridicule, with which they were poſſeſſed, depraved their taſte, and corrupted their hearts. When the wiſeſt and beſt of their citizens was to be made the victim of their folly

and

and caprice, he was firft made contemptible and ridiculous upon the ftage.

As public virtue is, in an efpecial manner, the bafis of a democratical government, when this was impaired, their very conftitution muft have contributed to hurry on their ruin. The final determination of all public affairs was in the popular affembly; and this affembly was now made up of feveral diftinct factions, which almoft always purfued their own particular views and interefts; as to be excufed from perfonal fervice in war; from contributing their fhare in the public expences; or the like. The public leaders, and fpeakers, perceived and flattered this weaknefs. They were the fprings which moved the whole community; the adminiftration was, in a great meafure, committed to them; and they had, [A] fome time fince, learned the art of applying it to enriching and aggrandizing themfelves and their families. Many

Dem. in
Philippicis
paffim.

[A] ARISTOPHANES, in many of his plays, is particularly fevere on the corruption, and fervile adulation, of the Athenian orators. An ancient poet, from whom Athenaeus hath preferved fome fragments, in reckoning up the feveral wares and commodities, which were fold at Athens, clofes his catalogue, with Κλεψυδραι, Νομοι, Γραφαι. The decifions of judicial caufes, laws, and decrees.

ATHEN. l. 14. p. 640.

of

of them were already the penfioners of Philip; and, while they earned his pay, at the fame time fecured their own power, and acquired the favour of the people, by flattering their fupinenefs, and recommending pacific meafures, under various plaufible pretences. Sometimes the enemy was too weak, and inconfiderable, to be an object of terrour to the great fovereigns and arbiters of Greece: fometimes he was too powerful and formidable; it was rafh and impolitic to provoke his refentment; a war was burdenfome and expenfive; the balance of power a romantic confideration; and the true intereft of the ftate. to attend to her domeftic affairs, and to fecure and improve the advantages of commerce. If fome bold attempt, upon their dominions, roufed them from their infenfibility, then their national pride and vanity dictated the moft magnificent and pompous decrees and refolutions: armies were to be raifed, and navies fent abroad: but, in thefe magnificent decrees, their courage all evaporated. Affected delays arofe; their love of eafe returned; they fent out fome mercenary troops (for to thefe were their interefts now entrufted) commanded by a general, chofen by cabal and intrigue. He fails out, dreaded and fufpected by their allies, whom he oppreffes and pillages; defpifed by the enemy, whom he takes care to avoid; and, when he

at

at laſt appears before the place he is appointed
to relieve, it is in the hands of the beſiegers.
Thus, like unſkilful boxers (to uſe the ſimili-
tude of their own * orator) they think of defending themſelves, when they have already received the blow. And this defence generally
proves weak and inſufficient, even if exerted
ſeaſonably. Their forces then return; their
general is brought to a trial; and either condemned raſhly for not performing what, with a
wretched collection of mercenaries, unaffected
by any ſentiments of honour, or regard for the
public cauſe, and unprovided with pay or pro-
viſions, he could not perform; or elſe he ſcreens
his cowardice and bad conduct, under the protection of a powerful faction, and ſo eſcapes
from public juſtice. It is true, that, even in
this ſtate of their degeneracy, ſome acts of valour were performed not unworthy of their early
and uncorrupted age: nor did they want able
ſtateſmen, or valiant, judicious, and faithful
generals: but the firſt had the vices and prejudices of their countrymen to encounter, as
well as the oppoſition and eloquence of corrupted leaders: and their greateſt commanders
were either laid aſide by the power of faction,
or their abilities were rendĕred ineffectual by the
general indolence and miſconduct of the ſtate;
or, laſtly, they were condemned raſhly and un-
juſtly,

* Dem. Phil.
1. ſect. 14.

juſtly, and diſqualified from ſerving the public, at the time when their ſervices were particularly demanded.

It may not be thought unworthy of attention, to examine what was the manner of private life, in Athens, at the eve of its downfal, when every part of its government betrayed ſuch total corruption and depravity: and of this * Athenaeus hath particularly informed us. A love for public ſpectacles was the firſt thing which the youth was taught. There every object, which could inflame their paſſions, was preſented to their view: they hung with an effeminate pleaſure on the muſical airs, with which women were employed to enervate and captivate them: they waſted their important hours, which ſhould have been devoted to diſcipline and inſtruction, in wanton dalliance with the performers; and laviſhed their fortune, and their vigour, in an infamous commerce with theſe, and other women of abandoned characters. The ſchools of their philoſophers were in vain open for their inſtruction; and, poſſibly, theſe might have been held in ſome contempt, as fitted only for the formal and recluſe, and beneath the notice of the man of buſineſs, deſtined to the exalted and active ſcenes of life. Thus, the younger men entered into what is now called the world, totally igno-

rant,

* L. 12. p. 534.

rant, and confiderably corrupted: already ac-
cuftomed to regard all felfifh gratifications, as
their chief happinefs; and prepared to acquire
the means of thefe gratifications, by the moft
fordid, or the moft iniquitous practices. Their
love of money, or their incapacity for more
rational entertainment, engaged them in gam-
ing; which, when frequently indulged, is well
known to grow into an infatuating habit, which
tafte and reflection cannot always fubdue. Magnificent and coftly feafts were now alfo become
honourable diftinctions at Athens. The fordid
gratification of their palate became the ftudy,
and exercifed the invention, of its inhabitants.
Thus was their wealth lavifhly and ignobly
wafted, while the public exigencies were fparing-
ly and reluctantly fupplied. Athenaeus * hath
even recorded one almoft incredible inftance of
their depravity. They had lately, as we learn
from this author, conferred the freedom of their
city (the higheft compliment ufually paid to
kings and potentates) on two men, whofe only
merit was, that their father had been eminent
in the art of cookery, and was famous for having introduced new fauces.

SUCH was the people with whom the king of
Macedon was principally engaged. Their infolence

lence and oppreffion had, at this time, involved them in an important conteft with their allies and dependent cities, whom they had driven into rebellion. They began their operations, againft thofe revolters, by the fiege of Chios; where Chabrias, one of their commanders, re- markable for vigour, humanity, and integrity, unhappily attempted to pufh up to the city with a fingle veffel; and, in a tranfport of romantic valour, leaped on fhore; difdained to retire, though deferted by his foldiers; was furrounded and killed. Every lofs of this nature, at a time fo critical, was of the utmoft importance to this people. Yet thofe generals, whom war fpared, their own caprice, and blind prejudices, frequently deftroyed.

Nep. in
Chab.

Of the other ftates of Greece, Sparta ftill was confidered as the moft eminent; though its power had received the deadly wound by the fucceffes of Epaminondas. Agefilaus, who had raifed this ftate to the fummit of glory, lived to be witnefs of its fall. Archidamus, his fon, never failed to watch all occafions of recovering fome fhew of that power which Sparta had formerly poffeffed. The fucceffes of Epaminondas had been particularly favour- able to many of the inhabitants and people of Peloponnefus. His truly humane difpofition,

and

and his juft and extenfive policy, both deter- Sect. III.
mined him to reftore thofe to their liberty and
independence, who had been haraffed and op- Xenoph.
Hift. Grae.
Diod. Sic.
l. 15.
preffed by Sparta; and to fupport the interefts
of thofe neighbouring ftates, who had experienced the feverity of her dominion. Hence
were the people of Argos (who remembered,
with pleafure, the generalfhip of Agamemnon,
and entertained high notions of their own dignity) encouraged to avow that enmity which they
had ever harboured againft the Spartans. The
Arcadians, by the advice and with the affiftance
of the Theban general, according to Paufanias *, * In Arcad;
confulted for their fecurity by collecting all
their force into one common city, which they
built, and called Megalopolis, or the great city.
The Meffenians, after a difperfion of many Diod. ut
fupra.
ages, were alfo reftored by Epaminondas, and
rebuilt and fortified the city, from which their
anceftors had been driven by the Spartans. Thus
was Sparta furrounded by many fecret or declared enemies, who had felt, and therefore
dreaded, her oppreffion; ever watchful to maintain their prefent liberty, and ever jealous of
their ancient mafters; who, on their part, regarded them as revolted fubjects, and fhewed
fufficient inclination to reduce them to their
former obedience. Hence arofe a fpirit of dif-
content and diffenfion among the inhabitants of

Pe-

Book I. Peloponnefus, which it was Philip's intereft to foment, and from which he afterwards derived confiderable advantage.

Olivier l. 3.
p. 114.

Suspicion, ftupidity, and bravery, formed the character of the Thebans. Thefe qualities, united, frequently produced the moft fingular refolutions in that people: but, while Epaminondas was at their head, no defects appeared in their minds: this great man rendered them fovereigns of Boeotia, and arbiters of Greece. But with him their glory was extinguifhed. They retained only a brutal fiercenefs, and an inveterate hatred of their neighbours. The only general they had, after Epaminondas, was Pammenes, who, in his youth, had been attached to Philip by the ftricteft and tendereft friendfhip.

Ibid.

The Phocians were naturally obftinate; and did not want valour. They were oftentimes unjuft, and fometimes generous. Their minds were open; their genius fufficiently cultivated and elevated. Their mifconduct involved them in calamities, which were attributed to their impiety, and, therefore, lefs pitied; yet, in thefe calamities, they difcovered a remarkable firmnefs and greatnefs of foul. The moft diftinguifhed part of their character, was an un-
                              furmount-

furmountable antipathy to the [B] Thebans,
Locrians, and Theffalians, their neareft neighbours.

THE Theffalians were fufceptible of all im-   Olivier, ut
preffions, and incapable of preferving any;   fupra.
equally forgetful of the good and evil which
they received: ever ready to fubmit to tyrants,
and to implore the fuccour of their neighbours
againft them.   They now obeyed Tifiphonus,
Lycrophon, and Pitholaus, who had removed
Alexander of Pherae, only to have an opportunity of continuing his injuftices.

[B] Some particular caufes of enmity feem to have lately
arifen between Thebes and Phocis, and to have effaced the
memory of that alliance which fubfifted between them in
the late war with Lacedemon.   Juftin (in l. 8. c. 1.) hints
at fome outrages and devaftations committed by the Phocians in the territories of Boeotia; of which the Thebans
complained in the council of Amphictyons, and which therefore feem to have been committed before any hoftilities were
declared, though that hiftorian appears to be of a contrary opinion.   And we learn from Athenaeus, (l. 13.
p. 560) that Duris, an ancient hiftorian, recorded one particular act of violence in the Phocians, fome time fince committed againft Thebes.   Theano, a Theban lady, was
feized, and forcibly borne away from her hufband, by fome
lawlefs inhabitants of Phocis: nor could the remonftrance
made to that ftate prevail to have her reftored.   Such actions had, in ancient times, produced the bloodieft contefts:
and the hiftorian above mentioned makes this particular
outrage the real caufe of the facred war.

VOL. I.   L   THIS

THIS Alexander was the moſt deteſtable tyrant that Greece ever knew. He had maſſacred, in cold blood, his father-in-law, his uncle, and a number of his ſubjeĉts. Nor was he ever known to have diſcovered the leaſt feelings of humanity, but at the repreſentation of a tragedy of Euripides; from which he retired with ſhame and confuſion, for being betrayed into tears, at the ſight of imaginary misfortunes, after all the horrid cruelties which he himſelf had committed.

THEBÈ, the wife of this Alexander, quite tired out by his barbarity, and ſpirited up by the interviews which ſhe had with Pelopidas, at the time when he had been ſeized and confined by Alexander, at laſt reſolved upon his deſtruĉtion. The execution was difficult: the tyrant's palace was always filled with his guards: and even in theſe he did not wholly confide. He lay in a high and retired chamber, to which he mounted by a ladder. This he drew up after him; and the paſſage was guarded by a furious maſtiff, whom nobody dared to approach, but Alexander, his wife, and the ſlave who fed him.

THEBÈ concealed her brothers Tiſiphonus, Lycophron, and Pitholaus, in the palace. And, at night, having come to the tyrant's apartment, ordered the slave, who had the care of the maſtiff, to remove it, as it diſturbed the king's reſt. She then went down the ladder, which ſhe had taken care to cover all over with wool to prevent the leaſt noiſe ; brought up her brothers, poſted them at the door, and ſhewed them the ſword of Alexander, which was the ſignal agreed on. Juſt at the point of execution, the youths began to heſitate ; but Thebè threatened that ſhe would awaken the tyrant ; they reſumed courage ; one of them ſeized him by the feet, another by his hair, and the third buried a dagger in his heart.

Tisiphonus, Pitholaus, and Lycophron, were now regarded as the deliverers of their country. But they did not long appear ſolicitous to maintain this honour. Tempted by the ſplendour of a ſtation, which their father Jaſon had poſſeſſed, they aſſumed the power, and, in a great meaſure, imitated tne conduct of Alexander. They hired a large body of foreign troops to ſupport their uſurpation ; and puniſhed, or baniſhed, all thoſe who attempted to oppoſe them : until the nobility of Theſſaly, with the Aleuadae deſcendents from Hercules, at their head, finding themſelves oppreſſed by three tyrants inſtead of one, declared openly againſt them :

Diod. Sic. l. 16 ſect. 14.

L 2

and

and implored the affistance of Philip, now confeffedly the greateft of all the neighbouring powers.

NOTHING could have poffibly been more flattering than this invitation. The honour of affifting the Aleuadae, who were defcended from the fame race with himfelf; and of imitating the renowned Pelopidas, in giving liberty to Theffaly; the long wifhed-for opportunity of interfering honourably in the affairs of Greece; of affecting a natural connexion with that nation, and appearing interefted in the peace and liberty of its ftates; all confpired to determine Philip at once to fufpend the progrefs of his Thracian conquefts, and to march againft the tyrants. Delighted with the profpect of difplaying his power in the moft honourable manner, and having firft feized Lariffa, according to Juftin *, he advanced, with all his force, towards Pherae, fituated between Magnefia and the Pelafgiotae, at a little diftance from mount Pelion, which feparates thefe provinces from Macedon. The tyrants, who had collected their army to oppofe this invafion, met the Macedonians, and determined to try their fortune in the field. Here the abilities of Philip, and the fuperiour zeal and vigour of his foldiers, foon determined the fortune of the battle. The army of the tyrants

* l. 7. c. 6.

was

was totally defeated; and they themselves, pressed by a victorious enemy, and deserted by their adherents, were soon obliged to acknowledge the superiority of the conquerour, and to submit implicitly to his decisions. He now compelled them to resign their usurped authority, and to leave their country in peace and freedom: while all Greece resounded with the praises of the great protector and defender of liberty; the avenger of tyranny; and generous patron of the oppressed.

But renown and popular applause were not the only advantages which Philip derived from this expedition. The nobility of Thessaly imagined, that they never could sufficiently express their acknowledgments to their noble and humane deliverer; and, in the first heat and violence of a zealous gratitude, concluded a treaty with him, by which he was empowered to command all the conveniencies of their ports and shipping. Their cavalry was remarkably the best and most celebrated in Greece: and these were now obliged to attend him in all his wars. Such an acquisition only was wanted to render his forces complete: and he is said, by the abbreviator * of Trogus, to have been prompted to this expedition by the hopes of obtaining it. In effect, Philip had too much penetration, not to

L 3   foresee

Sect. III.
Diod. Sic.
ut supra.

Dem. Phil.
1. sect. 10.
Tourreil.
Not. in
Phil. 1.
Olynth. 3.
sect. 9.

* Justin. l.
7. c. 6.

foresee all the good consequences of his undertaking; and too much vigilance and policy, not to secure them. His conduct in Theſſaly, as it is described by Polyaenus *, was the exact epitome of his whole ſyſtem, and general courſe of his addreſs and artifice. He watched the contentions in the ſeveral cities, with a ſtrict and attentive regard; encouraged or allayed, fomented or decided, thoſe quarrels which different opinions and attachments had produced among a diſtracted people, juſt as his own views and intereſts directed. He was ſo complete a maſter of diſſimulation; he appeared ſo gentle, ſo humane, ſo affable, and obliging, ſo amiable, even to the conquered, that the Theſſalians reſigned themſelves to him with a total confidence. Thus was he enabled to ſet himſelf up in the place of thoſe he had ſubdued, not by open force, but by gentle and unſuſpected, and not leſs effectual, methods.

* Strat. l. 4. c. 19.

Tourreil. Not. in Olynth I.

PHILIP was now returned to his own kingdom in all the pride of conqueſt; honoured, admired, and applauded; when Olympias, the young princeſs, whoſe charms had engaged his affections at Samothrace, was conducted, with all due magnificence, to his court, and their eſpouſals were publicly celebrated. Neoptolemus, king of Epirus, the father of this princeſs, had

Juſtin. ut ſupra.

lately

lately died, and was fucceeded by his brother
Arymbas (or Arybbas, as he is called by Paufanias and Juftin). The better to fecure the
peaceable poffeffion of his throne, he determined to unite, in his perfon, all the rights of his
family, and married Troas, one of his nieces:
and, to purchafe the favour and alliance of a
prince, whofe reputation was become great and
extenfive, he now gratified Philip's paffion for
her fifter Olympias.

Sect. III.

The queen of Macedon had beauty, fpirit,
and elevation. She appears to have at firft
loved her hufband with fufficient tendernefs;
till the repeated inftances of his unfaithfulnefs
raifed other fentiments in her mind. Thefe
could not but fufficiently affect her, although
her refolution enabled her to conceal the impreffion for a while. She was at one time told of a
beautiful Theffalian lady, called Philinnè, with
whom Philip was faid to have been defperately
enamoured. In compliment to the queen, her
courtiers affected to afcribe this to fome charm
or philtre, which forced the affections of the
king from their proper object. Olympias defired to fee her: and, finding that her beauty
and graces far exceeded report, " Yes!" faid
fhe, " I now perceive what are the enchantments
" this fair Theffalian employs."

Oliv. l. 3.
P. 124.

L 4   The

Oliv. p.125.
Solin.

THE nuptials of Philip and Olympias were celebrated with the utmost splendour. The superstitious observed, that a dramatic performance was exhibited, on this occasion, called the Cyclops; and that soon after Philip lost an eye. This loss was even said to have been occasioned by a jealous curiosity of prying into the conduct of his queen, who is accused thus early of unfaithfulness, with many fabulous and extravagant circumstances, calculated to make the birth of Alexander appear the more extraordinary. The ancient writers, indeed, imagined, that every thing, relating to this hero, should have an extraordinary and important appearance; and have taken care to furnish a series of dreams, prodigies, and predictions, all expressive of his future fortune, from the moment of Philip's nuptials, down to the birth of Alexander. Olympias is said to have dreamed, the night before the consummation of her marriage, that a thunderbolt fell upon her body, which kindled up a conflagration, whose flames dispersed and raged to a considerable extent, and were then extinguished. Philip also had his dream a little after, in which he fancied himself employed in sealing up the womb of his queen with a signet, whose impression was a lion. Some interpreted this, saith Plutarch *, as a warning to the king to watch over the behavi-

Plut. in
Alexand.

* in Alex.

our

our of his wife: but Ariftander, his favourite interpreter of divinations, reflecting that it was not ufual to feal up any thing that was empty, affured him that this dream denoted, that the queen had now conceived a fon, who fhould hereafter prove bold and courageous as a lion.

FLATTERY, and indulgence to the weaknefs of Alexander, who, when intoxicated with his fucceffes, conceived the vanity of being thought the fon of Jupiter, feem to have given rife to the fiction of an enormous ferpent difcovered by Philip in ftrict intercourfe with his queen. The fight of a ferpent in her bed, fome of the anci- ents do not allow to have been fo very extraor- dinary, in a country where they were tame and harmlefs; and as Olympias, who was remark- ably devoted to the celebration of the enthufi- aftic rites of Orpheus and Bacchus, is faid to have danced in thefe ceremonies with great tame ferpents twining round her, fometimes inter- woven with the ivy of the facred fpears, or with the chaplets of her attendants, in order to in- fpire fpectators with the greater awe and hor- rour. Yet, from henceforward, faith Plutarch, his affection fenfibly abated; and, whether he feared her as a forcerefs, or imagined that fhe held a commerce with fome god, and was afraid of offending a fuperior rival, his correfpondence

with

See Bayle in
Art. *Olym-
pias.*

Plutarch. in
Alexand.

with her became lefs frequent: and, having fent to confult the Delphian oracle on this alarming occafion, he received for anfwer, that he was to pay peculiar honours to Jupiter Ammon, and muft expect to lofe that eye, which had pre-fumptuoufly intruded on the fecret communication of a divinity with his wife. According to Juftin*, Olympias herfelf firft fuggefted the account of the ferpent; and is faid by Erato-fthenes, an ancient hiftorian, to have informed her fon, as he was preparing for his expedition into Afia, of the fecret of his birth. But this information was poffibly nothing more than clearing up the fufpicions of his legitimacy; and affuring him, that he was really the fon of Philip, whofe actions might, with all propriety, have been urged as an incitement to his fon to approve himfelf worthy of fo great a father. This fentiment feems to be confirmed by the well known anfwer of Olympias to her fon's letter, in which he ftyled himfelf the fon of Jupiter. For, when the queen complained, that Alexander *made mifchief*, (if I may be allowed the expreffion) between her and Juno, I cannot conceive it in any other light, but that of rail-lery on his fantaftical vanity [c].

* l. 9. c. 9. Plutarch. in Alex.

Aul. Gellius, l. 13. c. 4.

[c] So Gellius underftood it.—*Olympiadem* FESTIVISSIME *refcripfiffe legimus*——*Amabo mi fili quiefcas, neque deferas me,*

The present nuptials seemed to have entirely SECT. III. engaged the court of Macedon, which now became a scene of general pleasure and festivity, in honour of the royal lovers. The secret and avowed enemies of Philip thought this a favourable opportunity to attempt the recovery of that power, and those dominions, which his arms had won from them; and, by one sudden and united effort, to crush his rising greatness. The kings of Illyria, of Paeonia, and of Thrace, joined in a strict confederacy, and meditated an invasion of Macedon with all their powers. Their scheme was artfully conceived, conducted with all secrecy, and had the fairest prospect of

Diod. Sic. l. 16. sect. 22.

me, neque criminere adversus Junonem, l. 13. c. 4. But, though Bayle allows that this has an air of raillery, yet he does not admit, that it warrants us to suppose, that Olympias denied any connexions with Jupiter, or intended to discredit any such reports; but only would persuade her son not to boast publicly of his birth. The terms, saith he, which Plutarch makes use of, signify no more, than that she recommends it to her son to be silent. (See Bayle Dict. Hist. in Art Olympias.) The words to which he refers, and which Plutarch ascribes to her, are these: Οὐ παύσεται μι διαβαλλων Αλεξανδρος προς την 'Ηραν; which the Latin interpreter renders non definet Alexander in crimen me apud Junonem vocare? But διαβαλλειν, διαβολη, and ΔΙΑΒΟΛΟΣ, are Greek words generally agreed to relate, not so properly, or, at least, not so usually, to accusations founded on truth: but to express something of malice, or falsehood, in the action or person, not barely of indiscretion.

success.

succefs. But, in the midft of all his gaiety, Philip's attention was not a moment diverted from his more important concerns. Among all the neighbouring nations he had his fpies and emiffaries, ftudious to merit his liberal pay by their vigilance, who never failed to inform him faithfully, and minutely, of every motion and tranfaction, by which he might be affected. While thefe new allies, therefore, were yet employed in making their preparations, Philip ordered Parmenio, the general in whom he moft confided, to march into Illyria, while he himfelf furprifed the Paeonians, and reduced them to fuch a ftate of fubjection, as appears to have rendered them incapable of giving him any farther oppofition: (for, from this time, hiftory makes no mention of any attempt to recover their independence.) Hence he marched into Thrace, to confound the fchemes of his enemies, and to chaftife their defigns againft his peace. Here, while engaged in fpreading the terrour of his arms, he received the pleafing news of a victory, gained by Parmenio over the Illyrians. His couriers, at the fame time, arrived to inform him, that the chariots, which he had fent to the Olympic games, had obtained the prize. Proud of this event, the moft authentic proof of his being acknowledged a true and legitimate fon of

Greece, he determined to preferve the memorial of it, by impreffing thofe victorious chariots on his coins. But, fcarcely had thefe joyful advices been received, when another, of ftill greater moment, was now brought to Philip, that his queen was delivered of a fon at Pella. A prince, born in the midft of fuch joy and fuccefs, his diviners affured him, muft neceffarily prove invincible; and the king, deeply affected by thefe inftances of good fortune, breathed out his prayer in rapture, that the gods fhould fend him fome misfortune to temper all his accumulated happinefs.

THE moft accurate chronologers fix the birth of Alexander to the firft year of the hundred and fixth Olympiad, in the month called by the Macedonians Loüs, which, at this time, anfwered not to the Attic month Hecatombaeon, as Plutarch afferts, but to Boedromion, the third of the Attic year, as appears from a letter of king Philip, preferved in the oration * of Demofthenes on the crown. Nor can we agree with Plutarch in fixing it to the time of the reduction of Potidaea, without contradicting, not only Demofthenes †, but Diodorus ‡, who is moft accurate in his chronology; and exprefsly determines the taking of that city to the third year of the hundred and fifth Olympiad. An-

2   tiquity

SECT. III.

Plutarch.
Apophth.

Plin. l. 36.
c. 14.
Eufeb. Cappel.

* fect. 51.

† in Orat.
Lept.
‡ lib. 16.
fect. 8.

Mela, 2, 3.
Serv. in
Virg. Georg.
4. 278.

tiquity hath been careful to furnish his birth with a number of presages and omens of his greatness. Thunderings, and lightnings, and earthquakes, were said to have announced this extraordinary event; and two eagles, by perching on the palace in which his mother lay, to have foretold his future empire over Europe and Asia. But his birth was really attended by one incident, which may, with some appearance of propriety, be called a presage of his future actions. On that very day, in which he first saw the light, Eroftratus, (for historians name him, notwithstanding the decree of the Ephesians to forbid it) set fire to the temple of Diana at Ephefus, from the fole motive of immortalizing his name. And this accident seemed so expreffive of the character of Alexander, that, poffibly, the imagination of historians invented the relation which Plutarch gives us, that the priests and diviners at Ephefus, looked on the ruin of their temple as the forerunner of some other terrible calamity; and ran frantic through the city, crying out, " This day hath brought forth " something, which will prove destructive to all " Afia."

Plutarch. in
Alexand.

The famous letter, which Philip now wrote to Ariftotle, muft not be omitted in this place.
The

The king had always affected an extraordinary reverence for this philosopher; and condescended even to attend with deference to his precepts of morality, and maxims of government. On the present joyful occasion, he expressed his sense of the sage's merit, and of the importance of making the earliest and most effectual provision for the future instruction of his infant son, by addressing the following letter to Aristotle:

SECT. III.

Ariflot.
Epiſt. in
Fragment.
Ælian. l. 8.
c. 15.

" King Philip, to Aristotle.   Health!

Arist. ut
supra.

" YOU are to know, that a son hath been
" born to us.   We thank the gods, not so
" much for having bestowed him on us, as for
" bestowing him at a time when Aristotle lives.
" We assure ourselves, that you will form him
" a prince worthy to be our successor, and a
" king worthy of Macedon.   Farewel!"

SUCH instances of his respectful attention to men of learning have made historians speak in the highest terms of his greatness of mind, and justness of sentiment.   Nor could they have failed to raise his reputation in Greece, where philosophy was held in such veneration, and accounted one of those honourable distinctions, which marked out the superiority of that nation over the barbarian world.   Nor can it seem im-

probable

 probable to thofe who confider the character of this prince, that a politic regard to his reputation might have had as great a fhare in thefe condefcenfions, as his real fenfe of the value and dignity of thofe men, who devoted themfelves to the ftudy and propagation of knowledge.

THE birth of Alexander was an event which might naturally have been expected to cement the union between Macedon and Epirus: and yet it feems probable, from a paffage in the third Olynthiac * oration of Demofthenes, where the orator traces the progrefs of Philip's conquefts, that, about this time, he committed fome hoftilities againft Arymbas, either to punifh fome fecret practices, into which this prince's jealoufy of Philip might have betrayed him, in favour of the late attempts of Illyria and Paeonia; or to gratify Alexander, the brother of Olympias, by difmembering the kingdom of Epirus, in order to inveft him with fome of its dominions. Hiftory fpeaks but obfcurely of his conduct with refpect to this prince, and the affairs of Epirus; and fometimes with apparent inconfiftency, which hath occafioned a difference in the reprefentations of modern critics and compilers. But to difcufs thefe particularly might lead us too far from the principal fubject:

nor

* fect. 6.

Juftin, l. 8.
c. 6. l. 17.
c. 3.
Tourreil.
Not. in
Olyn. 3.
Rollin Hift.
de Philippe.

nor is it neceffary to the underftanding the ge-neral tenour of this hiftory.

To Thrace we now return, where Philip was at leifure to purfue his advantages; to attend to the contefts and diftractions of the native inhabitants, and to the motions of the Athenians, whofe ancient valour had here gained fome fettlements, which, by their mifconduct, were now either loft, or rendered precarious; and who made fuch efforts to regain them, as their corruptions or embarraffments could admit; and watched and thwarted the attempts of Philip with an impotent jealoufy. This prince, who knew the importance of gaining an extenfive power and intereft in this country, the fource of wealth and commerce, the magazine from whence Greece was fupplied with many of the neceffaries and conveniencies of life, advanced as far as Maronea, where he was joined by Pammenes the Theban, with a confiderable reinforcement, fent to favour the attempts of the enemy of Athens. He held a private correfpondence with Charidemus, and might have completed the conqueft of this country, had he not been oppofed by Amadocus, affifted by the Athenians, with whom good policy did not as yet permit him to come to an avowed rupture. Diffenfions and contefts were arifing among the Grecians:

Demoft. in Ariftocr.

Grecians: many of whom any open and violent attack on a principal ſtate might have quieted and united. An affected regard to his treaty, a patience even of ſome hoſtilities and inſults, might give an appearance of ſelf-defence, or juſtifiable revenge to any hoſtilities, which he might hereafter find it convenient to commit, while his enemies were loaded with the odium of being the firſt and unprovoked aggreſſors. A fatal mixture of ſtrong national vanity and degeneracy, which prevailed at Athens, was every day rendering that ſtate leſs formidable and powerful, and encouraged their enemy to wait till their capricious and violent paſſions had totally waſted their ſtrength.

THESE had already operated in a manner which muſt have been highly pleaſing to Philip, by depriving them of the ſervice of two illuſtrious generals, Iphicrates and Timotheus. When Chabrias fell (as hath been related) in the ſocial war, the confederates laid ſiege to Samos, with all their force, which amounted to one hundred ſhips. The Athenian navy, commanded by Chares, the undeſerving favourite of the popular aſſembly, conſiſted but of ſixty. As it was therefore neceſſary to relieve a place, which had ever been firmly attached to them, and, as they were alſo alarmed by Philip's progreſs, another

fleet

fleet of equal force was fitted out, and entrusted to the command of Menestheus, the son of Iphicrates, and son-in-law to Timotheus, with instructions that he should conduct himself entirely by the advice of these two great men, who embarked with him. Upon the junction of the two fleets, it was agreed to make a diversion, by laying siege to Byzantium, one of the principal cities in the confederacy. The allies abandoned the siege of Samos, and the two fleets were upon the point of an engagement, when a sudden storm arose. Chares confidently proposed to begin the attack: but Timotheus and Iphicrates, more cautious and experienced, saw the disadvantage, and declined the engagement. For this they were accused by Chares of cowardice, and neglect of duty. Their countrymen, impatient of every disappointment which did violence to their prejudices and exalted notions of their own power and importance, recalled these commanders, and brought them to a trial. Timotheus relied entirely on his integrity: but Iphicrates thought himself obliged to use some artifice for his preservation. He dispersed certain young officers through the assembly, who were at his devotion, armed privately with swords, which, as if by accident, they took occasion to discover. The judges were intimidated, and, instead of condemning to death,

Sect. III.

Nep. in Timoth.

Diod. Sic.
l. 16.
sect. 21.
Nep. in.
Iphic. &
Timoth.

M 2

as

as was originally intended, impofed a fine on them, which both the one and the other was utterly unable to pay. And thus thefe **two** commanders, of the moft diftinguifhed merit and abilities, were driven difgracefully from their country, to languifh out their lives in an inactive exile, at a time when Athens required all their fervices.

Nor was it lefs fatal to the interefts of the Athenians, or lefs pleafing or promifing to their enemy, that Chares now became the principal commander of their fleets. He was a man poffeffed of all the exteriours of merit, without real and intrinfic abilities. His perfon was robuft and vigorous; his addrefs haughty and affuming; his prefumption not only impofed on his fellow-citizens, but concealed his incapacity even from himfelf. His infatiable avarice rendered him intolerable to the allies, and dependents of Athens, whom he plundered with a cruelty and rapacioufnefs more becoming an enemy than a protector. They dreaded his inhumanity, and defpifed the weaknefs of a general, who came attended by fingers, dancers, harlots, and other like infamous attendants on luxury; and who recommended himfelf to the favour of his officers, by indulging them in an

absolute

Oliv. l. 3. p. 109.

Athenae. l. 12. p. 534.

absolute contempt of all discipline and regularity
befitting a military life. But his fellow-citizens
could not divest themselves of their prejudices
in favour of a man, who asserted positively, and
promised boldly ; and who had his orators and
popular leaders constantly in pay, to defend or
palliate every instance of his misconduct. By
intrigue and cabal he had been raised ; on these
he depended for his support ; nor was inclined
or enabled to execute any enterprise of honour
or importance. Such was the consequence of
the indolence and the scandalous profusion of the
public money at Athens, that the fleet was entirely forgotten, and the commander reduced
to the utmost difficulty for the support of his
soldiers. At least such was the pretence by
which Chares concealed his avarice, and neglect of his commission, in deserting the war,
which had been entrusted to him, and hiring
himself, and his forces, to Artabazus, a revolted satrap of Ionia, who had occasion for immediate assistance against a large body of Per-
sians sent to reduce him to obedience. He relieved him from his danger, and returned with
magnificent presents, and all manner of provisions and necessaries for his fleet.

THE Athenians, who saw their navy thus
provided, without any burden to themselves,

SECT. III.

Demost.
Phil. 1.
sect. 9.
Diod. Sic.
l. 16.
sect. 22.

M 3

or

Diod. Sic.
ut supra.

or any neceffity of retrenching thofe expences which were lavifhly beftowed upon their plea-fures, liftened willingly to thofe who defended the conduct of Chares, and urged the neceffities which were faid to have driven him to this mea-fure; and, without any great difficulty, were perfuaded to approve of his expedition into Afia. But they were foon made to think of this affair in a different manner. Ambaffadors arrived with formidable remonftrances from the king of Perfia; who declared, that, in revenge of this their outrage, he had three hundred fhips ready to be fent out to the affiftance of the allied cities. Intimidated by thefe menaces, the A-thenians inftantly concluded a peace with the confederates, who were declared entirely inde-pendent, and exempted from all fubfidies, and from furnifhing their contingents in the wars of Athens. Thus the terrour of the Perfian power had more effect in the Athenian affembly, than the dictates of equity and moderation, which their ingenuous and honeft citizen, [D] Ifocrates, had

[D] The difcourfe which he addreffed to his fellow-citi-zens for this purpofe is ftill extant. In it we find him re-proaching them, with great freedom, for abandoning them-felves to the infinuations of thofe orators who flatter their paffions, while they treat thofe with contempt, who give them the moft falutary counfels. He particularly applies himfelf to correct their violent paffion for the augmentation

of

had urged, with all his candid eloquence, to SECT. III.
perſuade them to this meaſure: and thus the
ſocial war, which had continued for three years
to haraſs the Athenians, and had been one cauſe
of the weak and ineffectual interruption which
they had given to Philip's earlier deſigns, was
now concluded.

of their power and dominion over the people of Greece,
which had been the ſource of all their misfortunes. He re-
calls to their remembrance thoſe happy days, ſo glorious
for Athens, in which their anceſtors, from a noble and generous diſintereſtedneſs, ſacrificed every thing to the ſupport of the common liberty, and the preſervation of Greece;
and compares them with the preſent times, wherein the ambition of Sparta, and afterwards that of Athens, had,
ſucceſſively, plunged thoſe ſtates in the greateſt misfortunes.
He repreſents to them, that the real and laſting greatneſs
of a ſtate, doth not conſiſt in augmenting its dominions,
and extending its conqueſts, at the expence of humanity
and juſtice; but in the wiſe government of the people, a
juſt attention to their happineſs, and to the protection of
their allies; in being beloved and eſteemed by their neighbours, and feared by their enemies.— I he whole piece ex-
preſſes a mind poſſeſſed with the warmeſt ſentiments of benevolence, and a moſt moderate and equitable regard to
the common rights of mankind; together with a juſt contempt of falſe greatneſs, the fatal object of the heroes and
ravagers of the world. He concludes, that Athens, if it
would preſerve its happineſs and tranquillity, ought not to
affect the empire of the ſea, for the ſake of lording it over
all other ſtates; but ſhould conclude a peace, whereby every
city and people ſhould be left to the full enjoyment of their
liberty; and declare themſelves irreconcilable enemies to
thoſe, who ſhould preſume to diſturb this ſyſtem.

M 4

THE HISTORY

OF THE

LIFE AND REIGN

OF

PHILIP

KING OF MACEDON.

BOOK THE SECOND.

BOOK II. SECTION I.

CONTENTS.

—*The*

THE
LIFE AND REIGN
OF
PHILIP
KING of MACEDON.

BOOK the SECOND.

SECTION I.

THE Athenians were now recovering from the alarm occafioned by the menaces of the king of Perfia, and, being relieved from the burden of the late war with the confederates, were principally attentive to the motions and defigns of Philip; when the violence of mutual jealoufy and animofity burft forth fuddenly in Greece; and the feveral ftates confpired to favour the defigns of the great enemy of their liberty,

liberty, and to precipitate their own ruin, by arming againſt each other in the famous SACRED WAR.

THE Theban intereſt had been, for ſome time, predominant inthe great Amphictyonic council: and that venerable aſſembly, formed originally to ſupport the general intereſt of the whole Hellenic body, now ſhared ſo largely in the corruption and degeneracy of the time, that it was totally guided and directed by ſome one ruling power, and ſervilely echoed the dictates of the revenge or ambition of that ſtate, which could moſt effectually influence and corrupt its members. The authority which the Thebans acquired in this aſſembly, in conſequence of their late ſucceſſes, they ſoon determined to exert againſt thoſe whom they ſecretly or avowedly hated: and Phocis and Lacedaemon were the deſtined victims of their pride and oppreſſion. The firſt of theſe ſtates had been accuſed of occupying and cultivating ſome lands ſituated on the banks of the Cephiſus, to the eaſt of Mount Parnaſſus, which the religion of ancient times had conſecrated to Apollo, and, of conſequence, conſigned to perpetual deſolation. A large fine was impoſed on them by the Amphictyons, the guardians of religion and the rights of the god. At the ſame time, the Thebans, not contented

with

with the revenge which their arms had executed
in Sparta, prevailed upon the council to take cognizance of the conduct of Phoebidas, and to con-
demn the Lacedaemonians in a fine of fifty talents,
for their breach of public faith, and violation of
the general peace of Greece, in seizing the citadel of Thebes. The two states, affected by
these sentences, were by no means ready to pay
the due deference to such severe decisions; and
possibly the Amphictyons themselves were not
very zealous to enforce the execution of their decrees; till, again solicited by the Thebans, the
council, at length, resolved, that the Phocians
should instantly comply, and pay their fine, on
pain of being stripped of all the fruits of their
sacrilege: and that the Lacedaemonians also
should, without delay, submit to the authority
of the general council, and make the appointed
atonement for their crime; or, in case of a re-
fusal, be regarded and treated as rebellious
against the sovereign power of the Amphictyons,
and as the enemies of Greece.

THE Phocians, who were pursued with the
greatest zeal, as the most odious and criminal
party, were thus on the point of having all the advantages, which the labour and industry of years
had with difficulty procured, at once wrested
from them; and many of themselves and families
exposed

Diod. Sic.
ut supra.

Book II.

expofed to want and diftrefs; driven from the lands and habitations they had long occupied, and deprived of the means of fubfiftence. Murmurs and complaints arofe naturally among a people of fpirit to exprefs their indignation at this extreme feverity. Nor did they want turbulent and defigning men, to inflame their difcontents, and aggravate their grievances. Philomelus, one of the moft confiderable members of their community, was a man poffeffed of all the qualifications neceffary to recommend him to the popular favour. He had that infinuating eloquence, which at once feizes the attention, and engages the affections. Under the appearance of a tender regard for the welfare of his fellow-citizens, he concealed a turbulent and violent ambition, which his daring foul prompted him to gratify at the expence of dangers and toils, and in defiance of juftice, and of all thofe rights, which the general opinion and principles of mankind had fanctified. This man now affembled the Phocians, and, in an artful harangue, exerted all his addrefs to lead them to his purpofes.

Diod. Sic. ut fupra.

He began with declaring, that, gallant and courageous as they were, he could not in the leaft fufpect that they would fubmit to the unjuft fentence of the Amphictyons; and, by paying

ing

ing the fine required, brand themfelves and their country with an ignominious ftain, which no time ever could efface : but that, if their fpirit was really loft, if they were determined to fubmit to the arbitrary decifions of their enemies, ftill the fum demanded far exceeded their abilities. He expatiated on the injuftice and cruelty of the Amphictyonic decree, which had impofed a fine fo enormous, on account of a fmall portion of land, which their neceffities had forced them to occupy. If they could be fo patient as to fuffer, this land to be taken from them, and united to the ancient patrimony of the god, befides the difgrace of a fubmiffion fo abject and daftardly, the lofs of their liberty, the utter deftruction of their properties, and their lives, he declared muft prove the inevitable confequence. All the fatal effects of the cruelty of their enemies he knew how to reprefent in the moft lively co-lours, and to inflame the imaginations of his hearers with affecting pictures of the future di-ftrefs of his dear fellow-citizens. One way yet remained to obviate all thefe melancholy confe-quences. If they would entruft him with the command of their army; if they would refign themfelves abfolutely to his direction, he made no doubt of proving fufficient to extricate them from the prefent difficulties, and to affert their

 ancient

 ancient dignity and privileges. To them, and
to them alone, had been entrufted the temple
and the oracle of Delphi in ancient times; their
anceftors were acknowledged as abfolute proprietors of the whole city and all its territories.
Hear, faid he, the teftimony of Homer, the venerable and authentic recorder of the ancient
glory of Greece, and of all the rights of its feveral inhabitants:

[A] The Phocians next in forty barks repair;
Epiftrophus and Schedius head the war;
From thofe rich regions, where Cephifus leads,
Her filver current thro' the flow'ry meads:
From Panopëa, Chryfa the divine,
Where Anemoria's ftately turrets fhine;
Where Pytho *, Daulis, Cypariffus ftood.————
Pope.

Let us then boldly draw the fword, and affert
the honours of our fathers, and the rights of
their pofterity.

These artful reprefentations had the defired
effect: the Phocians created Philomelus their
general, with full powers to conduct them as

[A] Αὐταρ ΦΩΚΕΩΝ Σχεδιος καὶ Ἐπιστροφος ἤρχον————
Οἱ Κυπαρισσον ἐχων ΠΥΘΩΝΑ τε πετρηεσσαν, &c.
Iliad. B. I. 516.

he

Diod. Sic.
ut supra.

he thought proper: and he proceeded to concert the neceſſary means of anſwering the expectations of his countrymen. He began with making a journey to Sparta, where he had a private conference with king Archidamus. He repreſented to this prince, that the intereſt of Sparta was no leſs concerned than that of Phocis, in reſcinding the late decrees of the Amphictyons. He diſcovered his ſcheme of ſeizing Delphi, with aſſurances, that his firſt care ſhould be to efface all the memorials of the diſgrace of their two ſtates; and deſired the aſſiſtance of the Spartans, in a cauſe, in which they and the Phocians were equally concerned. Archidamus was pleaſed with a deſign formed againſt the enemies of Sparta, and ſenſible of the advantages which that ſtate might derive from its ſucceſs; yet, being duly affected by the odiouſneſs and danger of it, and too cautious to commence or to join in this hazardous war, till the effects of the firſt bold experiment had appeared, and the other leading ſtates had diſcovered their diſpoſitions, declared to Philomelus, that he fully approved of his plan; and that, although it was not at preſent convenient openly to avow his attachment to the Phocians, yet that he might depend on ſome private reinforcements, beſides ſupplies of money. To evince the ſincerity of theſe declarations, he accompanied

N 2

them

 them with a present of fifteen talents, to which Philomelus added the same sum of his own; and thus was enabled to raise a large body of mercenary troops, who were encouraged to crowd to his standard by the liberality with which he paid them.

 THE army he had thus collected he proceeded to model; and, in imitation of other great generals and masters of the art of war, incorporated a thousand chosen Phocians into one distinct body, whom he called Πελτασαι, his targeteers; and, having thus provided for the execution of his designs, he appeared at the head of his forces, and directed his march to Delphi. Certain inhabitants of the neighbouring district, called Thracidae, attempted, in vain, to oppose his entrance into the city. They were defeated, and cut to pieces, and their possessions given up to the will of a rapacious soldiery. The Delphians trembled in expectation of the like fate; but Philomelus quieted their apprehensions, by assuring them that he entertained no hostile intentions against their city; no sacrilegious designs against their temple: he came but to assert the just rights of his country to the guardianship thereof, and should ever preserve a due reverence to the god, and an exact attention to the welfare of his votaries. And thus this enter-
prising

prifing chief gained poffeffion of the city, and
affumed the cuftody of the temple, with all its
immenfe riches [B].

THE Amphictyons, on their part, could not
behold this outrageous oppofition to their authority, which they affected to confider as a violence to all rights divine and human, without
the utmoft emotion.   By a formal decree, they
pronounced thefe profane Phocians enemies to
Heaven and to Greece; and invited all thofe
who acknowledged their fovereign authority,
and who retained a regard for religion, to draw
the fword againft facrilege, and fo to difcharge

[B] THE marbles of Paros fix the commencement of the
Phocian war to the archonfhip of Cephifodotus, the third
year of the hundred and fifth Olympiad: which was probably the date of the decree of the Amphictyons, which
produced it. We know, befides, from Æfchines, Demofthenes, and Paufanias, that it lafted ten years. The laft
mentioned author places the invafion of the temple under
the archonfhip of Agathocles, the fourth year of the hundred
and fifth Olympiad. Thus then we may reconcile thofe
different authorities with Diodorus.

The decree of the Amphictyons, under Cephifodotus.
The fpeech of Philomelus, and the infurrection of the
  Phocians, under Agathocles.
The journey of Philomelus to Sparta, in the archonfhip
  of Elphines. Olymp. 106. Y. 1.
The feizing of Delphi, under Calliftratus. Olymp 106. Y. 2.
OLIVIER.

N 3

thofe

thofe facred obligations, which they owed to their country and to Heaven.

Diod. Sic. ut fupra.

THE Locrians, who inhabited the neighbourhood of Delphi, were the firft to exprefs their zeal, by rifing fuddenly in arms to attack Philomelus. But this chief found no difficulty in defeating a tumultuary body, that fought with more valour than difcipline. Encouraged by this victory, which feemed a prefage of future fuccefs, he returned in triumph into the city; tore down the records of the Amphictyonic decree from the pillars to which they were affixed; deftroyed the brazen tablets on which the fentences againft Sparta and Phocis were infcribed; and difperfed his declaration through Greece, that he had poffeffed himfelf of the temple, not with a defign of violating the rights of Apollo, but only to refcind the unjuft and oppreffive decrees of the Amphictyons; and to affert the ancient prerogative of the Phocians, which his countrymen juftly confidered as the moft valuable inheritance their anceftors had tranfmitted to them.

† In Phoc.

THE Boeotians, with the Thebans at their head, influenced by private animofity, as Paufanias † exprefsly obferves, much more than by the nobler motive of religion, foon imitated the example of the Locrians, and raifed confiderable

levies

levies for the relief of the temple, and to avenge the majefty of the offended deity. Philomelus, informed of thefe motions, furrounds the temple with a ftrong fortification, fo as to render it a kind of citadel to the town; collects new forces from all the adjacent diftricts; augments the pay of his mercenary troops; encamps before Delphi with five thoufand chofen men; and thus becomes no lefs formidable to Thebes, than Thebes could poffibly appear to Phocis. His enemies had not yet appeared; he therefore determined to intimidate them by an inftance of vigour; and having left a fufficient body to guard the avenues to the city, marched down againft the Locrians, and ravaged their territories. This people were foon obliged to arm in defence of their lands, and found the Phocian general befieging a fortrefs on the banks of one of their rivers. The ftrength of its fituation had checked the progrefs of his arms; and he now found himfelf obliged to abandon the fiege, and to march againft his affailants. An engagement immediately enfued, in which twenty of the Phocians fell. The conteft for their bodies, according to the cuftom of the ancient Greeks, was violent and obftinate: but the Locrians at length prevailed, and obliged Philomelus to fend an herald to demand them. The enemy anfwered, with feverity, that, by the laws of

N 4   Greece,

Greece, facrilegious perfons were denied the rites of interment. Philomelus, provoked at their refufal, and ftill more irritated and alarmed at the harfh reafon on which they founded it, once more led out his forces, renewed the engagement, and, remaining mafter of the field of battle, obliged the Locrians to exchange the dead. Thus, with a large acceffion both of wealth and reputation, he returned to Delphi.

HE knew of what confequence it muft neceffarily be to remove the odious appearance of impiety by which his caufe was difgraced; and therefore determined, if poffible, to obtain fome oracle, which he might interpret as a fanction to his attempts. For this purpofe he applied to the Pythian prieftefs; and commanded her inftantly to afcend her facred tripod, and to declare the will of the god, and the event of the prefent war. The prieftefs, either dreading her danger, or from a regard to the ceremonials of her religion, reprefented to him, that the god could not be confulted but [c] at certain ftated times,

Diod. Sic. l. 16. fect. 27.

[c] IT may not be difpleafing to the reader, to have fome account of thofe times and preparatory rites laid before him. For which purpofe I take the liberty of making ufe of the accurate and copious collection from ancient authors, by Monfieur Hardouin, in his differtation on the oracle of Delphi,

times, and after all the preparatory rites and fa-
crifices regularly and exactly performed. Philomelus,

Delphi, publiſhed in the memoirs of the academy of Belles
Lettres. Tom. 3.

In the earlier times of the oracle, the Pythian prieſteſs was
inſpired but once in a year, in the month which the inhabitants
of Delphi called Βυσιον, which was the firſt month in the Spring,
called Βυσιον for Πυσιον formed from the word πυθανεσθαι, to
enquire or *interrogate*. Afterwards, Apollo was prevailed on
to inſpire the prieſteſs once in every month. But the preciſe
day was by no means an article of an indifferent nature. Some
days were ſtiled ἀποφραδες, nefaſti, *unlucky days*, on which it
was abſolutely forbidden to conſult the oracle. We do not
know, preciſely, whether the day of conſultation in every
month was fixed and determined, or whether the prieſts had
the liberty of chuſing it. We only know, that the Pythian
prieſteſs never mounted her tripod but on one day in the
month, and that the other days were employed in preparing
every thing neceſſary for this ceremony. Sacrifices made a
principal part of this preparation: without the due performance of theſe, the god was deaf, and the prieſteſs mute.
The utmoſt care was taken, that the victims ſhould be found
pure, without ſpot or blemiſh. When they received the
effuſions of wine, or water, they were to tremble, and feel
an univerſal palpitation in all parts of their body, without
which propitious ſigns, the prieſteſs could not preſume to
do her office. She herſelf was alſo obliged to a particular
preparation. She began with an abſtinence of three days,
which greatly increaſed the diſorder of her mind. On the
day of conſultation, ſhe bathed in the fountain of Caſtalia,
and drank a certain quantity of its water, to which Apollo
had communicated a portion of his enthuſiaſtic virtue. She
then chewed ſome leaves of laurel that grew near this fountain.

lomelus, influenced only by political regards, in-sisted on his demand, and declared his resolution of forcing her to do her office. The priestess cried out, in indignation at his violence, that he commanded there, and might act as he pleased. This answer he pretended to regard as the effect of enthusiasm, and the genuine dictate of Apollo. It was instantly published through his army; it was engraved on a brazen tablet, and exposed to public view, that all men might know that the god had granted him permission to act as he thought proper; and, having convened his people, he declared and interpreted this pretended oracle, and earnestly recommended to them to adhere firmly to a cause, which Apollo himself had sanctified by his approbation.

Diod. Sic. l. 16. sect. 27.

To the affairs of war, he again began to apply with due vigour; but, at the same time, took care to provide his people with a prodigy, in order to animate them still further. An eagle was

tain. This laurel was the symbol of divination; and no small assistance to enthusiasm. The priestess being thus prepared, Apollo did not fail to give notice of his approach. A laurel, which grew before the portal of the temple, by its motion, announced the god. The temple itself was shaken; at least, the priestess felt the presence of the deity: and then her attendants conducted her, with all due so-lemnity, to the sanctuary, and placed her on the sacred tripod.

seen

seen to hover round the temple, then to enter in, and to pursue some doves that were bred there, with such violence, that some of them he killed at the altar. Diviners were found to pronounce this to be an omen, which promised the sovereign power of Delphi to Philomelus and his Phocians. The event was capable of a different application; yet the present interpretation, purchased no doubt by corruption and intrigue, was eagerly received, and industriously propagated, to serve the present purposes of the Phocian general; who, while he thus wrought on the ignorance and superstition of his followers, was, at the same time, attentive to the more important means of assuring his success. He chose out those of his followers, who seemed best qualified for negociation, some of whom he dispatched to Athens, others to Lacedaemon, and others even to Thebes. In like manner he applied to the other considerable states of Greece; and gave them all the most solemn assurances of the rectitude of his intentions. He repeated his declarations, that the sole motive of possessing himself of Delphi was to assert the right of Phocis to the patronage of the temple; that he abhorred the thought of sacrilege, and was determined to preserve the treasures of Apollo inviolably; that he was ready to render an account to Greece of all the gold and silver, all the rich and

and magnificent offerings, their weight, number, and condition, with an exactnefs which
fhould demonftrate the juftice of his caufe, and
the fincerity of his intentions; and concluded
with entreating, that they would diveft themfelves of thofe unwarrantable prejudices conceived againft him; acknowledge the juftice of
his procedure, and unite their arms with Phocis;
or, at leaft, continue neuter in a war, by which
the public interefts of Greece, either civil or religious, were by no means affected.

THE chief attention of the Athenians was at
prefent to the actions and defigns of Philip, who
was now engaged in Thrace, where he was ever
labouring to gain fome new acquifitions, either
by force or intrigue. Their arms were wholly
employed in fome indirect and weak efforts to
oppofe or harafs him; and were no longer pro-
feffedly engaged in any important quarrel. They
remembered, with gratitude, that Phocis had
expreffed a regard for Athens in its ftate of de-
preffion at the conclufion of the Peloponnefian
war: they looked with indignation at the arrogance with which their late fucceffes had infpired
the Thebans; they harboured a warm refentment of every inftance of oppofition or enmity
that had appeared in Thebes through the courfe
of the Grecian contefts; they hated and determined

Demoft. de
falfa Leg.
fect.22. cum
Schol.

mined to oppofe any people who prefumed to appear as their competitors for fovereign power; and, in fuch difpofitions, received the ambaffadors of Philomelus with the utmoft favour; and, by a formal decree, entered into a ftrict mutual engagement and alliance, offenfive and defenfive, with the Phocians, whom they affected to confider as men driven to extremities by the tyranny and oppreffion of their enemies.

THE Lacedaemonians alfo had particular reafons for liftening to the overtures, and efpoufing the caufe, of Philomelus.   The Amphictyons, as hath been already obferved, had condemned them in a fine of five hundred talents to be paid to Thebes.   As this fum was not paid at the appointed time, the penalty was doubled by a fubfequent decree of the great council, and no lefs than one thoufand talents was impofed on the Lacedaemonians: a fum, which, exorbitant as it was, they muft neceffarily pay, or be expofed to all the rigour of the general laws of Greece.   To recur to the fame pretence which the Phocians had ufed, and to cry out loudly againft the injuftice of the decree, feemed the only means of eluding the blow.   But remonftrances, however violently urged, could have no effect, unlefs feconded by arms, and fupported by an appearance of warlike power.   And then,

to

to take up arms in the character of men condemned by the council of Greece, would be to
expofe themfelves to all the weight of popular
odium and indignation.   If, on the contrary,
they appeared only as affiftants to the Phocians,
they might obtain their grand point in a manner
apparently more honourable.   All the odioufnefs of rebellion would fall on thofe who had
been the firft to take up arms ; while the Lacedaemonians would be fuppofed to act only
from pity to their friends, who were driven to
the very brink of ruin.

THESE are the motives to which * Diodorus
afcribes the prefent conduct of Lacedaemon.
And, from the character of Archidamus, a
fubtle,   penetrating,   and defigning prince,
ftrictly attentive to every event from which he
might derive advantage to his country, and indefatigable in projecting the means of recovering its ancient fplendour, we may probably
conclude, that, in engaging to affift the Phocians, he was influenced by another particular
view of intereft.   The Lacedaemonians, as
there will be hereafter occafion to obferve, had
themfelves an ancient claim to the poffeffion and
patronage of the Delphian temple ; he therefore readily favoured an attempt to wreft it from
the late poffeffors.   The Phocians, by difputing

their

their right, deprived it of the reverence paid to   SECT. I.
a long undisturbed possession; and when they
were so far weakened, as to be no longer able
to support their pretensions, he might then,
with more ease, and less odium, assert those of
his own country.

OTHER states of less moment were also found,   Diod. Sic.
who, from their connexions, passions, or inte-   l. 16.
rests, favoured the cause of Phocis. But, at   sect. 27, 29.
Thebes the ambassadors of Philomelus were received with indignation; and warned to expect
nothing but hostilities and just resentment. The
Thebans freely declared, that they were arming
against the Phocians to avenge the majesty of
the deity, whom this people had offended by
their sacrilegious enterprize. The Locrians,
Thessalians, Perrhibaeans, Dorians, Dolopians,
Athamantians, Achaeans, Phthiotes, Magnetes,
Ænians, and some others, influenced either by
their attachments to Boeotia, their ancient ani-
mosities to Phocis, or the popular motives of
religion, and veneration for the temple, all
united against Philomelus and his adherents.
And thus this quarrel, at first seemingly inconsiderable, became gradually to appear important
and alarming: and divided all Greece with the
greater animosity, as their passions and interests
                                             had

 had the specious shew of religion to disguise them, and to sanctify their most bloody consequences.

It doth not appear, that Philip was as yet invited, by either party, to share in this dispute: but a prince of his consummate policy could not have regarded it with indifference: and, although he had no prospect of immediate advantage from it, yet, by his conduct, he seems to have duly weighed its remote consequences, and, from the beginning of this fatal contest, to have justly considered it as the foundation of his future greatness. He looked on with secret satisfaction, while these people rushed to war with an inconsiderate fury, which rendered them blind to their real danger; and waited till they should exhaust and weaken each other, so as to enable him to attack them all with greater advantage.

The first year of the sacred war had now elapsed, (for it must be thought an essential part of the present history to trace the progress of this important contest) when Philomelus began to find himself engaged in a truly dangerous and momentous enterprise. He perceived the dreadful storm which was preparing to burst upon

Diod. Sic. l. 16. sect. 28.

upon him from different quarters, and saw the
necessity of guarding effectually against it.
He drew together a large body of new mercenaries, to which he added a number of such
Phocians as were capable of service, but as yet
had not been incorporated in his army; and as
it was absolutely necessary to procure a large sum
of money for the support of these forces, and
as policy forbad him to commit any outrage on
the riches of the temple, he conceived a less
odious method of raising the necessary supplies;
which was to tax all the inhabitants of Delphi,
who had been enriched by the devotion of
Greece, and by the continual resort of various
nations to the celebrated oracle. By these means,
he was enabled to take the field with a formidable power, and to present himself in readiness
to oppose all the enemies of Phocis. The Locrians, who were still the first to express their
zeal against him, now again met him in arms,
and came to an engagement near to those rocky
precipices, called by the Grecians, Phaedriades.
The battle was fought, on each side, with sufficient valour; but, in spite of their bravest
efforts, the Locrians were defeated, pursued
with considerable slaughter, many of them made
prisoners, and many driven down headlong from
the rocks. The event of this engagement serv-

ed to inflame the spirit of the Phocians, but threw the Locrians into the deepest consternation. They instantly dispatched their deputies to Thebes, to represent their deplorable condition, and to urge that state to hasten to their assistance, and that of the god.

AND now the Phocians were threatened with the immediate appearance of the Thebans, and of the other states, which paid deference to the decrees of the Amphictyonic body. Philomelus could not yet think himself sufficiently armed against so formidable an association, and therefore determined to reinforce his army with still greater numbers. To this it was previously necessary to find new supplies of money. As all his former resources were exhausted, as neither Athens nor Lacedaemon had as yet sent him the stipulated succours, he was at last obliged, however invidious and unpopular it might appear, to lay his sacrilegious hands on the treasures and rich offerings of the temple; and, having taken as much from this large fund as he judged necessary, he was enabled to augment the pay of his mercenaries by one half of the former sum. By these means, he instantly found himself surrounded by great numbers from all parts of Greece, of desperate fortunes

and

Diod. Sic.
l. 16.
sect. 30.

and abandoned characters; immoral and profligate contemners of the national religion, and influenced only by the hopes of sharing a rich spoil. They were all supplied and gratified; and thus Philomelus was enabled to march into the Locrian territory, at the head of above ten thousand horse and foot; a large army for a Phocian general, and much beyond what might have been expected in his circumstances. The Locrians, now reinforced by some of the Boeotians, came out to meet him. The cavalry on each side engaged, and the Phocians were victorious. The Thessalians, with the auxiliary forces, which their neighbouring states had raised, having made up a body of six thousand men, next march down into Locris, and meet the enemy at the foot of an hill called Argolas: but here the Phocians are once more victorious. A formidable body of thirteen thousand Boeotians now arrive, and join the confederates; while Philomelus is reinforced by fifteen hundred Achaeans sent from Peloponnesus. This chief, though now considerably inferiour in numbers, yet disdained the thoughts of a retreat. Both armies were collected on the same plain, and incamped in view of each other.

Frequent excursions were necessarily made from each army, on account of foraging; and,

on

on one of these occasions, it happened, that a number of mercenary forces, in the service of Philomelus, had the misfortune to be surrounded, and taken prisoners, by a superiour body of Boeotians. The wretches were brought in triumph to the camp; proclamation was made with all solemnity, by an herald, that, by the sentence of the great council of Amphictyons, these men were condemned to die, for having served in the army of sacrilegious violators of the rights of Apollo; and this sentence was instantly executed without mercy. The soldiers, in the pay of Phocis, were fired with fury and indignation at the cruel and disgraceful fate of their comrades: they seized the first opportunity of surprising a party of the enemy: they led them to their general's tent: they called loudly for revenge: nor could Philomelus oppose their urgent remonstrances: the prisoners were delivered up to their fury, and put to death with every circumstance of cruelty that had been practised in the enemy's camp.

Diod. Sic. l. 16. sect. 31.

At length both armies decamped at once, and began to march the same way, which the the conveniency of forage seems to have pointed out. After some motions, in a close and woody country, which concealed the approach of each from the other, until they were just in view,

5

their

their vanguards firſt met unexpectedly, and began to ſkirmiſh. The action ſoon became general and violent; and the Phocians, after ſome
reſiſtance, were forced to yield to ſuperiour numbers. The country, in which they fought,
filled with rocks, and precipices, and pathleſs
woods, impeded their retreat, and expoſed them
to all the fury of the victorious enemy, who
made great ſlaughter both of the Phocians and
the mercenaries. Philomelus exerted all his
valour and abilities to correct this diſorder, but
without effect. Unable to ſtop the flight of his
ſoldiers, covered over with wounds, pierced
with anguiſh and deſpair, he, at length, yielded
to the torrent, and ſoon found himſelf puſhed
to the brow of a frightful precipice, which cut
off all further flight. The enemy were preſſing
cloſe upon him; he knew the treatment he was
to expect, were he to fall alive into their hands;
his deſperate reſolution was, in the ſame moment, formed and executed; and, from the
precipice on which he ſtood, he boldly leaped
down, and paid the puniſhment due to his turbulent ambition. The command of the army,
by this means, devolved to Onomarchus, his
brother and colleague, who, with great difficulty, collected, by degrees, the ſcattered remains
of the defeated army, and retired to Phocis.
The Thebans, and other confederates, having

O 3

cloſed

clofed the campaign fo fortunately, returned to their own territories, expatiating on the fate of Philomelus, as a manifeft indication of divine wrath; and being, by this fuccefs, confirmed in their refolutions to purfue the enemies of heaven and of Greece, they declared their firm purpofe of afferting this righteous caufe, and of punifhing all thofe facrilegious wretches, who might be taken in the courfe of the war, in the fame manner as their chief had fuffered, the manner which Apollo himfelf, by this execution of his vengeance, feemed to point out to them.

The Athenians, as we have already feen, were engaged by a formal treaty to fend affift-ance to thefe unhappy Phocians. But their indolence had as yet prevented them from performing their engagement, and they had now the mortification to find their acknowledged friends and allies defeated, and almoft totally deftroyed, by means of their defertion. While they thus neglected a conteft, which raged in the heart of Greece, and now began to threaten moft important confequences, their vanity prompted them to extend their views to Afia, and to affect an attention to the motions and defigns of the great king. The thoughts of their ancient glory were too flattering ever to

fubfide,

subfide, even amidft all their corruptions; the ancient caufes of enmity, between them and Perfia, were ftill remembered, and, on many occafions, oftentatioufly recounted. The late conduct of their general Chares, in affifting a rebellious noble, had raifed a juft and warm refentment at the Perfian court; and their notions of their own importance made them readier to fufpect, that the vaft armaments, which were now preparing by Artaxerxes Ochus, threatened them, and that fome important blow was meditated againft their dominions. The orators of Athens feemed ftudious to flatter the weaknefs and vanity of the people on this occafion, and exerted all their eloquence to engage them in a vigorous oppofition to the ancient enemy of Greece. All the actions of their great anceftors were recalled to their remembrance; the names of Miltiades, Themiftocles, Cimon, and the other illuftrious enemies of Perfia, refounded through the affembly; all the force and artifice of language was employed to adorn their actions; and their pofterity were pathetically invited to imitate thefe renowned patterns of virtue, and to rife up in arms againft the Barbarian. It is not impoffible but that the agents and partifans of the king of Macedon might have regarded this as a favourable occa-

Demoft. Orat. de Claff.

fion

Book II.

fion to advance their mafter's intereft; and that by joining violently in the outcry againft the Perfian, by fomenting the fufpicions of his defigns, and by flattering the national pride of the Athenians, they endeavoured to divert their attention from the actions of Philip, whom they feem to have reprefented as a powerful prince, ready to lay afide all private animofities, and to unite with them againft the common enemy. The artifice of thefe fecret friends of Macedon, or their own terrours, fo far wrought upon the Athenians, that they refolved to fend a deputation to all the Greeks to invite them to fufpend their private quarrels, and to unite againft the defigns of Perfia; and they themfelves fo far forgot all private animofities; and poffibly were fo far influenced by the artifice of corrupted hirelings, that they refolved, on this occafion, to acknowledge Macedon as a member of the Hellenic body, and to invite Philip to join in the general confederacy. Olivier * thinks it probable, that Ifocrates was the perfon who anfwered for the conduct of Philip, and induced his countrymen to this refolution. This old, reclufe, and virtuous rhetorician was eafily flattered by the attention which Philip paid to him, as well as other men of learning; and, convinced, himfelf, of the fincerity of his declarations, might naturally have laboured to convince his

fellow-

Liter. Philip.

* Lib. 4. P. 175.

fellow-citizens, and to remove their prejudices, by echoing thofe plaufible pretences with which Philip difguifed all his hoftilities, and which might have had their full effect upon an honeft mind, unacquainted with the artifices of public life. Add to this, that Philoftratus tells us (as the French writer obferves) that at one time Ifocrates reconciled Philip to the Athenians; which could not poffibly have happened but in the prefent conjuncture: as in the grand treaty, executed by the ten orators, Ifocrates had no fhare: and the peace which fucceeded the battle of Chaeronea was not made till after his death. However this may be, no overtures could poffibly be made to Philip more agreeable to his policy and ambition, nor more likely to engage his whole attention; and poffibly the fecret practices of this prince, or the vanity of Athens, might have had more material confequences in this conjuncture, had not Demofthenes now appeared, for the firft time, in a debate about the public intereft, and exerted his addrefs and energy to moderate the exceffive and ill-directed zeal of the Athenians.

THIS illuftrious orator and ftatefman, whom we fhall hereafter find acting fo confiderable a part in the courfe of this hiftory, was born in the laft year of the ninety-ninth Olympiad, according

cording to Dionysius, who, in his epistle to Ammaeus, hath accurately distinguished the different periods of his life, and the times in which his several orations were delivered. He was the son, not of a mean and obscure me-

chanic, as the Roman satyrist hath represented him, but of an eminent Athenian citizen, who raised a considerable fortune by the manufacture

of arms. At the age of seven years he lost his father; and, to add to this misfortune, the guardians to whom he was entrusted, wasted and embezzled a considerable part of his inheritance. Thus oppressed by fraud, and discouraged by a weak and effeminate habit of body, he yet discovered an early ambition to distinguish himself as a popular speaker. The applause bestowed on a public orator, who had defended his country's right to the city of Oropus, in an elaborate harangue, inflamed his youthful mind with an eager desire of meriting the like honour. Isocrates and Isaeus were then the two most eminent professors of eloquence at Athens. The soft and florid manner of the former did by no means suit the genius of Demosthenes. Isaeus was more vigorous and energetic, and his style better suited to public business. To him, therefore, he applied; and, under his direction, pursued those studies, which might accomplish him for the character to which he aspired. His

first

firſt eſſay was made againſt his guardian, by whom he had been ſo injuriouſly treated. But the goodneſs of his cauſe was here of more ſervice than the abilities of the young orator; for his early attempts were unpromiſing, and ſoon convinced him of the neceſſity of a graceful and manly pronunciation. His cloſe and ſevere application, and the extraordinary diligence with which he laboured to conquer his defects and natural infirmities, are too well known, and have been too frequently the ſubject of hiſtorians and critics, ancient and modern, to need a particular recital. His character, as a ſtateſman, will be beſt collected from the following hiſtory; as an orator, the reader, perhaps, is not to be informed of his qualifications. I take the liberty, however, of tranſcribing a brief account from a former work:

" ENERGY and majeſty were his peculiar ex‑
" cellencies. From the gravity of Thucydides,
" the pomp and dignity of Plato, the eaſe and
" elegance, the neatneſs and ſimplicity of the
" Attic writers, he formed a ſtyle and manner
" admirably fitted to his own temper and genius,
" as well as that of his hearers. His own ſeve‑
" rity determined him to the more forcible me‑
" thods of aſtoniſhing and terrifying, rather
" than to the gentle and inſinuating arts of
" perſua‑

" perfuafion; nor did the circumftances and
" difpofitions of his countrymen admit of any
" but violent impreffions. As many of thofe to
" whom he addreffed himfelf were men of low
" rank and occupations, his images and ex-
" preffions are fometimes familiar. As others
" of them were themfelves eminent in fpeaking,
" and could readily fee through all the common
" artifices of oratory, thefe he affects to defpife;
" appears only folicitous to be underftood; yet,
" as it were, without defign, raifes the utmoft
" admiration and delight : fuch delight as arifes
" from the clearnefs of evidence, and the fulnefs
" of conviction. And, as all, even the lower
" part of his hearers, were acquainted with the
" beauties of poetry, and the force of harmony,
" he could not admit of any thing rude or
" negligent; but, with the ftricteft attention,
" laboured thofe compofitions, which appear fo
" natural and unadorned. They have their
" ornaments; but thefe are auftere and manly,
" and fuch as are confiftent with freedom and
" fincerity. A full and regular feries of dif-
" fufive reafoning would have been intolerable
" in an Athenian affembly. He even contents
" himfelf with an imperfect hint: a fentence,
" a word, even his filence is fometimes pregnant
" with meaning. And this quicknefs and ve-
" hemence flattered a people, who valued them-
          " felves

" felves upon their acutenefs and penetration.
" The impetuous torrent, that in a moment
" bears down all before it; the repeated flafhes
" of lightning, which fpread univerfal terror,
" and which the ftrongeft eye dares not encoun-
" ter; are the images by which the nature of
" his eloquence hath been exprelfed."

He was now twenty-eight years old, when
the Athenians affembled to confider of the meafures to be taken in confequence of this alarm
from Perfia, and particularly of the manner of
raifing an armament proper to defend them
againft the fuppofed danger, and of the funds
required for preparing and maintaining it. Luccefini, in his notes on the oration which Demofthenes now delivered, propofes a difficulty, that,
by the eftablifhed laws of Solon, no man was
allowed to fpeak in public, who had not attained
the age of thirty; which law, as it appears
from the oration of Æfchines againft Timar-
chus, was ftill in force: but this law, as the
fame learned commentator hath abundantly
proved, only regarded thofe ten public orators
who were annually chofen and paid to fpeak in
the affairs of ftate : who, as they were frequently to addrefs the fenate, muft neceffarily be of
the fenatorial age. All the other citizens were
freely allowed to declare their fentiments in the
affembly,

 affembly, and to propofe any thing which they deemed of advantage to the ftate; with a due deference, however, to feniority; though the law, which gave to the elders a prior right of fpeaking, was now abrogated, according to another interpreter of this great Athenian orator.

Tourreil. Not. in Phil. 1.

Olymp. 106. Y. 3.

THIS privilege, therefore, Demofthenes now affumed, but not before he had heard the full fpirit of national vanity break forth in the affembly, in magnificent harangues on the ancient glory of Athens, and the neceffity of curbing the pride of the Barbarian, and of calling upon the Greeks to unite againft their common enemy. He feems to have formed jufter notions of the prefent ftate of his country, of its connexions, interefts, and corruptions. As yet, however, it became his age to fpeak with due caution, and to curb that feverity with which he afterwards combated the errours of his countrymen; he begins with tempering their heat and extravagant zeal, without abfolutely fhocking their prejudices.

Oratio de Claff. init.

" THE men, who thus dwell upon the praifes
" of our anceftors, feem to me, ye men of
" Athens, to have chofen a fubject fitted rather
" to pleafe and gratify the affembly, than to do
" the due honours to thofe on whom they lavifh

7   " their

“ their applaufe. As they attempt to fpeak of
“ actions which no words can worthily defcribe,
“ the illuftrious fubject adorns their fpeech,
“ and gives them the praife of eloquence; while
“ their hearers are made to think of the virtues
“ of thefe heroes with much lefs elevation than
“ thefe virtues of themfelves infpire. To me
“ time itfelf feems to be the nobleft witnefs to
“ their glory. A feries of fo many years hath
“ now paffed over: and yet no men have yet
“ appeared, whofe actions could furpafs thofe
“ confummate patterns of perfection. It fhall
“ be my part, therefore, folely to endeavour to
“ point out the means which may enable you
“ moft effectually to prepare for war. For, in
“ fact, were all our fpeakers to proceed in a
“ pompous difplay of their abilities, fuch pa-
“ rade and oftentation could not poffibly be of
“ the leaft advantage to the public. But if any
“ man whatever will appear, and can explain,
“ to your full fatisfaction, what kind of arma-
“ ment, how great, and how fupported, may
“ ferve the prefent exigencies of the ftate, then
“ all thofe alarms muft inftantly be difpelled.”

From the circumftances of Greece, the contefts which now reigned, the difpofition of the
principal ftates, the dangers which were nearer,
more certain, and more alarming than thofe apprehended

prehended from Perſia, he proceeds gradually to inſpire them with ſentiments of greater moderation, to recall them from all romantic purſuits, and to confine them to defenſive meaſures, to the care and attention due to their military preparations, that ſo they might appear amply provided againſt any attack whatever. The method he propoſes for raiſing their armament, diſcovers an extraordinary attention to the conſtitution of his country, and ſhews that it was not only by forming his voice, his ſtyle, and his pronunciation, that Demoſthenes prepared himſelf for public buſineſs. His ſcheme, if particularly diſcuſſed, might lead us too far away from the principal ſubject. It ſeems equitably and happily conceived, calculated for expedition, and to obviate all difficulties and murmurings. Though poſſibly the great deſign of the orator was not ſo much to point out the means of guarding againſt the ſuppoſed danger, as to divert his countrymen, by a delicate addreſs and artifice, from an affair, which had no other foundation than in the over-heated imaginations of ſome orators, who were poſſibly intereſted in fomenting and increaſing the preſent emotions of the aſſembly.

It was one great corruption in the ſtate of Athens, that the richer members of the community

munity employed all their influence (in the general decay of public fpirit) to fhift off from themfelves the burdenfome and expenfive duties of an Athenian citizen. It was their province to equip and to maintain the fhips of war: and, by the difpofition which prevailed at prefent, the richeft citizen was only obliged to contribute a fixteenth part to the fitting out of one veffel. So that the poor alone felt the public burdens, and many irregularities and deficiencies were found in their marine. In the place of this, Demofthenes propofed a new regulation, whereby every citizen, poffeffed of ten talents, was obliged, at his own fole expence, to equip one fhip of war : they who poffeffed lefs, were to unite their fortunes, fo as to make up this fum, and to contribute in proportion to their wealth; and they, whofe fortunes exceeded ten talents, were alfo obliged to contribute an additional fum, rated according to their abilities; and, if poffeffed of twenty, were to fit out two; if of thirty, three fhips; which number, together with one tender, was the greateft that any citizen was obliged to provide by the new regulation. This propofal, equitable as it was, yet gave occafion to a profecution: but the accufer had fcarcely that number of voices in his favour, which could fcreen him from the confequences of a malicious accufation.—The people

Demoft. de
Corona, fect.
30.

 saw clearly the advantages of the scheme which Demosthenes proposed ; and, without any difficulty, adopted and confirmed it.

THEIR late debate only served to demonstrate what high notions they had formed of the merit and power of Philip : their magnificent schemes quickly vanished, when it began to appear, that the designs of Ochus were all directed against Egypt ; and the precarious condition of many of their dependent cities roused them from their dream of glory, to an humble and mortifying sense of their weakness and danger. The possessions which they were labouring to maintain, or to recover, in Thrace, were every day threatened by some new attempt made by the vigilant and active king of Macedon, who was continually engaged in weakening their interest there, while his hostilities were apparently aimed against those petty sovereigns who divided that country, and who, by their mutual contentions for power, gave him a fair opportunity of carrying his arms into their territories, under pretence of succouring the oppressed and weaker party. Cersobleptes, who commanded in the Thracian Chersonesus, soon perceived that he could not long defend that important district against the claim of Athens, and the arms of Philip : in order, therefore, to gain the friendship of the Athenians,

Demost. in
Aristocr.
Olymp.
106. Y. 104.

Diod. Sic. l.
16. se t. 34.

nians, he now determined to make a formal re- Sect. I.
signation of the Cherſoneſus to this people:
hoping, by this method, to attach them to his
intereſt, and, by their aſſiſtance, to eſtabliſh
himſelf in the reſt of the kingdom, on the ruin
of Beriſades and Amadocus, the other two co-
heirs. · This ceſſion was in the higheſt degree Demoſt. in
Ariſtoc.
pleaſing to the Athenians: Cerſobleptes was de-
clared a citizen of Athens; the ſame honour Epiſt. Phil.
was conferred on Charidemus, who was then
engaged in his ſervice, and aſſumed the greateſt
ſhare of the merit of this conceſſion to himſelf; Demoſt. in
Ariſtoc.
and flattered the people with hopes of ſtill far-
ther advantages. In the ardour of their acknowledgments, the Athenians paſſed a decree, enjoin-
ing all the allies and ſubjects of Athens to deliver up, alive or dead, any perſon who ſhould
make an attempt on the life of Charidemus;
which produced that oration againſt Ariſtocrates,
the author of this decree, to which we are indebted for many particulars relating to the affairs of Thrace.

CHARES, who was now coaſting along the
Helleſpont, was directed to receive thoſe places
in the Cherſoneſus, which were thus yielded to
the Athenians. He proceeded to execute his Diod. Sic.
u ſupra.
commiſſion, but found a vigorous oppoſition at
Seſtos, one of the principal of theſe cities. He
P 2 was

 was obliged to befiege it with all his force, and, having taken it by affault, treated the inhabitants with a feverity capable of intimidating all the other fettlements from any further oppofition.   All thofe, who were of age to bear arms, were put to the fword without mercy; the reft reduced to flavery, and an Athenian colony immediately fettled at Seftos.

BUT there was one circumftance which, in a great meafure, defeated all the advantages which the Athenians might derive from the poffeffion of the Cherfonefus.   Cardia, the moft confiderable city of this peninfula, had ever appeared averfe to the Athenian government: it was fituated on the ifthmus, of confequence commanded the entrance from Thrace, and was enabled to preclude the inner fettlements from all the advantages of commerce.   Its fituation afforded room for fome difpute, whether it was to be confidered as a part of the Cherfonefus, or of the Thracian continent.   It had been excepted in feveral treaties, by which the right of Athens to the Cherfonefus was acknowledged; and now Cerfobleptes exprefsly referved Cardia to himfelf.   The Athenians, on their part, though unable to fupport their pretenfions to Cardia, yet ftill afferted them; and thus a field was opened for perpetual difputes, and Philip had

a fair

Demoft. in
Arifloc.
Diod. ut
fupra.

a fair occasion of distressing the Athenians, by
uniting with the Cardians, and supporting their
independence: a design which he was afterwards
enabled effectually to execute.

In the mean time, this prince, ever restless
and aspiring, ever attentive to the schemes which
his ambition dictated, and ever provided with
some pretence to justify his hostilities against
those who were obnoxious to him, turned his
thoughts to Methonè, as a city which his interests required him to reduce.   Ancient geogra-
phers mention several cities of this name: the
principal of which were Methonè in Peloponnesus, situated between Epidaurus and Troe-
zenè; another of the same name in Thessaly,
built on the coast of Magnesia; and a third,
called the Thracian Methonè, situated on the
Thermaïc bay, at the distance of * forty stadia
from Pydna.   This last city it was, to which
Philip now laid siege, (as the authority of
Strabo †, as well as that of Eustathius, in his
notes on the second book of the Iliad, directs us
to determine.)   By its situation it was capable
of serving as a kind of citadel to favour the excursions of the enemies of Macedon into the
heart of his dominions, whether of Cersobleptes,
against whom he made no scruple to avow his
enmity; or of the Olynthians, on whose ruin

* About
four miles.

† In Ex-
cerpt. l. 7.

Oliv. l. 5.
p. 189.

P 3   he

he now feems to have refolved, and who, on their part, had good reafons to fufpect and dread his rifing power. Nor was this city lefs convenient to the Athenians, or lefs favourable to any attempts which they might make to invade his kingdom. Thither were their forces tranfported, as we have already feen, in the expedition in favour of Argaeus: and, in earlier times, as we learn from Thucydides [*], they had experienced the convenience of this port, in making their defcents on Macedon. He could not think of leaving fuch a city open to his fecret or declared enemies; and therefore determined to deftroy it. The Methonèans, to whom his defign could not be long a fecret, prepared and exerted themfelves as men who fought for their very being; and, for a while, fuftained the fiege with an obftinate valour. One of the cities, called Methonè, had been employed in its fortifications from the time of the Trojan war: which the Greeks imputed to an imprecation pronounced by Agamemnon, who, when the inhabitants alleged this their engagement as an excufe for not uniting their arms with him, prayed that thefe walls, which thus prevented them from joining in the common caufe of Greece, might never be finifhed. Theopompus, as quoted by Strabo [*], underftands this of the city which Philip now befieged: and, if fo,

the

the Methonèans had ſtrength, as well as valour, to oppoſe Philip: while the Athenians, on their part, alarmed at this new inſtance of his reſtleſs ambition, were preparing to ſend powerful ſuccours to the beſieged.

During the operations of the ſiege, as Philip was employed in viewing the works, and directing the approaches, an arrow, ſhot from the town, wounded him dangerouſly in the eye, and caſt the beſiegers into the utmoſt confuſion. But they were ſoon re-animated by the vigour and reſolution of their prince, who gave orders, with the utmoſt calmneſs and intrepidity, for continuing the ſiege, and committed himſelf to the care of Critobulus, a chirurgeon, whoſe ſkill, in ſo important a cure, hiſtory has thought worthy to be recorded: and who, though he could not ſave his eye, yet contrived, by his dexterity, to take away all the blemiſh which might have been expected from ſuch an accident. When the arrow was extracted, this inſcription is ſaid to have appeared on it, Aster to Philip's right eye; a circumſtance on which ſome relations have been founded, that are unauthorized, and unſupported, by the more authentic writers. It is ſaid, (as the reader, who is at all converſant in modern compilements,

P 4

perhaps

Sect. I.

Phil. 1.
ſect. 13.

Suidas in
Καβαιος.

Plin. l 7.
c. 37.

Suidas
Solin. c. 14,
15.

Tourreil.
Not in
Philip 1.

perhaps need not be informed) that one After
of Amphipolis, or of Olynthus, according to
others, recommended himself to the service of
Philip, by assuring him, that his skill in shoot-
ing was so accurate, that, with his bow, he
could strike down birds in their full flight:
to which Philip answered with contempt, " It
" is well ! I shall make use of thee when I wage
" war with starlings:" and that After, stung
with this neglect, threw himself into Methonè,
whence he shot the arrow with the inscription
above mentioned. It is also added, that Philip
sent back the arrow, when extracted from his
eye, with another inscription, importing, that,
if once master of the town, he should hang up
After; and that this threat was afterwards executed. These last circumstances entirely depend on the authority of Suidas and Ulpian;
and are thought to be sufficiently overturned by
the honourable testimony which Justin * gives
to the general clemency of Philip on this occasion: but if the particulars, which Monsieur
Tourreil relates, be really authentic, (his authority, indeed, I confess, I have not been able to
discover) it must be submitted to those who are
acquainted with the laws of war, how far an
extraordinary severity may be justified against a
man, who took so severe a method of approving
his

lib. 7.
in fine.

his ſkill, and, at the ſame time, revenging the king's neglect. It is certain, that, whatever were the circumſtances really attending this wound, they muſt have reflected ſome degree of diſhonour upon Philip; as Lucian *, in his method of writing hiſtory, mentions, as an inſtance of the freedom with which hiſtorians ſhould write, that ſuch particulars as Philip's wound in the eye, or Alexander's killing Clitus, ſhould, by no means, be paſſed over. And, if his wound was the conſequence of a raſh and wanton neglect of a ſoldier's extraordinary abilities, his enemies muſt have triumphed, and he himſelf been aſhamed of his miſtake and his misfortune. Such a ſuppoſition may account for that ſenſibility which Philip is ſaid to have felt ever after, to ſuch a degree, that the bare repetition of the word EYE was painful and offenſive to him. As to any wounds received nobly in the courſe of war, it cannot be ſuppoſed, that a prince of his exalted ſentiments, and thirſt for glory, could have conſidered them in any other light, but as the memorials of his valour. But if the recollection of them ſuggeſted the idea of his miſtaken conduct, and unwarrantable inattention to his intereſt; then it muſt neceſſarily have covered him with confuſion. Indeed as to the word CYCLOPS, by which his enemies frequently pointed him out; the

offence,

 offence, which he is faid to have conceived at it, may as well be fuppofed to have arifen from its conveying the idea of a cruel and barbarous monfter, incapable of the fentiments of humanity.

THE wound of their prince, which had at firft caft the Macedonians into confufion, now ferved only to animate them, when they found the danger over, and that Philip was ftill enabled to direct the fiege with unabated vigour. The inhabitants of Methonè, on their part, continued to make an obftinate defence. The Macedonians were ordered to prepare for a general affault; and, animated by the prefence of their royal general, encouraged by his promifes, and inflamed by the example of his refolution, they preffed forward with fufficient eagernefs, and boldly mounted the walls. The oppofition of the befieged could not prevent confiderable numbers from gaining the battlements; when, to cut off all retreat, Philip inftantly ordered the fcaling ladders to be removed; thus leaving his men to the defperate alternative, either of dying, or purfuing their advantage. The Methonèans foon found all refiftance vain; laid down their arms, and fubmitted to the mercy of the victor; who, if we may believe Juftin *, treated them, on this occafion, not only. with moderation,

Polyaean.
Stratag.
l. 4.

* l. 7. in fin.

ration, but kindnefs. Diodorus † informs us
more explicitly, that the conditions which he
granted them were thefe : that the inhabitants
fhould be fuffered to march out unmolefted,
with one fuit of apparel only ; and that the city,
with all the reft of its poffeffions, fhould be
delivered up without referve. And, in thefe
times, when flavery was generally the unhappy
lot of the conquered, and their enemy was
deemed abfolute proprietor of their perfons, as
well as their poffeffions, fuch terms muft have
defervedly been efteemed moderate and favourable.

THUS was Philip in poffeffion of Methonè,
while the Athenian fuccours were failing to its
relief.   The city was rafed to the ground ; and
the lands divided among his foldiers : and thus
were his enemies deprived of a ftation which
they might have occupied with advantage, and
a colony planted there entirely in the intereft of
Macedon, ready to watch their defigns, and to
give the alarm on the leaft appearance of commotion, bound particularly to Philip by all the
ties which could engage men ; by the opinion of
his power, his abilities, and his merit ; and by
the benefits which he well knew how to beftow
upon them, with the appearance of the moft

5   cordial

SECT. I.
† l. 16.
fect. 34.

Demoft.
Phil. 1.
fect. 13.
Diod. ut
fupra.

 cordial and undefigning affection and liberality.

Oliv. l. 5.
p. 195.

THE French author of his life here feems
ftrongly affected by his hero's laudable difpofition, equally influenced by the pleafure of be-
ftowing, and that of animating the virtue of
his foldiers, by the rewards which his bounty
dealt to them.   In one inftance he obferves this
happy temper engaged him in an act of injuftice,
which gave him much uneafinefs, but which
he found means of repairing.   The reader may,
perhaps, not be difpleafed at having the narration fufpended by the introduction of this
anecdote, which Seneca hath preferved.

Seneca de
Benef. c.
37.

A CERTAIN foldier, in the Macedonian army,
had, in many inftances, diftinguifhed himfelf by
extraordinary acts of valour, and had received
many marks of Philip's favour and approbation.
On fome occafion he embarked on board a veffel,
which was wrecked by a violent ftorm, and he
himfelf caft on the fhore, helplefs and naked,
and fcarcely with the appearance of life.   A
Macedonian, whofe lands were contiguous to
the fea, came opportunely to be witnefs of his
diftrefs, and, with all humane and charitable
tendernefs, flew to the relief of the unhappy
                                        ftrange-

ftranger. He bore him to his houfe, laid him in his own bed, revived, cherifhed, comforted, and, for forty days, fupplied him freely with all the neceffaries and conveniencies which his languifhing condition could require. The foldier, thus happily refcued from death, was inceffant in the warmeft expreffions of gratitude to his benefactor, affured him of his intereft with the king, and of his power and refolution of obtaining for him, from the royal bounty, the noble returns which fuch extraordinary benevolence had merited. He was now completely recovered, and his kind hoft fupplied him with money to purfue his journey. In fome time after, he prefented himfelf before the king, he recounted his misfortunes, magnified his fervices; and this inhuman wretch, who had looked with an eye of envy on the poffeffions of the man who had preferved his life, was now fo abandoned to all fenfe of gratitude, as to requeft that the king would beftow upon him the houfe and lands where he had been fo tenderly and kindly entertained. Unhappily Philip, without examination, inconfiderately and precipitately granted his infamous requeft; and this foldier now returned to his preferver, and repaid his goodnefs, by driving him from his little fettlement, and taking immediate poffeffion of all the fruits of his honeft induftry. The poor man, ftung

with

Book II. with this inftance of unparalleled ingratitude and infenfibility, boldly determined, inftead of fubmitting to his wrongs, to feek relief; and, in a letter addreffed to Philip, reprefented his own and the foldier's conduct in a lively and affecting manner. The king was inftantly fired with indignation; he ordered that juftice fhould be done without delay; that the poffeffions fhould be immediately reftored to the man whofe charitable offices had been thus horridly repaid; and, having feized his foldier, caufed thefe words to be branded on his forehead, THE UNGRATEFUL GUEST: a character infamous in every age, and among all nations; but particularly among the Greeks, who, from the earlieft times, were moft fcrupuloufly obfervant of the laws of hofpitality.

BOOK II. SECTION II.

CONTENTS.

HISTORY of the sacred war continued.—Onomarchus created general of the Phocians.—His assiduity and address.—He prepares vigorously for action.—Takes Thronium, Amphissa, and Orchomenus.—Is defeated before Chaeronea.—Philip, at length, engaged as a party in the sacred war.—The disorders in Thessaly.—Philip marches against the tyrants who had attempted to resume the sovereign power, and defeats them.—Onomarchus prepares to support them.—Philip receives a signal defeat.—Onomarchus ravages Boeotia.—His secret practices with Lycophron,—discovered by Philip,—who marches once more against Lycophron and the Phocians.—Gains a complete victory.—The death of Onomarchus.—Philip's measures to secure the attachment of the Thessalians.—His reputation.—The jealousy of the Athenians.—An union between their state and Olynthus.—Commotions in Thrace.—Philip besieges Heraeum.—Confusion at Athens.—

Sickness

BOOK the SECOND.

SECTION II.

THE defeat of Philomelus, as hath already been obferved, clofed the fecond year of the facred war; when the confederates, who had united to defend the authority of the Amphictyonic council, retired into their own territories; and the Phocians were led back to Delphi by Onomarchus, delivered for a time from the horrours of a war, in which they had already fo feverely fuffered. This interval of reft they firft began to employ in convening a general affembly of their allies and auxiliaries, to confult about the war, and the meafures to be purfued in their prefent diftrefsful circumftances. In this affembly, the opinions were confiderably divided, according to the different paffions or interefts which influenced that great variety of members who compofed it. Many, deeply affected by the profpect of their danger, and the odioufnefs of their caufe, judged that an accommodation fhould be purchafed on any terms, and declared violently for peace. Others, who

Vol. I.   Q   dreaded

dreaded the refentment of the enemy, or who had engaged in this unpopular quarrel, merely from expectation of large pay and rich plunder, and whofe abandoned manners rendered them infenfible of difgrace and infamy, declared as violently for the continuance of a war, on which alone their rapacious hopes and profpect of fecurity were founded ; and inforced their opinions by every plaufible argument which might have weight in a popular affembly. After fome paffionate debates, each party was for a while filent ; while the leaders turned their eyes around, to look for fome man of confequence, whofe opinion might determine the fate of this important deliberation.

THEY did not long continue in this fufpenfe. Onomarchus, who was fully prepared for the part he had now to act, rofe up, and inftantly engaged the attention of the whole body. This chief, who had a peculiar intereft in the continuance of the war, addreffed himfelf to the *Died. Sic. l.* affembly in an artful and premeditated harangue, *16. fect. 32.* calculated to diffipate their fears, and to enliven their expectations. With a confummate addrefs he inforced every plaufible argument for war, every motive of intereft and of honour, which might induce the Phocians, and their allies, to purfue the plan which their late general had

.5   formed.

formed. His harangue was fpecious and infi-
nuating; and numbers were found in the affembly to echo his fentiments. All opinions
of moderation, all reprefentations of difficulty
and danger, were drowned in the violence of
acclamations and tumultuous applaufe; without further confultation, it was refolved to purfue the moft vigorous meafures for fupporting
the war: and Onomarchus was invefted with
full powers, as commander in chief of the Phocian army.

No fooner was he thus raifed to the dignity
which had been the object of his wifhes, but he
began to exert himfelf in fuch a manner, as to
confirm the expectations his people had conceived from him. He applied himfelf, with
the utmoft diligence and vigour, to the re-efta-
blifhment of his army, which the late engagement had confiderably weakened. Every part
of Greece was ranfacked for mercenaries, whom
he enticed to his ftandard by his munificence
and flattering affurances. By thefe, (whom he
incorporated with thofe companies in which the
greateft havock had been made) he not only
reftored, but augmented, his army: and once
more enabled the Phocians to threaten their inveterate enemies with a formidable oppofition.

Q 2

And,

And, while thus employed in making every neceffary provifion for war, he alfo took care, in imitation of his predeceffor, to work on the fuperftition and ignorance of his people, and to find out dreams and portents, in order to infpire them with hopes of fuccefs. While his mind was poffeffed with magnificent fchemes and defigns, he dreamed, or pretended to have dreamed, that he was employed in raifing a coloffal ftatue, which the Amphictyons had dedicated to Apollo; and that it appeared to grow greater under his hands. This Diodorus * ferioufly interprets as a declaration, that this general fhould be the means of making thofe wretched Phocians doubly repay the outrages committed againft the deity and his temple. But Onomarchus was furnifhed with diviners, who explained it in a quite different manner, as an indication of that great acceffion of glory and honour, which his army was to acquire under their new commander.

His vigour and affiduity gave weight to this interpretation. To repair every damage fuftained in the laft battle, he applied himfelf to provide weapons for the numbers he had now levied. All his armourers were employed inceffantly; and vaft quantities of arms, offenfive and defenfive, were provided with all expedition.

* l. 16
fect. 33.

Ibid.

tion. The gold and filver, which the rapine Sect. II.
of his predeceffor, or his own induftry or violence, had amaffed, was quickly coined; and
his agents difperfed through the neighbouring
ftates that were in alliance with Phocis, where
they diftributed his money to the magiftrates
and citizens of eminence, to attach them the
more firmly to his intereft, and to bear down all
oppofition in their popular affemblies. Nor
were even his enemies entirely proof againft the
powerful temptations by which he fecretly af-
failed their fidelity. Numbers of them were
found, who eagerly received his bribes, and
were prevailed on to revolt to the Phocians, or,
at leaft, to obferve a neutrality: fuch was the
power of gold, and fuch the univerfal degeneracy and corruption which now prevailed
through Greece. And while he thus laboured
to increafe the number of his friends, and to
weaken his enemies, by thefe his fecret practices,
he, at the fame time, eftablifhed his intereft at
home, by the moft arbitrary and defpotic meafures. Murmurings and difcontents, which the
calamities of war naturally excited, and which
that fenfe of the odioufnefs of their caufe, ftill
remaining among the more moderate and virtuous of his countrymen, could not but increafe,
were inftantly ftifled by the moft tyrannical feverities.

rities.   If any prefumed to exprefs the leaft diffatisfaction at his conduct, they were loaded with chains, defpoiled of their poffeffions, and put to death with every circumftance of cruelty: a procedure which not only ferved to weaken and intimidate the party which oppofed him, but enabled him to promote his defigns, by the additional wealth acquired from thefe confifcations.

AND now, having made all the neceffary preparations, Onomarchus marched out, at the head of his forces, and made an irruption into the territories of the Locrians, called Epicnemidii.   Here he began with attacking Thronium, a city on their confines; and, having taken it by affault, expofed it to the rapacioufnefs of his foldiers, and made flaves of the inhabitants.   Thence he proceeded to Amphiffa, a town of the Locrians, furnamed Ozolae. The Amphifsèans, intimidated by the feverities inflicted on the people of Thronium, did not attempt the leaft oppofition: but inftantly fubmitted to fuch terms as the conquerour was pleafed to dictate; and, probably, by a large fum of money, refcued their city from the infatiable fury of his army.   Hence he poured down on the territories of Doris; where, having

ing taken some cities, and, desolated the lands, he traversed his own country, and, by a forced march, pierced into Boeotia. Here he seized the famous city of Orchomenus : and, having spread the terrour of his arms, rushed forward with a precipitate fury, and prepared to lay siege to Chaeronea ; when the Thebans, who were now ready to stem the torrent, marched out to meet the Phocians, by this time considerably weakened by their repeated conquests and the garrisons they had stationed in the several conquered towns. A general engagement ensued, in which Onomarchus was defeated, and driven back to Phocis.

HITHERTO we have seen this contest carried on independent of Macedon, and Philip viewing, with a seeming unconcern, the havock, the variety of fortune, the victories and calamities of the contending powers. But, at length, the time was come, when his honour and policy required that he should take some share in this quarrel. Lycophron, whom Philip had obliged to resign his usurped authority in Thessaly, had not yet lost all hopes of re-establishing his power; but secretly formed and strengthened his party, waiting for some favourable opportunity to avow his intentions. To him, among

Q 4

other

other confiderable perfonages, Onomarchus had applied, and, partly by the intereft which Lycophron maintained among the Theffalians, partly by the natural inconftancy of this people, his intrigues and bribery proved fo fuccefsful, that Theffaly feparated from the confederates, and profeffed to obferve a neutrality in the facred war. The Phocian chief, juftly confidered himfelf principally indebted to Lycophron for this important fervice, and that his intereft muft be greatly advanced by the reftauration of this

tyrant. By his means, and in his name, he even hoped to gain the abfolute command of Theffaly, and to become the real fovereign, while Lycophron, who was to govern by his fupport, could govern only for his purpofes. Seven thoufand of his forces, therefore, were difpatched to Pherae, under the command of his brother Phayllus, to fupport the tyrant; who, encouraged by this powerful alliance, eftablifhed himfelf in that city, and openly afferted his pretenfions to the fovereign power.

THE defertion of Theffaly was regarded by the Thebans with an affected contempt. This people, refolving to convince the world that they could not poffibly be diftreffed by fuch inftability, detached five thoufand men into Afia,

under the conduct of their general Pammenes,

to

to affift Artabazus, (who ftill continued his rebellion; but, when Chares was obliged to quit
his fervice, found himfelf reduced to confiderable difficulties.) Here Pammenes gained repeated victories; and, by his conduct, gave
peculiar pleafure to the Thebans, who, ever
fince the famous Perfian war, in which they had
united their arms with the Barbarian, eagerly
wifhed for any glorious opportunity of retrieving
their honour, by fome gallant exploits againft
the ancient enemy of Greece.

BUT the king of Macedon could not look
with indifference on this conduct of the Theffalians, which feemed to argue the declenfion of
his influence in their ftate; nor could his honour
permit him to fuffer the total fubverfion of thofe
glorious regulations, thofe provifions for the
peace and liberty of Theffaly, which his arms
had lately made. The folicitations with which
his friends and adherents, in that country, now
urged him to take up arms in their defence,
were not wanted to prevail upon him. He inftantly marched into Theffaly. (I follow the
opinion of a learned commentator * in fuppofing, that) on this occafion it was, he formed
the fiege of Pagafae, which Demofthenes fo
frequently mentions. The Athenians were informed of this tranfaction; they refolved to

fend

8

Sect. II.

Dem. Orat.
de Claff.

* Luccefini
Not. in Phil.
I.

send succours to the town; and, as usual, executed this resolution, when the address and valour of the Macedonian had already rendered him master of it. Lycophron, and his auxiliaries, prepared to meet the enemy, but soon proved unequal to Philip and his valiant army. Onomarchus, sensible of their danger, marched out with speed to join them, but could not arrive till they had received a total defeat, and were chaced out of Thessaly.

And now Philip, having reinforced his army with those Thessalians who still continued well-affected to him, prepared to meet Onomarchus, who was advancing with all his powers. The Phocians were superiour in numbers: but the Macedonian Phalanx was, by this time, renowned through all Greece. Onomarchus dreaded its attack, and justly conceived that his success wholly depended on breaking this formidable body. The two armies met, and, at the very first charge, the Phocians gave way, and were pursued to some high mountains contiguous to the field of battle. The Macedonians pressed on, confident of victory; but soon had horrid proof, that the retreat of their enemy was no more than an artifice, which the sagacious foresight of their general had suggested

and

and contrived. The Phocians now began the attack in earneſt, and made effectual uſe of thoſe weapons, which had been provided for the execution of their deſign. Stones, and fragments of rocks, of an enormous ſize, were rolled down upon their aſſailants, whoſe ſanguine hopes were quickly loſt in amazement and confuſion; whole files were, in an inſtant, cruſhed to pieces, with every circumſtance of horrour. The Phalanx, whoſe cloſe order ſerved but to increaſe the havock, was broken, and, in that ſtate, unable to ſuſtain the aſſaults of their enemy, who now marched down in good order from the mountains, and fell, with all their fury, upon an army already vanquiſhed. The valour and activity of Philip here proved, for the firſt time, ineffectual: the Macedonians were forced from the field of battle, which was become a horrid ſcene of ruin and carnage. Their prince, however, after many fruitleſs efforts, at length brought off his forces to an even ground, out of the reach of the enemy, where he, with difficulty, reſtored their order, and revived their courage. But as the Phocians had been at firſt ſuperiour in numbers, and as great havock had been made in his army, he found it moſt adviſable to march back to Macedon; obſerving, on this occaſion, that his

ſoldiers

foldiers did not fly from the enemy, but, like rams, retired, in order to make their fhock the more forcible and furious [A].

LYCOPHRON was thus enabled to return triumphant into Theffaly; while Onomarchus, elevated by his victory over a prince who had hitherto been regarded as invincible, marched into Boeotia, where he gained another victory, and then proceeded to attack the city of Coronea. This city was built on an eminence near mount Helicon. On the eaft, it was defended by the lake Copaïs, which prevented it from being entirely invefted, and ferved to convey a conftant fupply of provifions, by water, from the other cities of Boeotia. The river Curalius, as it winded round to fall into the lake, formed a natural fofse on the fouth: but, on the north, the city was entirely open, as the Thebans, in order to preferve their fuperiority in Boeotia, and to fecure the dependence of this city, had

[A] ACCORDING to Diodorus, (l. 16. fect. 35.) Philip renewed the engagement, and was again defeated; which reduced him to the greateft danger and difficulty. A confiderable part of his army deferted; and the reft were, by the utmoft efforts of his addrefs and policy, fcarcely prevailed on to adhere to him. By chufing to follow the account of Polyaenus, I apprehend the greater honour is paid to Philip's conduct and abilities as a general.

filled

filled up the trench, and demolished the forti-
fications on that side.   A city, thus dismantled,
was by no means capable of opposing a numerous and victorious army.   Onomarchus entered without any considerable opposition, and
insulted and terrified the Thebans, by the de-
vastations which he committed, without controul, in the very heart of their dominions.
Thus chastised for their vanity in weakening
their strength by the Asiatic expedition, this
people looked on Philip as their most effectual
resource, and expected, with impatience, the
moment when he should be enabled to make a
diversion in their favour.   He had been dili- Diod. Sic,
gently engaged in re-establishing and strength- ut supra.
ening his forces, and now appeared once more
in Thessaly at the head of a formidable army,
and advanced boldly upon the tyrant.

LYCOPHRON, fully sensible of his own weakness and insufficiency, made the most pressing
instances to Onomarchus, to march immediately
to his relief.   He lavished the most flattering Diod. Sic.
promises on this crafty and ambitious chief; he l. 16.
assured him, that the Phocians should absolutely sect. 35.
command Thessaly, and all its forces; and that
he, and those dominions which he was labouring
to maintain, should be ever at the devotion of
their protectors and deliverers.   Pleased with

the

the profpect of fo important an acceffion of power, Onomarchus did not hefitate a moment to comply with the tyrant's defires. He was now at the head of an army capable of undertaking the moft hazardous enterprifes; he imagined himfelf already fovereign commander of all Theffaly, and marched boldly to reinforce his ally with twenty thoufand foot and five hundred horfe. The forces which Philip had brought from Macedon, he was fenfible, were, by no means, able to encounter fo formidable and numerous an army: to the Theffalians, therefore, he was obliged to addrefs himfelf, whofe caufe he affected to affert, and for whofe liberty he profeffed himfelf wholly folicitous.

Diod. Sic. I. 16. fect. 35.

He induftrioufly and artfully reprefented to them, that the junction of Lycophron and Onomarchus muft prove fatal to their freedom and happinefs; that their tyrant, not content with haraffing and oppreffing them himfelf, had now fold them to a foreign power for a vain fhew, and empty title of fovereignty; that even of that he muft be quickly ftripped, and Theffaly totally loft in a mean dependence upon Phocis. In the facrilegious quarrels of this people, the braveft among the Theffalians muft be forced to fhed their blood ignobly; to fee their poffeffions torn from them, and all their fertile plains ranfacked and ravaged to fatiate the avarice

rice and rapine of a chief, impiously rebellious against heaven and Greece. All these, and suchlike remonstrances, he knew how to enforce with consummate artifice; and so inflamed the minds of the generality of the Thessalians, that they breathed nothing but fury against Lycophron and Onomarchus; they acknowledged the king of Macedon their leader, their protector, and deliverer; and crowded to his standard with a warm and cordial zeal. By these means, Philip soon found himself at the head of twenty thousand foot, and three thousand of the best cavalry in Greece.

THE two contending armies now advanced against each other, equally eager to engage, and equally possessed with hopes of victory. Glory and ambition were motives sufficiently animating to Philip; and his soldiers also he well knew how to animate. His cause was fair and popular: he fought against tyranny and oppression, against sacrilege and profanation, in defence of liberty, of Greece, but particularly in defence of Apollo. He ordered all his men to crown their heads with laurel, a tree sacred to that God; and his ensigns he adorned with the emblems and attributes of his divinity. And thus the Macedonians and Thessalians marched on with an enthusiastic valour, as if

com-

Diod. Sic. l. 16. sect. 35.

Justin. l. 8. c. 2.

commiffioned by heaven to inflict its vengeance on facrilege and profanation. The Phocians, whom the appearance of the enemy had ftruck with a confcioufnefs of their guilt, were charged with all imaginable fury; yet fought like men animated by defpair, and fenfible of the neceffity of defending their iniquity. The infantry, on each fide, equal in numbers, and equally obftinate, kept the victory for fome time doubtful; till the Theffalian cavalry advanced, and determined the fortune of the battle. The Phocians, unable to fuftain their force and valour, were broken, defeated, and purfued with confiderable flaughter. Horrour and difmay hurried great numbers of them towards the fea, which was contiguous to the field of battle; and, among thefe, their general Onomarchus. Here they beheld, at fome diftance, a fleet which feemed to advance towards the fhore, and which they juftly concluded to be the fuccours which Athens had fent to them under the command of Chares; and which arrived only to be witneffes of their ruin. Inftead of attempting to ftem the torrent of the victorious enemy, and to make fome ftand till this fleet might advance fo far as to afford them, at leaft, the opportunity of an orderly retreat, their terrour and impatience plunged them headlong into the fea, in hopes, by fwimming, to find their fecurity

in

Diod. Sic.
l. 16.
fect. 36.

in the ſhips. Here numbers of them faint with the loſs of blood, and confounded by their fears, ſunk under their wounds and fatigue, or were forced down by the tumult. Onomarchus, himſelf ſhared this unhappy fate; or, as Pauſanias * hath aſſerted, fell a victim to the revenge and indignation of his own ſoldiers; who imputed their ruin to his ignorance and cowardice, and forced him down into the deep, covered over with wounds. More than ſix thouſand Phocians periſhed in this precipitate flight. and on the field of battle: three thouſand were made priſoners, and reſerved for all the ſeverity which the general laws of Greece denounced againſt ſacrilege. To expreſs the warmer zeal for religion, Philip ordered his ſoldiers to ſearch for the body of that impious chief, whoſe profane arms heaven had thus puniſhed; and cauſed it to be hung on a gibbet, as a dreadful memorial of iniquity and divine vengeance. The other bodies of the ſlain he caſt to the waves, as of wretches unworthy of interment, and the common rights of mankind. He was alſo authorized, by the laws of Greece, to inflict the ſame rigour on thoſe who had fallen alive into his hands: but whether he cauſed them likewiſe to be caſt into the ſea, ſeems not entirely clear from the expreſſion of Diodorus; though a

* in Phoc.

Philo. Ind. in Fuſ-b. l. r-p. l. 8. p. 392.

VOL. I. R French

French compiler of this history suppofes, that the dead only were thus treated, and that it is probable he contented himfelf with reducing his prifoners to the condition of flaves, the mildeft punifhment denounced againft facrilege: but whether fuch mercy was confiftent with Philip's prefent political views of fetting up for a prince of the moft confummate piety, and a zealous avenger of the god's injured honour, may, on the other hand, be juftly made a queftion. So that the fate of thefe unhappy captives muft for ever remain in obfcurity.

THIS victory convinced Lycophron of the neceffity of once more refigning his pretenfions to the government of Theffaly; and obliged him to retire from Pherae. That city, together with Pagafae, his late conqueft, and Magnefia, another town of confiderable note in Theffaly, Philip referved to himfelf, the better to fecure the dependence of the inconftant Theffalians; who were, at prefent, unwilling and unable to difpute the decifions of their deliverer, and, without difficulty, fubmitted to thofe regulations which he made under pretence of reftoring their tranquillity, but, in reality, to keep them firmly attached to Macedon. Thither he now directed his courfe, crowned with glory and victory; the

fubject

ſubject of univerſal praiſe through Greece, where, from this time, he began to be regarded as a prince really great and powerful. Stateſmen admired the depths of his policy, and generals acknowledged the ſuperiority of his military conduct and abilities; while the lower orders of men, who were incapable of penetrating into his real deſigns, and were affected only by thoſe fair appearances with which he veiled them, revered and applauded him as a religious prince, the ſcourge of ſacrilege, and defender of Apollo.

AT Athens, his great actions ſeem to have been received with envy and jealouſy. A people enervated by indolence and luxury, devoted to ſelf-enjoyment, and, at the ſame time, elevated with pride and national vanity, were no longer able to ſupport their ancient reputation, yet could not give up the flattering remembrance of it: they perceived the gradual advances, of a new and unſuſpected rival, to conſummate greatneſs and ſovereignty; but perceived them with an impotent indignation. Convinced of the abſolute neceſſity to check the progreſs of his arms, yet fatally averſe to thoſe vigorous meaſures which ſo important a deſign required, they amuſed themſelves with ſchemes of raiſing up ſome other enemy to Philip, who

Demoſt.
Olynth. 2.
ſect. 4.

R 2   might

might divert him from thofe excurfions which threatened Greece in general, and particularly the Athenians. The confederated ftates of Olynthus feemed to be the only power fitted for this purpofe. It was urged vehemently, that the Olynthians, if poffible, were to be engaged in a quarrel with Macedon, as the only means of confining the views of this enterprizing prince to his own neighbourhood; and, while they were thus folicitous to throw the bufinefs of their own defence on others, they applauded the defign, as the refult of deep and extenfive policy, though really dictated by their love of eafe. The Olynthians, on their part, encouraged them in thefe their fchemes of depreffing their rival, by the uneafinefs and fufpicions of Philip, which they now difcovered. The late reduction of Methonè, which implied a peculiar diffidence of them, feems to have alarmed them with a lively fenfe of the danger to be apprehended from their afpiring neighbour. They envied, they dreaded, they fufpected him, in fpite of all the favours he had, fome time fince, conferred upon them; they deemed it abfolutely neceffary to guard againft the defigns of a prince inceffantly employed in enlarging his power, and extending his dominions. They regarded the ftate of Athens as the only balance againft Macedon; and, about this time, applied to the

Athenians,

Demoft. in. Ariftocr.

Athenians, to propose an accommodation of all
ancient differences, and to enter into such terms
of friendship, as might be the basis of a future
strict connexion, and of an alliance defensive
and offensive. Overtures, so consonant to their
own sentiments, were readily embraced by that
people, whose assemblies, the only scenes in
which their vigour was displayed, seem to have
been constantly engaged in deliberations about
the conduct of Philip, the tendency of his designs, and the means of guarding against them.
But, while the Athenians were consulting, the
Macedonian pursued his conquests; and, by
new instances of his active spirit, cast them into
new dismay and consternation.

FRESH commotions, which arose in Thrace,
determined this prince, ever indefatigable in
the pursuit of his designs, once more to march
into that country. Here Berisades, one of the
coheirs of Cotys, was dead; and Cersobleptes,
without regard to those engagements which he
had entered into with Athens, and which secured
the interests of the other brothers, and probably supported and secretly encouraged by the
king of Macedon, attacked the sons of Berisades, and his brother Amadocus, and seemed
determined, if possible, to gain the entire sovereignty of Thrace. The several members of

.   R 3   this

this family, who had oftentimes experienced the vanity of a dependence on Athens, now began to find it expedient to court the friendſhip of Philip. To him their differences were ſubmitted: and, in the diſpoſitions which he now made, his own intereſt only was conſidered. Amadocus, and the family of Beriſades, ſeem to have been driven by him from their dominions, (for ancient authors ſpeak but obſcurely of theſe tranſactions) and Cerſobleptes, who had, by this time, gained the friendſhip of Philip, eſtabliſhed on their ruin. Teres, another petty prince, who claimed a part of this country, but of whom we have no particular accounts, ſeems alſo to have had his power eſtabliſhed and enlarged by Philip, who thus diſtributed dominions as he pleaſed, and, by his nod, determined the fate of contending potentates.

While he was thus engaged, his attention, fixed eternally on the purſuit of new conqueſts, directed him to an attempt, which diſcovered the depth of his penetration, and the extent of his views. Heraeum was a fortified place, built by the Samians in Thrace, over-againſt Chalcedon, and ſo called from the name of Juno, who was worſhipped in that country with peculiar honours. The place was of no great conſequence in itſelf; its harbour was dangerous

I

and

Demoſt.
Olynth. 3.
ſect. 6.
Juſtin. l. 8.
c 3.

Dem. Olyn.
3. ſect. 6.
Dem. in
Ariſt.

Phil. Liter.
Lucceſini
in Olyn. 1.

Stephan. in
voce Hjæa.
Herod. l. 4.
Harpocrat.

Lucceſini in
Olynth. 3.

and deceitful; but it ferved as a kind of citadel Sect. II.
to Byzantium, an eminent Thracian city, and
of the utmoft confequence to the Athenian intereft, as it was one great mart from which the
barren land of Attica was fupplied with the neceffary means of fubfiftence for its inhabitants.
With a view, no doubt, of facilitating the conqueft of fo important a city, Philip now laid
fiege to Heraeum. The Athenians, though too
inattentive and fupine to guard againft their danger, yet had penetration to conceive it in its full Demoft O-
lynth. 2,
fect. 3.
extent, and to fee through the whole fcheme of
their enemy. The news, therefore, of this attack,
raifed a commotion, hitherto unknown, in the
affembly at Athens. Some of the orators exerted
all their powers in reprefenting the danger which
threatened the ftate, and in inveighing againft the
injuftice and ambition of Philip: others, in defending or palliating the conduct of a prince,
who had attached them to his intereft by the
power of gold. After fome time fpent in the
warmth of mutual oppofition, a decree was formally made, that forty fhips of war fhould be
inftantly fent to fea; that all the citizens of
Athens, within the age of five and forty years
(though ufually exempted at forty from military
fervice) fhould now embark on board this fleet,
as in a time of urgent diftrefs and difficulty;

R 4   and

and that fixty talents fhould be raifed to fupport this formidable armament.

But new advices were now received to fuf-pend the effect of thefe refolutions, and to lull this infatuated people into their former ftate of infenfibility. The fatigue of conftant action, joined to the effects of the wound which Philip had received at Methonè, threw him into a dangerous fit of ficknefs, which alarmed the Macedonians, and interrupted their military operations. The news of this event was foon received with the utmoft joy at Athens, and, as is ufual in fuch cafes, was propagated with circumftances far exceeding the truth; fo that the people were now flattered with affurances, that the king of Macedon was dead. They refigned themfelves, with the utmoft credulity, to the pleafing hopes of being thus eafily delivered from their dangerous enemy: their late decrees for war, and vigorous meafures, lay totally neglected and forgotten; months paffed away in indolence and pleafures: their entertainments, and religious ceremonies, were deemed objects worthier attention than their defence and fecurity: nor did they ever once think of executing their late refolutions, till a full year elapfed; and, even then, all their projected preparations were reduced to ten veffels, under the command

2   of

of Charidemus, (who was, at this time, engaged in their service) without soldiers sufficient to man them, and with an inconsiderable sum of money to support them.

But while the Athenians were gradually sinking into this dangerous state of security, Philip's happy temperament, and robust habit of body, freed him from his present disease, and enabled him to proceed in the execution of his designs. It doth not clearly appear, whether his attempt against Heraeum was successful, or whether his sickness saved that place. But, from a passage in the third Olynthiac oration of Demosthenes *, compared with one in the first Philippic †, it appears, that, immediately upon his recovery, he made an inroad into the territories of the Olynthians; possibly in revenge of their late practices at Athens; and might have pursued his hostilities still farther, had not the disorders and commotions in Greece diverted his attention, and, for a' while, suspended the final ruin of Olynthus.

The remains of the Phocian army, which had escaped the fury of the victorious Macedonians in the late engagement, retired into Phocis, still obstinate and undismayed; and, still resolving to pursue the war, chose Phayllus, the last sur-
viving

Sect. II.

* sect. 6.
† sect. 7.

Olymp. 107.
Y. 1.

viving brother of Onomarchus, for his fucceffor.
This chief was actuated by the fame fatal paffions as his predeceffors, equally ambitious,
equally vigorous, and equally a contemner of
the national religion. Inftructed by their conduct, he determined to purfue the fame meafures; he employed the large fund of wealth
which he poffeffed, in collecting great numbers
of new mercenaries, and in augmenting thofe
fubfidies which the Phocians had been obliged to
pay to feveral people; and went in perfon to
folicit their fpeedy and effectual affiftance. At
Athens he received affurances of powerful fupport. At Sparta, in ancient times fo renowned
for a contempt of money, his gold now found
an eafy accefs. To Denicha, the wife of king
Archidamus, the Phocian, it is faid, particularly applied [B]. Her perfon expreffed her
mean and fordid mind; and, by gratifying her

Diod. Sic.
l. 16. fect.
37.

Paufan in
Lacon.

[B] She was remarkably low in ftature, and poffeffed of
none of thofe graces, for which the Spartan women were in
general famous. We learn from Heraclides Lembus, an
ancient writer, quoted by Athenaeus, (l. 13. p. 566.) that the
Ephori impofed a fine on Archidamus for preferring her to
another lady of diftinguifhed beauty, but of inferior fortune.
The Spartans, who were ever attentive to the conftitution
of their offspring, expreffed their fears on this occafion, left
fuch a match fhould produce a diminutive race of kings.
Βασιλικους αντι Βασιλεων.

paffion

paffion for money [c], he was confiderably af-
fifted in his defign, and found but little difficulty
in gaining a renewal of the alliance, and a promife of affiftance.

THE fubtle and defigning temper of Archidamus, inceffantly employed in forming fchemes
for reviving the power of his country, had, at
this time, engaged him in a conteft with his
neighbours, which made a ftrict connexion between him and Phocis ftill the more neceffary.
He had conceived a plan for reconciling the dif- Oliv. l. 6.
ferent interefts of the Grecian ftates, in appear- p. 213.
ance advantageous to the principal members of
the great Hellenic body, but, in effect, only
calculated to reftore the fuperiority of Sparta.
He propofed to re-eftablifh the feveral cities in
the fame condition as before the late wars.

[c] ACCORDING to Paufanias (in Lacon. p. 91.) Archidamus himfelf had no fmall fhare of the facrilegious fpoils
of the temple. To this circumftance the author of the Iti-
nerary fubjoins another more for the honour of this prince.
That, at fome time in the courfe of the facred war, when
the Phocians had formed a cruel and defperate refolution,
of putting all the inhabitants of Delphi, who were capable
of bearing arms, to the fword, and felling their wives and
children for flaves; Archidamus prevented the execution
of this defign, and faved the Delphians.

ATHENS

Demoft.
pro Megal.

ATHENS would thus have recovered the city of Oropus, to which they ftill afferted their claim, but which the Thebans kept in their poffeffion [D]. Thefpia and Plataea, two eminent cities in Boeotia, that had felt the jealoufy and revenge of Thebes, and now lay fubverted and depopulated, were, by the fame plan, to be reftored and fortified.. The Phocians were to give up their two important conquefts, Orchomenus and Coronea. But thefe, and the other Boeotian cities, were only to acknowledge Thebes as the principal and leading city of Boeotia, without any abfolute fubmiffion or depend-

[D] THESPIA was a city of Boeotia, at the foot of mount Helicon. Its inhabitants accounted it an honour to be totally ignorant of all arts, even argiculture not excepted. The Thebans, after their victories over Sparta, to punifh the pretended difaffection of the Thefpians, facked and razed their city, without fparing even the temples.——Plataea was another city of Boeotia, famous for the victory which the Greeks gained there over Mardonius. It had been twice demolifhed by the Thebans. In the fifth year of the Peloponnefian war, the Spartans blocked it up, and obliged the inhabitants to furrender; on which occafion, the Thebans, who were then united with the Spartans, infifted on the demolition of Plataea. The peace of Antalcidas reftored this city. But the Thebans, three years before the battle of Leuctra, provoked at the refufal of the Plataeans to join with them againft Sparta, again reduced it to a ftate of 'defolation.　　　　TOURREIL, Not. in Orat. de Pace.

ence,

ence, and without obedience to that jurisdiction which the Thebans claimed over them. On the other hand, Meſſene and Megalopolis, the two barriers which Epaminondas had raiſed up againſt Lacedemon, were to be deſtroyed, and their inhabitants diſperſed. Thus, while the Thebans were to loſe that power, which their late conqueſts had acquired in Bœotia, all the regulations, which the equity of Epaminondas had eſtabliſhed in Peloponneſus, as barriers againſt the Lacedaemonian ambition, were to be totally ſubverted, and the Spartans to be reſtored to a power of reſuming that tyrannical dominion, which they had formerly exerciſed over their neighbours.

In order to facilitate the execution of this plan, he firſt endeavoured to gain that authority in Peloponneſus to which he aſpired. A diſpute was ſoon raiſed between Sparta and Argos, about the boundaries of their dominions. To Nicoſtratus, an eminent citizen of Argos, Archidamus ſecretly applied, and, by many artful and flattering promiſes, endeavoured to prevail upon him to put him in poſſeſſion of one of the gates of the city. But the illuſtrious Argian rejected his offers with indignation. "Is "this," ſaid he, "the language of a deſcendent "from Hercules? he deſtroyed villains, you "would

Plut. in Apophth.

" would make a villain." The king of Sparta, confounded by this gallant rebuke, refolved to have recourfe to arms, and, by engaging the feveral ftates of Greece in a new conteft, increafed the diforders and inflamed the commotions of this diftracted nation; and thereby gave new hopes to the common enemy, the Macedonian, who faw, with pleafure, the commotions in Peloponnefus, and waited for an occafion of interfering in them with honour and advantage.

But, whatever diftant hopes Philip might have now conceived from this new difpute, the facred war was defervedly the more immediate object of his regard. Archidamus had fent one thoufand Spartans to the affiftance of Phayllus; the Achaeans two thoufand; the contingent of the Athenians was ftill more confiderable, for they detached five thoufand foot, and four hundred horfe, under the command of Naufieles, one of their moft experienced generals. The tyrants of Theffaly, lately driven out of that country, without any hopes of a reftoration, reinforced the Phocian army with two thoufand Theffalians, who had followed their fortune. Nor did thofe illuftrious ftates, which Phayllus had laboured to gain over, alone engage in this difpute. Many of the lefs confiderable communities were enticed by the profpect of advantage, and joined with

no

no lefs ardour in this odious and unpopular
caufe.   And, having thus formed a numerous
army, the Phocian chief determined to ftrike
terror into his enemies, by proceeding to immediate action : for this purpofe, he entered into
Boeotia ; and, having advanced as far as to Orchomenus, encountered the enemy ; but, to mor-
tify his afpiring hopes, received a fignal defeat,
and was obliged to retire with the lofs of a confiderable part of his army.   Without allowing
his followers time for any melancholy reflections,
he inftantly fought an occafion of reviving their
hopes, and retrieving the honour of his arms.
He again marched againft the Boeotians, and
engaged them near the river Cephifus : but this
attempt was ftill more unfuccefsful : four thoufand of his men were killed ; above four hundred fell into the hands of their unrelenting enemy, who remained abfolute mafters of the field
of battle.   Yet, ftill undifmayed, Phayllus renewed the combat in a few days, and, in this
weak and unfuccefsful effort, fifty of his Phocians were flain, and one hundred and thirty
made prifoners.

In the mean time Philip, ever ftudious to
derive the full advantage from the opinions and
paffions of other men, was preparing to improve
his late fuccefs.   The honours of his victory

over

over Onomarchus were ftill frefh and blooming: even his enemies admired him; and his partifans were inceffant in founding his praifes: the minds of the Grecians were inflamed againft facrilege and profanation; and every defeat, which the Phocians received, was induftrioufly reprefented as a manifeft indication of the divine difpleafure. This Philip therefore conceived to be the favourable moment for an attempt to penetrate into the very heart of Greece; there to appear the umpire in all difputes, and to render his decifions abfolute and irrefiftible. He flattered himfelf, that his defigns muft be perfectly concealed by the veil of religion and veneration for the gods; he declared his refolution of entering into Phocis, and executing full vengeance on that profane and obftinately hardened people; and, with a numerous and formidable army, already provided for the purpofe, marched towards Thermopylae, thofe famous ftreights, which commanded the entrance into Greece. The Athenians, too acute and penetrating not to fee his defign in its full extent, or to imagine that any motive could really prompt him to this attempt, but that of gaining the abfolute command of Attica and Peloponnefus, were ftruck with terrour and aftonifhment at the approach of fo formidable a· prince to what they juftly efteemed the very borders of their territories,

Boeotia

sect. 38.

Juftin, l. 8. c. 2.

Demoſ. Phil. 1.

Boeotia alone intervening. They imagined that
they already faw the powers of Macedon and
Thebes united, pouring down and overwhelm-
ing their country, and fpreading like a deftruc-
tive inundation over all Greece. This fudden
and violent impreffion roufed them from their
indolence. No difficulties were thought of, no
fupplies wanted; the richer citizens, in this
preffing emergency, fupplied the public amply
from their private fortunes; a formidable armament was inftantly provided at an expence,
which plainly demonftrated the general fenfe of
the impending danger. They failed to the
ftreights, poffeffed themfelves of all the paffes,
and ftood prepared to oppofe the invader.

Demoft. de
falfa Leg.
fect. 29.

THEIR army was now pofted between inac-
ceffible mountains on one hand, and frightful
precipices on the other, which terminated in the
fea. Valour and difcipline muft have proved
ineffectual againft fuch advantage of fituation,
even if it had been confiftent with policy to
have attempted to force a paffage. But fuch
an attempt muft have been too flagrant a declaration of his defigns againft a people with whom
he was ftill concerned to keep fome meafures;
Philip, therefore, chofe to lead his forces back
to Macedon, and to load the Athenians with all
the odium of the defence of facrilege.

VOL. I.   S   THIS

Book II.

Dem. Phil.
1. sect. 5.

THIS unexpected disappointment irritated the mind of Philip to a degree of acrimony, which plainly discovered that his own interest and designs were much more affected by it, than the cause of heaven. His resentment against the Athenians was expressed in the bitterest and boldest denunciations of vengeance; and, if we may believe Justin, his present vexation of mind appeared in some actions quite inconsistent with his general conduct; in which he seldom failed to assume the appearance at least of justice and lenity, and especially where some material point of interest was not concerned. But it is asserted

· l. 8. c. 3.

by that historian *, that he now turned his arms against those very cities which had been attached and allied to him, which had marched under his command, and congratulated both him and themselves upon his victories; that he ravaged and plundered these cities, and sold the wives and children of the inhabitants for slaves; that, in the places where he had been just received with all the marks of hospitality, he spared neither their temples nor their gods, so as to appear not so much the avenger of sacrilege, as solicitous to abandon himself to all the excesses of impiety and profanation. Paulus Orosius, who laboured to find out crimes and calamities in profane history, dwells with seeming pleasure on this description of Justin; but neither the

vehemence

vehemence and acrimony of Demofthenes, nor
the authentic hiftorical remains of antiquity,
have given any particulars of thefe pretended
outrages: neither can they be reconciled to
Philip's acknowledged good fenfe, and his conftant attention to his future intereft.

THE late precaution of Athens foon became
a general topic in Greece, and was varioufly
received and reprefented from the variety of
tempers, opinions, and interefts. "How dif- Juftin, l. 8.
"ferent," did Philip's favourers and partifans   c. 2.
now cry out, "was this action of the Athenians
"from the glorious effort of Leonidas at the
"fame place! That illuftrious Spartan marched
"to Thermopylae to defend the Grecian temples
"from the ravages of the Barbarians; the Athe-
"nians, to defend the ravagers and impious
"profaners of the Delphian fhrine, and to op-
"pofe a glorious zeal for the honour of Apollo; Meurfii
"that divinity, whom they had the vanity to   Athen. Art.
"account among their anceftors; that divinity, Ariftid.
"whom they had ever confulted in all their dif- p. 169.
"ficulties; that divinity, by whofe directions fupra.
"they had made fo many conquefts, and had
"gained fuch extenfive empire. Before this time,
"this degenerated people had difcovered their
"contempt for all things facred; we all remem-
S 2   "ber,

" ber, that, when [E] Iphicrates had intercepted
" some statues of gold and ivory destined for the
" service of the gods by Dionysius the Sicilian,
" they ordered him to sell them publicly, tho'
" dedicated to the Olympian Jupiter and Del-
" phian Apollo : they have now repeated their
" impiety ; an impiety the more shocking, when

[E] Diodorus relates this transaction at large, as an instance of the present impiety of the Athenians. Iphicrates,
a little before the commencement of the sacred war, had
been at anchor with his fleet before the island of Corcyra,
when the Sicilian vessels, which were laden with these statues, fell in with some of his ships, and were taken. When
the admiral had examined the lading, he sent to his state
to desire instructions how he was to proceed ; and received
for answer, that the affairs of the gods were by no means
his concern ; that a commander was to confine his attention
to the support and maintenance of his forces. Thus encouraged, Iphicrates instantly converted the statues into money.
Dionysius, to express his resentment at this impious outrage, addressed a letter to the Athenians, in which he pur-
posely omitted the usual formulary χαιρειν και ευπρατlειν. The
letter is preserved, and was expressed in this manner :

" Dionysius, to the senate and people of Athens."

" Happiness I cannot wish you with propriety ; as you
" commit sacrilege against the gods, both by sea and land.
" The statues which were sent by us, those holy offerings,
" dedicated to the divinities, you have seized and destroyed,
" in an open and impious violation of the reverence due to
" the greatest gods, Delphian Apollo and Olympian Ju-
" piter."

" com-

" committed, not by the ignorant and lawlefs,
" not by the rude and barbarous, but by people
" refined and polifhed, inftructed and directed
" by wife and humane laws and inftitutions, by
" the example of their anceftors, and the me-
" mory of their former virtue."

Thus did the honeft and undefigning, who
were fenfible of the corruption of Athens, and
the creatures of a fubtle prince, who had received
his pay, and were ever ready to echo his dictates, exprefs their real or pretended fentiments.
On the other hand it was urged, that " the af-
" fectation of a zeal for religion, was but too
" plainly a pretence to conceal the dangerous
" defigns which the extravagant ambition of the
" Macedonian had formed. The prefervation
" of a juft balance of power had been originally
" the great object of Athens, in the affiftance which
" that ftate granted to the Phocians; the junction
" of Macedon and Thebes threatened Greece
" with many dangerous confequences; and com-
" manded all the attention of the Athenians, who,
" from the early ages of antiquity, had ever ap-
" peared the patrons and protectors of Grecian li-
" berty, the enemies of oppreffion, and the fcourge
" of lawlefs and extravagant ambition. But their
" own immediate welfare, the very being of their
" ftate, had now called forth their arms, and en-

S 3

" gaged

" gaged them to defeat the pernicious schemes
" of Macedon. The total subversion of Athens,
" and the sovereignty of Peloponnesus, were the
" immediate objects of Philip's views. Caution,
" vigilance, and vigour, were ever to be exerted
" against so politic and enterprizing a prince ; a
" prince, who, from an obscure and contemptible
" corner of the world, presumes to give law to all
" his neighbours ; leads out his armies, extends
" his conquests, foments divisions, arms nation
" against nation ; equally the enemy of all, and
" really attentive only to the establishment of
" his own greatness.   Ever since the famous vic-
" tory of Plataea, no Barbarian had ever pre-
" sumed to set his foot in Greece. Philip is
" equally alien, equally barbarous with the Per-
" sian, more the object of indignation, and much
" more to be dreaded and suspected. The op-
" position, therefore, now made to his audacious
" attempt, was dictated by the same glorious
" zeal for the common cause, which animated
" Leonidas and his Spartans ; and should be
" received with equal gratitude, and held in
" equal honour. The valour of the Athenians
" had obliged the common enemy to retire in
" shame and confusion ; and defeated the de-
" signs of the man, who, under pretence of suc-
" couring the weak, and punishing the guilty,
" sought only to erect his own power and sove-

" reignty

"reignty on the ruin of all, friends and enemies,
"allies and competitors."

Sect. II.

DIOPHANTUS, who had commanded the Athenian forces on this occasion, was received, at his return, with the same joy and acclamations, as if he had obtained a signal victory. Crowns were decreed to him, and prayers and sacrifices offered up to thank the gods for the deliverance of Athens. Yet, notwithstanding the retreat of Philip, the impression of their late danger still remained in full force: it was now but too apparent, that indolence and misconduct, on the part of Athens, had raised up an enemy capable of forming and executing the boldest designs. They saw their fatal errour in neglecting and despising a power which should have been crushed in its infancy, and were at times, tempted to believe, that all opposition was now too late. They could scarcely persuade themselves, that Philip had abandoned his enterprise, but were possessed with the imagination of his appearing every moment at their gates. To guard their territories from invasion, to defend themselves against the menaces of Philip, which were now resounded in their ears, both by those who were employed to magnify his power, and by those who inveighed against his insolence, they posted a con-

Demost. de falsa leg. sect. 30.

Dem. Phil I. sect. 2.

S 4   siderable

fiderable body of forces, either at the entrance of Attica, or at Thermopylae, (for interpreters are divided in explaining that paſſage in the firſt Philippic oration, which alludes to this tranſaction.) Their former ſolicitude, to prevent his entrance into Greece, makes it more probable that their forces were now ſtationed at the very ſtreights ; for it could hardly be conceived, that, if Philip returned, was allowed to paſs through Thermopylae, and to unite with his allies in Boeotia, any body of forces, occaſionally raiſed, and ſtationed ever ſo advantageouſly at the entrance of Attica, could poſſibly bear up againſt ſo formidable an inroad of two ſuch united powers, or prevent them from burſting in, and over-running that country. It is but juſtice, therefore, to the penetration of this people, to believe, that, on this occaſion, they took the moſt effectual precaution. Yet ſtill their corruption appeared in this inſtance of timely zeal and vigour ; for, inſtead of entruſting a ſervice of ſuch conſequence to ſome citizen of worth and character, regularly choſen by the voices of the people, intrigue and cabal were ſuffered to procure the command for Menelaus, an obſcure foreigner. It is indeed hard to think with Tourreil, that this Menelaus was a natural brother to Philip, whom his jealouſy had driven out of Macedon : or that the Athenians would have

intruſted

intrufted their army to one fo nearly allied to
their enemy.   The conjecture of Luccefini feems
better founded, that he was fome Phocian officer, who might have been recommended on
this occafion, as from his] knowledge of the
country, where the forces were to be ftationed,
he might be fuppofed capable of pofting them
to the beft advantage, and, from his intereft
there, might gain them provifions with greater
eafe and readinefs.

HAVING thus provided for the defence of
their territories, their next care was to con-
vene an affembly to deliberate on the means of
correcting paft errours, and controuling the ambitious fchemes of their formidable rival.   This
was but refuming a fubject, which had frequently engaged their attention.   Every inftance
of ill fuccefs abroad, every motion and tranfaction of their enemies, was fure to raife a fer-
ment in the Athenian affembly, where the pride
of that people was flattered by the thought,
that, thus convened, they decided the fate of
ftates and nations, of enemies and allies, and
where their orators acknowledged, and fervilely
ftooped to the fovereign authority of the people;
and either by condemning and inveighing againft
the conduct of thofe to whom their affairs were
intrufted, or by defending the public meafures,

afforded

Book II.

afforded them perpetual fubjects of conteft and debate; and frequently acquired an intereft, which no fufpicions of their want of integrity, and fometimes even avowed corruption could not fhake. At prefent they affembled with lefs pride, and lefs paffion, than they had on fome occafions difcovered: inftead of indignation at the conduct of Philip, they felt terrour and difmay: inftead of hearing their greatnefs, and glory, and power, refounded by their flattering leaders, they now found a counfellor in Demofthenes, who had courage to oppofe their prejudices, and to difplay their errours and mifconduct; and integrity and prudence to point out the meafures neceffary for their defence and fecurity. This renowned orator now rofe up, for the firft time, againft the Macedonian; and difplayed thofe abilities, which, through the whole courfe of Philip's reign, proved the great obftacle to his defigns.

Phil. 1.
fect. 1.

In the oration which he delivered on this occafion, and which is ftill extant among the invaluable remains of this illuftrious Athenian, we find him introducing his fentiments with an apology for that zeal which prompted him (now but twenty-nine years old) to appear the foremoft in the caufe of his country, without regard to the precedence ufually granted to the elder fpeakers.

speakers. They had frequently been heard upon
the present subject, and the insufficiency of
their counsels plainly appeared from this single
circumstance, that it was a subject which the
people now found themselves obliged to resume.
The present melancholy state of their affairs he
imputes not to any want of power and abilities,
but to supineness and inaction; and from this
cause of their distress, derives fair hopes and
prospects of future fortune. He reminds them
of their glorious and successful efforts to reduce
the power, and curb the insolence, of Lacedaemon; and to regain that sovereignty which they
had lost by the victory of Lysander.

" If there be a man in this assembly" (thus
doth he continue his spirited address) " who
" thinks that we must find a formidable enemy
" in Philip, while he views, on one hand, the
" numerous armies which surround him; and,
" on the other, the weakness of the state thus
" despoiled of its dominions; he thinks justly.
" Yet let him reflect on this: there was a time,
" Athenians! when we possessed Pydna, and
" Potidaea, and Methonè, and all that coun-
" try round: when many of those states, now
" subjected to him, were free and independent,
" and more inclined to our alliance than to his.
" Had then Philip reasoned in the same manner,
" How

" How shall I dare to attack the Athenians,
" whose garrisons command my territory, while
" I am destitute of all assistance! He would
" not have engaged in those enterprises, which
" are now crowned with success; nor could he
" have raised himself to this pitch of greatness.
" No, Athenians! he knew this well, that all
" those places are but prizes, laid between the
" combatants, and ready for the conqueror:
" that the dominions of the absent naturally de-
" volve to those who are in the field; the pos-
" sessions of the supine to the active and intrepid.
" Animated by these sentiments, he overturns
" whole nations; he holds all people in subjec-
" tion: some, as by right of conquest: others,
" under the title of allies and confederates: for
" all are willing to confederate with those whom
" they see prepared and resolved to exert them-
" selves as they ought.

" And if you (my countrymen) will now,
" at length, be persuaded to entertain the like
" sentiments; if each of you, renouncing all
" evasions, will be ready to approve himself an
" useful citizen, to the utmost that his station
" and abilities demand; if the rich will be
" ready to contribute, and the young to take
" the field: in a word, if you will be your-
" selves; and banish those vain hopes, which

" every

" every single person entertains, that while so
" many others are engaged in public business,
" his service will not be required; you then (if
" Heaven so pleases) will regain your dominions,
" recal those opportunities your supineness hath
" neglected, and chastise the insolence of this man.
" For you are not to imagine, that, like a god, he
" is to enjoy his present greatness forever, fixed
" and unchangeable. No, Athenians! there are
" who hate him, who fear him, who envy him,
" even among those seemingly the most attached
" to his cause. These are passions common to
" mankind; nor must we think that his friends
" only are exempted from them. It is true,
" they lie concealed at present, as our indolence
" deprives them of all resource. But let us
" shake off this indolence! for you see how we
" are situated; you see the outrageous arrogance
" of this man, who does not leave it to your
" choice, whether you shall act, or remain quiet;
" but braves you with his menaces; and talks
" (as we are informed) in a strain of highest ex-
" travagance; and is not able to rest satisfied
" with his present acquisitions, but is ever in
" pursuit of further conquests; and, while we
" sit down, inactive and irresolute, incloses us
" on all sides with his toils.

" When

" When therefore, O my countrymen! when
" will you exert your vigour? when roused by
" some event? when forced by some necessity?
" what then are we to think of our present con-
" dition? to freemen, the disgrace attending on
" misconduct is, in my opinion, the most ur-
" gent necessity. Or, say, is it your sole am-
" bition to wander through the public places,
" each enquiring of the other, What new ad-
" vices? Can any thing be more new than that
" a man of Macedon should conquer the Athe-
" nians, and give law to Greece?—Is Philip
" dead?—No, but in great danger.—How are
" you concerned in those rumours? suppose he
" should meet some fatal stroke; you would
" soon raise up another Philip, if your interests
" are thus regarded. For it is not to his own
" strength that he so much owes his elevation,
" as to our supineness. And, should some ac-
" cident affect him; should fortune, who hath
" ever been more careful of the state than we
" ourselves, now repeat her favours, (and may
" she thus crown them!) be assured of this,
" that, by being on the spot, ready to take ad-
" vantage of the confusion, you will every where
" be absolute masters: but, in your present dis-
" position, even if a favourable juncture should
" present you with Amphipolis, you could not

" take

" take poffeffion of it, while this fufpence pre-
" vails in your defigns and in your councils."

From thefe bold and animated expoftulations, he proceeds to lay down a plan of operation. Their force, he obferves, was not fufficient to meet Philip in the field ; they were to be guarded againft his excurfions ; and, by depredations on the coaft of Macedon, to confine his attention to the fecurity of his own kingdom. For this purpofe he recommends to them to prepare fifty fhips of war, with tranfports and other neceffary veffels for a body of horfe, ten light veffels for a convoy, two thoufand infantry, and five hundred cavalry, of which number five hundred foot and fifty horfe to be citizens of Athens. He then computes the fupplies neceffary for this force, and propofes a fcheme, in form, for raif-ing them.

It doth not appear, that the fpirit which ani-mated this harangue, and the accurate know-ledge of the interefts of Athens, which the great fpeaker difplayed, had that effect which might naturally have been expected from them. The people feem to have attended with pleafure and applaufe, without duly weighing the force of his remonftrances, or the wifdom of his counfels. Probably, the affiftance they had already fent to

Phocis,

Phocis, rendered them averse to new expences and new armaments; and, probably, Philip had his agents and partisans in the assembly, who, ever attentive to the service of a master by whom they were magnificently paid, recommended less vigorous measures, under various plausible pretences; which had but too much weight, as they flattered the indolence and unsurmountable aversion to public cares, which were ever predominant at Athens, notwithstanding any temporary interruptions and transient fits of zeal. The dispositions, the prejudices, the errours, and the corruptions of this people, were ever watched by Philip with the most attentive regard: while they were amused and deceived, his restless mind was secretly employed in meditating his revenge: the late sudden effort of their zeal was just sufficient to convince him, that they were to be regarded as his principal rivals; and that nothing but their opposition could raise up any material obstacles to those schemes, which his ambition, enlivened by success, was daily forming and extending: and the general weakness of their conduct encouraged him to hope that this opposition would, in the end, prove ineffectual; and that art and resolution would render him superiour to their power.

BOOK

BOOK II. SECTION III.

CONTENTS.

HISTORY of the sacred war continued.—The death of Phayllus.—He is succeeded by Phaleucus.—Actions of this general.—Commotions in Peloponnesus.—The Argians and Megalopolitans assisted by the Thebans, Eleans, &c.—Letter of Archidamus to the Eleans.—The Spartans supported by Phocis.—Orneum taken.—Thebans defeated.—Their confederates retire.—Oration of Demosthenes for the Megalopolitans.—Action near Telphusa.—A truce granted to Megalopolis.—Probable reasons for this truce.—Philip's expectations from the disorders of Peloponnesus.—The continuance of the Phocian war highly agreeable to his views.—The Thebans exhausted.—Apply to the king of Persia.—Philip's attention to the affairs of Greece.—His influence in all popular assemblies.—Justin's account of his expedition into Cappadocia.—Difficulties attending this account.—Philip resides for some time in Macedon.—His buildings.—He borrows money from the men of affluence in Greece.—This conduct

<table><tr><td>VOL. I.</td><td>T</td><td>explained.</td></tr></table>

BOOK the SECOND.

SECTION III.

THE sacred war still continued to rage in Greece, to harass and weaken the contending parties, and to prepare the way for the power of Macedon. Phayllus, the Phocian general, having been driven out of Boeotia by repeated defeats, led his forces into the territories of the Locrians, surnamed Epicnemidii, and there possessed himself of several cities. At Aryca, a town of considerable note in this district, he first found his progress checked; and as his arms could not readily subdue it, he entered into a secret conference with some traitors within the walls, who prevented the delay and danger of a formal siege, by betraying the town to the Phocians. Here he left a small garrison, lest he might too far weaken the main body of his army, and marched back to Phocis; when the Locrians, by means of some private intelligence, surprised the town which they had

Book II. Sect. III.

Diod. Sic. l. 16. sect. 38.

so

so lately lost, and put the Phocian garrison to the sword. The news of this event determined Phayllus to enter once more into Locris, where he again invested Aryca with a considerable body, and led the rest of his army against Abae, a city of eminence in Phocis, where there was an ancient and splendid temple of Apollo, in which the god delivered his oracles; whose inhabitants had for ages paid, and still continued to pay him peculiar honours; and, from their veneration to the divinity, had refused to join with Phayllus and his Phocians in their irreligious attempts.

Diod. Sic.
l. 16.
sect. 58.
Herod.
Urania.
cap. 134.

THE Boeotians thought themselves obliged to succour this place; and, marching with incredible diligence and expedition, fell by night upon the camp of Phayllus, defeated the Phocians with considerable slaughter, and, having ravaged and laid waste their territories with an uncontrouled fury, elevated by their success, and laden with booty, they returned into Locris to raise the siege of Aryca. But Phayllus, whom they fondly supposed to have been ruined beyond all recovery, instantly rallied and collected his forces; and, when the victorious army arrived at the town, they were surprised and mortified, by finding, that he had already joined the besiegers; and was so well prepared to give

Diod. Sic.
l. 16.
sect. 58.

them

them battle, that, before they could be regularly formed in complete order, he fell furiously
upon them; and, having gained a complete
victory, took the city of Aryca, and rafed it to
the ground.

THIS was the laft military exploit of Phayllus,
and the only one in which his arms had been
crowned with victory. In fome fhort time after,
he was attacked by a confumption, which abfolutely prevented him from action. He ftruggled
for fome time with his diforder, but, at length, D'rd. Sic.
was obliged to yield to the violence of it; and l. 16.
died in fuch excruciating torments, as made his fect. 38.
death to be regarded by the religious, as the
manifeft judgment of heaven [A].   He named
Phaleucu?, the fon of Onomarchus, for his
fucceffor, with directions, that, in confideration
of his youth and inexperience, Mnafeas fhould

[A] THE heathen hiftorians, who all exprefs a ferious
regard to their religion, and a deep fenfe of the veneration
due to the national worfhip, fpeak of all the events of this
war, and all the calamities of the Phoians, in that manner. Paufanias (l. 10 p. 318.) makes Phayllus have fufficient warning of this his miferable end in a dream. Among
the facred offerings of the temple was an artificial fkeleton
of brafs, faid to have been depofited by Hippocrates the
phyfician. The chief is faid to have dreamed, immediately
upon entering on his command, that his body was become
exactly like to this figure.

T 3

he

be appointed his coadjutor, an ancient friend of the family, a man well verfed in arms, and in every refpect capable of forming a great general. In fome time after, the Boeotians, as if refolved to make a trial of this new general and his director, took advantage of the night, and fell on the Phocian camp with fo much fury, that the whole army was thrown into the utmoft diforder. Mnafcas, who exerted himfelf with due vigour to repel this unexpected attack, fell in the engagement, together with two hundred of the Phocians; and thus the young Phaleucus loft all the advantage of his counfels. This chief, now left to his own guidance, foon felt the fatal confequences of a precipitate valour: With all his cavalry he marched againft that of the enemy, and came to an engagement before the city of Chaeronea, where he received a total overthrow, after a bloody and obftinate conteft, in which a confiderable number of his troops were flain.

And now, while Thebes and Phocis were purfuing each other with fuch unrelenting fury, efforts were made by each in favour of their allies. The hoftile intentions of Archidamus had been fufficiently declared againft the Argians, whofe independent condition he beheld with impatience and indignation; and againft

the

the Megalopolitans, whofe fettlement he confidered as the difgrace of his country, and the
odious memorial of the triumphs of Epaminondas. The Thebans, on their part, were
bound in honour to fupport the eftablifhments
of their illuftrious general ; and had, therefore,
difpatched four thoufand foot, and five hundred
horfe, under the command of their general
Cephifion, to the affiftance of the Megalopolitans and Argians. Encouraged by this fupport, the Megalopolitans took the field, and
pitched their camp near the fources of the Al-
pheus, fo as to cover their city and territories :
and here they received additional reinforcements
from the Eleans, Meffenians, and Sicyonians.
The Eleans had no great military reputation,
and were, at this time particularly, weakened by
inteftine diforders; which made Archidamus
exprefs his contempt of their preparations in
the following Laconic letter :

> " Archidamus to the Eleans."

> " Peace is a valuable thing. Farewell."

THE Spartans, on their part, were affifted by
the Phocians, who, for this purpofe, detached
three thoufand foot, and one hundred and fifty
of the famous cavalry of Theffaly, who had

T 4

followed

SECT. III.

Diod. Sic.
l. 16.
fect. 39.

Paufan. in
Eliac.

Plut.
Apoph.

followed Pitholaüs: some of their Peloponnefian allies also united with them: and Archidamus took his station near Mantinea, in the prefence of the enemy. The vicinity of the two armies made a general engagement to be regarded as inevitable; when Archidamus suddenly decamped, entered the territories of Argos, and feized the town of Orneum, which had engaged in an alliance with Megalopolis. The Argians were the firft to oppofe this attempt, but were foon defeated, with the lofs of about two hundred men. The Thebans followed, and renewed the engagement, in full reliance on the fuperiority of their numbers; but the exacter order and and difcipline of the Spartan army fupplied the deficiency of their force: the conflict was maintained with equal ardour on each fide, till night put an end to it, and left the victory undecided; when the Argians, who had now experienced, and feem to have dreaded, the vigour of Archidamus, retired, and the reft of the allies alfo marched back to their particular cities. The Lacedaemonians, thus left mafters of the field, made an inroad into Arcadia, where they ftormed and plundered the city of Heliffon, and then returned in triumph into Sparta.

In

In this short respite from war, Olivier asserts, that we must necessarily fix the embassy of the Megalopolitans and Spartans to Athens, where each of these states pleaded their cause before the assembly, the one to gain assistance, the other to persuade the Athenians to continue neuter: on which occasion Demosthenes appeared the advocate for Megalopolis. Dionysius of Halicarnassus dates his oration for the Megalopolitans somewhat earlier; and an attentive perusal of the oration itself may possibly suggest some arguments to confirm us in the deference due to the accuracy of that critic. From its general tenour, it appears, that the application of the Arcadians was really made, at the first beginning of this quarrel, while the Lacedaemonians were as yet but preparing to attack them. But the learned reader may think the precise time, in which the oration was delivered, a matter not so worthy his attention, as the artifice, the delicacy, the insinuating address, the exact knowledge of the interests of Athens, of the dispositions, opinions, passions, and designs of the leading states, the penetration and extensive policy, and all the qualifications necessary for an accomplished statesman, which are eminently displayed in the oration itself. Yet we must conclude, that his eloquence and abilities

 lities were unfuccefsful, as Diodorus does not mention the Athenians among the people who fent fuccours to the Megalopolitans on this occafion.

THE hoftilities, on each fide, were now continued for fome time longer. The allies, as hath been obferved, retired from the fcene of action: and the Thebans, in their retreat, met with a party of the Lacedaemonians, near the river Telphufa, commanded by Anaxander; and, after an engagement fufficiently obftinate and bloody, took the general prifoner, together with fixty of his foldiers. This fuccefs determined them not to haften their march : they again attacked two different detached parties of the enemy with repeated fuccefs; but in a more general engagement, which thefe fkirmifhes produced, the Lacedaemonians gained a victory, which put an end to the campaign : and, a truce being now concluded between Sparta and Megalopolis, the Thebans had no opportunity of retrieving their late difgrace, but retired into Boeotia with the remains of their army.

HISTORY doth not affign any caufe for this appearance of moderation in the Spartans, in granting a truce to a diftreffed enemy, deferted by their allies, and weakened by the taking of Heliffon.

SECT. III.
Olivier, l 6.
p. 236.

Heliſſon. The French hiſtorian conjectures, that they might have been determined to this by the arrival of ſome ſuccours from Athens, in favour of Megalopolis. But, as to any ſuch ſuccours, hiſtory is ſilent; and, if it be allowed to indulge conjectures, his apprehenſions of Philip may, not without reaſon, be ſuppoſed to have influenced the king of Sparta on this occaſion. The Macedonian Prince's early connexions with Epaminondas, gave him a plauſible pretence of interfering to ſupport the eſtabliſhments of that renowned commander: and we ſhall find, in the courſe of this narration, that in a little time after this, Philip had acquired conſiderable intereſt among the enemies of the Spartan power in Peloponneſus. Demoſthenes * aſſerts, in his oration on the Crown, that, from the time when theſe commotions firſt broke out in that country, he had a particular attention to them, and took care to gain over a number of partiſans in every city, who were employed to keep up and to foment all diſorders. He was concerned, ſaith Olivier *, more particularly than any other, to prevent the execution of that plan which Archidamus had formed. It would have deprived him of ſome maritime towns, which he had gained in Thrace; the cities which he poſſeſſed in Theſſaly muſt have been given up; and his connexions there

* ſect. 7.

* ut ſupra.

entirely

entirely broken. The Olynthians, whose ruin he now meditated, and who, on their part, hated and suspected him, must have recovered those places in their district, which Lacedaemon had kept possession of, since the late war with Olynthus, or had rendered independent. It might therefore have been naturally urged by his creatures and agents in Argos and Arcadia, that the most effectual method to curb the pride and insolence of Sparta, was to seek the assistance and protection of the king of Macedon. To defeat a design of this nature, from which Archidamus might have foreseen very momentous consequences, it was obvious to amuse those people by a truce, and the hopes of a future accommodation of all differences. Philip, on his part, though exceedingly desirous of interfering in these disputes, could not think it necessary to prevent the present suspension of them. Archidamus, he knew, however he might dissemble at present, would not willingly resign his scheme. The different powers would act with vigour sufficient to prevent the execution of some part of it; but, as every one of them had some favourite articles in this scheme, which they were desirous of preserving, it was not possible they could act in concert: the contending parties would mutually weaken each other; and the

Arcadians,

Arcadians, and other enemies of Sparta, at laft
find themfelves obliged to have recourfe to Macedon. Some fortunate event might hereafter open him a paffage into Peloponnefus, where his arms and policy could not fail to decide their quarrels, and make him equally the mafter of all the contending parties, while he only affected a tender concern for the oppreffed, and an honourable zeal for defending the eftablifhments of Epaminondas.

Nor was it lefs confiftent with his views, to fuffer the facred war to wafte and harafs the feveral combatants ; particularly, as the late oppofition of the Athenians, prevented any impeachment of the fincerity of his zeal for religion. The Thebans, when the truce granted to Megalopolis obliged them to return into Boeotia, found that country wafted by the Phocians. Phaleucus, their chief, had juft now reduced the city of Chaeronea, when the Thebans came opportunely to drive him from his conqueft, and to revenge the depredations he had made in their territories, by an inroad into Phocis. Here the whole country was expofed to their fury; they ravaged and laid wafte the lands, the houfes, the poffeffions of the wretched Phocians; and having taken and plundered fome

Diod. Sic.
l. 10. fect.
39.

cities

cities of lefs note, returned into their own country, laden with the fpoils of the enemy. All this variety of fortune ferved effectually to weaken the contending parties. The Phocians, quite exhaufted by their loffes in the field, as well as by their conquefts in Boeotia, where they were obliged to maintain numerous garrifons, appeared ready to fink under the attack of the firft powerful enemy who fhould declare againft them. The Thebans, equally exhaufted, faw fome of their moft confiderable cities in the hands of an enemy, whom they were unable to difpoffefs; and who, on their part, were obliged to exert all their efforts to maintain thefe pofts. Military perfons were, at the fame time, allured from every part of Greece, by large pay, and the fair profpects of advantage, to fhed their blood in the fervice of Phocis. And thus this fatal conteft not only ferved to harafs thofe who were immediately engaged in it, but proved the means of draining away, and gradually confuming, the natural ftrength of every Grecian ftate. No wonder, therefore, that Philip did not appear extremely folicitous to put an immediate end to this war. His defigns were, by this time, become great and extenfive; he had penetration and fagacity to fee through the incidents and tranfactions which

might

might facilitate them; and temper and resolution to wait, with patience, the favourable moment for carrying them into execution.

Sect. III.

It was not the least part of the distress which the Thebans now experienced, that their finances were entirely exhausted, by the expence of constant armaments. To the king of Persia, therefore, they applied; and, by their ambassadors, entreated this prince, by whose opulence the Greeks were on many occasions obliged, to relieve their present necessities by a sum of money. Artaxerxes Ochus, who now reigned in Persia, was, at this time, meditating an expedition against Egypt, where he had, some time since, fought with ill success: and had sent to the leading powers of Greece to desire assistance. The Athenians and Spartans declared their resolution of adhering to the interests of Persia, but, at the same time, pleaded their inability to send any troops [B]. The Argians, on the

other

Diod. Sic. l. 16. sect. 40.

Sect. 44.

[B] They had already sent out Phocion, with some ships, to the assistance of Hidriaeus, king of Caria, who was endeavouring to oblige Cyprus to return to its obedience to the king of Persia. Hidriaeus was the successor of Artemisia, so famous on account of her grief for the death of her husband. Possibly this reputation had no other foundation than in the imaginations of those men of genius who disputed

the

Book II. other hand, fupplied the great king with three thoufand men, commanded by Nicoftratus, a general

the prize in the games, which fhe exhibited in honour of Maufolus. This Maufolus was a weak prince, governed entirely by his wife; to whom the ambaffadors of foreign ftates were always privately inftructed to addrefs themfelves. It was fhe who had been the means of kindling up the focial war: nor did fhe, after her hufband's death, appear to act as a widow totally inconfolable, and regardlefs of the world. Vitruvius hath preferved the memory of a ftratagem which fhe employed to poffefs herfelf of Rhodes. The Rhodians held a private intelligence in the city of Halicarnaffus, the capital of Caria; and hoped that the inhabitants would willingly unite with them, in order to fhake off the yoke of a woman. In thefe expectations they fent a fleet thither. But Artemifia, having difcovered the plot, ordered the inhabitants to range themfelves under their walls, and to receive the Rhodians as their expected deliverers. Deceived by this appearance, the Rhodians landed, and left their fhips deferted: they were furrounded and cut to pieces. Artemifia, who had ordered her gallies to fall down fome canals which communicated with the port, and to feize their fhips, now fet fail in the Rhodian fleet, and appeared before their city. It was fuppofed by the people of Rhodes, that their own army had returned victorious from Caria. The Carians were mafters of their city before the fatal miftake was perceived: where Artemifia changed the form of government, from a democratical, to that of an oligarchy. This produced an application to the Athenians from the people of Rhodes, in order to engage that ftate to reftore their ancient government. The caufes of complaint, which they had given to the Athenians in the courfe of the focial war, it was hoped, would not be remembered; or, at leaft,

would

general equally eminent for his vigour and abilities; though his great qualities were, in some
sort,

would not prevent the Athenians from embracing the honourable occasion of re establishing a government of the
same form with their own. Demosthenes pleaded the cause
of Rhodes, in the oration on this subject, which is still extant among his remains. He begins with felicitating his
countrymen, that their enemies were now obliged to implore their assistance against those who had engaged them to
declare against Athens. He freely acknowledges the misconduct of the Rhodians, and confesses that they are themselves unworthy of that protection which they are imploring; but, at the same time, addresses himself entirely to the
generosity of his countrymen, which hitherto had ever
proved the great resource of the distressed, without regard
to their deserts. He expresses a greater dependence on the
misfortunes of the Rhodians, than on their gratitude; and,
to give more elevation to the sentiments of his hearers, artfully mixes with his reflections the praises of Athens, and
urges the advantages which this state must derive from increasing the number of democracies. He labours to dissipate
any apprehensions from Caria or Persia, which might prevent the Athenians from acting, on this occasion, agreeably to the dictates of generosity; and concludes with recommending the noble conduct of their ancestors to their
present imitation. There is one particular stroke in the
oration with respect to Philip, which deserves a place here:
—" Some of you, I find," saith the orator, " treat Philip
" with disregard, as if beneath their attention; and yet ex-
" press the greatest apprehensions of the KING, as an ene-
" my who must prove highly dangerous to those who may
" be the objects of his resentment. If then we are never to
" oppose the one, because he is weak; and if we are to

fort, difgraced by a wild and whimfical affectation of imitating the garb and manners of
Hercules, and appearing in the field armed
with his club, and cloathed in his lion's hide.
The Thebans alfo detached one thoufand of
their infantry, under the command of Lacrates,
one of their generals ; and the Perfian, in return
for this fervice, granted their prefent requeft,
and immediately fupplied them with three hundred talents.　Yet this could not enable them
to gain any material advantage over Phocis.　A
whole year was wafted in mutual incurfions and
depredations, or, at moft, fome flight actions,
which hiftory hath not thought worthy of being
particularly recorded.

Diod. Sic.
l. 16.
fect. 40.

During this interval, Philip was feated in his
own kingdom, watching the feveral commotions
which raged all around him ; ftrictly obfervant
of the errours and diftreffes of every ftate and
government, concerting his defigns, and preparing for new conquefts.　His forces, and par-

Demoft.
Phil. 1.
fect. 2.

" fubmit, in every inftance, to the other, becaufe he is for-
" midable; againft whom, ye Athenians, fhall we ever
" draw the fword ?"

These particulars, which I have contented myfelf with
tranflating from Olivier, and which he hath inferted in the
body of his hiftory, I thought might, with greater propriety,
be prefented to the reader in the form of a note.

ticularly

ticularly his marine, were conſtantly receiving ſome acceſſion or improvement; and new creatures were every day, and in every community, gained over to his intereſt, by the power of gold, whoſe buſineſs it was to raiſe confuſion and diſorder, to inflame all conteſts and animoſities, to magnify, or depreciate, the power of their maſter, to repreſent him as formidable or weak, juſt as his ſervice required them to inſpire terrour or ſecurity; to miſguide public councils, to betray public truſts, and to practiſe all the infamous arts of men, attentive only to gratify a ſordid luxury or avarice, and regardleſs of the moſt ſacred duties of civil life.

ABOUT this time, if we may depend on the copies of the abbreviator of Trogus, Philip made an excurſion into Aſia, where he reduced the whole province of Cappadocia to the power of Macedon, having firſt treacherouſly ſeized and put to death ſome neighbouring kings. We find, ſaith * Olivier, that Theopompus particularly and largely deſcribed this province, which ſeems to imply, that Philip, whoſe actions he related, muſt have had ſome intercourſe with Cappadocia, or that it was the ſcene of ſome of theſe his actions. But whether thoſe, whom Juſtin calls the neighbouring kings, were ſatraps who had revolted from the king of Perſia,

U 2 or

or governors of a part of Pontus, who supported themselves independent of that monarch, is left entirely to uncertain conjecture. As the records of antiquity have not preserved the least traces or circumstances of an expedition so remarkable as this must have been, the learned have been induced to suppose, that the copies of Justin are corrupted; and, instead of Cappadociam, we should read Chalcidem, or Chalcidicam. If so, the corruption must have been very early; for we find Paulus Orosius copying after the common reading. And although such an amendment, by supposing Justin to refer to his attempts on Euboea, or his war against the Olynthians (of which we shall have immediately occasion to speak) at once removes the difficulty which arises from the silence of other writers; yet another difficulty remains which might have deservedly been considered by those who suggested or adopted this amendment; and that is, that neither in the territories of Olynthus, nor yet in Euboea, can we find those *finitimos reges*, whom Philip treated with so much cruelty and treachery. If we suppose first, that Justin is relating his invasion of the Olynthian territories, and his reduction of the Chalcidian region; then, by those neighbouring kings, we must understand the kings of Thrace. But Philip's conduct to those princes, whatever it was, does

not

not appear to have been at all connected with this expedition; to have at all contributed (directly) to its fuccefs, or even to agree with it in point of time.   And as to Euboea, though Chalcis, and its other cities, had their diftinct governors and petty tyrants, yet we fhall find the power, which Philip gained in thefe cities, was by no means purchafed by the blood of thefe governors.   But, without further anticipating this hiftory, let us leave thefe matters in their original obfcurity, and return to this prince's conduct in his own kingdom, where we may pronounce, with more certainty, that he refided for fome time, waiting the effects of his fecret machinations, and revolving his fchemes of greatnefs.

Arts and elegance were but little known or cultivated in Macedon before the reign of Philip, when the poverty, the weaknefs, and barbaroufnefs of that country, confined the attention of its princes and inhabitants to the bare neceffaries for their fubfiftence and fecurity. But Philip had tafte, and now poffefled riches to adorn and polifh his kingdom; nor did he want the due attention both to its ftrength and fplendour.   Able architects, and fkilful engineers, were invited to embellifh, and to fortify, the feveral parts of Macedon.   Temples, pala-

Juſt. l. 8, c. 3.

ces, theatres, now began to rife in all his cities; and, as artifice and policy had ever fome fhare in all parts of this prince's conduct, under pretence of being the better enabled to erect thefe coftly edifices, he had recourfe to a fcheme with which later ages have been well acquainted. His emiffaries were difpatched through all Greece, where they folicited the men of affluence in every ftate, and, by promifes of large returns of intereft, engaged them to lend their money to the king of Macedon. Numbers were found, whofe avaricious expectations, or whofe vanity in obliging a prince who condefcended to requeft their affiftance, prompted them to empty all their hoards of wealth into the coffers of Philip. And, if we may believe Juftin, the expectations of thefe unwary men were fatally difappointed, and they themfelves reduced to beggary and ruin. He afferts, that neither their intereft nor principal were ever paid; but that, when thefe proprietors came to Macedon to folicit their feveral demands, after many delays, they were at length threatened with the royal difpleafure, and obliged to retire. It cannot reafonably be fuppofed, that this premeditated breach of truft fhould have efcaped the notice of Demofthenes, who reprefented all Philip's actions in the worft and ftrongeft light. Yet we find him quite filent on a fubject, which

Juft. l. 8. c. 3.

must

muſt have afforded ſuch an ample field for his
ſeverity. It ſeems therefore more reaſonable to
attend to thoſe who repreſent the preſent ſchemes
of Philip, as partly intended to conceal thoſe Olivier,
penſions which the intereſt of his affairs required I. 7. P. 250.
him to diſtribute. Theſe were received by num-
bers in every public aſſembly; and it was more
honourable, both for him who gave, and for
thoſe who accepted them, to diſguiſe theſe penſions under the name of debts. They to whom
he gave his own money, and they to whom he
paid high intereſt for the ſums he borrowed,
were indeed equally obliged, and, of neceſſity,
equally attached to him; the one for fear of
loſing his pay; the others to ſecure that property which they had depoſited in his hands.
Beſides, the fair pretence of tranſacting buſineſs,
and taking care of their private affairs, enabled
his partiſans to appear at any time in Macedon,
and to concert their ſecret practices without
ſuſpicion; as we may hereafter have occaſion to
obſerve.

But the attention of this prince was, for ſome
time, diverted by new commotions, which be-
gan to riſe in Theſſaly. Here the fickle inhabi- Olymp. 107.
tants became impatient for new revolutions. Y. 4.
They complained, that Philip had but expelled Dem. Olyn.
their former tyrants to eſtabliſh himſelf in their 3. ſect 8.

U 4

place:

place: they actually opposed him in an attempt to fortify Magnesia, and clamoured loudly for the restitution of that city, and of Pagasae, where he still maintained his garrisons. Their ports and harbours, they cried, were only made subservient to the interests of Macedon, instead of enriching the natural and original proprietors; and urged the necessity of confining these advantages to themselves, and excluding those, who, whatever their pretence had been, really appeared indifferent to the interests of Thessaly; and, notwithstanding their pretended zeal, suffered the Phocians to harass them and the other confederates, without that vigorous interposition which they had been made to expect. Pitholaüs, encouraged by these dispositions of his countrymen, and aided by Phocis, once more appeared at Pherae, and asserted his ancient title. Philip was equally concerned to regain the affections of the Thessalians, and to oppose the open force of Pitholaüs. He therefore marched to Pherae, obliging his soldiers to observe the exactest discipline, and declaring, that his sole design was to dispossess the tyrant. This was effected without any violence; for Pitholaüs, incapable of opposition, instantly disappeared at the approach of Philip, who was now left at liberty to make such further dispositions in this country as might secure the affections of

the

the people. He assured them, with all the appearance of a warm and sincere friendship, that he really intended, and that his affairs would soon permit him, to give them up entire possession of Magnesia; that the sacred war should be the principal object of his attention; that the Thessalians, and their confederates, should be freed from all the expence and burden of this quarrel, the final decision of which nothing but the unjust suspicions of Athens had prevented: that all his forces, and all his treasures, were devoted to this righteous cause; and that the enemies of Thessaly should soon experience the sincerity of these his declarations. Thus did his artifice calm the jealousies of this people, who resigned themselves once more, with full confidence, to the promises which Philip freely lavished, regarding them only as expedients; and, having thus diverted and allayed a storm which might have proved dangerous, he returned to pursue the means of increasing the lustre and magnificence of his own kingdom.

PHILOSOPHERS, poets, actors, musicians, men of genius, and artists of every kind, were received, caressed, and rewarded, at the court of Macedon. If a man of merit, in any part of Greece, suffered by the caprice, neglect, or envy of his countrymen, he was sure to be received

Æfchin. de
falf. Leg.
fect. 10.
cum Schol.

ed by Philip with the diftinction due to his abilities. Thus when Leofthenes, an Athenian eminent for his eloquence, was driven from his own country, by the envy of his enemies, or the fufpicions which the people were made to entertain of his integrity; he found fuch effectual protection, fuch marks of affection, and refpect from Philip, as made his countrymen afhamed of their conduct; and taught them to regret their errour, in giving their enemy a citizen of fo much merit. But what feems ftill a greater proof of the reputation which this prince had already acquired, and ferved to extend and to increafe it, was, that unfortunate princes and nobles crowded to his court, and there found a fecure afylum. When Egypt was at length fubdued by Ochus, and Nectanebus obliged to abandon his dominions, this prince is faid to have taken refuge, not in Ethiopia, as * Diodorus relates, but in Macedon, with the only prince whom he thought capable of protecting him againft the Perfian: and here he was received and entertained with fuch intimate affection and confidence, that fufpicions were fuggefted of an unwarrantable correfpondence between him and queen Olympias. Hence authors, who were inattentive to the period of time in which Nectanebus could have come to Macedon, have fuppofed, that to him Alexander

* l. 16.
fect. 51.
Solin, c. 14.

der really owed his birth; and hence all the fan-
cies of lefs ancient and authentic writers, and the
accounts of thofe magical arts by which they
fuppofe that this prince gained the affections of
Olympias.   But, whatever may be objected
againft the refidence of Nectanebus at Macedon,
it is certain, that Artabazus and Memnon, two
rebellious fatraps (the one of whom had for a
long time maintained a war againft his mafter,
and the other afterwards proved the moft dangerous enemy to Alexander) lived with their
families at Pella, fupported and protected by
Philip, until Mentor the Rhodian, who had
done the Perfian great military fervices, inter-
ceded for thefe his kinfmen, and made their
peace.

To his own fubjects Philip appeared to act
with that tendernefs and moderation, that affability and condefcenfion, which rendered him
infinitely dear to them, notwithftanding all the
toils and diftreffes, by which they were continually haraffed and wafted, under fo warlike
and enterprifing a prince. His ears were ever
open to their complaints, and every day, before
he gave audience, an officer was employed to
remind him in form, that HE WAS MORTAL:
thus did he contrive to affect an appearance of
humility; and, at the fame time, to remind
                                    his

Sect. III.

Glycas.
Cedrenus.
Syncellus.
Chronogr.

Diod. Sic. l.
16. fect. 51.

his fubjects of his real greatnefs, to give them high ideas of his elevation as a prince, and to affure them of his tender feelings as a man, and juft concern for their welfare.

It once happened, that a poor woman appeared before him to demand an audience; and, according to the cuftom of Macedon, to requeft, that he would hear and determine her fuit, which had been long depending, and which various engagements had obliged him to poftpone. Still he pleaded his embarraffments, and carelefsly put her off to fome time of greater leifure. Provoked at thefe repeated delays, fhe now anfwered boldly : " If you cannot find time to do me " juftice, diveft yourfelf of your office; ceafe to " be a king." He at once conceived the full force of this remonftrance, which a juft indignation had extorted from this oppreffed creature; and, far from being fhocked or difpleafed at her freedom, he inftantly heard and decided her fuit. He acknowledged, that to be a king and a judge was, in effect, the fame : that the throne was ftrictly a tribunal, and not only gave him the power, but laid him under the inviolable obligation of diftributing juftice; and that to grant all the time and attention, neceffary to fo important an office was not a favour, but a duty which he owed to his fubjects. All this,

faith

faith Monfieur Rollin, is contained in that ex- Sect. III.
preffion, fo fimple, and, at the fame time, fo
pregnant with good fenfe, *ceafe to be a king*.

We have an inftance alfo of his unbiaffed regard to juftice, in that noble anfwer which he
made to a perfon who folicited him to exert his Plut. in
influence and authority in favour of a man, Apophth.
whofe reputation, it was faid, muft be ruined
by a fentence which was going to be pronounced
againft him. " I had rather," faid Philip, " that
" he fhould lofe his reputation, than that I
" fhould deftroy my own." Nor in his quality,
as a judge, did he affume any rigid feverity, or
auftere appearance. On the contrary, his natural gaiety was fometimes fuffered to break
forth, as in the cafe of two notorious villains,
who accufed each other before him; one of
whom he fentenced to be banifhed; and, when
the other began to exult in his fuppofed victory,
the king, with an affected gravity, pronounced
that he fhould follow his adverfary.

In effect indeed, the illuftrious warriour, and
the wife and gracious prince, was no lefs diftinguifhed by his wit and feftivity, his eafe and
gaiety in private life. The diftance and haughty
retirement of Afiatic courts were utterly unknown in Macedon. Philip had thofe qualities

which

Book II. which could bear the teſt of a conſtant and familiar intercourſe. He converſed with his nobles, and ſhared in their diverſions and entertainments, with all the freedom of an equal.
His viſits to them were not announced in form:
he oftentimes ſurpriſed them totally unprovided
for his reception and entertainment. On one of
theſe occaſions, he is ſaid to have relieved his hoſt
from his confuſion and diſtreſs, by an artifice,
which it may be thought beneath the dignity of
Plutarch. hiſtory to have tranſmitted to us. The ſupper,
in Apophth. to which he came uninvited and unexpected, appeared ſcarcely ſufficient to ſatisfy the train
which attended him. He ordered that it ſhould
be privately intimated to the gueſts, that a ſecond
and better courſe was ſoon to make its appearance. The expectation of more delicate entertainment made moſt of them eat leſs freely:
the prince, and they who were in the ſecret,
feaſted fully, and afterwards indulged their mirth
at the diſappointment of the reſt.

Demoſt.
Olynth. I.
ſect. 7.
    But it is by no means honourable to the cha-
racter of Philip, that, in theſe his hours of feſti-
vity, his companions are ſaid to have been frequently choſen for the extravagance of their
humours, the livelineſs and bitterneſs with which
they expoſed each other to ridicule, and the in-
geniouſneſs,

genioufnefs, and abject fubmiffion, with which
they flattered their royal hoft. One Clifophus is
recorded to have aped his mafter with fuch infamous fervility, as to ufe but one eye, when Philip had loft one of his; and to halt, when
Philip had been wounded in the leg. If the
prince betrayed the leaft diflike of what he eat
or drank, the countenance of the flatterer at
once expreffed the fame fenfations. With this
he fometimes mixed an affectation of bluntnefs
and rudenefs, which rough difguife oftentimes
conceals the moft delicate flattery. When Philip one day upbraided him with his infatiable
importunity. " Why then," faid he, " do you
" allow me time to forget your favours ?" And
when he was upon fome occafion particularly
fevere upon him, " a truce to your raillery,"
replied Clifophus, " if you expect that I fhould
" give you a good character at court."

THE entertainment which he derived from
the extravagance and follies of thofe with whom
he converfed, appears from the ftory of Menecrates the phyfician. This man was mad enough
to fancy himfelf Jupiter, and is faid to have
written a letter to Philip, conceived in thefe
terms :

" Mene-

" Menecrates Jupiter, to King Philip,
" health !"

" You reign in Macedon.   I am fovereign in
" phyfic. I fave the fick. You deftroy the
" healthy. Farewell."

To which Philip returned this anfwer :
" King Philip, to Menecrates, wifhes [c]
" good fenfe !"

Athenae.
l. 7. p. 289.

To expofe his madnefs, Philip made a mag‑
nificent entertainment, to which Menecrates was
invited. While the other guefts indulged them‑
felves in feafting and drinking, the phyfician
was treated like an immortal, and entertained
with perfumes and incenfe. The firft tranfport
of joy, at feeing his divinity thus acknowledged,
made him, for a while, refign himfelf up to the
delufion : hunger, at length, forced him to re‑
collect his condition ; and, quite tired of this
exalted character, he abruptly left the company
to flatter the humour of their prince, and ridi‑
cule this deity who was obliged to eat, in order
to fubfift.

[c] Φιλιππος Μενεκρατει. Ὑγιαινειν. The fpirit of this fhort
epiftle, which is alfo attributed to Agefilaus, confifts in the
equivocal fignification of the word ὑγιαινειν ; which is indif‑
criminately applied to foundnefs either of mind or body.

BUT

But flattery, fervility, and abfurdity, were not the worst of thofe qualities by which Philip's companions were distinguished, if the remains of thofe authors, who have written largely of his conduct, have been tranfmitted faithfully and exactly. "In the choice of his courtiers "and confidents," faith the hiftorian Theopompus, as quoted by * Athenaeus, "he confulted "neither merit nor probity; Greeks and Bar-"barians were entertained by him indifcriminate-"ly, according to the degrees of their aban-"doned impudence and diffolutenefs: and this "infamous collection were called the friends of "Philip. All his efteem, all his liberality, was "confined to men plunged in debauch, and "given up to the groffeft exceffes of a licentious "life. What forts of infamy, what kinds of "vice, were they not guilty of? Some of them "affected the exterior and deportment of the "other fex, and, by their fhocking commerce, "might rather be called Philip's miftreffes than "his friends: equally abandoned to pollution "and cruelty, to murder and proftitution. Ene-"mies of honefty and good faith, and fhame-"fully triumphing in perjury and perfidy. No-"thing could efcape their rapine, or fatisfy their "avarice. So that this collection of wretches, "though not exceeding eight hundred men, "enjoyed a greater revenue than ten thoufand

* Lib. 4.
p. 167.
Lib. 6.
p. 260,
261.

 " Greeks peaceably settled in the most fertile
" soil."

Photius bib.
in Art. *Theopompus.*

THIS picture, shocking as it is, is yet said to be taken from an historian who flourished in the reigns of Philip and Alexander, who was connected with their friends, favoured by Alexander, and whose works were carefully collected and digested by the latter Philip, king of Macedon, to do honour to the memory of his illustrious predecessor. It is well known, that severity and acrimony were the peculiar characters of Theopompus: and such severity, when justly merited, Philip frequently received with the utmost patience and indulgence. Yet, in justice to this prince, it must be acknowledged, that the whole passage is quoted by Athenaeus from the forty-ninth book of the history of Theopompus; and that Diodorus * observes, that the last six books, from the forty-eighth to the fifty-fourth, are at least suspected [D]. The expression of Diodorus hath even been thought capable of a stronger signification, *That these last five books were entirely lost in his time.* These descriptions, which Athenaeus hath preserved,

* l. 16.
sect. 3.

[D] ἐξ ὧν πεντε διαφωνουσιν. *De quinque tamen inter haec discrepatur.* RHODUM. *Ex quibus quinque interciderunt.* G.J. VOSSIUS.

are

are rather ſtronger and more offenſive than thoſe
of Demoſthenes; and yet we know, that the
orator was at leaſt as remarkable for his ſeverity,
and for his force and art in aggravation, as the
hiſtorian. We know too, that the colourings
of oratory are generally higher and more ſtrik-
ing than thoſe of hiſtory. It muſt therefore be
ſubmitted to the judicious, whether there be
not reaſon to ſuſpect, that ſome later writer
might have attempted to ſupply the loſs of the
laſt books of the hiſtory of Theopompus; and
unwarily indulged his imagination, in enlarging
on the deſcriptions of Philip's diſſolute manners,
which he found in the great Athenian. If the
ſtyle of this hiſtorian, as * Suidas informs us, * in Αναξι-
was ſo exactly imitated in his own days, as to μενης.
deceive the Greeks, much more might ſucceed-
ing ages receive ſuch a ſpurious addition as the
genuine remains of Theopompus: and if the
exquiſite taſte of the Athenians could not immediately diſtinguiſh between the original and an
ingenious copy; it is ſcarcely preſumptuous to
ſuppoſe, that Athenaeus, Photius, and ſome
other writers, might have been deceived.

But however this may be, or however Philip
might, at ſome times, indulge himſelf in pleaſure and ſenſuality, his attention was not one moment diverted from his grand deſigns. The

 iſland

Book II.

Olymp.
107. Y. 4.

island of Euboea, and the territories of Olynthus, were now the immediate objects of his machinations. The situation and importance of Euboea, which he justly called the fetters of Greece, determined him to establish such an interest there, as might facilitate the conquest of the island; and, with Olynthus, he was now no longer obliged to dissemble; but resolved to seek an occasion of coming to an open rupture, as with the only powerful neighbouring state which he had left unsubdued; the only state, which, by uniting with the Athenians, might enable them to harass his frontiers, or distress his kingdom.

Æschin. in
Ctes. lect.
31.

When the Athenians had driven out the Thebans from Euboea, they left the island free, and demanded no other acknowledgment for their protection, than the advantage of those provisions, which the fertility of the soil enabled the islanders to supply. The country was divided into several distinct and independent states, and every city governed by those whose influence and address could raise them to the supreme command. These petty tyrants soon began to have frequent disputes and contests with each other, which Philip, no doubt, took care to foment, until they at last produced an open rupture. On this occasion, Philip espoused the interest of

Callias,

Callias, the governor of Chalcis, (a city neareſt SECT. III. to the continent, and, at this day, joined to it by a bridge) and ſent Eurylochus, one of his generals thither with ſome forces and money. Plutarch, who commanded in Eretria, inſtantly diſpatched ambaſſadors to Athens, expreſſing his apprehenſions of the Macedonian power, and the conſequences of Philip's interfering in the diſputes of the iſland; intreating the protection of the Athenians, and offering to ſubmit to their juriſdiction. They had, at this time, ſome Demoſt de falſa Leg. ſect. 82. Schol. forces in Euboea, under the conduct of one of their generals, named Hegeſilaus, who ſupported the propoſitions of Plutarch, and anſwered for the integrity of his intentions.

DEMOSTHENES, though an inveterate enemy Dem. Orat. de Pace. to the encroaching power of the Macedonian, oppoſed Plutarch, and adviſed his countrymen to reject his overtures. No other motive hath been aſſigned for this conduct, but a ſovereign contempt which he entertained for Plutarch and the Eretrians. Poſſibly he might have conceived, and not without reaſon, that this tyrant was ſecretly in the intereſt of Philip; and that the whole affair was no more than the conſequence of a ſcheme, concerted between them, to engage the Athenians in an expenſive and inglo-

X 3

rious

rious expedition, fo as to fatigue and exhauft them.

· If fuch was the opinion of Demofthenes, it was fully juftified by the event: but, at prefent, he was fingle in this opinion; and it was received with fo much indignation, that the people, who naturally fufpected this apparent inconfiftency with his former fentiments, and were particularly inflamed by the party, whofe private defigns made them earneft to engage their countrymen in this expedition, were fcarcely reftrained from tearing the orator to pieces. Demofthenes himfelf imputes this heat and violence to the latter caufe. "You may remem- "ber," faith he, in his oration on the Peace, "that during the diforders of Euboea, when "certain perfons perfuaded you to affift Plutarch, "and to engage in an inglorious and expen- "five war, I was the firft, the only one, who "rofe up to oppofe it; and fcarcely efcaped their "fury, who, for a trifling gain, were urging "you to many highly pernicious meafures." But, although he thus affects to confider this fury as the mere artifice of intrigue and corruption, yet it is certain, that any oppofition to the paffions and reigning fentiments of the Athenians, was frequently received with impatience and refentment;

ment: and never were they hurried on with greater ardour, than to this expedition. Men of diftinction and eminence vied with each other in their zeal for the public fervice. They were for rufhing, all at once, into the ifland, till Phocion, who was appointed general, obliged them to be content with ferving by turns. The orator, Hyperides, who was bound to equip a fingle veffel, infifted on fitting out two; one on his own account, and one for his fon. Niceratus, the fon of Nicias, embarked, notwithftanding a lingering diforder with which he was afflicted, and the recent lofs of his two children, which he then felt in all its force. Eretemon, Mantitheus, Euthydemus, Cleon, Ariftocles, Pamphilus, all illuftrious Athenians, fitted out their gallies: the three laft commanded them; the others ranked with the cavalry, where Æfchines, of whom we fhall hereafter fpeak, and Demofthenes alfo ferved. Thus did this people, whofe impreffions were ever violent, and who always acted in extremes, rufh on to an expedition calculated to ferve the purpofes of Philip.

Plutarch in Orat. Vit. p. 849.

Demoft. in Midiam. p. 408.

Æfchin. de falfa Leg. fect. 53. Dem. ut fupra.

THEIR forces landed at Eretria, where affairs appeared in a much worfe condition than had been imagined. The troops of Philip were fo difpofed as to command every advantageous post.

Plut. in Phocion.

post.   He had sent in but few Macedonians.
The greatest part of his force was formed of
auxiliaries, who rather appeared to be employed
and paid by Chalcis, than as mercenaries in the
service of Philip.   With these was also joined
a large body of Phocians, (though enemies of
Macedon, and allies of Athens) engaged by
ampler pay than they received at home: and
Plutarch himself gave many indications of disaffection and treachery.   Those whom they
came to relieve, were found equally corrupted,
and equally the enemies of Athens with those
whom they were to engage.   Thus was the
snare discovered: but, happily, the abilities of
their leader extricated them from the danger.

THIS man would have done honour to the
early and least corrupted times of the Athenian
state.   His manners were formed in the academy
upon the models of the most exact and rigid
virtue.   It was said, that no Athenian ever saw
him laugh or weep, or deviate, in any instance,
from the most settled gravity and composure.
He learned the art of war under Chabrias; and
frequently moderated the excesses, and corrected
the errours, of that general: his humanity he
admired and imitated; and taught him to exert
it in a more extensive and liberal manner. When
he had received his directions to sail, with twenty

ships,

Æschines
in Ctesiph.
sect. 32.

Plut. in
Phocion.

ſhips, to collect the contributions of the allies and dependent cities; "why that force?" ſaid Phocion; "if I am to meet them as enemies, it is "inſufficient; if I am ſent to friends and allies, a "ſingle veſſel will ſerve." He bore the ſeverities of a military life with ſo much eaſe, that, if Phocion ever appeared warmly clothed, the ſoldiers at once pronounced it the ſign of a remarkably bad ſeaſon. His outward appearance was forbidding, but his converſation eaſy and obliging; and all his words and actions expreſſed the utmoſt affection and benevolence. In the popular aſſembly, his lively, cloſe, and natural manner of ſpeaking, ſeemed, as it were, the echo of the ſimplicity and integrity of his mind; and had frequently a greater effect than even the dignity and energy of Demoſthenes; who called him "the pruner of his periods." He ſtudied only good ſenſe and plain reaſoning, and deſpiſed every adventitious ornament. In an aſſembly, when he was to addreſs the people, he was ſurpriſed by a friend wrapped up in thought. "I am conſidering," ſaid he, "whe- "ther I cannot retrench ſome part of my in- "tended addreſs." He was ſenſible of the ill conduct of his countrymen, and ever treated them with the greateſt ſeverity. He defied their cenſures, and ſo far did he affect to deſpiſe their applauſe, that, at a time when his ſentiments extorted their approbation, he turned about, in

ſurpriſe,

surprise, and asked a friend, " if any thing " weak or impertinent had escaped him." His sense of the degeneracy of Athens made him fond of pacific measures. He saw the designs of Philip, but imagined that the state was too corrupted to give him any effectual opposition. So that he was of the number of those men, who, according to Demosthenes, in his third Philippic oration, " gave up the interests of the " state, not corruptly or ignorantly, but from " a desperate purpose of yielding to the fate of a " constitution thought to be irrecoverably lost." He was, of consequence, ever of the party opposite to Demosthenes; and, having been taught by experience to suspect the popular leaders, considered his earnestness to rouse the Athenians to arms, as an artifice to embroil the state, and, by that means, to gain an influence in the assembly. " Phocion!" said Demosthenes, " the people, in some mad fit, will cer- " tainly sacrifice thee to their fury." " Yes!" replied he, " and you will be their victim, " if ever they have an interval of reason." Yet they often prevailed on him to act against his judgment, though never to speak against his conscience. He never refused or declined the command, whatever might be his opinion of the expedition. Forty-five times was he chosen to lead their armies, generally in his absence；

and

and ever without the leaſt application. They
knew his merit; and, in the hour of danger,
forgot that ſeverity with which he uſually treated
their inclinations and opinions.

THE preſent occaſion demanded all his abilities. Pompous aſſurances of the aſſiſtance
and concurrence of the Euboean ſtates had determined him to lead but a moderate number of
forces into the iſland. He now ſaw the vanity
of theſe expectations: nor were his ſoldiers duly
obedient to military diſcipline. Immediately
after the deſcent, numbers of his cavalry quitted
him and diſperſed; but theſe he would, by no
means, recal or wait for: " all that could be
" of real ſervice," he obſerved, " continued
" with him: the mutinous and diſobedient
" would not only prove uſeleſs and ungovernable
" themſelves, but impede and corrupt others.
" And, as they are conſcious of their own miſ
" conduct, they will be the leſs apt (ſaid he) to
" miſrepreſent or calumniate us at our return."

THUS were the Euboeans much ſuperiour in
numbers, an inconvenience which Phocion determined, if poſſible, to remedy by the advantage of ſituation. The Euboeans are celebrated
by Homer for their firm and cloſe manner of
engaging. They valued themſelves on verify

ing

SECT. III.

Plutarch. in
Phocion.

ing this elogium; and, by a law, which Strabo mentions to have seen engraven on a column in the midst of the island, forbad the use of missive weapons; which they never employed, at least in their civil wars. This made Phocion chuse for the situation of his camp, an eminence near the plain of Tamynas, which it was probable the enemy would occupy, and separated from it by a piece of rough and rocky ground, inclosed with a deep ditch. Here he intrenched himself, and waited the approach of Callias, who encamped on the opposite plain, and exerted all his efforts to surround him. Some days he remained besieged in his camp: the news was brought to Athens; and reinforcements were decreed. In the mean time the enemy prepared for a general assault. As they advanced, Phocion ordered his men to stand to their arms, while he himself went to sacrifice: in which, either his religion, or artifice, engaged him for some time. His soldiers began to be impatient for the charge: but, as he observed on this or a like occasion, "They could not then make him va-"liant, nor he make them wise." Plutarch, who probably saw his design, and was willing to defeat it, began to utter many insinuations to the disadvantage of the general's courage; and, in a pretended fit of zeal, charged the enemy himself at the head of the auxiliaries.

When

When the cavalry faw this, they forgot the or-
ders of their leader ; rufhed out without forming, and fpurred on againft the enemy. Plutarch's attack was weak and fallacious : he fled
at once, and, falling back upon the horfe,
fpread terrour and confufion among them : feveral were killed, and the reft reached the camp
in the utmoft diforder. The Chalcidians, in
their turn, purfued with a rafh and intemperate
ardour : and, in full confidence of the victory,
marched up boldly to the intrenchments, and
began to level them. Phocion now put an end
to his facrifice: the enemy was engaged in an
uneven and difadvantageous ground : he fallied
out with his infantry ; made great havoc among
them ; and quickly drove them to the plain they
had at firft occupied. Here he halted, to give
time for his cavalry to rally : and, having collected round him the braveft of his forces, fell
furioufly on the center of the Chalcidians. The　Plutarch. in
fight was bloody and obftinate, and Phocion in　Phocion.
the utmoft danger of being overpowered by　Æfchin. in
numbers, when Cleophanes, a gallant Athenian,　Ctefiph.
who, by this time, had formed the cavalry on a　fect. 32.
plain which had been ufed for a horfe-courfe,
charged the right wing of the enemy. This
wing was quickly broken ; the center gave way,
and the victory was complete. It was obferved,

that

Book II.
Demoft. in
Midiam.
p. 399.
Æfchin. de
falfa Leg.
fect. 53.

that Demofthenes was by no means the firft to return to the charge. He was even accufed as a deferter of his rank. Æfchines indeed behaved with an intrepidity which was honoured and rewarded ; and was appointed, by Phocion, to bring the news of this victory to Athens.

Plutarch. in
Phocion.

THE conduct of Plutarch, in the late engagement, rendered him juftly fufpected. And fome further practices and intelligences, in which he was difcovered, or the declaration and open avowal of his attachment to the Macedonian intereft, determined Phocion to treat him as an enemy. He drove him out of the ifland, and then proceeded to attack the fort of Zaratra, fituated advantageoufly on that part of the ifland which projects, as it were, into an ifthmus, fo as to command the fea on each fide. The garrifon furrendered, but Phocion would not fuffer any one of the Greeks to be made a prifoner: "left the Athenians," faid he, "fhould at fome "time be inflamed by their popular leaders, and, "in a fudden fit of fury, wreak their vengeance "on them."

Demoft. in
Midiam.
p. 408.
Plutarch. in
Phocion.

THUS had Philip the mortification to find his fecret practices, for this time, ineffectual. The expedition ended to the immortal honour of the

illuftrious

illuftrious Athenian, who re-embarked at Styra, 

with his victorious army; and, with all his fhips collected and drawn up in order of battle, crowned with garlands, and enlivened by the found of flutes, with which the rowers kept time, entered the port of Athens, amidft the joyful acclamations of his foldiers and fellow-citizens.

END OF THE FIRST VOLUME.